THE BEST FRIEND

LIZ HARRIS

HEYWOOD PRESS

PROLOGUE

S *unday, 18th June, 1989*

THE DULL ROAR of an engine broke into the silence of the early afternoon.

Caroline ducked in her seat.

A moment later, she heard a powerful engine sweep past the car, she'd hired and then slow down. Raising her head to look through the window, she saw it turn on to the brick driveway at the side of a mock Georgian house on the opposite side of the road.

The blood drained from her face.

It's him, she thought, her heart pounding fast. And she was sure there was someone next to the cheating bastard. Probably the bitch who'd persuaded him into walking away from nine years of marriage to a woman who adored him and who'd given him two lovely children.

Tears sprang to her eyes. Impatiently, she brushed them away—she'd cried enough. She seemed to have been crying since the moment she'd found the note he'd so cruelly left her at the beginning of the week, and she must stop. If only till she'd confronted the woman he was with. She mustn't let the woman see her cry.

Wiping her tear-stained face, she focused her gaze on the gleaming white doors of the double garage at the bottom of the drive. They began to open. The car inched into the gloom of the garage, and stopped. The driver's door swung open, and a man got out.

Her husband.

Swallowing hard, she blinked her tears away, leaned forward. And stared hard at the passenger side of the car, waiting to see the woman he was with.

The garage door began to close and she felt a surge of panic.

She absolutely had to see the woman. She knew she wouldn't recognise her—it had to be someone he'd met through work. None of her three closest friends would've betrayed her in such a way, and nor would any other of her friends. Nor would anyone on the PTA, nor any of those who helped with the Rotary Club activities. They weren't like that.

But nevertheless, she just had to know what the woman looked like.

The passenger door opened. She caught her breath and grasped the handle of the car door.

The garage door clicked shut.

The blank white face of the garage door stared back at her.

She inwardly swore.

They might not go out again that day, or at least not for a

while. It meant that she could go home. After all, she now knew where they were living. It was only an hour or so away, so she could easily come back another time if she wanted.

But she didn't want.

She couldn't leave. Not till she'd seen the woman.

When she'd seen her, the woman would be real to her and her husband would be truly gone in a way that he wasn't yet. She'd stop going to bed in tears, and opening her eyes in the night, hoping to find him next to her, hoping that this had all been a horrible dream. And she'd be able to think more clearly about what to do next.

She took a deep breath. There was no alternative—she was going to have to go up to the house and knock at the door.

Before her resolve could weaken, she opened the car door, and got out.

Her heart beating fast, she tucked her auburn hair behind her ears, and walked as steadily as she could across the road and down the path to the front door. When she reached the two white pillars that flanked the door, her steps faltered. She took a step back, and stopped.

No, she could do this, she told herself. She had to do it.

She took a small step forward, and then another, and then the door was inches from her. She raised her hand to the bell, hesitated a moment, and then pressed it firmly.

'Get that, will you, darling? My hands are full,' she heard her husband call from somewhere inside the house.

'Will do. I'm right by the door, anyway,' came a voice she knew very well—a voice she'd first heard eleven years earlier, on the day that she and the three girls who'd become her closest friends had met each other in the Camden Town house they were going to be sharing.

Her stomach gave a violent lurch.

Her face ashen, she shook her head. It can't be, she thought.

The door opened.

'You!' Caroline gasped. 'My God, it *is* you!'

1

ELEVEN YEARS EARLIER

 *ctober, 1978*

CAROLINE REDWAY LOOKED around the empty classroom on the Friday evening and wondered if she'd the guts to jack it all in after only a month. Her first four weeks as a probationary English teacher had felt the longest four weeks of her life, and been the most miserable. Her gaze came to rest on the large black letters that headed the display that ran across the back wall—someone had changed the final 'r' of 'Carrie's War' to an 'n' and added a 'k'.

Her eyes brimmed.

How could she have failed to realise that a large comprehensive in London would be very different from the rural secondary school in Cheshire that she'd attended? There the teachers had automatically been respected, and the pupils well behaved. Nothing in her experience had come near to preparing her for the sort of kids she'd been facing every single gruesome day for the past month. Every lesson had felt like a battle against an implacable enemy. And depressingly, the enemy kept on winning.

The one bright spot in her life was that she'd a nice place to which to retreat at the end of each horrendous day. She'd been really lucky to have seen the letting agent's ad about rooms in a Camden Town house, which was to be let for the first time. And she'd been even luckier that the other three girls she was sharing with seemed very pleasant.

They were certainly a varied bunch.

Louise was friendly and down to earth, and was bound to be successful in her chosen field of public relations. Emily, whose head was forever in a law book, could be more than a little prickly, and was clearly something of a loner, but on the whole she seemed all right. Terri Lee was the proverbial dumb blonde, set on being an actress. She was obviously obsessed by her boyfriend, Hugh, who sounded truly ghastly.

She couldn't imagine what the others thought of her, with her dream of finding a man who wanted her to stay at home, raise beautiful children and give dinner parties for his business colleagues. Probably the same as her school friends. They'd thought she was mad to want to be a full-time housewife rather than have what they saw as a proper career. But making a home for her Mr Right was all she'd wanted to do for as long as she could remember.

Unfortunately, she'd yet to meet that Mr Right.

As she hadn't met the right person at university, she'd come down to London in search of him. Teaching was to be her means of paying the bills until the day she married.

But she was never going to meet such a person, the way things were going, she thought in despair. After only a month in the job, instead of feeling like a vibrant young woman on the threshold of life, she permanently felt like a limp rag that had been screwed up and discarded, and fulfilling her dream had never seemed further away.

Her door opened and a man looked into the room.

She glanced up and gave him a wan smile. 'Hi, Tom.'

'You about ready to leave?' Tom asked. 'A few of us are going for a drink. Why don't you come along, too? It'll help you to put the week behind you.'

'It sounds tempting, but I don't think I will this time, thanks. I ought to get off home. We're having a fish and chips evening. It's a sort of celebration at the end of our first month of sharing. But thanks for suggesting it.'

'If you're sure?'

'I am. You have a good time, though.'

The door closed behind Tom.

She stared at the spot where he'd been. Meeting a kind person like Tom had been another stroke of luck.

If it hadn't been for Tom, she'd have almost certainly walked out by now and got a job as a temp, like her house-mate, Terri Lee. No matter what Terri Lee said, temping couldn't be worse than the life she'd got herself into. But deep down she knew that if she'd left teaching so soon after starting, she'd have always felt a sense of failure. For her own satisfaction, therefore, she needed to get through the probationary year, even if it was her first and last year in teaching, so she owed a debt of gratitude to Tom.

CAROLINE HAD BEEN INTRODUCED to Tom Slater in her first week at the school, but had been in too much of a whirl to notice him. It had all been a hazy blur of teachers, pupils and lessons, and Tom had been part of that blur. Things hadn't been much better in the second week. But by the beginning of the third week, Tom had started to stand out from the others.

At first he'd just been an English teacher in a nearby classroom—someone who was handy when she'd a question to ask or an urgent problem with discipline. Which had been often. Now in his fourth year of teaching, Tom seemed to have everything cracked.

His advice had been to plan her lessons so that there'd always be something else for those who finished first. But despite the hours she spent on her class preparation in the evenings, she couldn't get the hang of this. As a result, the faster pupils became bored and restless, and amused themselves by distracting the slower pupils, and her classes invariably slid into noise and chaos.

By the end of her first month, she found herself looking out for Tom in the staffroom, and stopping and chatting to him whenever they passed each other in the corridor. And not just out of gratitude—he was easy to talk to and she enjoyed his company. In fact, the more she saw of him, the more she liked him.

It wasn't that he was particularly good-looking, although he had a pleasant face, with brown eyes full of laughter, and an almost boyish look that was strengthened by his fondness for wearing faded brown cords, a university scarf slung around his neck and a tweed jacket. No, it was quite simply that he was fun to be with. And if she was truly honest with herself, his obvious interest in her was also both flattering and a great boost to her self-confidence at a time when she desperately needed it.

Never before—not at school, not at university—had she felt such an abject failure.

She glanced down at the pile of exercise books on her desk, stood up wearily and started cramming the books into her large black bag. Yet another weekend of marking and lesson preparation lay ahead of her, with no hope of meeting interesting people.

But it wasn't too late to get her life back on course, she thought with a sudden burst of determination as she snapped her bag shut. She was being defeatist, and that wasn't like her, or it used not to be. She was going to snap out of it, take her life into her hands, and do something to improve it. She didn't yet know what, but she'd come up with something. She just had to.

Feeling better in herself, she crossed the classroom, switched off the light and closed the door behind her.

'THAT OLD FART I've been working for all week ought to be put down!' Terri Lee Taylor exclaimed as she sank down on to one of the wooden benches lining the wall opposite the bar. She picked up the glass of white wine on the table in front of her, raised it to the man next to her, and took a long drink.

'You poor baby,' Hugh Waverley soothed, and he raised his glass to her.

'Thanks for the wine, Hughie,' she said, cradling the glass as she leaned back against the wall. 'That hit the spot —or it will do in a minute. It's been one hell of a day. First, I found out that I wasn't being called back for a second audition, even though I know I was bloody good, and then I was sent to work for that over-sexed goat. Being a temp is deadly —I've just gotta get an acting job soon.'

'And you will, honey,' Hugh murmured.

'You don't know how awful people can be! I swear that randy lech only asked for the records on the top shelves so I had to keep going up the ladder. He got a right eyeful every time, and he didn't even try to hide it, the pig. And whenever I walked past him, he pinched my bottom.'

'Well, it *is* a lovely bottom.' Hugh slid his arm around her shoulders. Bending slightly towards her, he moved a blonde curl away from her ear and nibbled her lobe. 'It's your fault for being so beautiful, babe.'

'It's all right for you to fancy me, Hughie,' she said, moving her head back a little and pouting glossy pink lips in his face, 'but you've no idea how foul it is to be pawed over all day long by some slob with dirty fingernails, a fat belly and bad breath.'

'But I can imagine it, babe, and that's why your restorative was awaiting you. So drink up and be restored.'

She took another sip of her wine. 'When I'm a star,' she went on, 'I'm going to be dead nice to all the people working their way to the top, and I'll be especially nice to secretaries, 'cos I'll know their life is shit.'

'I'm sure you will, sweetie. But drink up now. I ought to be going—you know, things to do. I've told Charlie we'll join them at the club tomorrow evening—Alastair's hosting a small party in the back lounge. I'll pick you up around nine.'

'Oh, no! Must we? You said we were gonna have an evening by ourselves, just the two of us together for a change. Charlie's as bad as that perv today.'

'Surely not.' Hugh raised his fair eyebrows in mock disbelief. 'I know for a fact that he has a weekly manicure. But admittedly, I've never got close enough to his mouth to speak with authority about his breath.' He kissed her lightly on the cheek.

'I don't know, Hughie. Charlie's such a pig.'

'You'll be doing me a big favour, babe, if you come along tomorrow and are really nice to Charlie. He likes you, and we want to keep him on side, don't we? You know how much I need his help with setting up my practice—Harley Street's not cheap. I think you can swing it for me. The sooner I can start earning real money, the better, and then we can think about our future together. So what about it, then?'

At his mention of seeing a future with her, a warm glow of happiness swept through her.

She leaned against his shoulder. 'I guess I can endure him leering at me for one more evening.'

'And am I forgiven for having to leave you now?' He blew gently into her ear.

'I suppose. It's probably just as well, anyway. We've sort of planned to get some fish and chips this evening and have a catch up. It suits me as I don't want a late night. I'm meeting someone tomorrow morning about being a film extra, and I've gotta look my best. Being an extra would be miles better than working for any agency. I might get noticed on the set.'

'You could never look less than stunning, lover, sleep or no sleep. Now finish your wine, there's a good girl, and we can get off. Wear something sexy tomorrow, something real tight and low that shows off those beautiful boobs. I promise that this is the last time I'll drag you to a party you don't want to go to.'

'I'm pleased to hear it. We never do anything by ourselves these days.'

'We will soon, believe me.' He stood up and started moving towards the door.

She finished her wine and hurried after him.

Never before had he promised that she could stop going to those dreary parties, and never before had he made such an obvious comment about them having a future together. He wouldn't have said those things if he didn't mean them.

An important man like Hughie, who was a consultant, wouldn't go back on his word. Of that she was sure.

EMILY BYCROFT DRAGGED herself up the stairs past the empty rooms. Having the house to herself wouldn't last long, alas. The others would be back early that evening as they'd planned to eat together. She wasn't looking forward to the fish jamboree one little bit, but if she didn't join in, they'd think her even more anti-social than she was sure they already thought her.

Reaching her bedroom on the top floor, she went inside, dropped her briefcase on to the floor next to her desk, kicked off her low-heeled black shoes, fell back on to her bed and gazed up at the ceiling. Her first month as a pupil barrister was over and done with, she thought, running her fingers through her short mid-brown hair. And what an amazing month it had been!

It was hard to believe that she'd been in Chambers for four weeks only.

It seemed an eternity ago that she'd clung to a rail on the underground train that was taking her to the Temple that first Monday morning, dreading that her pupilmaster was going to turn out to be unhelpful or difficult to get along with, or impatient with her, or that he'd expect her to know instantly the answer to every legal question thrown at her.

No matter how often she'd told herself that she was no longer the isolated, frightened child she'd been throughout her early years in Weymouth, that getting a First in Law, and subsequent sponsorship by a local educational charity, which had come into effect as soon as the period covered by her grant had ended, and would support her for her year as a pupil in one of the best Chancery Chambers, which showed that people thought she could do the job, she hadn't been able to stop herself from panicking.

Everyone there had been new at some point, she told herself as she arrived at the Chambers. She took a deep breath, and fervently hoping that she'd have time to find her feet before she met the barrister who'd be supervising her throughout the year, she went in.

As luck would have it, the first person she met when she reached the clerks' room was Gordon Orpington-Smith, her pupilmaster. But to her great relief, he seemed all right— quite flamboyant in a brocade waistcoat that was taut across his belly, and with extravagant whiskers, he was a bit of a blusterer, but not really forbidding. He'd warmly welcomed her and told her that she shouldn't hesitate to ask him anything she was uncertain about, and had then disappeared down a corridor.

With the worst over, she'd immediately felt more at ease.

Next, she'd met the other two new pupils. The female, Venetia, was beautiful and clearly knew it. She'd come across as cold and somewhat full of herself. But the other pupil, Paul, seemed really pleasant, and she was pretty sure that she and Paul would get along well and help each other a lot, especially with things they were afraid to ask the other barristers.

Although, she thought wryly, she'd be wise to remember that at the end of the year, all of them would be hoping to be offered a tenancy by the Chambers, so in a way they were rivals.

As the three of them had been taken around and introduced to the clerks and some of the other barristers, she'd felt a sense of relief that the black wool suit she'd bought at a rock-bottom price in a sale had been exactly the right thing to wear, and her confidence had grown.

Even the Head Clerk hadn't been able to faze her, although he'd seemed scary. He'd welcomed them briefly when they'd been introduced to him, indicated their pigeon-holes with a wave of his hand and wished them good luck.

By the end of the day, her fears had gone, and she'd been amazed at how relaxed she felt.

THE FOUR WEEKS between then and now had been everything she'd hoped for, and more. She'd found the crock of gold at the end of the rainbow. Let other people have their families: she had the Law, and that was all the family she wanted.

2

T *he following day*

As she ran up the wide stone steps leading to Ethan Ford Electronics, Louise Crawford glanced anxiously at her watch. Three minutes to nine. Phew! She'd made it in time, but only just. The last thing she'd wanted to do was be late for her appointment that morning.

Her past year's placement in Ethan Ford's PR department had been brilliant.

They'd given her a large number of products to place, far more than she'd expected, and although she'd had to work extremely hard, she'd learned a fantastic amount by being thrown in at the deep end, and she'd enjoyed every single minute of her time there.

And she been overjoyed when the company had more or less promised to give her a job after she'd completed her marketing course at West Hampstead Business School, which she'd been lucky to get on as it was one of the first such courses offered by a business school. She was about to go back to the school for her final year, but after that, if nothing went wrong, she'd return to the electronics company. If she'd been late that morning, it might have jeopardised that.

Panting by the time she reached the top step, she all but ran through the swing doors. Normally it wouldn't have mattered if she was a minute or two late as her hours were flexible, and they knew she frequently worked longer than she'd had to, but just before she'd left the office the night before, Ethan Ford had sent a message via his secretary saying that he'd like to see her at nine o'clock the following morning.

She'd struggled to join in with the fish and chips evening with the others, and had been unable to sleep all night for worrying about what she could've done wrong. And now, flustered and out of breath from rushing, she was unlikely to have her wits about her when she most needed them.

And it was all Terri Lee's fault.

Yet again, Terri Lee had monopolised the main bathroom that the four of them shared.

They all knew about her summons from Ethan Ford, and they realised they'd have to be quick in the bathroom— all except Terri Lee. Saying that she'd an important meeting, too, she'd been even longer than usual.

Damn her!

She was totally selfish. True, there was probably quite a nice person underneath all the make-up, but there'd be an even nicer person lurking there if she gave a thought to someone other than herself at times.

Waving at the receptionist, she ran past the reception

area, and reached her desk at two minutes to nine. She propped her leather bag next to her desk, paused momentarily to tuck some stray strands of dark brown hair into the tortoiseshell claw that was securing her hair on top of her head, and to smooth down the jacket of her pale grey trouser suit, and then started towards Ethan Ford's private office.

She went a few steps, and paused. Then she turned, went back to her desk and picked up a large file. He might want to see her about her ideas for marketing the latest bipolar transistor, so it'd be wise to have all the facts at hand.

'BUT IT WASN'T about the bipolar transistor or any other transistor,' she told the others later that evening as the four of them sat in the sitting-room with their coffee. 'Ethan Ford and I are off to California in a couple of weeks!'

The surprise on their faces was mixed with envy.

When she'd gone to see him that morning, she told them, he'd begun by praising her work. It hadn't gone unnoticed, he'd said, that she'd successfully placed an unusual number of products for someone still at a business school, and as her placement year with them was coming to an end, the company wanted to thank her. The way they often expressed their gratitude was by sending the employee on a trip. Although it might involve a small amount of business, there'd be a whole lot of free time. He'd been hoping for a while that something suitable would present itself.

And indeed it had.

That something was a ten-day visit to his San Francisco branch.

Apparently, they were having difficulty in placing one of

their cameras on the back of a cable car for a commercial that was to be shot in the city. Such a placement would result in a huge surge in sales, and anxious to secure the deal, they'd asked for some first class PR help from the London office. He'd decided to go himself, and he wondered if she'd like to go, too.

She thought she'd squeaked something at that point, but she wasn't quite sure what.

Fortunately, he'd carried on as if she hadn't made any sound at all, and had asked if there was anything in her life outside the office that would make it difficult for her to leave the following week and be away for ten days.

What life outside the office, she'd asked him.

'You're right there,' Terri Lee said. 'All you ever do is work. You were dead smart to land a job in a company that deals with rich men's toys. You get to meet loads of gorgeous men, but you never take advantage of it, you mad woman. Go and have some fun for once.'

'And that's just what I'm going to do.' Louise beamed at them, her dark eyes shining. 'We'll be spending the Friday, Saturday and Sunday nights near Monterey to unwind, as he put it—but I think he really wants to play golf—and then we're off to San Francisco on the Monday morning. We're staying in the Fairmont Hotel, which is at the top of Nob Hill.'

'How much work d'you think you'll have to do?' Emily asked.

'Not much. Just a product demo, with the focus on placing the camera. For the rest of the time, I can do what I want.'

'What will your college say?' Caroline asked. 'Your term starts in just over a week, doesn't it?'

'They won't mind. After all, it might help with my dissertation.'

'You really are a lucky sod, being taken to California for a dirty weekend. Or a dirty however long it is,' Terri Lee said, her voice tinged with jealousy. 'I wish my Hughie would suggest something like that.'

'I'm sorry to disappoint you, Terri Lee,' Louise said with a laugh, 'but I'm sure Mr Ford isn't like that. Nothing will be further from his mind.'

'He's a man, isn't he?' Terri Lee retorted.

'Terri Lee might be right, Louise. Somehow I can't see you shaking hands at the end of a wonderful day and saying a chaste goodnight. Even *I* think that sounds unlikely,' Emily commented drily.

'Is he dishy?' Terri Lee asked.

'I suppose so. The girls in the office certainly seem to think so. But I've never let myself think about him like that—there'd be no point. It's widely known in the office that he never dates people who work for him. And I work for him, don't I?'

Terri Lee raised her eyebrows at Louise. 'Get real, gal. You'll be alone in a glamorous place with a bloke who owns a company, and who'll be used to women being all over him. He's bound to come on to you. I certainly wouldn't say no.'

'No surprises there, then,' Emily murmured.

Terri Lee glared at her.

'Don't start, you two,' Caroline cut in. 'We haven't asked if he's married. Is he?'

'He can't be. Not if he's got a rule about not dating employees.'

Terri Lee laughed. 'Where've you been living, Louise?'

'I know you said that after your parents were killed in an accident, your older sister—Nicola, isn't it—gradually became so over-protective that you decided to move out,' Caroline went on. 'But Terri Lee's got a point. You'll need to be careful, unless this is something you want.'

Louise shrugged. 'You can think what you want, but I know that this is Mr Ford's way of thanking me, and he's nothing else in mind. But if he has, he'll be disappointed. I'm hardly going to do anything that might jeopardise being given a permanent job in his firm when I've finished my course.'

'YOU'RE REALLY LUCKY,' Caroline told Emily as they carried the empty mugs into the small kitchen leading off the sitting-room. 'Like Louise, it's clear that you love your job. If you're not talking about it, you're reading up about it, and I bet that when you're in bed, you're dreaming about it. And everyone in your Chambers sounds really pleasant.'

'That's the impression they give, but you never know what's under the surface.'

'That's the lawyer in you talking.' Caroline gave her a weak smile. 'Whatever you say, I do think you're lucky to be dealing with documents, not teenagers. Documents don't answer you back. If only I'd thought of reading Law. If I had, I wouldn't be stuck in a nightmarish school for a year, and I'd be working with interesting people, not truculent kids.'

'It's early days for us all, Caroline,' Emily said gently. 'It's obvious you're finding it tough, but I'm sure it's just a matter of classroom management, and that'll come with practice.'

'I suppose you're right,' Caroline said, putting the clean teaspoons back into the knife drawer.

Caroline's eyes were suspiciously bright, Emily noticed.

'Not everyone I work with is nice,' she added. 'Venetia's a stuck-up cow, and quite lazy, I suspect, and the Head Clerk is scary. The person I see most of is Gordon Orpington-Smith, and although he's bearable, he's a pompous windbag who's very full of himself.'

'Is he fanciable?' they heard Terri Lee yell from the sitting-room.

Emily rolled her eyes at Caroline. 'D'you only think about men in terms of sex, Terri?' she shouted back.

'It's Terri Lee, if you don't mind! You mean there's another way of thinking about them?' Terri Lee's voice rose in mock surprise.

3

Emily glanced in annoyance at Gordon Orpington-Smith. He was sitting at the far end of the room, hunched over his desk, leafing frantically through a large pile of papers. His customary flamboyance had deserted him, and for once he looked stressed and harassed.

Which was exactly the way she felt.

A late night phone call had woken her up when she'd just got to sleep.

She'd picked up the receiver and had heard Gordon Orpington-Smith shouting down the phone that she must get to Chambers as early as possible in the morning. He'd got an urgent disclosure for her to deal with. He looked like being in danger of having to take the case to court, but he'd no intention of doing so. If he did, he risked losing a hefty fee. The only way of ensuring that he and his client's solicitor, and also the lawyers for the other side, would make money out of the case was to settle before it got to court. It was down to her, he'd told her grimly, to find a way to make a settlement happen.

And then he'd hung up.

With the result that she was going to feel exhausted all morning.

And it was entirely his own fault that he was in such a mess. He should never have agreed to take on a conditional fee case as he knew that if the case was lost, no payment would be made.

She'd discovered by then that barristers generally tried to avoid such cases as they were frequently a cause of problems, but having accepted the case in a moment of rashness, her pupilmaster ought to have got down to studying the papers a good few weeks before his date for court. Instead, he'd sat back and waited for the other side to make an offer that could lead to a settlement.

But the offer hadn't come in, and that morning, two days before they were due in court, she'd been told to work out why. And then she was expected to come up with something that would get Gordon Orpington-Smith off the hook.

FINALLY, four hours after she'd started to study the disclosure, she'd discovered the reason for the lack of offer from the other side. They weren't the ones who should be making the offer—they were almost certain to win if the case ever went to court owing to discrepancies in the evidence given by her pupilmaster's client. Safe in that knowledge, they would've been waiting for Mr Orpington-Smith to make them an offer.

She'd immediately told him what she'd discovered, and he'd realised that because of the discrepancies, he and his client's solicitor, who had as much to lose as he, would have to pressure their client at once to agree to a settlement. Gordon was confident that the solicitors for the other side would be willing to settle no matter how strong their evidence, as going to court was always a gamble.

By settling out of court, everyone walked away with some money.

'He didn't even say thank you,' she told Paul at a late lunch. 'All morning, he's acted like everything was my fault, when it was down to his laziness. How unfair is that!'

'He doesn't know how lucky he is to have you for a pupil, Emily—you're bright and you work really hard. It's a shame he didn't get landed with Vile Venetia—they'd have made a right pair. If he had, you might have had John Northwood as your pupilmaster. Venetia's a jammy individual to be working for John—he seems really nice.'

She shrugged. 'It's the luck of the draw, I suppose. You're okay with Andrew, though, aren't you?'

'Absolutely! He's easy-going, but he works hard and he knows what he's doing. I struck lucky with him.'

'Unlike me with Gordon O Smith,' Emily said with a sigh. 'Anyway, let's forget about him. After this year, I'll be free of him.' She looked at her watch and stood up. 'I'd better get back. This isn't the day to take a full hour for lunch.'

'Right you are. By the way, Em,' Paul said, standing up. 'A group of us are going to The Seven Stars on Friday evening. Why don't you come along, too?'

'I don't think so, thanks. I'm always shattered at the end of the week, and this week's proving even more tiring than usual.'

'All the more reason to go for a drink. Some of the clerks will be there and you want to keep in with them, don't you? We'll all be looking for a tenancy when our year is up, and there'll be stiff competition. I know that I'd like to be taken on here. Despite Gordon O, this is an excellent set. If you want to be in with a chance of being considered, it might be an idea to show that you're prepared to drink with the boys, so to speak.'

'When you put it like that, I suppose I'd better. Will you come by for me on Friday when you're ready to set off? I don't like going into pubs on my own. I don't like going into pubs, period.'

'Will do. See you later. And chin up—it can only get better.'

SURREPTITIOUSLY GLANCING AT HER WATCH, she took another sip of her red wine. How she wished she hadn't listened to Paul, but had gone straight home, as she'd done every other Friday.

When Paul had phoned to say that he'd finished for the week and would meet her at the entrance, she'd been completely absorbed in doing a Particulars of Claim for an eviction. Reluctantly, she'd had to close her computer and leave the final details for the following week. She'd have enjoyed the evening a whole lot more if she'd skipped the pub and carried on working.

It was fine for Paul—he fitted in well—but making small talk really wasn't her thing. And there was nothing worse than having to paste a smile on your face and try to look as if you were having a good time, just in case anyone noticed you.

Not that anyone ever did.

She looked at her watch again. She'd shown willing for long enough, she decided. She'd finish her drink and go. No one would notice. And if they did, so what? She wouldn't want to work in a place so shallow that it awarded a tenancy on the basis of a pupil's skill at socialising!

'I'm afraid you don't look as if you're enjoying yourself...
Emily, isn't it? Would another glass of wine help?' she heard
a voice behind her ask.

'No, it most certainly wouldn't,' she snapped.

'Oh, dear,' said the voice. 'Is the prospect of having a
drink with me that terrible?'

She swivelled on the bar stool to see who'd spoken
to her.

'Mr Northwood!' she exclaimed, and she went bright
red. 'I'm really sorry—I must've sounded so rude. Having a
drink with you wouldn't be terrible at all. In fact, it would be
very pleasant. It was tiredness talking. It's been a long week
and I'm done in.'

'Gordon said something earlier this week about both of
you working against the clock. You managed to beat the
clock, I hope.'

'Yes, we did, thank you.'

The sound of a girl's loud laughter pierced the air, and
they turned simultaneously towards the sound.

Across the bar, Emily's fellow pupil, Venetia, was
laughing with a couple of pupils from a different set of
Chambers, her head thrown back and her hand resting
lightly on the shoulder of one of the men.

'Typical! It's Vile Venetia,' she said, turning back to John
Northwood. Her hand flew to her mouth. 'Oh my God, I
can't believe I said that! She's your pupil, isn't she? I think I'd
better leave right now—I dread to think what my third *gaffe*
might be.' She slipped down from the stool. 'You'll have to
excuse me.'

'Of course. Your name *is* Emily, though, isn't it?'

'That's right. Emily Bycroft. I'm sorry to leave, Mr Northwood, but the phrase 'foot in mouth' is hovering above my
head, and I really don't want it to sink lower.'

'That's a shame. It could be rather entertaining. It has been so far. But if you're going to deprive me of a third *faux pas*, perhaps you'll keep it safely in reserve and allow me to take you to dinner some time so that I can enjoy it on a later occasion.'

Emily laughed. 'You don't have to make the supreme sacrifice,' she said. 'I'm not even sure it'd stop at three *gaffes*. I fear there'll be plenty more such slips during the rest of my year with you. Goodnight.' She started to move away.

'It wouldn't be a sacrifice, Emily,' he said quickly. 'It'd be a pleasure, with or without a slip of the tongue to enliven the occasion.'

She stood still. 'Are you asking me out?' she asked in a tone of amazement.

'Indeed, I believe that *is* what's happening,' he said mildly.

She stared at him. He must be at least ten years older than she was, she thought, but the lock of brown hair that fell over his forehead somehow made him look much younger, and the dark brown eyes that were smiling at her from behind tortoiseshell-framed glasses were warm and friendly, and a little nervous. He actually had a very pleasant face, she thought.

Her eyes slipped to his tweed jacket, the collar of which was half up and half down, and she noticed that he'd spilt coffee or something similar on his tie.

She looked back up at his face, and knew that she'd like to spend some time with him.

'I'd very much enjoy going out with you one evening, Mr Northwood,' she said.

'Thank you, Emily. Shall we say next week—on Saturday, perhaps? I know you want to get away now. I'll confirm the time at the beginning of next week when I've made a booking for us. Or is that too soon for you?' he asked, his voice reflecting a sudden anxiety.

'No, it isn't. That would be lovely. Well, goodnight again, Mr Northwood.' She turned to go.

'My name's John,' he called after her.

She looked back at him and smiled. 'Goodnight, John,' she said.

4

onterey, California
Mid October

M

LOUISE JUMPED out of the large bed and slipped into the white towelling bathrobe that she'd thrown over one of the armchairs the night before. Tying the belt, she crossed to the French windows, flung them wide open, and stepped into the autumn sun that had been trapped between the walls of the private patio.

White jasmine curled up the walls of the garden room she'd been given, its delicate scent mingling with the heady fragrance from the multitude of flowers around her. In one corner of the patio stood a jacuzzi, and set in the wall opposite the French windows, a gate opened out on to a narrow pathway.

She took a deep breath—she was living the dream!

Mentally hugging herself with glee, she turned, went

back into her bedroom and crossed the room to the creamy vanilla bathroom.

Minutes later, her jet lag washed away, she stepped out of the glass-fronted shower cubicle on to heated limestone tiles, took a white bath sheet from the folded pile on a long glass shelf next to the cubicle, wrapped it around her, and with a second towel, rapidly dried her hair.

Fifteen minutes later, she was heading through the patio gate, and on her way to the courtyard that, she'd seen from the plan in her room, lay at the heart of the hotel. She knew that an alley leading from the courtyard would bring her to the grill where she was meeting her boss.

She hoped he'd think she looked all right in what she was wearing.

She'd done her best with her clothes, given her limited wardrobe, to solve the thorny problem of what to wear on a day that was both work and not work. In the end, she'd chosen a cornflower blue cotton dress with shoestring straps, and low-heeled gold strappy sandals. Over her arm, she carried a lightweight gold leather jacket. As her hair was still damp, she'd pulled it loosely back from her face with a pale blue velvet ribbon that she'd tied in a bow at the nape of her neck.

Walking along, she looked with interest around her. Yellow and white clematis rose up from the hard ground and clung to the stone walls that enclosed the patios she was passing, and small cypress trees grew intermittently along the grassy border between the walls and the path, their slender trunks and branches bleached a greyish-white by the wind and the sun.

It had been too dark to see much of the small Mediterranean-style hotel when she and Ethan Ford had arrived late the evening before. They'd had a quick drink in the hotel lounge, and had then turned in for the night. Before separating, he'd suggested that they meet for breakfast at the nearby grill.

It was no more than a short walk from the hotel, he'd told her, but if she preferred, she could always have breakfast in her room. He'd suggested the grill as he thought she might like to look at a view during her first breakfast in Pebble Beach, and she'd readily agreed with him.

When she reached the restaurant, she found that her boss hadn't yet arrived. A waiter showed her to a table on the outer edge of the patio deck, and brought her a glass of water and coffee. Then he gave her a menu, and put another menu on the opposite side of the table.

She stared at the empty chair facing her, and felt a sudden panic. What on earth would they find to talk about?

She was twenty-two, and he must be at least ten years older. She was a student, and he owned an electronics company with overseas branches. She'd had a couple of boyfriends at university, neither of whom was special, and he dated women who were both beautiful and sophisticated, or so she'd heard. People said she was quite pretty, but he was drop-dead gorgeous. She'd seen enough of him in the past twenty-four hours to know what the office girls had been raving about!

And this was going to be the first time thèy'd really talked to each other.

They'd been in different parts of the plane during the flight from England. And on the short helicopter ride from San Francisco International Airport to Monterey, both had been quite tired and had sat in silence and stared at the sea-blue view beneath them.

The more she thought about it, the more she wished

she'd opted for the solitary breakfast on her patio, and to hell with having a view!

And it wasn't only that morning that they'd have to find things to say to each other—it would be every day of the ten days, too. That was a really scary thought.

Making a determined effort to stop worrying, she picked up her coffee, turned her head towards the sea and tried to focus solely on the manicured lush green grass that stretched from the patio deck as far as the deep-blue crescent that was splintered with gold in the morning sun.

'That's some view, isn't it?'

Startled, she turned sharply, and saw Ethan Ford standing by the table. She almost dropped her cup.

'God, you frightened me!' she exclaimed, putting the cup back on to its saucer.

'That bad, is it? I wouldn't know—I try to avoid the mirror at this early hour.' Grinning ruefully, he rubbed his chin as he sat down.

'Christ, no, I didn't mean that,' she said, staring at him, aghast. 'No, it's an amazing view.' He raised his eyebrows. 'The sea, I mean.' He raised his eyebrows even higher. 'I didn't mean that you're not an amazing view,' she added hastily.

She felt herself going red and cursed inwardly. With her pale skin, blue dress and bright red face, he'd think he was sitting opposite the Union Jack.

'You seem to be digging yourself into a proverbial hole,' he remarked with a smile. 'If I were you, I'd stop before you run out of deities to call upon.'

'I'll take your advice,' she said with an awkward laugh. She inclined her head towards the expanse of grass. 'To change the subject, that's part of the golf course, isn't it?'

'Indeed, it is. But I wouldn't let any keen golfer hear you

refer to that patch of green with such a lack of reverence—that's an extremely famous eighteenth hole. No other finishing hole has had more written about it over the years.'

'I'm afraid none of that writing was on the business school syllabus.'

'If only everyone was as delightfully ignorant of its place in golfing history. If luck's against us when we come back this evening for their wonderful red clam chowder, which I hope we'll do, hordes of people will be blocking our view as they try to photograph the hole. But if we strike lucky and there's an absence of photographers, we might actually see the ghost of Bing Crosby tapping in a short one for birdie.'

'You sound as if you're a keen golfer. Do you play well?'

He laughed. 'I would say so, but I rather suspect my friends might say otherwise. My handicap's sixteen, which I suppose is quite respectable as I don't get much time to play. I try to keep my hand in, though, as it's useful for business.'

The waiter materialised with coffee and water for Ethan, and then disappeared.

'Since you're clearly not a golf enthusiast,' he said, picking up his coffee, 'I won't expect you to cheer me on tomorrow when I meet some friends for a game. I'm sure the pool will have greater appeal, and you must order any treatments at the spa that you'd like.'

'I won't ask what treatments you think I ought to have, as you could end up digging yourself into that same hole,' she said lightly. She felt a momentary panic—perhaps she'd been too informal with him.

But he burst out laughing. 'Well-restrained,' he said. 'Thank you for saving me from blundering so.'

She smiled across the table. His eyes were an amazingly deep shade of blue, she noticed, and the way they crinkled in the corners showed that he laughed a lot.

'Right, Miss Crawford,' he said, glancing to his left as a waiter hovered near the table with a refill of coffee. He picked up his menu. 'We're now about to face the first of today's major decisions; namely, what to have for breakfast. Have you looked at the menu yet?'

'I was waiting for you.' She opened her menu and glanced down at it. 'Wow! Americans certainly like to have a choice.'

'You must try their granola. It's fantastic. And I also recommend the Spanish tortilla and the pastries—not just the Danish, but also their ham and cheese. It's a great way to start the day.'

'If I ate all of that, Mr Ford, the emphasis would be on great,' she said, 'and you'd be spoilt for choice when it came to suggesting the treatments I needed.'

He looked up from his menu. 'Oh, I don't really think there's much likelihood of that,' he said with a smile. 'Not even if you added to your order a stack of pancakes with butter, lashings of maple syrup and a huge dollop of cream.' He looked back down at the menu.

She did the same.

'I'm wondering if Miss Crawford and Mr Ford don't sound a little formal for the setting,' he said a few moments later, glancing at her above the menu.

She cleared her throat.

'Why don't I call you Louise? Just while we're away. And you can call me Ethan, again just while we're away.'

Help, she thought inwardly.

'If you think that's all right,' she said hesitantly. She heard the nervousness in her voice at the thought of sounding so familiar with her boss, and gave a slight cough.

'I do. So to continue with what I was saying, Louise,' he went on smoothly, 'I'm going to begin with one of their fresh juices and then have the granola. But you must order what you want. When we've eaten, I'll show you around the area. It's always fun to show a place you love to someone who's seeing it for the first time. In a way, you get to see it through new eyes yourself.' He smiled warmly at her, and gestured for the waiter to approach.

To hell with getting new eyes, she thought—his old ones were absolutely perfect.

5

Caroline sat at her heavy oak desk and stared across the classroom to the far window. Rain beat noisily against the mud-spattered panes, gouging a path to the wet ground below. It had rained all the way to the school that morning, all through break, all through the lunch hour, and it looked set to rain all the way home.

Before long, the leaves, still beautiful in their various shades of gold and brown, would fall from the trees and gather in soggy clusters along the sides of paths and in gutters and drains, where they'd gradually blacken beneath a never-ending stream of grey days, intermittent drizzle and pounding shoes.

Those sad, wet leaves said it all, she thought miserably.

She turned from the window and stared at the two piles of exercise books on her desk that would have to be marked that evening. Thank goodness she had her date with Tom to look forward to. She'd been wise to have given up waiting for Tom to ask her out, and taken the matter into her own hands.

Enjoying Tom's company in the staffroom as much as

she did, and sensing that he felt the same about being with her, she'd been rather expecting that he'd ask her for a date. But time had gone by and that hadn't happened, and she'd been surprised at how disappointed she felt.

Finally, she'd resolved that as soon as an opportunity presented itself, she'd invite him to go for a drink. If he said no, she'd know that she'd misread the signals.

Luckily for her, a moment had presented itself almost at once.

A couple of days after she'd formed her resolution, one of the Science teachers had flown into a temper when Caroline had mistakenly made her morning coffee in that teacher's special mug. Tom had been in the staffroom at the time and he'd instantly leapt to Caroline's defence. The Science teacher, completely taken aback when Tom had rounded on him, stopped ranting, gave them both an unpleasant knowing glance, and moved off in a huff to another part of the staffroom, leaving Caroline still holding the offending mug.

She'd turned gratefully to Tom and insisted that he let her thank him for his support, and she'd invited him to go for a drink after work that evening. The pleasure on his face as he'd accepted her invitation had made her spirits soar.

That drink had been the start of their out-of-school relationship. And not long after that, when they'd staggered back to Caroline's room after an evening with some of the other teachers, their relationship had been firmly cemented when they'd fallen into bed together. It had seemed the natural thing to do.

Since then, in the morning assembly, their eyes would meet across the hall above the heads of the pupils; during the day, they were often overcome by the need to go into the other's classroom for a highlighter or a board marker or anything; at lunchtime, they'd sit side by side at a table in the corner of the staffroom, marking their books and sharing their sandwiches, oblivious to the glances of the teachers around them.

Even though it was still early days, she'd even begun to ask herself about where she'd like this to end.

'Bad day?' She jumped at the sound of Tom's voice and looked up from the exercise books. 'You look exhausted,' he said sympathetically, coming into the classroom and pushing the door shut behind him.

'Oh, Tom, what a day,' she wailed. 'But what else is new? You must've heard the din the last class was making. No, don't say you didn't—I know you did. I can't seem to do anything right.'

'You'll be fine. It's hard for everyone at first. The kids smell inexperience and nervousness, which are like red rags to a bull. It isn't easy, but you'll get there.'

'It's nice of you to lie like that, but I should be beyond that stage by now. If it weren't for you, I'd have walked out weeks ago. You're the one bit of sanity in this place.'

He grinned at her. 'I'm not sure that I'd choose to be seen as a symbol of sanity. I'd much rather be an icon for something more exciting—a symbol of sex, for example. Let's you and me slide between the sheets tonight and work on a change to my iconic status. I obviously haven't done a good enough job so far. What d'you say?'

'I'd love to, Tom, but I can't,' she said woefully.

'Don't tell me—you're going to mark.'

She nodded. 'I've got to. I've got the monsters again tomorrow.'

'Then here's the plan. I'll come back to your house with you now, and we'll divide your marking between us.'

Her spirits leapt.

'But there's a hefty price for you to pay,' he went on. 'When there are no books left to feel the touch of that all-knowing red biro, you, Miss Redway, overcome by gratitude, will ravish me to within an inch of my life, and then you'll allow me to take you out for food to give you the strength to start all over again. How does that sound?'

'You're nuts!' she said with a laugh. 'But it sounds great. Are you sure you don't mind helping me out like that?'

'Not one little bit. Come on, let's go.'

SAN FRANCISCO, CALIFORNIA

LOUISE AND ETHAN stood side by side on the deck of the ferry, watching the small rocky island of Alcatraz, which rose from the deep blue sea, recede in the distance behind them. Then they turned to face the way they were going.

'Wow, look at that!' Louise exclaimed, staring at the sun, which was beginning to sink behind the Golden Gate Bridge, setting the sky and sea on fire with crimson and burnished gold. 'You timed it brilliantly!'

'If you keep your eye on the bridge, you'll see why that red bridge is called the Golden Gate.'

'Oh, I see what you mean,' she cried out a few minutes later, looking back up at him. 'Every window in the city is reflecting the sun, and you can't even see the bridge for the mass of gold.'

He looked down at her upturned face. 'And it's not only the bridge that seems to be made of gold—you've a tiny fleck of sun trapped in the centre of each of your eyes.'

With a self-conscious laugh, she put her hand to her cheek. 'I must look like a zombie.'

He opened mouth as if to say something, closed it, and turned back to the bridge.

She stared at his profile, her eyes slowly tracing the slope of his forehead, his straight nose, the curve of his mouth, his strong jaw, and she swallowed hard.

'I'd have hated to be a prisoner on Alcatraz,' she said, looking back towards the island in the hope of squashing the sudden strangeness she felt. 'Being stuck in a miserable little cell, able to see the city across the water, but unable to get there because of the currents and sharks and everything. It must've been awful.'

'I'm sure it was.' He raised his hand to run his fingers through his hair, and his arm brushed against hers. She shivered.

What was wrong with her!

'You're cold. I should've realised. Here, take this.' He took off his jacket and wrapped it around her shoulders. 'I should've warned you that a light cardigan probably wouldn't be enough for the ferry—it gets quite cool on the sea in the evening.'

'Oh, no, I can't—' she began, and she started pushing the jacket from her shoulders.

He put his hand on top of hers and stopped her. 'Yes, you can,' he said firmly, 'and you will. I'm fine as I am, I assure you.'

His hand rested on top of hers for a moment longer, and then fell to his side.

Clasping the collar of the jacket with both hands, she pulled the jacket tighter around her neck. 'Thank you,' she said, looking down at the deck again, the back of her hand tingling where his hand had lain.

She sensed him nod in acknowledgement, and turn his attention to the water passing beneath the ferry.

'We'll have dinner at the hotel when we get back,' he said after a few minutes, 'but we'll go somewhere else for dessert. I know a place where the desserts are unbeatable. Then we'll go back to the hotel for a nightcap. You've got to have a Mai Tai in the Tonga Room at least once before we leave. How does that sound?'

'Fantastic,' she said. She paused for a moment, and then went on. 'This has been an amazing trip, Mr Ford. I never expected anything like it. I thought I'd be doing a product demo, and any other work that was needed, and when I wasn't wanted, that I'd be left on my own to amuse myself as best I could. I didn't for one minute imagine that you'd take it upon yourself to see that I had a fabulous time.'

'It's still Ethan—we haven't gone home yet,' he said with mock admonishment. 'But you know,' he went on, leaning against the railing and looking back at the water, 'you're not the only one who's having a fabulous time, to use your word.'

'What d'you mean?' She felt herself going red, and pulled the jacket higher over her chin.

'Tut, tut, Louise.' He straightened up and looked squarely at her. 'You forget I saw you in action earlier today. Anyone who can tell the techie exactly how Wednesday's demo and reception has to go, who can list the equipment required and insist that it's at the hotel in time for the run-through tomorrow, who can set in place a tight security procedure for checking the new products in and out, might just be able to work out the meaning of what I said.'

'You mean, you're genuinely having a good time, too?' she asked hesitantly. 'You're not bored to death, spending so much time with me?'

'Not at all.'

Her mouth framed the question why.

He gave a slight shrug. 'This has been a very good visit, work-wise, and I feel completely relaxed, despite the importance of why we're here. I haven't always been able to say that on past visits. And out of hours, I've had a really good time. Being here with you must be the reason why I'm enjoying myself so much this visit. Or put more simply, you're good company, Louise. Will that do for an answer?'

Biting her lip, she nodded slowly.

At the expression in the blue eyes that stared down at her, her heart missed a beat.

Their eyes locked for a moment, and then both turned away.

6

God, she was bored!

Wandering through the large French windows that had been thrown wide open, and out on to the plant-fringed roof-top patio of the club, a champagne flute in her hand, Terri Lee felt thoroughly fed-up. Once again, it was the same old thing, despite it being more than a month since Hugh had promised an end to their constant partying.

And it didn't help that her dream of being extra had come to nothing. That sleazy bod at the extras' agency had obviously been lying when he'd told her she'd be in great demand, looking so good and all that. She'd not had a single phone call.

She glanced around her and sighed deeply.

At first it had been exciting, going with Hugh to different clubs and parties. They'd often been held in large, high-ceilinged rooms that were imposing with their sense of faded grandeur, and she'd walk in and find herself surrounded by beautiful people. Pencil-slim women, all dressed in the height of fashion, would glide around the room on the arms of men in exquisitely tailored suits—men who exuded power and confidence—and she'd actually pinch herself to believe that she, Susan Lesley Taylor from Derbridge, a nothing town in the West Country, was really there among them.

But the novelty had long worn off. The name of the host might change, and the venue might be different, but before long every party had come to seem the same as the one before and the one before that.

The same posse of identical waiters, in crisp white shirts and black bow ties, would weave a path between the glamorous people, their trays held high above their heads as they made their way to the gleaming bars where the bartenders knew how to mix every kind of cocktail imaginable.

The same crop of young waitresses, identically clad—maybe in short frilly dresses with tight, low cut bodices; maybe in something more outré—would wander among the guests, offering cigarettes, cigars and lighters, and discreetly offering, Terri Lee was sure, the harder stuff for any guests so inclined. And clearly many were.

The same guests turned up at the different parties, perching themselves on high stools or gathering in groups of varying sizes, helping themselves to drinks from the passing trays while hardly missing a beat of their conversation. Among them were the same repulsive slobs who turned up everywhere, panting as they glanced at her boobs, and feeling her bottom as she passed by.

But deals were made in such places, she knew; big deals. Hughie had told her so often enough. And he was after a deal himself, which was why they were on the party circuit. But although she still felt lucky to be moving in such circles —after all, you might meet a producer of director at any of the parties—she was now thoroughly bored by it all.

It wouldn't be so bad if she and Hugh spent at least some of the time at the parties together, but they didn't. He disappeared almost as soon as they got there, leaving her on her own or, even worse, in the company of a lech.

It was true that every so often, Hugh would look around for her, beckon to her to go over to him, slip his arm casually around her shoulders and pull her close to him. But she soon caught on that he was making sure that his companion feasted his eyes on the generous cleavage displayed in front of him.

And she knew all too well what she was meant to do, and did it.

She'd run her tongue along her lips, pout prettily, and then pull back from Hugh and slide her hands down the front of her dress to smooth out non-existent creases, all the time glancing saucily at the leering man from under her eyelashes. Hugh would laughingly release her, excuse himself for a moment and she'd be left alone with a man who couldn't even be bothered to raise his eyes from her chest.

Although she'd try to make some kind of conversation, it was clear that no one in the parties they went to was interested in anything she had to say, nor in saying anything to her. She was there to be seen and to make Hugh look good, and that was all.

But she didn't blame Hugh for taking advantage of the fact that he had a sexy girlfriend who could act, and was using her to make himself noticed by men with money. It was unfortunate that the men with financial clout were frequently loud and overweight, and always seemed to have beads of perspiration trickling down their faces, but she knew that by softening them up, she was helping Hugh to get financial support for the Harley Street practice he wanted to open. And that was all that mattered.

She and Hugh were a partnership. She loved him, and she knew he loved her, and she was glad she was able to help him. It was just that it had become so bloody boring, and she couldn't wait for the day when he had all the backing he needed, and they'd no longer have to party so.

Idly, she crossed to the balustrade running around the edge of the patio, leaned over and stared down at the illumi-nated street below. How she'd love to be down there, making her way home, close to being able to kick off the flimsy high-heeled sandals that were killing her feet.

'If I were Hugh, I wouldn't let you out of my sight for so much as one minute,' a deep voice said from behind her.

She sensed that the owner of the voice had come to stand alongside her at the balustrade.

Straightening up, she glanced at him. Like she'd been doing, he was staring ahead at the view of Central London by night.

He was a fairly tall, distinguished-looking man with a strong profile, grey-flecked wavy hair and broad shoulders. The immaculate charcoal grey suit he was wearing had obviously been made by a first-class tailor. She'd now been around wealthy men long enough to recognise a well-cut suit when she saw one. She guessed he must be in his fifties, but whatever age he was, he looked good, she thought as she looked back at the view.

'Beautiful, isn't it?' he murmured. 'As, indeed, are you, Terri Lee,' he added, his eyes still firmly fixed on the lights of London.

She turned to him sharply. 'How d'you know my name? Did Hugh send you over?' she asked, suddenly wary.

'Indeed, Hugh did no such thing. And as for your name,

I make it my business to find out the names of the women I'm interested in.' His clear grey eyes locked into her startled blue gaze. His mouth curved into an amused smile.

'What do you mean, you're interested in me? No, don't answer that—I can guess. We'll stick to the scenery, thank you. You're right—it *is* a beautiful view. I always like London at night.'

'That's why you're becoming a regular part of London night life, is it? To enjoy the views of the city?' he asked. 'I've lost count of the number of parties I've seen you at in the past few months.'

'I'd like to say I've noticed you, too, but I haven't,' she said stiffly. 'However, since you seem to know so much about me, you'll know that Hugh Waverley and I are together. Wherever Hugh goes, I go. And he's been invited to lots of parties recently.'

'Yes, your Hugh does seem to be a busy boy.'

'And your name is?'

'Marcus Shaw.' Marcus held out his hand to Terri Lee. She hesitated a moment, and then took it. 'It's a pleasure to meet you, Terri Lee,' he said smoothly. 'I've been watching you work and you're to be congratulated upon the way in which you conceal your boredom, and upon the ease with which you find something to say to people who are—let's be honest—more interested in your attributes than in your conversation.'

She pulled her hand away. 'I'm not working,' she said shortly. 'I'm here with Hugh. Now, you'll have to excuse me—'

'Here *for* Hugh, rather than *with* Hugh, if I might venture to suggest.'

'I'd rather you didn't venture to suggest anything at all, thank you very much. I haven't a clue what you're talking about, and I've got a feeling that if I did know, I wouldn't like it.'

Marcus laughed. 'That's a bit too convoluted for me! I'll put it bluntly then. You're nice to the men who are introduced to you by Hugh. Although you're bored by them, you don't show it.'

'I don't know about being bored by the men I meet with Hugh, Mr Whatever-your-name-is, but I certainly know *you're* boring me at the moment, and I don't in the least mind showing it.' She started to turn away.

'You're not alone, you know.'

'I know I'm not. I'm with Hugh, aren't I?' she said haughtily.

'You're not alone in being here for someone else's benefit, and you're not alone in having to spend the evening entertaining dull people, who are interested solely in what's under your dress,' he said quietly.

She glared at him. 'D'you get off on sticking your nose into other people's business? What's my life got to do with you?'

'But you *are* alone in the fact that you're the only one getting nothing out of it for yourself. You're very alone in that, Terri Lee,' he went on as if she hadn't spoken. 'There are other women like you here tonight, but they're making very good money for what they're doing. I'm guessing you're not making a penny.'

'I'm helping my boyfriend, that's what I'm doing. And he appreciates it.'

He gave a dismissive shrug. 'If all you want is the knowledge that Hugh appreciates you helping him to make money, even though you don't get to see any of that money yourself, then you ask for very little out of life. Appreciation doesn't pay bills; it doesn't put bread and butter on the table;

it doesn't buy the sort of dresses you'd love to own, or jewels, or a car, or a stunning apartment. Still, if appreciation is all you want, I'm sure that Hugh appreciates what an asset you are, so you must be very happy.'

She stared at him. 'I'm not a prostitute, you know, and I never will be. I'm happy to help Hugh. I love him and he loves me. I'm going to be an actress, and that's how I'll earn the money you were talking about.'

He gave a slight bow. 'Then I wish you well. I'm sure you're an excellent actress, if the show you put on at these parties is any indication. I hope you get a lucky break. You'll need it if you're going to succeed in the face of all of the pretty young hopefuls arriving daily in London from the provinces, many of them already clutching equity cards in their hot little hands, all of them dreaming the same dream as you.'

She stared at Marcus in uncertainty. 'How d'you know all this? And about me?'

'I run an escort agency, Terri Lee. A large number of the women draped over the arms of the wealthy men here this evening are my girls. They're paid to spend the evening with the man. They're drawn mainly from the ranks of models, centre-folds and resting actresses. They're stunning girls who want to make a bit of extra easy money. But they're not prostitutes, any more than you are.'

He paused.

She frowned. 'What do they have to do for their money, these stunning girls?' she asked.

'Why, look stunning, of course,' he replied with an amused smile. 'They go to the function, whatever it is— maybe dinner, maybe the theatre, maybe a party—and they make conversation, perhaps with their date for the evening, perhaps with one of his friends. Sometimes they get some enjoyment out of the evening, sometimes they don't, but either way they make a large amount of money.'

'What else do they have to do to get all that money?'

'I'm not a pimp. I pay them to escort, that's all. And I pay them very well.' He made a gesture of helplessness with his hands. 'If they choose to make even more money by going beyond their contractual requirements, then that's up to them. But you don't need to offer extras to make big bucks.' He fixed his grey eyes on her face. 'You have the right look, and you relate well to men. I'd be happy to put you on my books.'

'I don't think so, thank you. I'm not interested.'

'That's fine. No need to decide anything now. All I ask is that you take my contact details and think about it. Here, let me give you a card.'

He slipped his hand into his pocket, brought out a small white card embossed with black lettering, and handed it to her. She took it from him and tucked it into the bodice of her dress.

'Don't lose it now,' he said with a smile. 'Go home and take a look in the mirror, Terri Lee. You'll see a potential gold mine looking back at you. Give me a call when you're ready.' With a slight salute of his hand, he moved off and was absorbed immediately into the crowd.

She stood and stared after him long after he'd disappeared from sight.

Then she went back into the party venue, sat down on the nearest leather-backed chair and looked slowly around the room, studying the women there.

'TERRI LEE! Thank God, I've found you! Where the fuck have you been? I've been looking everywhere for you.

Charlie keeps asking where you are, and here are you, you're away with the daisies! What the hell d'you think you're doing?'

'I didn't know you wanted me, did I? I'm sick and tired of that bloody man, and I'm sick and tired of these bloody parties. I've had it up to here with them. This is the last one I come to, and I mean it. And for your information, I went outside to get some fresh air—I needed it after you left me with that perv.'

'Well, I've found you now,' Hugh said, visibly trying to control himself. 'Charlie's fucking mad that you've not been near him. I told you he liked you. Now get over to him before he's so pissed off that he takes his money elsewhere.' Grabbing her by the arm, he pulled her up out of the chair and started to drag her across the room.

'Slow down!' she exclaimed, half-running to keep up with him. 'Let me go! You're hurting. Let me go, I said.'

But his fingers tightened their hold on her, and he continued to pull her after him as he strode across to the long bar that filled one of the walls of the room. She saw Charlie at the bar, leaning against the counter, clutching a drink.

Hugh released her arm just before they got to him.

'That's better,' she said, standing still and rubbing the red patch where his fingers had been. 'That really hurt. To hell with Charlie—I want to go home now.'

'I'm sorry, babe.' Hugh gave her a rueful smile and ran his hands gently up and down her arms. 'Naughty Hugh got carried away. Put it down to stress. Would Hughie really want to hurt the woman he adores? Of course, he wouldn't.' He leaned towards her and kissed her lightly on the forehead.

She didn't say anything, but continued to rub her arm.

'I'm sorry, lover. But with Charlie wanting to see you, and me missing you like crazy and unable to find you, I rather forgot myself. Can beautiful Terri Lee ever forgive her naughty Hughie?'

'I suppose so,' she said, pouting. 'But I mean it, Hugh— this is the last party I come to with these arseholes. I've had enough.'

'Agreed, angel. Now come on over and say hello to Charlie for me, and then we'll go home. I can't wait to get you on my own. You know how much I love you, don't you?'

'Oh, Hughie. I feel the same about you.'

'Then let's get this over with. Just a quick hello to Charlie and then we'll split.' He kissed her lightly on the mouth. 'Come on now, lover.'

He put his arm around her shoulders and they went up to Charlie.

'Here she is, Charlie!' Hugh said with exaggerated effusion as they reached the large man who was frowning over a glass of whisky.

Charlie looked up at them, and she saw that he was drunk. His protruding eyes were bloodshot, his mouth was hanging open and there was a trace of dribble on his thick lips and chin. She felt herself recoil in disgust, and looked up at Hugh, expecting to see him struggling to smother a sense of repugnance, but he was smiling broadly at Charlie.

He clapped Charlie on the shoulder. 'I said I'd come back with her, didn't I, old boy, and here she is!' He turned to Terri Lee and gave her an encouraging nod. With a slight pressure of his hand on her shoulder, he pushed her closer to Charlie. 'Charlie's been looking for you, babe. He wants to say hello. I've got to have a word with a man about a dog. I'll be back in a minute.'

And he was gone.

Terri took a deep breath. That slob in front of her would be putty in her hands in minutes. Sex was power. If she'd learned anything, she'd learned that. If that escort man she'd just met could see her flirting with that drunken slob like she was about to do, he'd see how good an actress she could be, and how much money she was worth.

She caught her breath sharply. What was she thinking of?

This wasn't about money. It was about helping Hugh by indulging in some harmless flirting. It was no more than that, and never would be. Her days of being Susan Lesley Taylor were well and truly over.

7

D*erbridge*

'HOW MANY TIMES have I gotta ask you to give me a hand with the meal?' Susan Lesley Taylor's mother screamed at her from the kitchen.

Curled up on the threadbare brown sofa in the front room, Susan pressed her hands against her ears to block out her mother's shrill voice. She was going to play Nancy in 'Oliver Twist' and she'd two pages of lines to learn before the next rehearsal, which had been brought forward to the following day, and she hadn't a moment to lose.

Not that she was complaining about the pressure of time. In all of her fifteen years, she'd never been given such an important part in a play, and she was longing to show everyone what she could do. But that wouldn't be much if she didn't know her words.

And it wasn't as if she hadn't already helped her mother that day.

She'd made the breakfast, and then washed a pile of dirty clothes and pegged them on the line before leaving for school. As soon as she'd got home, she'd unpegged the clothes and folded them, washed up the breakfast things, swept the kitchen floor and peeled the potatoes for the evening meal. And it was she, Susan, who'd be doing all the ironing the following day. Not her mother.

She always did her bit, but it was never enough for her mother. All her mother had to do when she got back from her cleaning job was cook the meal. It wasn't fair—no one else at her school had to do as much housework as she did.

'Susan!' her mother shouted again.

Susan pressed her hands even harder against her ears.

This would be her last chance to act in a school production. In six months' time she'd be sixteen and she'd have left school before the next play.

She'd loved to have stayed on at school so that she could do some more acting, and she'd told her mother that if she let her stay on, and perhaps did something like the secretarial course, she'd work at the hairdresser's on Saturdays and every evening, and she'd give every penny to her mother. But her mother had said no.

'How any daughter be so ungrateful?' her mother snapped whenever Susan had tentatively raised the subject of staying on. 'You've not got a father helpin' out. That good-for-nothing bastard disappeared years ago, and I'm the one who's gotta pay for everything. I'm workin' my fingers to the bone for you, and that's all the thanks I get. You'll leave school as soon as the law says you can, and you'll go out to work and start payin' your way.'

But if her mother thought she was gonna leave school

and work in some crap job, and hand over every penny she made as well as do everything at home, her mother was in for a shock. The moment she left school, she was gonna go down to London and become an actress.

She knew it'd be harder to get a job in the theatre as she hadn't been to a drama school, but she was still confident she would get to the top. After all, everyone said how beautiful she was, with fair hair that fell in curls to her shoulders and large blue eyes with long lashes.

And she knew her curves were in all the right places. The fact that the girls in her class, although friendly, were clearly jealous of her, told her that. Even her best friend, Patty, could be a bit green-eyed. And the boys were always coming on to her, even though she made it clear she wasn't interested in any of them—she was waiting to meet someone in the theatre, a director or an actor maybe, someone who could help her get good parts. But the other kids being the way they were was proof that there was something special about her, which would make her stand out when she got to London.

And with her face and figure, and the natural talent everyone said she had, she'd soon put her moaning mother and dull Derbridge behind her.

First, though, she had some lines to learn.

'So that's where you are! I might've guessed,' her mother snapped, coming into the front room. She glared at Susan. 'I've been yellin' myself hoarse, tryin' to get you to give me a hand, and you're sittin' here doin' nothing.'

'I'm not doin' nothing—I'm learning my lines. The rehearsal's tomorrow.'

'Same difference. Well, you can stop what you're doin' and put the dinner on,' her mother said, and she walked out of the room.

'It's not fair,' Susan yelled after her. 'No one else has to do what I have to do. I've already done the potatoes and just about everything else that had to be done. I've gotta learn my lines.'

Her mother spun round, went back to the sofa and leaned over Susan. The acrid stench of stale cigarettes hit Susan in the face. 'There's a lot I'd like to do, madam,' her mother said, her voice bitter, 'but I can't because of you. You ain't a clue how much it takes to keep you in clothes and food, with a roof over your head. I could've got wed years ago if it hadn't been for you. What man wants to take on someone else's brat?'

'If you didn't smoke as much, we'd have more money, wouldn't we? Or go to the pub so often,' Susan shouted up into her mother's face.

Her mother's hand was hard against her cheek.

Tears sprang to her eyes. She blinked them away, determined not to give her mother the satisfaction of letting her see that she'd hurt her. She jumped up, clutching her script close to her chest.

'I hate you,' she hissed, inches away from her mother's pinched face. 'I can't wait to leave home. The minute I finish school, I'm going to get as far away from you as I can. I won't be sticking around this dump for a moment longer than I have to. Do the meal yourself—I'm not hungry.' Turning on her heels, she ran out of the room and up the stairs.

Alone in her bedroom, she threw herself on to the narrow bed, angry at herself.

She should never have told her mother that she intended to leave home. Her mother was bound to make her next six months a misery, and there was nothing she could do about it—she didn't have anywhere else to go. She didn't have any relatives, or if she did, she'd never met them. Her mother had never mentioned anyone else in the family, and apart from one occasion, had never mentioned her father. For as long as she could remember, it had been just her and her mother, a woman who didn't seem to like her very much.

The once she'd mentioned her father, Susan had been about five years old. Her mother had found a ten pound note in the street, and in a really good mood, had promptly taken Susan to the park, where they'd fed the ducks. Seeing her mother so happy and smiling, Susan had asked her where her daddy was, and if he, too, liked feeding the ducks.

Her mother had fallen silent for a moment, and then muttered something about Susan having the right to know something about her pig of a father. She'd told Susan that she and Susan's father had fallen in love when they'd been quite young. With both families against them because of their age, and because he didn't have a job, they'd run away together.

At first, things were all right. He found some casual labour which brought in a bit of money, and she got a job, cleaning every day in a grand house near where they lived.

But then Susan had been born and things had got difficult.

Her mother couldn't work because of Susan, and her father started staying out longer and longer. When he'd been home, he'd kept on complaining about the cramped conditions in which they were living, and being angry at Susan's frequent crying. Soon he was spending most of his wages on drink, and each week saw a struggle to pay the rent. One day, her father walked out and never come back.

For weeks after that day in the park, Susan had stared at every man coming towards them in the street, wondering if this was her father returning. But gradually, she'd come to realise that she'd never see him again, and had stopped looking.

The sound of the front door slamming shut broke into her thoughts.

She sat up on the bed and glanced at the clock on the chest of drawers on the opposite side of the room. It said six o'clock. It was very early for her mother to go to the pub, she thought with a sinking feeling—she'd be dead drunk when she got home, and could easily start creating. She must try to learn her lines before her mother returned.

Leaning over the side of the bed, she picked up the script that had fallen to the floor, and started memorising her words.

An hour later, feeling hungry, she ran downstairs, took two slices of bread and a lump of cheese from the pantry, and then hurried back up to her room with her food. As soon as she'd finished eating, she put on her nightdress, took her plate back down to the kitchen, came back up, washed quickly in the bathroom, returned to her bedroom, climbed into her bed and sat with her back to the pillow. Having arranged the script so that it rested against her knees, she carried on learning her lines.

Gradually, her eyes closed, and some of the sheets of her script drifted to the floor.

A few hours later, a burst of raucous laughter shattered the silent darkness that hung in the still room.

Susan's eyes sprang open.

The laughter sounded again. It seemed to be coming from somewhere beneath her. She shifted her position, and the last two sheets of her script floated to the floor.

Reaching over the side of her bed, she tried to push the script into a neat pile, her head coming close to the wooden floorboards, and she heard the sound of voices below. She glanced at the clock. It wasn't yet ten. She's back early, she thought in surprise, and she's not alone.

Leaning further over the edge of the bed, she tried to make out who was with her mother, even though she hadn't much chance of recognising the voice—she'd rarely met any of her mother's friends. They were pub friends, not real friends like she had at school, and she hadn't liked the ones she had met. They were creepy, always staring at her body in a nasty way.

At times like that, she wished she was flat-chested like her friend, Patty. If she didn't have any shape, men might actually look at her face.

Patty's brother, Terry, was an exception.

He'd always seemed really interested in her on the few occasions she'd met him, and he'd never gawped at her. If she hadn't decided to go to London, she'd have set her sights on Terry. He was two years older than she was, and was really fit. At the moment, though, there were more important things than boys on her mind, like her career.

She strained harder, trying to make out what they were talking about downstairs, but without any luck. She was pretty sure that there was one other person only with her mother—a man with a rumbling sort of voice. They were talking fairly quickly and at times broke out into laughter—not a sound she normally associated with her mother—but their voices were muffled.

Yawning, she picked up her script and lay back on to her bed. She wasn't going to be able to go back to sleep while they were making such a din, so she might as well look at her lines while the moonlight held out—she'd no intention of letting her mother know she was awake by putting the light on.

Her script in front of her, she struggled with it until the

room was too dark to see anything and she had to give up. She put the script quietly on to the floor, and curled up in her bed, hoping for sleep.

A few minutes later, she realised that it had gone very quiet downstairs. Sitting up, she listened intently. The house was definitely silent. She must have missed hearing the man leave, and her mother go up to bed.

Then she heard a slight sound, which seemed to come from just outside her door. The door handle turned.

Instinctively, she pulled her blanket up to her chin. The door opened wide and her mother stood framed in the doorway. In the light reflected from the bottom of the stairs, she could see that her mother's eyes glittered brightly. She could also make out a large shape behind her mother.

'What d'you want?' she asked sharply, drawing her knees up under the blanket, suddenly nervous though she wasn't sure why.

'That's no way to speak to your mother,' her mother said evenly, coming into the room. The shape behind her filled the doorway. It was a man she'd never seen.

'What d'you want?' she asked again. 'And who's that with you?'

'A friend of mine. His name's Mack. He's a good friend, and he wants to be a good friend of yours, too. A very good friend.'

The man gave a dry laugh.

She tightened her grip on the blanket. 'Get out and let me get back to sleep! I've got school tomorrow.'

'She's got a bit of spirit in her, Mack. You'll like that,' her mother said with a laugh, glancing at the man behind her. She turned back to Susan. 'You'll do as you're told, my girl. Mack's gonna join you for a bit, and you're gonna be very nice to him.'

'Get out!' Susan screamed in panic. 'Both of you, get out, or—'

'Or what, Susan? There isn't really an 'or', is there?' her mother said with a sneer. 'You're gonna walk out of the house in your nightdress, are you? No knickers on your fanny; no money in your pocket; nowhere to go. You're gonna do that, are you?'

Susan stared at mother, horror in her eyes.

'Because if that's what you wanna do, you can get right out this minute. No one's stoppin' you. But if you decide to stay, you're gonna start earning your keep right now. You plan on leaving me high and dry the minute you can, so I might as well get somethin' out of you for as long as you're here. Call it pay back for what you've cost me over the years. So, which is it gonna be—walkin' out, or stayin' and bein' nice to Mack? Stand aside, Mack. Madam might wanna leave.' She opened the door wider, and the man in the doorway stepped back on to the landing.

Her stomach turning over in fear, Susan shivered violently.

'I didn't think so.' Her mother's mouth twisted in triumph. 'It's gettin' late now and I've gotta get some sleep. In you go, Mack. In every sense of the word.' Laughing coarsely, she went out of the room, leaving Susan's door wide open.

She heard her mother cross the landing, go into her room and close the door firmly behind her.

The big man came into Susan's room and kicked the door shut behind him. Walking unsteadily, he went forward to the bed, unbuttoning his shirt and tugging it out of his trousers as he went. Coarse black hair covered a large, flabby belly that hung over his trouser waistband.

She recoiled in horror.

Unzipping his trousers, he threw back the covers and climbed on to the bed. The smell of stale sweat and beer filled her nostrils as he pushed up her nightdress. Looking down at her, he grunted. With his knees, he forced her legs apart, and she felt rough fingers push into her and feel around.

He thrust his fingers deeper, his breathing getting louder and faster, and she cried out in pain. Withdrawing his fingers, he lay heavily on top of her, raised his hips and reached into his pants. A moment later, something cold and wet touched the soft flesh of her inner thigh.

Swallowing her nausea, she gazed up at the ceiling as tears rolled down her cheeks.

I'M AN ACTRESS, and I'm helping Hugh by flirting with these jerks. But it's only flirting, no more than that, Terri Lee told herself. Just a bit of harmless flirting. Surreptitiously, she inched down the front of her bodice and moistened her lips.

'Hello, Charlie. How are you?' she murmured huskily.

'Huh,' he snorted, and his eyes slid down her cleavage.

8

S *aturday*

CLOTHES LAY SCATTERED on the floor of Emily's room, over her bed and on the back of her chair. Standing in the centre of the chaos around her, she clutched her jeans.

'Don't even think it,' Terri Lee told her, grabbing at the jeans. 'You're not wearing those on your first date with that guy—your first date with anyone since you moved in! No one expects you to appear in a ball gown, but wearing jeans is not on. No way. For once in your pig-headed life you're gonna listen to someone else. Tell her, Caroline.'

Emily glanced longingly at her jeans. 'He said it was casual, so why shouldn't I wear something comfortable? After all, he's not a trendy sort of person. I wouldn't be going out with him if he was.'

'There's casual and casual, Emily,' Caroline told her firmly. 'Terri Lee's right—jeans are unsuitable. For a start, you don't know where he's taking you. As a rule, it's better to risk being slightly overdressed than underdressed.'

'I can't believe this! I only asked you which top I should wear. I didn't expect a lecture.'

'None of those for a start,' Terri Lee retorted, indicating the pile on the bed. 'You've gotta get tarted up a bit. Hasn't she, Caroline?'

Emily winced.

'You don't have to go overboard, Emily, but I do think Terri Lee's right in saying you should make an effort,' Caroline said smoothly. 'After all, you've had a whole week in which to sort something out. What does it say to him if you haven't bothered?'

Emily threw her jeans on the bed. 'Okay, I give up. But what on earth can I wear? I've no time to get anything new before tonight. I can't go out to dinner in my work clothes, and that leaves only my casual things, which you're dead against.' She gazed helplessly in the direction of her wardrobe.

'Don't panic. We're gonna help you,' Terri Lee said cheerfully, and she stood up. 'It'll be fun. Skinny people like you can wear just about anything. Caroline and I will raid our wardrobes and see what we've got that would do. We won't bother with Louise's things as she's shorter than you. You won't recognise yourself when we've done with you.'

'That's what I'm afraid of,' Emily said, and gave a theatrical groan.

'And I'll bring up some wine to get us in the mood,' Terry Lee added.

'Not for me,' Emily said hastily. 'Not before I go out; thanks all the same.'

. . .

AN HOUR AND A HALF LATER, Emily stood in the sitting-room in front of Terri Lee and Caroline, who sat in the armchairs, a glass of wine in front of each of them.

She was wearing a short, slightly fitted three-quarter-sleeved black crepe jacket over straight black crepe trousers, with black patent leather heels. Around her neck was a shiny wide silver band, and in each ear she wore a silver earring. Her light brown hair was swept back from her face, in a style that, along with the touch of silver eye shadow that Terri Lee had put on her eyelids, and her black mascara, had made her hazel eyes stand out. On her lips, she wore a plum-coloured lipstick.

'It doesn't look like me,' she said. 'I feel strange. And as for my face—it looks scarily colourful.'

'You look stunning, Emily,' Caroline said, staring at her in amazement. 'You look absolutely lovely. You should dress up more often. You're going to knock him dead.'

'You don't think him being dead could make for a boring evening?' Emily said drily.

'Funny, I don't think,' Terri Lee said. 'You have a ball now, and don't do anything I wouldn't do. And don't say that gives you plenty of scope!' she added quickly as Emily opened her mouth. 'That'd be too corny for words.'

The doorbell sounded. The two girls raised their glasses to Emily, who gave them a nervous smile. She picked up the black cashmere cardigan coat that she'd borrowed from Caroline, and paused.

'I've never had friends like you before,' she said awkwardly, her eyes filling with tears. 'You've both been really kind.'

'Get off before you wreck your mascara,' Terri Lee said with a laugh. 'And have fun.'

.   .   .

'SO WHY DID you choose Property Law, and not Criminal Law or Family Law, Emily?' John asked, filling Emily's glass and smiling at her across the table.

'Non-Chancery lawyers often ask me that, but I'm surprised at *you* asking. Surely the answer's obvious to someone like you. After all, you chose Chancery work, too.'

He shrugged. 'I know what I like, naturally, but I'm curious about what motivated you. Criminal Law's the glamour profession. Wouldn't working with people, even criminals, or working in the field of Matrimonial Law, be more fun than burying your head in a volume of words and documents?'

'You mean because I'm a woman?' she asked, a trace of irritation in her voice.

'No, I didn't mean that at all,' he said gently. 'I'm just interested in why you made the choice you did; that's all.'

'I chose it because working with people is exactly what I don't want to do,' she said firmly. 'I've had enough of people to last me a lifetime. I'd rather spend my time with a dry old document any day.'

John sat back and stared at her across the table. Amusement flickered across his lips. 'So, I'm a dry old document, am I?' he said. 'In that case, what do you read on this ancient piece of parchment that is me?'

Her hand flew to her head. 'Oh, no, I've done it again! You know I wasn't talking about you, don't you?' she said, and she gave an embarrassed laugh. 'But since you ask, let me see.' She narrowed her eyes and stared at him thoughtfully. 'It's hard to say,' she said at last. 'You seem to be together in every way: you're well respected; you're successful in your job and you seem very nice. But I don't believe anybody's that perfect. There'll be a hidden sub-text somewhere. As I can't see it, it must be written in invisible ink.'

'Words written in invisible ink normally show up when exposed to heat. If you carry on scrutinising me as closely as you are now, I shall go even hotter under the collar, and who knows what words will then emerge?'

She burst out laughing. 'You're mad.'

He leaned forward. 'Then we'd better order our food without delay,' he said in a conspiratorial tone. 'If the rest of the world catches on to my madness, I might find myself being whisked away to an institution where the food isn't a fraction as delicious as the Italian food they serve here. Nor in such a lovely setting.'

'It *is* beautiful here,' Emily said, looking up from the menu and glancing through the panoramic window.

The River Thames was gliding silently beneath the illuminated Tower Bridge, a sequined band of ebony velvet that separated them from the city. Tall buildings, black silhouettes against the night sky, punctuated by pin-points of light, stood stark in outline against the amber halo that pushed back the darkness and hung above the city.

She looked back at John. 'D'you come here a lot?'

'Not as much as I'd like to. It's one of my favourite restaurants, but I need to be with the right company to enjoy the ambiance as much as it deserves.'

'You can't be saying that *I'm* the right company,' Emily said in a tone of disbelief. 'I'm useless at small talk, and in the short time we've known each other, I've either been snapping at you or making awkward *gaffes*.'

John raised his eyebrows. 'You don't think you're good company? Then it's my turn to say that I think *you're* mad, too. That being the case, we'd be wise to order now before we're both carted off. If that happened, I might be prevented from taking you out again. If you think you might like to come out with me again, that is.'

Emily stared at him across the table. A smile crept across her face. 'I'd like that very much,' she said.

'I DO HOPE Emily's having a good time,' Caroline said from the depths of the armchair. She leaned forward to the coffee table, poured half the remains of the wine into Terri Lee's glass and the rest into hers, and then sank back against the cushions.

Terri Lee nodded. 'Me, too. The thought of Emily being frequently out of the house in the future is quite appealing.' She reached for her glass. 'But how come you're home on a Saturday evening? Is Tom washing his hair?'

'He called earlier to say he wasn't feeling well. I can't say I was sorry—it's been a hectic week and I could use a quiet evening. With Louise back before long—I can't remember exactly when—we'll soon be a full house again. But as we were saying about Emily, she must really like this John. She'd never go out with anyone just for the sake of it. Not our Emily.'

'Well, she certainly needs someone—she's so bloody boring at the moment. All she ever does is rabbit on about her cases. It drives me mad. Having a bloke should help her lighten up.'

'Talking about men, you've never told me how you met Hugh.'

Terri Lee shrugged. 'There's not much to tell. I was brought up in a shit little town called Derbridge, by a mother you wouldn't believe. I came to London to be an actress, but when I stepped off the bus I hadn't a clue how to go about it. Some missionary bloke outside the bus station gave me a leaflet about a hostel, so I went there. By the end of the week, I'd got friendly with a couple of other girls there, and we decided to rent a cheap flat in Cricklewood.'

'How did you pay for that?'

'I'd saved a bit from working in a hairdresser's, hadn't I? And as soon as we moved into the flat, I got a job as a temp, which I thought I'd do till I found work as an actress. I'd done a bit of typing at school, so I did filing, typing, and things like that. At the weekends, there was always at a party. I met Hugh at one of the parties and we fell in love. Though why a consultant gynaecologist with a fab car, who lives in St. John's Wood, would look at me, I'll never know.'

'Lucky you.'

'Don't I know it! Cricklewood was a bit far out for him, so when he saw the ad for this place, he told me to apply. I'm really glad I did—I like the three of you better than those other girls, and Camden Town is a fun place to be. Also, it's nearer to Hughie.'

'Are you seeing him later on?'

'Nope, he's busy somewhere. It's something to do with his surgery, I think. To be honest, he was a bit vague. I only know that I won't be seeing him till next Saturday, when we're going to a small do at one of the clubs.'

'I don't know how you can bear the endless round of parties and the like. I'd hate it.'

'I'm not that keen, I must admit. I was at first, but not any longer. Most of the men there are morons and slobs.'

Caroline frowned. 'So why does he go there, and why d'you go with him?'

'It's work for Hugh. He's trying to get backing for the Harley Street surgery he wants to set up. He needs money for equipment and things. I go along with him because they like to see me—at least, that's what he says. And anyway, I want to be with Hugh, wherever he is, no matter how boring. You do when you love someone, don't you? But you must know that. You're nuts about Tom, aren't you? Anyone can see that.'

A wave of anxiety spread across Caroline's face, and she bit her lip.

Terri Lee's eyes narrowed speculatively. 'You *are* in love with Tom, aren't you? Everything is all right with you both, isn't it? Tell Auntie Terri Lee,' she coaxed.

'I'm afraid I *do* love Tom, but I wish I didn't.'

'That sounds weird. Why not? We all know how much you wanna get married. And if you love him, problem solved.'

'Not really, it isn't. Tom and I can never come to anything. I know exactly what I want out of life, and I know without a doubt that I wouldn't get it with Tom. You can't live on love alone. I know that if I married Tom, I'd come to regret it.'

Terri Lee opened her mouth to speak.

Caroline finished her drink and stood up. 'Please don't think I'm being rude, but I'd rather not talk about Tom and me. I'll say good night now.'

As she left the room and climbed the stairs, a sense of depression settled upon her, weighting her down.

9

Daylight was fading into darkness.

Sitting opposite each other at a table next to the wall of glass that rose from the floor to the ceiling of the restaurant, Louise and Ethan stared out across the darkening bay to the glittering skyline of San Francisco.

'I always eat in Sausalito on my last night in California,' Ethan said. 'There isn't a better view of the Bay Area to be had. For as long as there's still some light, you can see Angel Island, Alcatraz and the Bay Bridge. And if you look down there,' he indicated the strip of land to the side, 'you can see a small bit of the Sausalito waterfront. The view from this spot keeps me going till I return.'

'I can well believe that—it's an amazing view. It's the perfect way to end a fantastic ten days. Thank you for giving me such a brilliant time, Ethan. I'll never forget a single minute of the trip.'

Ethan smiled warmly at her. 'And I won't either. Apart from the demo being a great success, and getting us the camera placement we wanted, it's the ten days in which I got to know you.' He leaned back in his chair, folded his arms and stared hard at her across the table. His brow creased into a frown. 'Actually, it's not strictly true that I've got to know you. The truth is, I know very little about you. But I'd like to know more, so tell me something about yourself.'

'It's very boring so I'll do you a favour and let you off the hook,' she said with a laugh.

'But I don't want to be let off the hook. So tell me. I'm listening.'

She shrugged. 'Okay, then; you asked for it. On the career side of things, I've one more year at business school —that'll be mainly doing a dissertation. When I leave, I want to work in PR, as you know.'

'I'm glad to hear it.'

She smiled. 'On the family side of things, I was born in London and have always lived there. My parents were killed in a car crash when I was thirteen, and I went to live in Finsbury Park with my older sister and her husband. They'd just got married, and now they've got a son. I moved out in September and got a room in a house in Camden Town, sharing with three other girls. I got a full grant for business school, so I could afford the rent. My sister means well, but she can be somewhat smothering, and I needed some space of my own. That's it.'

'Sharing can't be easy when you're studying.'

'You manage. It's your turn now to tell me something about yourself. Or is that a step too far as you're my boss? If it is, I'll take back my words.'

'It isn't a step too far—remember, we're still on equal footing. And I introduced the topic so you've a right to ask me. If you really want to know, I've made quite a mess of some things in my life.'

'Who hasn't? The longer you live, the more time there is to make mistakes.'

'Ouch!' he said.

'I didn't mean to imply that you were old,' she said quickly, smothering a giggle. 'Not at all.'

'That's all right then,' he said. 'No offence taken. As an aged person, though, I'll give you one piece of advice, young Louise,' he added, and his voice took on a note of seriousness. 'Keep your distance from the people who work with you. If you want a happy life, that's essential. What happened to me illustrates that.'

'Well, are you going to tell me more?' she prompted after a moment or two.

'It was just something that happened years ago,' he said, shaking his head dismissively. 'I was in the early stages of developing my company, building up contacts and all that, and I had a brief fling with my secretary. It was a bit of fun for us both, but no more than that, or so I thought. It lasted for about a month, and then I ended it. Unfortunately, she wouldn't accept it was over, and she pursued me week after week, sending me gifts, cards with declarations of love, you name it. I couldn't get rid of her.'

'That must've been frightening.'

'It was. And then she became threatening, and I ended up having to go to court and taking out an injunction against her. That finally ended the whole thing. But she had the details of a number of deals I'd lined up, and she managed to scupper most of them, causing me to lose some valuable contacts in the process. She nearly destroyed my company before it had even properly got going.'

'That's awful!'

'For that whole long nightmare, I felt trapped. I'd learned an important lesson the hard way. Maybe it's made me somewhat bitter, I don't know, but it's certainly made me wary. The business relationships you make will be the key to your success. In order to protect those, it's safer never to mix business with pleasure.'

'But any relationship could end up with one person refusing to accept that it's over. It's not only in the workplace that it can happen.'

'True. But you've much more to lose when the other person knows the ins and outs of your business, in the way that colleagues and employees do. With people outside work, it's a different matter.' He paused. 'Do you understand what I'm trying to tell you, Louise?' he added quietly.

'Yes.' She tried to push back the huge wave of disappointment welling up inside her. 'I understand perfectly well.'

And she did.

She'd caught him gazing at her with obvious desire on several occasions when he'd thought she wouldn't be aware of it, and she'd frequently felt herself longing for him to take her in his arms. But to her great regret, he'd never made any attempt at all to change the nature of their relationship.

Yes, she'd got the point all right—she was strictly business. She was never going to be pleasure.

'Anyway,' he said, finishing his wine. 'That was a long time ago. But to get back to the present and to you, I'm surprised you haven't been snapped up yet—at least, I'm assuming you've haven't as you've not mentioned anyone. You're easy to talk to, as I've just proved, and you're not that unpleasant on the eye.'

'Why, thank you, kind sir; I'm overwhelmed!' she said, forcing a lightness back into her voice. 'But I don't want to be snapped up, as you put it, by just anyone—it's got to be by the right person. When I meet that person, I'll know it. And if I don't meet them, I'll stay on my own.'

'I wouldn't bet on the latter situation,' he said.

Their eyes met across the table, and held.

She felt a flush spread over her cheeks, and she turned swiftly to stare out of the window at the moonlit city. At the same moment, Ethan made a great show of looking at his watch.

'I think it's time I asked for the bill and we got back to the hotel, don't you? After all,' he went on, his clear blue eyes taking on an air of amusement, 'we ought to avoid me being up too late. At my age, one needs all the sleep one can get.'

She watched him as he raised his hand to call the waiter. His skin was lightly tanned from the sea and the wind, and his dark brown hair was streaked by the late autumn sun that had bathed the city throughout their visit. She ached deep within her.

Thank God they were leaving the following morning, she thought in relief. She was finding it nearly impossible to hide the way she felt about him, and she was dangerously close to ignoring his words, and throwing herself physically on top of him.

SHE STARED MOROSELY at the Camden Town house as the taxi came to a stop in front of the door.

'Thanks for coming all the way back with me, even though it's horribly late,' she said, turning to Ethan. 'I'm sure I don't have to tell you again how grateful I am for everything—you must already know it.'

'You don't have to thank me—I've loved every minute of our time together, Louise.'

'Ditto.' She cleared her throat. 'I shall be going in on Monday. At the end of the week, I'll clear my desk. I may or may not see you before I leave.'

'One of those possibilities is a pretty safe bet,' he said with a smile. She started to open her door. 'You know, Louise,' he added quickly. 'As of the end of next week, you won't be an employee any longer. It makes it a whole new ball game. I must go up to the Northumberland office next week and I expect to be there for a week or so—there's a problem with some of the manufacturers up there, and I'm not sure it's being handled as it should. But when I get back, would you mind if I got in touch with you? Perhaps took you out for a meal on English soil.'

An explosion of pleasure shot through her.

'That would be brilliant,' she exclaimed, her face lighting up. 'Absolutely brilliant.'

10

N*ovember*

TOM WAS CLEARLY head over heels in love with her, and Caroline knew she was close to feeling the same about him.

She frowned slightly and sat back at her desk, idly watching her pupils as they worked noisily in their groups.

Tom was a fantastic person, and she was delighted that he was as keen to do with her what they'd frequently have to do if she was going to have the number of children she wanted. But that had thrown up a problem: what to do about contraception.

Up to that point in her life, it hadn't been necessary for her to give much thought to birth control. Given the standard she was looking for in a man, she'd been quite fussy about the men she'd dated, and on the infrequent occasions she'd had sex, the man had put on a condom without being asked.

But her relationship with Tom was different. This was the first time she'd slept with anyone with any degree of regularity, and she needed to give serious thought to avoiding a pregnancy. Much as she wanted children, she fully intended to control when she had them, and with whom.

Tom generally used a condom as she couldn't get on with the cervical cap, but there'd been the odd occasion when neither had remembered the condom in time. Quite a few such occasions, in fact. As soon as she'd realised the risk they'd taken, she'd had a nervous week or two, although Tom hadn't seemed particularly bothered by it.

And she was also acutely aware that the condom had quite a high failure rate. So far, they'd been lucky, but the risk they were taking had become such a worry that she was actually thinking about going on the pill.

She'd read somewhere that the pill could make you infertile, and so far that fear had overridden every other consideration. But the situation had changed with Tom's arrival on the scene, and she was going to have to weigh up the risks involved, and balance them.

She knew that Tom would marry her like a shot if she fell pregnant. In fact, he'd probably be pleased as he was as keen as she on having children. And she knew that if she got pregnant, she'd have to agree to marry him.

Some women could go it alone, but she knew herself well enough to know that she wasn't one of them. She needed a husband to come with the children—preferably to come before the children—but whatever the order, a husband was a vital part of the picture.

But if she had a choice, would she choose to spend the rest of her life with Tom, she mused.

She liked him very much. No, it was more than that—

she loved him. He was kind and thoughtful, excellent company, and her very best friend, and she knew that he'd never let her down. But for as long as she could remember, she'd dreamed of being a full-time homemaker, looking after the house, her children and her husband.

And the sad reality was that Tom would never be able to make that dream come true.

He was a superb teacher and was sure to move up in the profession, perhaps even become a head teacher. But she knew him well enough to know that he lacked the kind of ambitious drive that would take him out of the school and into the higher administrative ranks, the ranks he'd need to be in if he was going to earn the sort of money that would support a full-time housewife and a lovely home, and that would ensure that their children were taught by better teachers than she.

If she were someone else, she could abandon that dream for the sake of staying with Tom.

But she wasn't that someone else.

As she stared around the classroom, willing the lesson to draw to an end, she knew in her heart that she wasn't prepared to abandon her dream so early on. Not even for Tom. She'd always wonder what would've happened if she'd stayed true to her priorities for a little longer, and she'd never have any peace of mind.

She hated herself for feeling that way, but she couldn't stop herself.

She still wanted to carry on seeing Tom, though. There was no reason to break with him just because she didn't think they had a future together, which meant that she was going to have to go to the doctor and be put on the pill. She sighed deeply. With luck, she'd get an appointment on Friday.

. . .

Terri Lee sat nervously on the edge of one of the chairs that lined the corridor. Another Friday: another audition. In her hands, she clutched her headshot, her resumé and the script extract.

Someone had told her that it was a good idea always to take a headshot with you, even to an audition for a play, and when she'd first met Hugh, he'd got a photographer he knew to do a headshot for her. But her hair was longer now and the photo was somewhat out of date. She'd have to ask him to get another shot done.

She glanced anxiously down at the script, hoping like mad that there wouldn't be any tricky words.

She was amazed that she was still as nervous as she was at auditions—she'd done more than enough of them to know the score. And there was seldom much to read, especially when it was for the part of a maid, which this one was. It must be that she desperately hoped each time that she was about to get the break she needed.

Deep down, though, she'd come to realise that the odds on her getting a role, which hadn't been great to begin with, were even worse with each passing month.

At audition after audition, she'd found herself surrounded by girls with good figures and pretty faces, girls full of enthusiasm and hope. At first she'd thought they were just like her. But as she'd got to know them while they waited in turn to be called, she'd learned that most had hidden extras.

Some had certificates to show that they'd been to theatre and dance schools, where they'd been taught how to act and how to behave in front of a camera. Others already had acting experience of a sort. Maybe they'd got it by doing commercials; maybe by touring the country with a repertory company; maybe by travelling from school to school, acting out Shakespeare plays for the kids. But however they'd got it, they'd had training and experience, and she hadn't.

As for her acting ability—she'd quickly realised that school plays and a natural flair couldn't compare with actual experience. Seeing that, she'd early on decided to join a repertory company so that she, too, could learn her trade, and would have something more than just good looks to offer when she went back to auditioning.

And then she'd met Hugh.

She'd realised from the outset that he wouldn't want her to join a company and go off touring for month after month, and she'd known that she'd lose him if she did so—he was a real catch and someone else would be sure to snap him up.

Also, as he'd pointed out, most of the people she met when she was with him were successful businessmen, important people with money, who knew other important people. They were going to help him, he firmly hoped, and if she played her cards right, they might help her, too.

But she couldn't quite bring herself to give up a plan that she'd felt so sure would help her to achieve her goal, and for a while, she was mired in indecision.

And then Hugh saw the advert for the house in Camden Town.

Hugh had instantly pointed out that living there would be better than living in her poky little room in Cricklewood. Camden Town was the right place to be: it was a good location, central to everything in London and, above all, it wasn't too far from where he lived.

That had decided her. Hugh clearly wanted her living near him, and that could only mean that he was serious about her. She'd promptly abandoned all lingering thoughts of joining a rep, and from then on had devoted herself to Hugh and to furthering his cause.

Sadly, Hugh's early hints that his friends might help her had come to nothing, and now, months later, she was still auditioning along with all the other hopefuls, who had so much more than good looks to offer.

As she glanced down at her script, not for the first time in recent weeks she wondered if she'd made the right decision.

She sat up straight and inwardly kicked herself—of course she had. She still had Hugh, didn't she? They'd been together for several months and he clearly loved her as much as she loved him. As soon as he'd got the financial backing he wanted from Charlie and the friends he hung around with, he was sure to ask her to marry him. He'd more than once hinted as much.

A door leading off the corridor opened. 'Terri Lee Taylor,' a weary voice shouted, and a head appeared through the gap.

She got up quickly and followed the man into a large room, and hesitated.

There were several people standing around, a couple of whom were eating sandwiches. She hadn't a clue who anyone was, but they all looked pretty bored, which wasn't surprising as they'd seen hordes of actresses before they'd got to her, and there were still a lot more waiting in the corridor.

A casually dressed man in a brown leather jacket was talking to a camera operator in the corner. That would be the director, she decided. You could never tell for sure, though. She remembered one ghastly audition where she'd mistaken the director for the caretaker, he'd looked such a mess, and she'd asked him to sweep up the crisps she'd dropped. After that embarrassing experience, she'd treated everyone as if they were someone important, no matter how scruffy they looked.

As no one came over to tell her what to do, she crossed to the centre of the room, and stood there, glancing around her while she waited, wondering where she should leave her headshot and resumé. Then the leather-jacketed man went and sat in the director's chair at the back of the room.

'Right, stand on that mark over there near the kitchen chair, so we can see you. We'll take a shot, and then you can tell us something about yourself,' a voice called from the side of the room.

She moved to the spot the voice had indicated, paused for the shot, and then briefly introduced herself.

'Okay. Now let's see you walk around, stand, sit in the chair, you know the sort of thing,' the voice instructed.

She did as asked—she'd done it often enough—moving around for a minute or two, trying to think how a maid might hold herself, especially in the scene she was going to be reading out. When she got back to the place where she'd started, she stopped.

'Start reading!' the director yelled.

'Where d'you want me to focus?' Terri Lee asked, glancing in his direction.

He shrugged. 'You choose,' he replied, and sat back.

Looking slightly to the side of the director to make sure that he saw her face from its best angle, she started to read the role of the maid, looking up from the script as much as she could, aiming to make eye contact.

In the early days, she'd tried to learn each script by heart, even if it had been handed to her only minutes before, but a friend of a director, who'd taken her out for a drink after one of her auditions, had told her that most of the girls didn't make any attempt to learn the words. They weren't testing her memory, he'd told her—they were testing her acting ability.

That had been a good tip, Terri Lee had often thought since then, as it had saved her from needlessly learning thousands of words, and from then on, she'd read the words, putting in as much emotion as possible.

'That'll do, Terri Lee. Check that the receptionist's got your details on the way out. Be sure to sign out and record the time, won't you? We'll be in touch.'

'I bet you will,' she muttered inwardly as she handed her photo, resumé and script to a woman sitting at a table a little way back from the door.

She walked into the bright sunlight outside the building, and stopped.

It hit her with the force of a thunderbolt that she'd had enough of chasing a dream that would never become a reality, and she'd had enough of agency work. She was going to have to find a different way of using what talent she had to make a living.

11

Caroline glanced at the clock on the wall. Thank God it was the last lesson of the week, and there were only a few more minutes left.

She stood up, told the class to pass their exercise books to the front and then put their chairs on their table. Walking from one side of the classroom to the other, she collected the books from each of the front tables, took them back to her desk and put them into her bag.

The bell sounded.

She opened her mouth to dismiss the class, but her voice was lost in the sound of chairs being knocked to the floor as the pupils pushed past each other in their haste to get to the door. Within a matter of minutes, the room was empty and in complete disarray. Wearily, she walked along the rows, picking up the chairs and straightening the desks. When she'd finished, she took her bag, switched off the light and went out into the corridor.

'I'm off, Tom,' she called as she opened the door to his classroom. He was still at his desk, she saw, and had a pupil in detention. 'Sorry!' she mouthed, with a little giggle.

He got up and came swiftly to the door. 'Are we meeting tonight?' he asked, keeping his voice low.

'Not tonight, I'm afraid,' she said. 'I'm shattered. I just want to crash out.' He opened his mouth to speak. 'By myself,' she added with a laugh. 'Come on over tomorrow and I'll do you a meal.'

'I wouldn't dream of it. You've worked all week so Saturday should be a day of rest. We'll go out to eat. I'll book somewhere. I'll come round at about seven thirty, if that's okay with you?'

'Sounds good.' She gave him a little wave, turned away and walked along the corridor towards the main entrance.

It was the right decision not to see Tom that evening, she thought as she left the school premises and headed for the underground station, and not just because she'd got a doctor's appointment—she felt totally drained and not at all in the mood to be social. She'd dump her bag in her bedroom as soon as she got home, and chill out downstairs until it was time to leave for the doctor's.

Part of her low mood, she knew, was depression at having to go on the pill. But she didn't really have any choice, not if she wanted to carry on sleeping with Tom, and she did.

Glancing up as she left the underground station, she saw that the sky was darkening. Tightening her hold on her bag of school books, which were getting heavier by the minute, she walked briskly up Camden Road, anxious to avoid being caught in the rain that threatened. When she reached the entrance to their road, she slowed down and fumbled in her bag for her key.

'Damn!'

She looked up, startled at hearing a man's voice.

A tall man in a dark grey pin-striped suit was standing

on the doorstep in front of their house, his back to her. His finger was on the door bell.

She cleared her throat and moved forward. 'Can I help?' she called. 'I live there.'

The man spun round. His face broke into a warm smile. A heart-stopping smile.

He's really good-looking, she thought, and she went closer.

'Since you live here, I wonder if you'd be good enough to let me into the house?' he asked.

She raised her eyebrows questioningly.

He laughed. 'I'd better explain. I'm Robert Chesterton. I own the house, which makes me your landlord, I guess. My letting agent, Manny Brown, was supposed to be meeting me here, but something seems to have held him up. I didn't bring a key as I was assuming that Manny would let us in. The last thing I want to do is hang around till he arrives, so I'd be very grateful if you'd do the honours.'

'You're here to do what exactly?'

'To look at the garden. It seems that none of you is particularly keen on cutting the grass, and the garden isn't your responsibility anyway—it's mine. I was thinking of having it shingled or paved. Either would look better than overgrown grass, and would need minimum work. I'd send a gardener about once a month to keep the weeds at bay. What d'you think?'

'I think it's a great idea,' she said enthusiastically. 'We'll want to be out there as much as we can next summer, but you're right, we're none of us keen gardeners. It's not that we don't want to do it,' she added quickly, 'it's just that we don't have the time.' She indicated the bag she was carrying.

'That's fair enough. As I said, it's not up to you: it's up to me. That's why I want to see what needs to be done.'

'That makes sense.' She smiled radiantly up at him.

'Well, shall we go in?' he asked a moment or two later, in obvious amusement. 'While it's very pleasant standing here, at some point it'll be too dark to see the garden, and if it rains, it'll be too wet.'

She laughed in embarrassment, tore her gaze from the dark brown eyes that were looking down at her with unmistakable appreciation, and dug deep in her bag for her key.

He must think her a real idiot, she thought as she pulled out the key, standing there staring at him, her tongue all but hanging out. But he really was very attractive: tall and well-built, with a suggestion of the sort of inner power she'd always dreamed of finding in a man. Yes, her landlord was quite something else.

As she unlocked the door, her heart thumped loudly. She pushed the door open, and stepped back. 'After you,' she said.

'Oh no,' he murmured, indicating that she should go first. 'I'm definitely going to go after you.'

Is he flirting with me, Caroline wondered. And as she stepped across the threshold, she realised how much she wanted the answer to be yes.

'WHAT SORT of day did you have, Caroline?' Terri Lee asked, looking up from *Glamour* as Caroline came down the stairs in the housecoat.

'Okay,' she said casually, going through to the kitchen.

'Okay, was it? Well, that's an improvement on what you normally say at the end of the day,' Terri Lee called after her. 'It must mean that you're getting on top of the job. Bully for you, gal.'

'Don't get excited—the job's just as awful as ever,' Caroline said, coming back into the sitting-room, a bottle in one hand and a glass in the other. 'I'm as useless today as I was the day I began. D'you want some wine before I drink it all?'

'You have it. I'm going out later and I'm saving myself till then. So what turned today into okay, rather than crap?'

'Haven't a clue,' Caroline said, settling into the armchair. 'To be honest, I don't even know why I said it.'

'To be honest, my arse! You said it for a reason. If work's not got better, it must be something Tom's done.'

'Listen to you! I'm telling you, it's not work and it's not Tom. It's nothing.'

'Pull the other leg. It's something, and because you're not saying what it is, I'm guessing it's about a man.'

'Honestly, it's not.'

'Yes, it is,' Terri Lee cried, her voice triumphant. 'You should know by now that redheads can never get away with lying. You should see the colour of your face! You've absolutely *got* to tell me what's going on.'

'Well,' Caroline said hesitantly. 'I might've met someone.'

Terri Lee squealed with delight. Curling her legs up under her, she leaned forward. 'Don't stop there. I want every bit of the nitty gritty.'

'You're going to be so disappointed,' Caroline said, laughing. 'There's nothing to tell. When I got home, I found a man on our doorstep, trying to get in. It was our landlord, so I let him in. He had a look at the garden and decided to get it paved, and I let him out. End of story.'

'And the bit you've left out is—?'

'He's drop-dead-gorgeous, Terri Lee,' Caroline said, her eyes shining. 'He's absolutely fabulous.'

'And?'

'That's it, I'm afraid. I doubt I'll ever see him again.'

'Then we're just gonna have to break the dishwasher or something, and get him back here,' Terri Lee said firmly.

'Don't think I haven't thought about that, but it wouldn't work—the letting agent deals with that sort of thing. And anyway, who's to say that I'd be the one he'd ask out if he came here and saw the three of you? In fact, I'd be far happier if he kept away from the house when you lot were in.'

'I'm not sure he'd go for Emily, make-up or not. Only a weird sort of person would fancy her, and our landlord doesn't sound weird from what you've said. And Louise could be a little too nice for him. With all that gorgeous money and those looks, I suspect he could prove to be a bit of a bad boy, and Louise wouldn't be his thing. As for me, I've got my lovely Hughie and wouldn't want anyone else.'

'I'd still rather not chance him meeting you before I've got my hooks into him.'

'And where does Tom fit into all this?' Terri Lee asked after a slight pause.

'I don't know,' Caroline wailed. 'I feel awful, Terri Lee, thinking about someone else in that way. Not when I've got Tom, who's lovely and who's saved my life I don't know how many times. I'm being so unfair to him.'

Terri Lee shook her head. 'No, you're not. Quite the opposite. If you find the dishy landlord's not what you hoped he was, and you spend the evening wishing you were with Tom, you'll know you love Tom. But if you do fall for the Greek god, then it'll show that you don't love Tom as much as you should, and it's better he knows that sooner rather than later.'

'My head tells me you're right, but it still feels wrong.'

'Forget about Tom for a minute, and let's work on a way to get lover boy here,' Terri Lee said. 'The three of us will go out before he arrives, I promise—not that he'd look at us with you around. I'm not saying we won't get an eyeful from around the corner, but he won't see us. Then, when you're into each other big time, we'll meet him.'

'And how exactly do you suggest we get him here? Therein lies the rub.'

'Oh, I'll find a way,' Terri Lee said cheerfully. 'You can be absolutely sure of that.

The clock on her bedside table said three in the morning.

Emily was furious with herself that she was still awake. The trouble was, she was just too excited after the evening she'd had, which had ended by John telling her that he loved her. And although it was over three hours since she'd said goodnight to him, she hadn't been able to shut down the memory of his face, or of the good time they'd had that evening and on all of the other occasions she'd been out with him.

She thought back to their first date, and smiled.

Terri Lee had told her to have fun, and she certainly had. And they'd had just as much fun—in a calm sort of way that the others would never understand—on all of the other dates that had followed.

She curled up in her bed and tried to think back to any time before she'd met John when she'd enjoyed life in the way she had since she'd met him. But she couldn't think of any.

Fun wasn't something that had figured largely in her early years.

The Lord didn't put you on earth to have fun, Prudence, she heard her mother snap at her. The Lord created you in His image to glorify Him and to follow in His path. Let other people have their fun: we have the Lord.

As her mother's words resounded in her head, Emily's smile faded.

WITH THE AID of her sleeve, Emily wiped the morning condensation from the front room window, pressed her nose against the glass and stared longingly at the children, who were meandering down the hill past her house.

It wasn't fair.

She was seven years old now, old enough to be walking down the road as one of their group. She should be swinging a school bag just as they were doing and joining in with their conversation. She knew the kind of things they talked about because once or twice when she was running an errand for her mother, they'd been coming out of school, and on each occasion, she'd followed them down the hill, keeping her distance, but trying to hear what they were saying.

To be able to watch them, she'd started sitting on the narrow window seat in the front room while she did the lessons her mother had given her. At first her mother had called for her to come and sit at the parlour table, but Prudence had told her that she preferred to be on her own when she did her lessons, and her mother had reluctantly agreed to let her stay where she was.

While she worked, she kept on glancing out of the window, and whenever she saw children of her age going down the hill, she'd run and ask her mother if there were any errands that needed doing. If she was really lucky, she'd be sent to the local shop on the corner, two streets away. If she wasn't, she could be asked to deliver a message to the Meeting Hall.

Going to the shop was the best. She'd rush out of her house, clutching a handful of coins, and walk as close to the children as she dared, listening to what they were saying. Although her mother was teaching her at home at the moment—except when she went to the house of her friend, Patience, to be taught by Patience's mother—she'd go to a big school one day, with children from the families that hadn't been saved, and she'd need to be able to talk to them.

She was always disappointed if the children were discussing television programmes as she'd never be able to talk about those. Television and radio were instruments of the Devil, her parents said. It was better when the children were chatting about things she knew about.

One of her and Patience's favourite topics was the suffering of the various martyrs, and they used to devour books about the martyrs' lives, their hands to their mouths as they read of the torments they endured to prove their love for the Lord. Perhaps the children at the big school also liked talking about the martyrs. She'd lend them some books if they wanted.

Yes, going to the shops, where she might see the other children, was definitely the best sort of errand. Being sent to the Meeting Hall in Bay Street was the worst.

Preacher Madson might be there.

Whenever Preacher Madson saw her, he'd stop whatever he was doing, come across to her, lay a long thin hand on her head and say a prayer that she be delivered from Evil.

She used to wonder why he was so worried about her doing Evil—she never had the chance.

She wasn't even sure that she really knew what Evil was. She supposed it must be something that the other children did, and that was why she wasn't allowed to talk to them.

But if doing Evil was such a terrible thing, she used to wonder, her nose flat against the window pane, why did other children always seem to be having such a good time as they walked along, laughing with each other?

She'd love to be allowed to play with them, so that she could laugh, too, but she didn't dare ask her parents if she could. Not again. The once she'd asked had been enough.

One of the girls walking past her house had seen her staring through the window and had waved at her. Thinking the girl wanted to be friends, she'd waved back. The girl had seemed about to stop, but had changed her mind and carried on walking down the hill.

She'd immediately run into the parlour to ask her mother and father if she could go out and play with the friendly girl. But before she'd finished her question, she'd seen a look of pain come over her mother's face, and her words had died in her throat.

'We are all born into Evil,' her mother had told her, her voice heavy with sorrow. 'But the Good Lord is merciful to those who follow in His path. Ungodly children ask not for the Lord's forgiveness, nor do they try to follow in His path, so we do not seek their company.'

'Perhaps they don't know what His path is. I could show them,' she'd eagerly suggested.

Her mother's lips had tightened. She'd put down the spoon with which she'd been stirring the stew, taken her headscarf from a peg on the wall and tied it around her hair, lamenting with every twist of the scarf that she'd borne a daughter who wished to mix with heathens. Then grasping Prudence firmly by the hand, she'd swept her out of the house, down the hill and along the road that led to the Meeting Hall.

Preacher Madson had been sitting on a chair in the Hall when they arrived. Grim-faced, her mother had explained the situation to him, and begged him to say the words that would cleanse her daughter of filial ingratitude.

Prudence wasn't sure what 'filial ingratitude' meant, but she never wanted to be guilty of it again—the memory of Preacher Madson's fingers on her shoulders as he guided her to the chair facing his, had haunted her for days afterwards.

He'd sat himself down, inches from her knees, and leaned forward to speak to her. She'd stared at her hands.

'Look at me, Prudence,' he'd instructed her. She'd looked up and smelt vinegar on his breath.

Peering intently into her face, his eyes pink and watery, he'd talked softly to her about the Lord's love for His children, witnessed on earth by a parent's love for a child, and placing a hand gently on her knee, he'd explained the duties of a loving child towards God and her parents, and the importance of unquestioning obedience to His will.

She'd felt the touch of his fingers through her thin cotton skirt, and goose bumps had prickled her arms.

'Unquestioning obedience to whatever they're told,' he'd repeated sternly, his hand sliding to her thigh. 'Now, Prudence; do you truly love and fear the Lord and long to do His will,' he'd asked solemnly. She'd seen a tuft of grey hairs hanging from his nostrils and she'd nodded vigorously.

His hand still on her thigh, he'd asked if she had anything to say to her mother. Anxious to escape his eyes, and the touch of his hand, she'd nodded again. He removed his hand and beckoned to her mother to step forward.

She'd apologised for being such a terrible daughter and for causing her mother and father to be so unhappy, and she'd promised that she'd always be good in the future.

'And do you still want to mix with heathens, Prudence?' Preacher Madson had quietly asked. She'd hastily assured him that she didn't.

His mouth a thin line of satisfaction, and his eyes cast down, he'd interlocked his fingers in front of his chest while her mother profusely thanked him for his words to her wayward daughter. It had been the Lord who'd spoken, he'd murmured. He'd merely been His instrument. Then he'd bade them all good day, and she'd walked with her mother out of the Meeting Hall, feeling Preacher Madson's eyes hot on her back.

But she *did* still want to be friends with the other children, even if they were heathens.

She longed to mix with them. More than ever, in fact. It was boring always being by herself. Of course she had Patience, and she liked her very much. But all they ever talked about was the Bible, and the martyrs. They never laughed together. There wasn't much to laugh about in the lives of the martyrs.

And then one day not long after that, she had an unexpected chance to make friends with the children who walked with Evil, and she jumped at it.

On the way to the shop for her mother, she'd turned the corner at the bottom of the hill and seen a group of children a little way ahead of her. Walking more quickly to get closer to them, she caught up with a girl who was bending down to do up her shoelaces. The girl had long fair plaits with red rubber bands at the end of them. It was the girl who'd once smiled at her.

'Can I play with you?' Prudence asked.

The fair-haired girl glanced up at her, and then stood up and stared at her. The surprise on her face changed swiftly to amusement.

'Hey!' she yelled to the others. 'Come and see who wants to play with us!'

Her friends turned and ran up to them. When they reached them, they stopped abruptly and stared at Prudence.

She smiled nervously at the children, who were standing in silence, their eyes running down the length of her body. Then one of the boys pointed to her, turned to the others, threw back his head and shrieked with laughter.

The others boys joined in, gradually followed by the girls. Soon all of the children were laughing at her, with tears of amusement streaming down their cheeks.

'Why're you wearing that funny long dress?' a boy with a large brown mole on his left cheek asked, wiping his eyes. 'It looks weird. Are you going to a fancy dress party or something?'

'It's my everyday dress,' she answered, increasingly uncomfortable. She suddenly wished she was at home. And that she hadn't spoken to the fair-haired girl with plaits. 'I only wear my best dress when I go to the Meeting Hall,' she added, trying to make things clearer for the children. 'I've never been to a party. But if I went to one, I think I'd wear my best dress to that, too.'

Again they collapsed in fits of laughter.

She stared at them in bewilderment. Putting her thumb in her mouth, she wondered what she'd said that was so funny. And what was so funny about her dress. All the girls who went with their parents to the Meeting Hall wore the same sort of long-sleeved cotton dress that almost reached their ankles, and most of their dresses were grey, too, and nobody thought they were funny.

She stared at the laughing children, puzzled.

'What've you got under your skirt?' the boy with the mole asked, and he winked at the others. 'Can I see?' He took a step forward, swaggering, and looked back at his friends.

'That's a rude thing to ask.' She stepped back and glanced anxiously at the fair-haired girl for support, but the girl was grinning at the boy.

She took another step back. She didn't want to be friends with them after all—not if they talked about rude things. That was the Devil's talk and it would lead to God turning his back on them. Only heathens talked about their bodies and showed them, and they wouldn't be saved at the Final Judgement.

A wave of pity shot through her as she gazed at the circle of grinning faces: they were all going to Hell and they didn't even know it!

Only the week before, Preacher Madson had told the community to pray for those who hadn't felt the healing grace of the Lord, and he'd said that if an opportunity presented itself, they should seek to lead the less fortunate out of darkness and into the love of God.

This was such an opportunity, she thought in excitement.

'Our body is the Lord's temple and should be kept pure,' she began, her face grave. 'We were all born into Sin. Christ's blood was shed for us to rid us of our sin, but we shall only be cleansed by His blood if we follow in the ways of the Lord.'

There was a moment's stunned silence, and then one of the boys said a word that she had never heard before, and they all ran off down the street, shrieking with laughter.

For a moment she stood there, staring after them, hearing the unkindness in their laughter long after they'd turned the corner and disappeared from sight. Then she slowly continued on her way to the shop. Patience and her parents were coming to tea that afternoon and she had to buy some margarine.

The thought of seeing Patience made her feel a little better.

She wondered what Patience would say about the children and their strangeness, but she knew she would never tell her what happened. Her friend would have been filled with dismay that she'd spoken to the ungodly children in the first place. Patience would never have done that.

WHY HAD those children been so nasty to her, Prudence was still wondering several days later as she sat by the front room window doing her arithmetic exercises.

But increasingly, she was coming to feel that she shouldn't hold their rudeness against them, but should forgive them. And she shouldn't give up trying to save them just because she'd failed the first time. After all, the martyrs persevered to the very end. Being laughed at was nothing compared with the sufferings they'd endured.

And it was also possible, she thought, that they *had* heard her words and had been thinking about what she'd said, and had been worrying about going to hell since she'd spoken to them. If so, it would be a kindness to teach them how to avoid the fires of eternal damnation.

Looking up from her exercise book, she saw two of the

girls from the week before. They were smiling at her in a pleasant sort of way. One of them waved. Hesitantly, she waved back. The other girl started to wave, too. Their smiling faces told her that they wanted to make everything better, and she waved at them with greater confidence.

The girl who'd been tying her shoelaces joined them, and she, too, waved. Then two boys joined the girls, one of them the boy with a mole. The smile left her face and she stopped waving. She didn't like that boy. He might even be Satan, trying to make the others fall into sin. He waved hard at her, but she didn't wave back.

The boy with the mole said something to the girls and they closed in around him, their backs to her. Hearing them giggling, she leaned closer to the window, watching them, wondering what they were doing.

Then they all turned to face her, smiling broadly. She gave them a weak smile back. The mole boy pushed to the front between two of the girls, and stood squarely facing her window. With his left hand on the buckle on his trouser waistband, he waved with his right hand.

She stopped smiling.

'Go to it!' the shoelace girl screamed.

The boy released his buckle. The girls on either side yanked down his trousers and pants. He pulled up his tee-shirt and thrust his body towards her.

She saw a small white thing hanging between pale thighs.

Screaming, she rushed into the back room where her parents were sitting. 'I hate children,' she sobbed. 'I hate them. The Devil's inside them all and they're nasty.'

13

She didn't tell Patience what had happened with the children on either occasion. She didn't tell anyone. But she didn't sit at the window seat again.

The years passed and she accepted without further protest being taught at home by her mother, happy to be away from other children, the memory of whose cruel laughter still kept her awake at night on occasions. Increasingly, though, her curious mind cried out for an input of facts and ideas that were beyond the scope of either her mother or Patience's. Both were doing their best, but by the time she reached her fifteenth birthday, she knew it was no longer enough.

By then, she'd started dropping into the local library whenever she was out on an errand, and she'd see pupils of her age studying the books there and making notes. Her need to know what they were learning was stronger than her hatred of them, and once they'd got used to the way she looked and ignored her, she would wander past them and glance at the books they were reading. It wasn't long before she realised that they had a body of knowledge far greater than hers.

From talking with the librarians during the summer holidays, she learned about the exams the pupils would take, and when they'd take them, and the careers they could choose from in the outside world. Consumed by envy for the choices they'd have, she decided that she, too, would take those exams so that she would have the same opportunities as they.

Her parents loved her, she told herself when she lay awake at night, mentally rehearsing what she'd say to them, so they were sure to want what was best for her. It was just a matter of finding the right words, and the right time, to raise the subject of going to a real school in order to learn what she needed to know to pass the exams.

But the weeks passed and the time never seemed right. When the summer holidays were drawing to a close, she knew that if she left it any longer, it would be too late to join a class, and she resolved to say something the following Tuesday evening when they'd finished their hour of prayer in the parlour.

Tuesday evening arrived. Throughout the prayers and readings, she sat motionless on her chair, petrified, unable to follow a single word. As the hour drew to an end, her mother closed the Bible. 'Praise the Lord,' she murmured, and set the book on the worn oak table beside her.

The moment had come.

Her heart beating furiously, she blurted out, 'I've something important to tell you.'

'What is it, Prudence?' her mother asked, her face registering displeasure.

'I want to go to university when I'm eighteen. To have any chance of getting accepted, I must study for the exams

I'll have to pass, so I'll need to go to school ... ' Her voice trailed off as she saw a guarded expression come into her parents' eyes.

They looked at each other. Her father shifted uncomfortably and pulled nervously at a loose thread in the upholstered arm of his chair. Her mother smoothed down her long worsted skirt.

'You're only fifteen, Prudence,' her mother said at last, her voice cold. 'Your father and I know what's best for you in the future, just as we've always known what was best for you in the past.'

'I'm old enough to know I want a career, though I don't yet know what. I don't just want to get married and have children. In fact, I don't ever want children—I hate them.'

Her father cleared his throat. 'University's out of the question, Prudence. We don't go to university. We walk with the Lord and do His will. To know His will, we study what He has said, and listen to Him. The more a person reads books that are not the words of God, the harder it is to hear God's voice.'

'But the Lord gave me a brain, Father, so surely He must want me to use it. By using it, I'll be thanking Him for His gift.' She looked hopefully from her father to her mother, but hope faded as she saw their mouths tighten.

'Universities are dens of iniquity,' her mother said in pained sorrow. 'Those who know the Lord stay as far from them as they can.'

'But I wouldn't be turning my back on the Lord just because I knew more things and met other people. I shall always love Him. It's just that I want an interesting career as well.'

'So you know better than Preacher Madson and the community, do you?' her father burst out, and he stood up, shaking. 'I'm ashamed that a daughter of mine is so filled with the sin of Pride.'

'I'm not.' She heard a trace of defiance come into her voice. 'I want a career, that's all. I don't want to have to marry for the sake of being supported. If I get a good job, I can support myself and also give money to the community.'

'I see.' Her mother's mouth was set in a grim line. 'And what does Patience say about this idea of yours?'

She hesitated. 'I haven't told her yet. I wanted to speak to you first.'

'You did the right thing by speaking to us first, Daughter. And I think we all know what Patience would say about this, don't we?' her mother said icily. 'Her parents are blessed in having a daughter who lacks unseemly ambition. Your wayward thoughts are a sadness for your father and me.'

'Patience and I are very different. She's happy to stay at home; I'm not.'

Her mother stood up. 'The subject is closed. Perhaps you'll set out the breakfast things before you go to bed.' Her mother moved towards the kitchen.

'Mother, please,' she begged, jumping up.

Her father put his hand on her arm. 'Time to stop this nonsense, Prudence,' he said quietly. 'Your mother is doing admirably with your education, and the inspector is satisfied with what she's teaching you. When you reach an age at which you could earn a little money, someone in the community will find you something suitable. You might join me in the back office at the bank, for example. In a few months, Mother and I will speak to Preacher Madson about a job for you until you marry.'

'That's not what I want, Father. I know Mother's taught me well, but she can't teach me everything. It's why I need to go to a normal school.'

Her mother appeared in the kitchen doorway. 'If you follow that course of action, you'll leave this house. No one in the community will ever speak to you again, not even your mother and father. Is that what you want?'

'Of course not! I couldn't bear it.' Prudence stared at her mother in horror.

'Of course, you couldn't,' her mother said steadily. She came in, sat again on her chair and indicated that Prudence sit, too. 'It's clear you hadn't really thought this through. Let us pray together as a family, and ask the Lord to give you the Grace to accept His will.'

Blinking back tears of misery and frustration, Prudence bowed her head.

'I SHOULDN'T HAVE THROWN it at mother and father all at once,' she'd told a stunned Patience the following day when they were sitting together in the gloom of Patience's parlour, her parents having gone to the Meeting Hall to collect some pamphlets for delivery. 'They think I'd leave the community. But I wouldn't—I couldn't ever leave it.'

'But's that's what *would* happen, isn't it?' Patience cried out in distress. She stared at Patience, shocked. She'd never heard her friend raise her voice before. 'We're forbidden to go to university to protect us from contamination,' Patience went on. 'Such contamination would rightly cause us to be cast out, as much to protect the community as for anything else.'

'But our faith is too strong for that to happen.'

Patience waved her words aside. She leaned over and grasped Prudence's hand. 'Without the community, we'd be lost souls. Please think again, I beg of you, dear friend.'

She smiled reassuringly, and squeezed Patience's hand.

'You're my closest friend. I can't begin to imagine what it would be like if you were forbidden to speak to me again, and I'll never let that happen. Taking a few exams doesn't mean I'll think any less of God and the community. You'll see that.'

'Oh, Prudence,' Patience said sadly. 'You aren't hearing us.'

TREMBLING, Prudence stood in the hall outside the office. On the front of the semi-glazed door across from her, she read the words, 'Miss Armitage, Pastoral Head'.

A pastor cared for his flock, she knew. Preacher Madson was always calling himself the pastoral head of their community. But Prudence wasn't part of Miss Armitage's flock. Those horrible children were, though. Perhaps Miss Armitage would be like them: taunting and mocking.

Her heart raced. She could walk out of the school and forget all about exams. No one at home would know where she'd been, and she could stay safely among those who loved her. She started to turn away, but the door opened and a short plump woman emerged.

'You must be Prudence,' she said. 'The office phoned me about you. Come on in, dear.'

She stood to one side to let Prudence pass in front of her. Then she closed the door and went and sat behind her desk, indicating that Prudence should take the chair opposite her.

'I understand that your name is Prudence Emily Bycroft, and that you don't go to this school, or indeed to any school, but that you'd like us to help you. Is that correct?' She smiled at Prudence.

'Yes, please,' she said, her voice a whisper.

'Why don't you tell me a little about yourself, dear,' Miss Armitage said. 'Take your time.'

Taking a deep breath, she began to tell Miss Armitage about her life and her hopes for the future. 'I *must* go to university, and that's why I need you to help me,' she finished. To her horror, she started to cry.

'That's quite a dilemma,' Miss Armitage said gently, and passed her the box of tissues that stood on the corner of her desk.

She took a tissue and blew her nose.

Miss Armitage stared at her thoughtfully for a few minutes.

'In all my years of being Pastoral Head, I've never been presented with such a tricky situation,' she said at last. 'You're asking us to go behind your parents' backs by giving you work on the subjects your mother isn't teaching you, and presumably you'd want us to correct that work. That's right, isn't it?'

She nodded slowly.

'Then, in a year you'd do the GCE exams. After that, you'd study for two more years, do your 'A' level exams, and then go to university.'

She nodded again.

'I'd like to help you in the way you suggest, Prudence, but I'm afraid I can't.'

'Please!' she cried, wiping her eyes with the back of her hand. 'I don't know who else to ask.'

'Don't despair just yet, dear. Listen to what I have to say. It would be wrong of us to help you deceive your parents. Moreover, in practical terms, what you're proposing wouldn't work. Each subject is taught by a different teacher, and it would be virtually impossible to co-ordinate them all. Furthermore, although you might be able to work through some of the GCE subjects by yourself, you wouldn't be able to cope with Science.'

'I learn very quickly,' she said, her voice shaking. 'My mother said so.'

'It's not that. There's a strong practical element in Science that couldn't be done at home. And then, to study 'A' level subjects at the depth required, without your parents knowing, would be virtually impossible.'

'So I won't be able to go to university?' Her voice broke.

'That's not necessarily the case,' Miss Armitage said. 'There's another way, one that could work, but it depends upon how patient you can be. I suggest that for the next couple of years you put thoughts of university out of your mind. You've said that your parents will help you find a job, and you could ask them to do so.'

She opened her mouth to protest.

Miss Armitage ignored her and continued. 'In a couple of years, you'll know with greater certainty what you want to do. If you still want to go to university, you'll have a little financial independence because of your job—not much, I know—but enough to pay for evening classes, where you'd be able to study for the necessary exams.'

'Evening classes! I didn't know there were such things!' Her face lit up.

'There are several venues in Weymouth, and I'm sure you'd be able to achieve everything you wanted at any of them. As for university, you'll probably need extra financial help for that. You'll find that there are several charitable scholarships you can apply to, which is something we can help you with in the future.'

'I don't know how to thank you, Miss Armitage.'

'However, there *is* one thing I can do to help you at the moment, dear,' Miss Armitage said, smiling at the relieved face on the other side of the desk. She reached in the drawer and took out a small card. 'Here's a membership card for the school library. With it, you'll be able to borrow books whenever you want. Or you can study in the library whenever the school is open, which might be wiser in the circumstances. You'll find careers' information in the library, too.'

Prudence took the card from Miss Armitage and clutched it tightly. 'Thank you so much,' she breathed. 'You don't know how much better I feel.'

'I think I've some idea,' Miss Armitage said with a laugh. 'Off you go now. Good luck with everything, and do drop by occasionally to let me know how you're getting on.'

'I will,' she said, and she left the office, a lightness in her step.

So she'd have to wait a bit longer to embark on her university dream, but it didn't matter—she'd get there in the end. In the meantime, she'd show her parents that she was a true believer, and that she'd always be a part of their family and the family of God.

14

The day that Prudence went to university, she started using her second name, which was Emily.

She'd wondered more than once in the years that followed how she'd been so naïve as to think that when she entered the outside world and filled herself with knowledge from the books that lined copious shelves, and spent hours listening to the exchange of ideas in animated discussions, she'd cling unquestioningly to her childhood beliefs.

The guilt she'd felt at taking those first hesitant steps away from the world into which she'd been born, and the guilt she'd felt as she rejected one by one the beliefs she'd been taught as a child, had gradually crystallised into a virulent hatred for the religion instilled in her since the day of her birth.

But she loved her parents, nevertheless, and Patience's family, too. If she hadn't, it wouldn't have hurt as much as it did when the community turned its back on her.

. . .

'IT'S ME—PRUDENCE,' she'd called through the letter box when she reached her parents' house on the day after she'd achieved a First in Law.

She knew they were home. She could hear movement inside and she'd noticed the net curtains flicker the first time she'd knocked on the brown-painted door. But no one answered. She knocked again. She hadn't brought her key with her, and even if she had, she'd have felt awkward using it as she hadn't been home for three years.

The day she'd left for university, her parents had stood at the bedroom window, watching the driver put her case into the taxi. She'd gone upstairs to kiss them goodbye, but each had turned away in silence, showing her their sense of betrayal that while doing the office job that Preacher Madson had got her, she'd secretly been studying for her GSE and 'A' level exams.

The evening class organisers had been brilliant. She'd told them she was working in the day, and had explained that her home situation made it necessary to study in secret, and that she'd probably miss some lessons. They'd been very understanding, and had given her the plan and notes for every missed lesson, and had then corrected her work when she'd finally been able to do it.

With their support, she'd passed her exams and got a place to read Law at a university in the north of England.

'Why Law?' Miss Armitage had asked her, when Prudence called into see her as she regularly did.

'Because it's precise. You know where you are with it. You can look at the Acts of Parliament and relevant cases, and you can go from there. I want something factual and logical, that isn't based on faith,' Prudence told her. 'Law will suit me down to the ground.'

When the syllabus for her university course arrived at

Miss Armitage's address, along with a reading list and details about halls of accommodation, she'd known that she had to tell her parents what she'd been doing.

They'd heard her in stony silence.

Then her mother had taken the Bible from the table and had stood up. 'If you choose to walk down this path, you know the consequences. Your father and I will pray that you step back from the brink before it's too late. If you move among the ungodly, you will become one of them, and we shall no longer have a daughter.'

SHE KNOCKED AGAIN on the front door and called through the letter-box, 'Please open the door.' She stepped back and waited.

The door opened. Her mother stood in front of her, her father half-hidden behind her.

Her mother looked older, more wrinkled and careworn, and the long hair that had been drawn tightly back into a bun at the nape of her head was streaked with grey. But she was her mother.

Emily felt a sudden surge of love for her.

A lump came to her throat. 'Hello,' she said, awkwardly. Her parents stood immobile, facing her. 'I've come home.' She took a step forward.

'We don't know who you are,' her mother said, and she shut the door in Emily's face.

She gasped with shock.

She stared blankly at the door, tears rolling down her cheeks. Then she turned and walked slowly down the hill. Before she'd realised it, she found herself in front of Patience's house.

She looked up and glimpsed Patience at her bedroom window. Then her friend was gone.

A movement in the front room caught her eye, and she saw Patience's parents rise from their hard-backed chairs and come over to the window. Side by side, they stared out at her. Then in a deliberate movement, Patience's father walked forward and pulled the curtains shut.

Shaking with grief and despair, she'd been able to think of only one other thing she could do—she could plead with Preacher Madson to help her with her parents. Picking up her suitcase, she half-ran to the Meeting Hall, oblivious to the rain that had begun to fall.

Preacher Madson was coming out of the low white hall as she arrived. Seeing her, he stood still in the open doorway. Even from a distance, she could see that his eyes were cold. She stopped in front of him. Recovering her breath, and at last able to speak, her words tumbled out chaotically, one on top of the other in her anxiety to explain the depth of her feeling for her parents.

'We'll not walk with you again, Miss Bycroft,' he told her as she fell silent. His words reverberated behind him in the hollow emptiness of the hall. 'You are not welcome in our community.'

'But—'

With an upturned hand, he silenced her. 'You have brought shame upon your parents, who had the right to hope for the same pride and joy that your former friend, Patience Collier, has brought to her parents,' he said quietly. 'She is shortly to be wed to a God-fearing man, who is to live in her family. Be assured, Miss Bycroft, that neither your parents nor Miss Collier and her parents will speak with you again. You walk alone, and will do so until the trumpet has sounded for the Final Judgement.'

Turning his back on her, he pulled the door shut, blotting out the cruel echo in the hall, locked it and walked past her without so much as a glance in her direction.

LATER, as she sat in the train taking her to London, staring blindly through the rain-streaked window at the outside world that was speeding by, her mind went back to the days when she'd stared with longing at the children walking past her window. In the silence of so many nights since then, their mocking laughter had rung in her ears.

She'd never been able to block it out.

Her childhood and her contact with theirs had left her with a legacy, and she was never, in all the years to come, going to have anything at all to do with children.

15

D *ecember*

JUST OVER TWO weeks after Caroline met Robert, they were in bed together.

As she lay curled up in his arms, she was full of wonder that things had moved as quickly as they had. From the moment she'd met Robert, her life had seemed one glorious blur.

Under his spell long before they'd completed their short tour of the garden, she'd spent the whole of Saturday wondering how she could contrive seeing him again. Neither she nor Terri Lee had been able to come up with any ideas. The problem had kept her awake for most of the night, and Sunday had been as fraught. And then the house phone had rung on Monday evening, and it had been Robert.

He'd been full of apologies for using a pretext to get the phone number from the letting agent.

'It's not a problem,' she'd said, laughing happily, and minutes later, she'd agreed to let him take her to a swish new restaurant in Hampstead the following Saturday night. It wasn't far from where he lived, he'd told her.

She'd gone through Tuesday in a hazy dream, hardly aware of what she was teaching her pupils, and pleading a headache to Tom to account for her abstractedness. As soon as she'd got back to the house on Tuesday evening, she'd sprung into panicked action about what to wear.

'He must be really special,' Louise said, staring from the doorway at the clothes that were strewn across Caroline's bed and floor. 'I've never seen your room in such a mess.'

'Don't be silly!' Caroline said sharply. 'All I know about him is that he owns this house, is quite attractive and looks good in a suit. I'm looking forward to a pleasant evening in agreeable company, talking about something that's nothing to do with school. But that's all it is. Obviously, I want to be suitably dressed for the occasion.'

'Of course you do,' Terri Lee called up the stairs, and she and Louise had burst out laughing.

ON SATURDAY EVENING, in a beautifully cut close-fitting black dress that emphasised the slender curves of her body, and with her auburn hair swept up in a gleaming mass on top of her head, she and Robert sat across the restaurant table from each other, a small candle in the centre of the table flickering between them. Whenever her eyes met his, a shiver ran down her spine and her mouth felt dry.

No one had ever made her feel that way before.

And Robert felt the same, too. She could sense it.

His dark brown eyes seemed to caress her whenever they lingered on her face, and for the first time in her life, she understood what authors had meant when they'd described someone's eyes as darkening with desire. As she tried to focus on the dessert menu, she wondered if this was going to be the first time she'd slept with someone on a first date.

In the past, her self-imposed rule had been to wait for a minimum period before allowing herself to be taken to bed.

'You aren't serious!' Terri Lee had exclaimed in amazement when Caroline had told the others not long after they'd moved into the house, that she always held off going to bed with a man for a suitable period of time. 'Sex gives you power over a man, gal. You wanna use that power from the word go,' Terri Lee advised. And she'd broken into incredulous laughter.

Emily and Louise had frowned at her.

'Give it a rest, Terri Lee,' Louise had said, and she'd thrown a cushion at her.

'Clearly, the concept of a woman respecting herself is foreign to you,' Emily had
said caustically.

'Talking of foreign,' Terri Lee had said, standing up and stretching, 'I need to get moving. Hughie's picking me up. We're off to dinner with a group of sheikhs.'

They'd heard her laughing all the way up the stairs to her room.

'Just coffee, thank you,' Caroline told Robert when he asked if she'd like any dessert.

Their dinner over, Robert took her back to the Camden Town house.

As they stood in front of the house, it seemed the most natural thing in the world for Caroline to put her face up to his, waiting to be kissed by him and to kiss him in return. But he leaned over, gently brushed her lips with his, and said softly that he'd ring her on Monday. And then he was gone, leaving her standing just inside the front door, frustrated.

She'd had to hover in the cool of the hall for a minute or two before she felt sufficiently composed to go into the sitting-room and face any of the girls who might still be up.

On the Monday morning, a bouquet of red roses addressed to her was delivered to the school office. 'The red beauty of these fades into nothing beside the beauty of the most gorgeous redhead I've ever met,' she read on the small card that was tucked into an envelope.

Her heart singing, she raised the card to her lips.

On the way home that evening, she took the bus to South Molton Street and went to Rigby & Peller, where she bought the most outrageously expensive underwear she'd ever owned. As she sat on the bus taking her back to Camden Town, feeling almost dizzy with excitement, she wondered where the unemotional, level-headed person she used to be had gone.

He phoned her that evening, as he'd said he would and as she'd known he would, and when he picked her up half an hour later, she was wearing her new bra and pants. He drove to Little Venice, parked his black BMW in front of one of the white stucco houses on Blomfield Road, and they strolled hand in hand along the towpath by the canal, eventually turning off the path on to a tree-lined road that led to a wine bar that Robert knew well.

As they sat close to each other in the bar, she found it hard to keep her hands off him. Much later, on their way back to the car, he wound his arm around her shoulders and she snuggled close to him, hot with longing.

He saw her to her house again. She asked him to come in for a late night coffee, but he refused.

'But if you can face two Saturday evenings with me on the trot, we'll go out to dinner again on Saturday. It means I'll have to wait four long days,' he'd said softly, putting his finger under her chin and bringing her face to look up into his. 'But our reward for waiting will be that we won't have to worry about getting up early the following morning for work.'

Then he'd kissed her lightly, and left.

She closed the door behind him, her heart full. Saturday couldn't come quickly enough.

'He's so easy to talk to,' she told Emily on the Friday morning as they'd walked together to the tube.

'What sort of things did you discuss?' Emily asked.

There was a moment's silence while Caroline struggled to remember any topic of conversation they'd had.

She giggled. 'I'm afraid I don't really know. All I can remember is that he's an accountant—he has his own firm —and he's thirty years old, ambitious and has never been married. Buying houses is a sort of hobby—he's building up a property portfolio.'

'He needs to watch for negative equity,' Emily remarked. 'I know it's not a big thing at the moment, but he'd be wise to keep it in mind.'

'Robert knows what he's doing. He wouldn't take silly risks, and he'd never pay an inflated price for a property. He's going to go far, I'm sure of that.'

'Well, for your sake, I hope you're around to see it, since that's what you clearly want.'

'Oh, I do,' Caroline said they stepped on to the escalator

going down. 'He's absolutely perfect for me, Emily. We want the same things out of life. And he's so fanciable. I can't believe how lucky I was to meet him. I can't wait for tomorrow night.'

Emily raised her eyebrows. 'Shall I mention Tom?'

'No, don't,' Caroline said quickly.

'THAT WAS A WONDERFUL DINNER, ROBERT,' Caroline murmured as Robert guided the BMW into a narrow space between two cars that were parked in front of a *pâtisserie*.

'Was it?' he replied, glancing at her with a wry smile. 'All I could think of was you.' He switched off the engine. 'Getting this space was a bit of luck. Parking's a nightmare in Hampstead. It's the one drawback of living here.'

'I'm sure it's outweighed by the compensations,' Caroline said with a smile. 'It's a lovely area and you've got Hampstead Heath on your doorstep. That's two compensations for a start.'

'True. But I think we'll leave the Heath for another day. There's a house that's waiting for us. And a bed.' He turned to her and looked deep into her clear green eyes. 'So let's go to bed, Caroline,' he said softly. 'If you want to, that is.'

'Oh, I do!' she cried. She went scarlet and put her hands to her cheeks in embarrassment.

He laughed. 'What are we waiting for, then?' He jumped out of the car, slammed the door closed and started round to the passenger side.

Caroline was already on the pavement by the time he reached her. He went straight up to her, slid his hand behind her head and kissed her hard on the lips.

'Come on, lovely lady,' he said. He pushed the passenger

door shut, locked the car, took her by the hand, and led her into the cobbled mews that ran alongside the *pâtisserie*.

A row of small brick houses flanked the mews, and Robert led her to one of the houses.

'Welcome to my home,' he said, and he unlocked the sea-green front door and pushed it open.

Hovering on the threshold, she glanced up at the outside of the house and saw that purple-flowering clematis had been trained to wind up and across the walls, and that on each window sill there was a sea-green window box that was overflowing with purple and white petunias.

'It's lovely,' she breathed as she stepped through the delicate scent of the flowers into the interior of the house. 'Oh, Robert!' she cried, dropping his hand and looking around the living-room. 'This is really beautiful.'

The walls of the room were crisp white. Running along one of the walls, there was a long white sofa scattered with a mixture of cushions that were white and stone in colour, with the occasional touch of sea-green. In front of the sofa stood a low medium-oak coffee table. Framed photographs were propped on a narrow white shelf that ran from one side of the room to the other. And higher on the wall, two more shelves spanned the width of the room, and were filled with books, some of which were standing vertically, some lying horizontally.

A hexagonal oak table stood at the far end of the sofa. On it, a couple of polished stones lay next to two ceramic dishes and a white-framed lithograph. A white spotlight shone down on the table, catching the simplicity of the arrangement and bringing out the warm subtle tones of the wood.

A large open hearth was cut into the wall opposite the sofa, with a Victorian wrought-iron fire basket standing inside. The hearth was framed by a white stone mantelpiece upon which stood a cluster of ceramic vases.

'This room tells me so much about you, Robert,' Caroline said turning to him.

'So tell me; what does it say?' he asked in amusement.

'It says that you've a truly artistic eye and that you're skilled enough, and bold enough, to mix the old with the new. Everything in here is clear-cut and minimal, so I know you're a tidy, organised person, who likes a calm environment. But you go even further than calm—you've aimed for an austere look. Yes, there's something in this room that's definitely austere, but very lovely. Above all, this room tells me you love beautiful things.' She stopped abruptly. 'I'm talking too much, aren't I?' she said and she gave a nervous laugh.

'I *do* love beautiful things. That much is certainly true. So come here, beautiful thing, and let me love you.'

'I thought you'd never ask,' she said, and she stepped into his embrace.

HE WAS ABSOLUTELY PERFECT, she thought happily as she lay in his arms, both of them bathed in the early morning sunlight that streamed through the windows, and he seemed to feel exactly the same about her. She snuggled closer to him, loving the rawness of his male aroma.

He stirred sleepily. With one hand, he pulled the sheet up over them, and with the other, he drew her closer to him. She lay still, enjoying the sensation of his hard chest next to her soft skin.

'Are you asleep?' he whispered. She glanced up and saw that he'd opened his eyes and was looking down at her.

She shook her head.

'Good, because I'm not, either. I seem to remember having a wonderful time in bed last night,' he murmured. 'But did I dream that wonderful time or did it really happen? I fear there's only one way to know the answer for certain,' and he gently rolled over on top of her.

'You are so very lovely, Caroline,' he murmured, looking down into her eyes, and he lowered his lips to her mouth.

THEY FELL BACK on the bed, their arms outstretched, struggling to draw their breath.

'That was bloody marvellous,' he was finally able to say. 'So I didn't dream it, then.'

'If that was a dream, please don't let me wake up!'

They rolled over on to their side, each facing the other, a smile on both their faces. Robert put his arms out to Caroline and she moved into them. Her final thought as she drifted into a satisfied sleep was that at last she'd found the man of her dreams. This was her Mr Right. And she hoped fervently that he thought she was his Mrs Right.

16

'And Tom? I'm going to insist on saying Tom's name this time,' Emily said, as she and Caroline stood on the platform on the Monday morning. 'You've not seen him all weekend. In fact, apart from at school, you've hardly seen him since you met Robert. He must be wondering what's going on. How does he fit into all of this?'

'Tom's a dear friend and I'll always love him as that. But what I feel for Robert is completely different. I've never felt like this about anyone before.'

'A dear friend that you've been sleeping with. Surely, sleeping with Tom means there's more than just friendship between you two. Or doesn't it? You're not Terri Lee, after all.'

'Of course it does. But Tom and I aren't the stuff that marriage and children are made of. I do love him, but it's not a passionate thing, not like it is with Robert. Obviously, I thought it was going to be like that with Tom or I'd never have let it go as far as it's gone, but I was wrong. I'd never known what real love was like till I met Robert.'

'Good grief, Caroline—you've only just met the man!

How can you possibly know it's real love? Real lust, I grant you. But real love, when you've only known him for a week... I don't think so!'

'You're so wrong, Emily.'

'Well, I admit I've never seen you as carried away as this, but don't let the sex side of things with Robert, or his money, stop you from seeing him clearly. You're longing to be a full-time wife and mother, and there's a danger that because of the trappings that come with Robert, you could easily lose sight of Tom's many strong points. Tom's one of the good guys—you struck gold with him.'

'I know that.'

'And you know he truly loves you and would never let you down. If you put aside that dream of yours, I think you'd realise you couldn't do better than Tom. After all, what d'you honestly know about Robert?'

'He's great company. He's got enough money for me to stay at home with the children. He's ambitious. He's good-looking. He's fantastic in bed. What more is there to say? He's perfect for me. He's everything I ever wanted.'

'Then I'm sorry for Tom.' She shrugged. 'But maybe it means you don't deserve him. You say that Robert is perfect for you, yet your list of his characteristics is somewhat deficient to my mind.'

'What d'you mean?' Caroline asked as they stepped into the train.

Emily shook her head. 'They're all superficial. I just hope you never regret throwing Tom away for someone you don't truly know. I feel really sorry for him.'

'He'll be fine,' Caroline reassured her, clinging to the overhead rail. 'You're right that Tom and I get on well, but I realised a while ago that it could never be anything more than friendship, and I think that in his heart Tom knows that, too.'

'I wouldn't bet on it,' Emily said drily.

'I can't help feeling you've been avoiding me for the past couple of weeks, both in school and out,' Tom said quietly as they sat in their favourite Italian restaurant in Chalk Farm.

'I've been waiting for a moment to give this to you,' he added, handing her a wood-framed photo, 'but that moment never seemed to come.'

Caroline looked down at the photo of the two of them at the school's Christmas Fair, and her eyes filled with tears.

'Is something wrong?' he asked anxiously.

Clutching the photo to her chest, she took a deep inward breath. 'I'm sorry, Tom,' she said, looking down at her plate, scarcely able to see her spaghetti through her blurred vision. 'I think we should stop going out with each other. It's just not working between us.'

She glanced up and saw shock in his eyes, followed swiftly by acute disappointment.

A wave of anguish swept through her, stabbing her with painful intensity, and she looked back at the table. Tears rolled down her cheeks and fell on her plate.

'I don't know what you mean,' Tom said, his voice shaking. He put down his fork, reached across the table and took Caroline's hand in his. She tried to pull it away, but he held on tight. 'I thought we were getting on pretty well,' he said, a note of desperation in his voice. 'We always have a great time when we're out together, and the bed side of things is pretty marvellous. At least it is for me and I thought it was for you. So what's not working?'

'I really can't explain; I wish I could. It's just something I feel. I do like you very much, Tom,' she said, forcing herself to look up and see his misery. 'You know I do. And you're right, we've had a brilliant time together. It's just that I feel we're not going anywhere long term, so it's best to end it now rather than carry on until we reach a point where we don't like each other any longer. This way we can stay friends.' She reached down for her bag, pulled out a tissue and blew her nose.

He frowned slightly. 'Why worry about long term at this stage? It's still early days. We're agreed that we like each other, and that sounds a pretty good basis on which to build. It's just a matter of going with the flow and seeing what happens.'

'Well, I don't agree. I think it's better to finish it now,' she said firmly, putting the tissue away. 'I'm sorry, Tom; I really am. But that's what I want.' She looked at her watch. 'It's getting late and I've a lot to do tomorrow. I can't eat any more so if you don't mind, could we leave now?'

He leaned back in his chair and stared at her across the table. His eyes bore into her. 'Is there someone else? Is that why you're blowing me out?'

She hesitated a minute. 'No, there's no one else.'

He sat upright. 'You're lying, Caroline, and don't say you're not. I know you well enough to know when you're lying, and you are now. I can see it in your face. So that's why you've been avoiding me. Who is he then? Let me guess —some rich bloke with money to burn? I'm willing to bet that whoever he is, he's not a poverty-stricken teacher. So tell me about him. You've just said we're still friends, and friends talk to each other about these things.'

Caroline heard bitterness creep into his voice, and despair.

'What makes you think it's anything to do with money?' she asked.

He gave a forced laugh. 'Oh, come on. I know what you want for the future; you've made that clear often enough. You want to have kids, live in a nice house, do lots of entertaining, and not work.'

'Most people would think that running a home and looking after children *was* work, and hard work at that! You, of all people, should know how much work children are— you teach them all day,' she said cuttingly.

'You know perfectly well what I mean. I'd never be able to support a family on my salary alone, not in the way you want to live. You'd have to bring in an income, too, and you don't want to do that; not even to stay with me.'

'Since you're accusing me of being materialistic, you can't think much of me, so it's just as well that we're finishing now. Wouldn't you agree?'

'I guess I've no choice,' Tom said, standing up and pushing back his chair. 'You know I love you, Caroline, and I believe you love me. In fact, I suspect you love me far more than you realise. We could've been really good together. I only hope the man you're after is worth it.' He put some money on the table and they walked out together.

'I'm sorry, Tom,' she said quietly as they stood facing each other in front of the restaurant.

He gave her a wan smile. 'I've a feeling I shall always love you, much as I hope I don't. If things go wrong, don't hesitate to call me. I'll always be your friend, even if I can't be more to you than that. Here.' He leaned across, took the photo from her, pulled a pen from his pocket, scribbled his phone number on the back of the frame, and returned it to her.

Raising his hand in a slight wave, he turned and walked away from her.

As she watched him go, she found herself trembling.

LATER THAT EVENING, she paused in the middle of applying cleanser to her face and stared into the mirror. Why did she still feel so distraught about Tom, she wondered.

It was normal to feel sad—after all, she and Tom had been together for several months and she was very fond of him—but she felt more than sad. She felt devastated. She'd done so since the moment she'd watched him walk away. But she knew she was doing the right thing, so why did she feel so grief-stricken?

The way she felt about Robert was very different from the way she felt about Tom. One glimpse of Robert was enough to make her break out in goose bumps. Whatever Tom might think of her, even if Robert had been poor, she would've loved him, and she would've willingly carried on working once they'd had children, had that been necessary. She was sure of it.

What she felt for Tom was a different sort of love.

But would she have finished with Tom if she'd never met Robert, she wondered, and she bit her lip.

Yes, she thought, and vigorously applied the cleanser to her chin.

By the time she'd met Robert, she'd already decided to make sure of not getting pregnant by Tom, and that spoke volumes about how she saw her future and Tom's. Falling for Robert had merely given her the impetus to finish with Tom, but no more than that.

And actually, she'd done Tom a favour by ending their relationship when she had. He wouldn't be wasting any more time on her, but was free to look for someone who'd love him in the way he deserved to be loved.

So she'd no reason to be feeling so deeply unhappy, she told herself firmly.

She screwed the top tightly back on to the cleanser, returned it to the shelf, picked up some pads, briskly wiped the cleanser off her face, and then climbed into bed. She wasn't going to let herself think about Tom again. From now on, it was just her and Robert and the glittering future she fervently hoped they were going to have together.

Turning on to her side, she remembered how Robert had lain back against his pillow on their second night in bed, a glass of champagne in his hand, and told her about the wonderful house he intended to look for in the country-side near London one day, and about the two point four children he was going to order to be delivered with it.

She'd giggled happily and suggested that he round the number up rather than down. With an amused smile, he'd looked deep into her eyes and murmured, 'Do you think so? That many? In that case, then, perhaps we shouldn't leave it too long before we begin.'

Yes, she and Robert definitely shared the same dream, she thought as she stared at her wall. Robert was her future, and she'd done the right thing that evening by finishing with Tom.

And she burst into tears.

17

J ohn put his head around Emily's door. 'Hello, Emily,' he said. 'Venetia mentioned you were still here. She was just leaving Chambers, and that's what you should be doing, too, especially with the weather as bad as it is.'

Emily glanced up at him, her cheeks wet with tears.

He stopped in surprise and came right into the room. 'Whatever's the matter?' he asked in concern. He came over to her desk and put his arm awkwardly around her shoulder. 'Is it anything I can help you with?'

'I'm just overtired; that's all.'

'I suspect it's a little more than that,' he said mildly. 'Won't you tell me what the problem is?'

'It's just this Skeleton Argument for Gordon's appeal tomorrow afternoon. It's about measure and loss. But I've never done a Skeleton Argument before, and I'm not sure I've done it right.'

'If you've run into difficulties, maybe I can help you work them out?'

She shook her head. 'Thank you, but no. I know you've

got to go to a drinks' party this evening. I'll sort it out.' She stared bleakly at the documents on her desk.

'Exactly where is the problem?' he asked, and he pulled up a chair and sat down next to her.

'It's these House of Lords' authorities,' she said miserably. 'It's so hard to get to grips with them, and I'm not sure if I've understood them correctly. There are three of them and the points in all three cases are really obscure. It *is* interesting, though. It's just that I've been tired all week. There's so much going on in the house at the moment—so many hormones flying about—that it's hard to relax in the evenings.'

'It can't be easy, sharing in the way you do.'

'It isn't. Anyway, I've finished writing the Argument, but I'm worried that I might have done it incorrectly, or missed a vital point. Gordon's introduction to Skeleton Arguments this morning lasted for all of ten minutes, and then he went off for the rest of the day. I've been working on it since he left.'

'You've written it, you say,' John said, taking off his scarf and hanging it over the back of his chair. 'Why don't you let me have a look at what you've done?' He took his glasses from his pocket. 'I can't bear to see you looking so unhappy.'

'If you really don't mind.'

'I don't.' He pulled the Argument towards him and ran his eyes down the page. 'Good,' he murmured to himself a couple of times. 'That's very good,' he said. He put the sheet of paper back on the desk and smiled at her. 'You've gone straight to the nub of the cases, Emily, and you've interpreted the crucial points correctly. This is excellent.'

Her pale face lit up. 'D'you really think so or are you just saying that?'

'I do think so, or I wouldn't say it. You can safely pack

away and go home. There's nothing you can do to improve this. All that will happen tomorrow is that the opponent will set out his grounds of appeal and put his arguments. Then Gordon will rise in all his glory and hand your Argument to the Judge. If the Judge doesn't have any questions about it, that will be that, and on the strength of this,' he tapped the Argument, 'Gordon should win the case.'

She relaxed visibly. 'Thank you so much, John. I feel a million times better now. I wish you were my pupilmaster, not Venetia's.'

'I don't,' he said quietly.

Her heart sank. 'Don't you?' she asked. 'Why not? Is it because she's so beautiful?'

'No, it isn't,' he said with a slight smile. 'It's because I wouldn't have been able to take you out to dinner as I've been doing if you had been my pupil—it would've been inappropriate. And by the way, Venetia's not the only one who's beautiful—you are, too, Emily.'

'No, I'm not,' she said sharply.

'It's that argumentative tongue of yours again,' he said, shaking his head. 'You must learn to accept a compliment. I think you're very beautiful. Every minute with you has been memorable. And I mean memorable for all the right reasons,' he added quickly, and he smiled again.

'Oh,' she breathed, looking wonderingly into his face.

'Do you still wish you were my pupil?' he asked, going slightly pink.

She shook her head vigorously. 'No. No, I don't.' She stared at him in growing wonder. 'No, I really don't,' she repeated.

A look of delight spread across his face.

He cleared his throat. 'Then we're both satisfied with the present working situation.' He looked at his watch. 'I really must get off,' he said, standing up and putting his scarf back on. 'I wish you could come with me. I intensely dislike these drink parties. Having you with me would make them bearable.'

'It's probably just as well that I can't—I'd be pretty bad company. I feel much better now, but I'm shattered. I'm better off going straight home after I've tidied up here. Thank you for the boost to my morale.'

'A pleasure.' He hesitated. 'There's something I have to do on Saturday, but if you're free on Sunday, perhaps we could go for a drive. We can't expect much from the weather at this time of year, but it might be relaxing to get out of London and have a bite to eat in the country. If you want to, that is. It'd give you a few hours away from the hormones in the house at the very least.'

'Yes, please,' she said at once.

NICOLA REACHED across the kitchen table for the tall bottle of olive oil, poured a few drops of the oil into the bowl in front of her and returned the bottle to the centre of the oak table.

'What's the matter, Louise?' she asked, glancing at her sister.

'Nothing.' Louise started chopping the parsley at a furious rate.

'There's certainly something. What is it?'

'I haven't a clue what you're talking about.'

'You're my sister, Louise. I know you like the back of my hand. A few weeks ago, when you got back from the States, you couldn't stop talking about your Mr Ford—how much you liked him, how much you thought he liked you—but now you never mention him. And you've got a face like a wet

Monday.' Her voice softened. 'I'm adding two and two together and I think I'm coming up with four. It hasn't worked out, has it?'

'There was nothing to work out.' Tears sprang to Louise's eyes, and she tried to blink them away.

Nicola stopped mixing the dressing, went across to the stove, stirred the casserole a few times, and then came back to the table and sat down on the chair next to where Louise was standing. Louise began to chop more quickly. Nicola put her hand on top of Louise's and held it still.

'Sit down, Louise. I can see you're unhappy and I want to help you, but I can't if you won't tell me what it is.'

Louise shook off Nicola's hand. 'Everything's fine, Nicky. Nothing went wrong because there was nothing to go wrong.'

Nicola frowned. 'I don't understand. I thought you and Ethan Ford liked each other.'

'So did I!' Louise sat down heavily on the nearest chair. A large sob escaped. 'I really thought there was something between us. I know we weren't in California for long, but we were together all day, every day. He said he'd contact me, but he hasn't. I haven't seen him since we got back. I must have got it wrong—he was just being pleasant, but no more than that.'

'But you said he'd gone away on work, didn't you? That's hardly his fault.'

'I know that. And I know he's been in Northumberland for longer than he'd expected. Barbara—she's his secretary—told me so when I phoned her on a pretext. But if he'd been at all interested in me, he'd have found time to ring. He can't want to see me again.'

'From what you've said about him, I don't think that's very likely—' Nicola began.

'I do,' Louise cut in. 'He must have changed his mind, now that life's got back to normal, or almost normal, and the magic of California's worn off. He might even have met someone else.'

'I'm really sorry, Lou.'

'Don't be.' Louise stood up, picked up the chopping board and scraped the parsley into a small porcelain bowl. 'It's all in the past. I'm going to stop thinking about him and I'll never talk about him again.'

'That might be best in the circumstances. Instead of moping at home, why don't you come out with Jim and me on Friday night? Jim's got a friend joining us, someone you haven't met before. You might like him.'

'From what I've seen of Jim's friends in the past, I'd much rather babysit Mark, thank you,' Louise said quickly.

'I know what you mean,' Nicola said with a laugh. 'Rest assured, I wouldn't force anyone on you. But you don't need to babysit Mark on Friday—I've already got someone lined up.'

'Well, if it falls through, let me know. I could do Friday, but not Saturday. We're meeting Caroline's new boyfriend, Robert, on Saturday. He's our landlord. He sounds quite nice. She's certainly mad about him, and I wouldn't imagine she's easy to please. We all really liked Tom, so if she prefers Robert, he must be quite something. Now, what else can I do to help?'

'It's almost done,' Nicola said, getting up and going over to the stove. She lifted up the casserole, and placed it on a hot plate in the centre of the table. 'You can put the dressing on the salad while I get the plates, if you like.'

'Markie's very quiet this evening,' Louise said, tossing the salad in the bowl.

'He's in the sitting-room. I've let him play some

computer games as a treat. You can get him if you want. The meal's ready.'

'Aren't we waiting for Jim?' Louise asked, moving towards the sitting-room door.

'Not today. He wasn't sure what time he'd be back. I'll put his on a plate. Now are you certain you don't want to come out on with us on Friday?'

'I really won't, thanks all the same. I'd rather stay in. But it's okay—I'm really over Ethan.'

'Is that so?' Nicola said.

18

Terri Lee lay back on the bed, stared at the ceiling and sighed. She could think of plenty of things she'd rather be doing on a Saturday evening than joining the others downstairs for a dinner to introduce Caroline's new boyfriend. Like being out with Hugh, for example.

If Hugh was coming to the meal, too, it wouldn't be as bad, but he wasn't.

When Caroline had suggested that she and Emily ask Hugh and John to join them, and that Louise ask anyone she wanted, she'd invited Hugh, but he'd told her he was being wined and dined by a medical supplier that evening, so couldn't come. It was a real shame as the others had hardly met him, despite the length of time they'd been together. It would've been the ideal occasion for them to get to know him better and see what good company he was.

And it wasn't only Hugh who couldn't come.

John told Emily that he was going to be out of town all day and wouldn't be able to get back in time, much as he would've liked to have been there. Emily would be seeing him the next day, though. Lucky Emily. Hugh didn't expect to surface till it was too late for them to get together that weekend.

Deep down, she suspected that Hugh's dinner engagement was just an excuse to get out of an evening he didn't fancy. John's was probably the same. Almost certainly, neither would want to spend an evening where Robert was the centre of attraction, and she didn't either.

Surprisingly, Louise hadn't asked anyone to the dinner.

She was a strange girl, Terri Lee thought. She was very pretty, and very nice with it, but she didn't yet have a boyfriend. And she didn't seem interested in finding one. When she'd given Louise a message from Hugh, saying he could fit her up with someone, Louise had burst out laughing and said a very definite no.

She'd obviously been keen on the electronic bloke she used to work for, but he'd been off the scene for ages. Louise had been an idiot to let a man like that get away. She needed to learn how to play her cards better.

From the sounds coming from downstairs, the other three girls were moving around, laughing and joking. They were probably trying to squeeze five place settings around the extended table. The ever-domestic Caroline had made a huge bowl of chilli and a mountain of rice, and the other two had thrown together a salad.

She hadn't done anything towards the meal, but cooking just wasn't her thing.

'Terri Lee!' she heard Caroline calling from the foot of the stairs. 'Can you come down and do the wine, please?'

'Just coming,' she shouted back.

She didn't move.

Let them wait, she thought. They might as well learn what waiting was like, just as she'd had to. Between waiting for Hugh to pop the question, and waiting to hear from her countless auditions, she seemed to have been waiting for something or other for a very long time.

For too long, in fact.

But there were some signs of a forthcoming improvement.

Hugh loved her, of that she was sure—he'd said so often enough. But with her engagement finger still horribly naked, she'd once or twice issued Hugh an ultimatum. Usually, he'd immediately say or do something very sweet, and that changed the subject. But at the last ultimatum, he'd told her that he was close to having all the money he needed, and all the required signatures.

Her heart had stood still.

They'd soon be able to live a normal life, he'd told her, just the two of them, and no more parties.

It was what she'd been wanting for so long, and her burgeoning impatience had dissolved in an instant.

When she'd married Hugh, tempting and auditioning would be things of the past, so there'd be more waiting for a phone call.

It was clear that he'd want his wife at his side, not playing to audiences every evening or away on a film location. He'd shown that in the way he'd been so against her touring with a company.

But she wasn't bothered about giving up any hope of a career as she and Hugh were going to have a wonderful life together.

She smiled up at the ceiling as she thought about becoming Mrs Hugh Waverley. That grey-haired man she'd met at the party ages ago, when she'd been alone on the roof-top patio, had been so wrong about her and Hugh. Fancy him thinking she might ever want to join his agency.

She couldn't even remember his name, with him having no place in her plans. Frowning, she tried to recall what it was.

Her mind a blank, she leaned across the bed, opened the shallow drawer in her bedside table and took out the small business card that was half-hidden beneath a packet of Kleenex. She lay back and looked at the name on the card: Marcus Shaw. That was it.

He'd been fairly good-looking for an older man, if she remembered rightly, and quite distinguished. His clothes showed there was money in what he was doing, but escort work would never have suited her. Whatever he'd said about the nature of the job, she knew that there could be an underside, and she'd no intention of ever going there again.

'Terri Lee!' Caroline called again. She heard irritation in Caroline's voice, followed by some giggling. Then she heard Caroline say, 'Right, you two. One...Two...Three...'

'Terri Lee!' the three girls shrieked, and they broke into peals of laughter.

She rolled off the bed and stood up. She glanced again at the card in her hand, screwed it up and threw it towards the waste paper basket under the table. She didn't need Marcus Shaw, not now, not ever.

The card landed on the pink rug under the table. She went over, picked it up and dropped it into the basket. Straightening up, she rearranged the row of soft toys that sat on the shelf above the table, and then moved languidly towards the door.

'At last!' Caroline said when she appeared in the sitting-room. 'The wine opener's on the kitchen shelf.' The door-bell sounded. 'Oh, God! How do I look?' she asked, pulling off her apron.

'Fine,' she said without looking, and she picked up the

first of the bottles of wine that were lined up on the kitchen worktop.

'Only fine?' Caroline wailed in dismay. She rushed across to the TV, knelt down in front of the screen, and adjusted her hair in the reflection.

'You look lovely, Caroline,' Louise said, laughing. 'Don't listen to Terri Lee; she's having you on. That shade of green with your hair is stunning. Go and open the door to the lucky man, and let the party begin.'

ALONE IN THE quiet of her room, long after Robert had left and the other girls had sunk wearily into their beds, Terri Lee drew back her curtains, leaned close to the window and peered out into the darkness beyond, her breath misting the glass.

In her mind, she went back over the evening.

It had been a great evening, she had to admit.

Caroline was a superb cook and the spices in the chilli had been perfectly balanced. Trust Caroline to get it right. Although chilli wasn't her favourite meal, for once she'd enjoyed it.

By the time she'd downed her second glass of red wine, she'd felt her bad temper evaporating and the evening had taken on an altogether more pleasant aspect. Caroline was right: Robert was charming. More than just charming—he seemed a really nice guy and was terrific company. Caroline was one lucky cow.

Or was she?

Using her forearm, she wiped the milky film from the patch of window pane in front of her.

Was Robert too good to be true?

There was nothing she could put her finger on, but she

had a niggling feeling that beneath his smooth exterior, there could be something quite complicated.

Maybe she was being fanciful, or maybe it was just that she couldn't believe that the height of ambition for such a sophisticated man could be domesticity, even if it did come equipped with an immaculate wife and a gourmet meal each evening. Wall-to-wall domesticity was boring. Robert didn't look as if he did boring.

Caroline should watch out, she thought as she stepped back from the window. If Robert was as good at acting as she was, Caroline could be in for a rocky ride.

She drew the curtains closed, went across to her bed, slipped beneath the duvet and hugged her favourite teddy bear to her chest. Perhaps she'd ask Caroline to give her a few cookery lessons. After all, when she and Hugh were married, they wouldn't want to eat out every evening, so she'd have to know how to make a few simple meals.

Her mother hadn't been much of a cook. There hadn't been the money, but even if there *had* been, her mother would've been too lazy. It was easier to sit on her arse and yell out for her daughter to boil a few potatoes or get in some chips.

But it was going to be different with her and Hugh. She was going to be the wife a man like him should have. As she leaned across to switch off the light, she wondered if he'd call the following day. Even if they couldn't meet, it'd be good to have a chat. She missed him like hell when she didn't see him.

Snuggling under the covers, she felt herself relax. A heavy torpor crept over her, and she closed her eyes. In the recesses of her mind, she wondered what Hugh had actually been doing that evening. Would he really have gone out

with a medical supplier on a Saturday evening? She didn't
think so.

She rolled on to her side and squeezed her eyes more
tightly shut.

She was being silly—he was sure to have told her the
truth, and she shouldn't be doubting him. He'd always been
honest with her in the past, and she'd no reason to suspect
he'd started lying.

She closed her eyes, and willed her mind to empty itself
of all such thoughts.

A few minutes later, with a sigh of resignation, she
opened her eyes again. She could just about make out the
shapes of her table and the waste paper basket beneath it.

Her gaze focused on the basket. She bit her lip. Maybe
she should've hung on to that card for a little longer. Just
because she had it, she didn't have to use it. And it didn't
exactly take up a lot of space.

She switched on her bedside light, got out of bed and
padded across the room to the basket. Bending over, she
retrieved the crumpled card, went back to her bedside table
and threw the card carelessly into the drawer. Then she
climbed back into bed, turned off the light, and closed her
eyes once more.

19

'So what did you think of Robert, Emily?' Louise asked, sitting down on the sofa. Slipping out of her trainers, she curled her denim-clad legs underneath her. 'A whole week's gone by since the dinner and I haven't had a moment to ask you. I couldn't ask when Caroline was around, or Terri Lee—not with Hugh and his disappearing acts.'

Emily looked up from the book she was reading. 'He seems fine, in as much as you can tell from one short meeting. He's nice looking, got bags of confidence, and is taller than Caroline, which I imagine's important to her. And equally important is the fact that he could obviously support her and any family they had. I don't mean that nastily, but she's clearly a home-maker. Me, I can't imagine anything more boring than staying at home all day.' She paused. 'What about you? Did *you* like him?'

'Yes, I did. I thought he seemed very nice, and very easy to talk to. He's been to San Francisco, too, so we discussed the places we visited. You seemed to be getting on well with him, too. What did you talk about?'

'He's trying to evict a tenant from one of his properties as the tenant's behind with the rent. It's not an easy thing to do, and he wanted advice. Reading between the lines, though, I suspect the real reason for wanting to oust the tenant is that he'd like to develop the property.'

'It seems a bit hard when you can't do what you want with your own property.'

'A landlord's got much more power under the law these days than in the past, but there's still a limit to what he can do, and rightly so. But I got the distinct impression that our Robert isn't going to be content with just buying houses and letting them out. I suspect he's set his sights on something more lucrative, such as serious property development.'

'Well, it'll be interesting to see what happens. I hope we'll know each other long enough to find out.'

Emily nodded. 'I can't see any of us moving far from London, so I'm sure we'll stay in touch. If anyone loses contact, it'll be Terri Lee. I can't fathom her out.'

'I hope Hugh pops the question soon, even though he sounds a real slime-ball. She deserves to be rewarded for that never-ending round of ghastly parties she has to go to. She's got another tonight, in fact. She told me she hates them.'

'Then more fool her,' Emily said sharply. 'No one can make you do what you don't want to do, not in this day and age.'

'That's easy enough to say, but not everyone's as strong as you, Emily. And it's not so easy when you're in love with someone. I feel really sorry for Terri Lee. It's obvious that Hugh isn't as keen on her as she is on him.'

'I'd put it more strongly than that—I'm sure he doesn't love her at all. And I'm equally sure he'll never marry her. He'll go for someone with money—not someone who clearly doesn't belong in his world. Look at her clothes for a start! Can you see a man with a Harley Street practice marrying a woman who looks like a tart?'

'People can change the style of clothes they buy. But she said he tells her what to wear, so he must like the way she looks. For her sake, I hope you're wrong about him.'

'I'm not, Louise, and if you're honest, you'll admit I'm not.' Emily put her book on the arm of the chair, stretched up her arms and locked her hands behind her head. 'And what about you?' she asked. 'If you make me a coffee, I promise to listen for the millionth time to the virtues of Mr Ford.' She paused, frowned slightly, unclasped her hands and dropped her arms. 'Come to think of it, you haven't said much about him for several weeks. Is someone else in the frame now? If there is, feel free to wax lyrical about him in return for that coffee.'

Louise unwound herself from the sofa and stood up. 'I'll make us a coffee because I want one, too, but you're spared any lyrical outpourings,' she said, moving towards the kitchen. 'As for Ethan, there's nothing to say. Terri Lee and I have something in common—the feelings are all on one side, and that's our side.'

Emily stared after her in surprise. 'But you really like him. What happened?' she asked as Louise came back into the sitting-room with two mugs of coffee, one of which she put on the table next to Emily, and the other she took to the sofa with her.

'Your guess is as good as mine,' Louise said flatly. 'I've not seen him for literally weeks, or months, in fact. I know he had to stay longer in Northumberland than he'd intended, but there's no way he'll have stayed this long. He's clearly not interested in me. But it doesn't matter—I ought to be focusing on my dissertation, anyway.'

'If I were you, Lou, I'd trust the instincts you had in California. You were sure he was keen on you then, and even more so when he dropped you back here. You won't have got that wrong. If he's not contacted you, it'll be because of work, not because of another woman.'

'Maybe so. But I can hardly compete with his job, can I? Not when I never see him. Any spark between us will have long gone out.'

'You don't know that for sure.'

'I do,' Louise said firmly. 'It was all in my head. Ethan belongs to the past—it's the future that matters. So, let's talk about something more cheerful. How are things with John? At least, I hope that's more cheerful,' she added quickly. 'This is the second Saturday in a row that you've not seen him.'

'They couldn't be better,' Emily said, cheerfully. 'He was sorry to miss Robert's dinner last week, but we made up for it on Sunday—we had a fabulous day at Windsor. It was great getting out of London for a while, and with someone who's such good company. He's at a conference today, alas, which is why we aren't meeting.'

'Are you spending Christmas with him or going back to Weymouth?'

'To Weymouth? Perish the thought! But I'm not spending it with John, either. He'll be playing happy families at his parents'. He asked me to go with him, but I can't think of anything worse than all that *faux* Christmas *bonhomie* among people I don't know.'

'But if he's your Mr Right, as Caroline would say, you'll have to get to know them at some point.'

Emily waved in dismissal with the hand that wasn't holding the coffee. 'It's much too soon to think about things like that. I'm putting the whole family thing off for as long as possible. If I had my way, I'd put it off forever. As I've no intention of having children, or going near anyone else's, why not? What about you, are you having Christmas at Nicola's?'

Louise nodded. 'I always do. It'll be fun, though—Mark's the perfect age for Christmas.'

'If you say so,' Emily remarked. 'What with Caroline in Cheshire, you in Finsbury Park, and Terri Lee probably mooching around with Hugh somewhere, the house is going to feel very empty over Christmas.' She held up her hand to stop Louise from speaking. 'No, don't mention Weymouth again. Empty sounds good to me.'

'I was only going to say that it won't feel empty once we've decorated it. I don't mind doing it. And I'm sure Caroline will give me a hand.'

Emily glanced at her watch, downed the last of her coffee and stood up. 'I'll go on up now. I might as well take advantage of not seeing John and do some work.'

'Why don't you take the evening off, Emily? It *is* Saturday evening, after all. We could open a bottle of wine. It'd be a chaser for our coffee. What d'you say?'

Emily hesitated. 'Oh, why not? I suppose there's nothing that's urgent. I'll get the wine as I'm already on my feet.'

She went through to the kitchen, opened a bottle, took two wine glasses from the shelf, and carried them with the bottle into the sitting room. She filled both glasses, handed one to Louise, and went back to her armchair with the other.

'Cheers,' she said, tipping her glass towards Louise. 'So, to go back to your Mr Ford—don't you think it worth finding out when he'll be in the office, and waylaying him?'

'Nope. It's over.'

The door bell sounded.

'I'm closer so I'll get it,' Louise said, standing up. 'But it's probably John for you.' She went into the hall, pulled the door open, and audibly gasped.

Ethan stood on the doorstep.

'Mr Ford!' she exclaimed when she recovered her voice.

'Good evening, Louise. Or rather, it's not such a good evening—it's a pretty cold one out here,' he said, his breath a column of white mist that hung in the chill air.

She frowned. 'What're you doing here?'

'I've just got back from Northumberland. The whole thing took a lot longer than expected. But the necessary structures are now in place to stop it ever happening again, and I'm delighted to say that today was the last Saturday I'll be waking up in Northumberland, beautiful county though it is. My mission accomplished, I got the first express train south.'

'I'm really pleased for you that it's finally sorted. It took long enough.'

'That's how it seemed to me, too,' he said, his clear blue eyes fixed steadily on her face.

Her heart missed a beat, and she felt herself reddening.

'I felt like celebrating,' he went on, 'so I dumped my things at the flat and came straight here. Are you busy, or will you come out and help me celebrate?'

Her face broke into a wide smile. 'It just so happens that I'm not doing anything particular tonight, Mr Ford. But you'll have to give me ten minutes to change. Come in and wait in the sitting-room.'

'It's not a work situation, Louise,' he said, following her into the house. 'You're not my employee now. You can use my first name.'

Glancing back at him over her shoulder, she smiled.

'Meet one of my housemates,' she said, leading the way

into the sitting-room. 'The other two are out. This is Emily. I'll leave you with her, Ethan. I won't be long.'

'Nice to meet you, Emily,' Ethan said easily. He slipped off his dark blue cashmere overcoat, and sat on the sofa opposite her. 'But please, don't let me interrupt whatever you were doing.'

'We were having a glass of wine.' She pointed to her glass, and started to rise from her chair. 'There's more in the bottle. Would you like a glass while you're waiting? Or a coffee?'

'It's fine, thanks—I'll wait till the restaurant. I'm driving so I've got to be careful,' he said. She sat down again. 'So,' he went on, 'what do you do when you're not drinking wine?'

20

As she stirred her after-dinner coffee, Louise realised that she couldn't recall a single word that she and Ethan had said to each other, not in the car, not during the meal.

After leaving Camden Town, they'd driven up to Haverstock Hill, found a parking place after a short search, and he'd taken her to a small French restaurant, where they clearly knew him well. He lived fairly close by, he'd told her, and he often went there.

She'd eaten what had been put on the table in front of her and she'd enjoyed it, but now, with the meal over, it would have been as difficult to say what she'd eaten as it was to remember what they'd talked about.

She took a *petit four* from a small dish in the centre of the table. The candle in the centre of the table trembled ominously in the slight movement of air that she caused, and she focused her gaze on the flame as it struggled to settle.

'Why don't you ask me what's been in the back of your mind all evening, Louise.' Ethan's voice broke into her thoughts, and she looked up from the flame. 'Go on,' he urged. Amusement flickered across his lips.

'I can't,' she said with a shy smile.

'Why not? Am I that forbidding?'

'No, of course not,' she said hastily. 'But I don't want to make a fool of myself.' To cover her awkwardness, she took another *petit four*.

'Go on; ask away. You know you want to,' he teased.

'Oh, all right, then.' She took a deep breath. 'I was wondering why you asked me out this evening.'

'Like I said, I wanted to celebrate the success of my Northumberland trip, and I couldn't think of anyone better to celebrate with than you.'

'But in all this time, you never called me. Why not?'

'I kept on meaning to. But then I wondered what I could say that wouldn't sound as if I was expecting you to feel something for me, when I didn't know if you were. If that makes any sense. My silence didn't mean I wasn't thinking of you, because I was—I missed you so much.'

Her heart leapt. 'Missed me?' she echoed, a thrill creeping through her.

'I've missed you every second of every day. And I've been rather hoping that you've spared a thought or two for me.'

'I think I'm dreaming.'

He laughed. 'Is that a woman's way of saying, Yes, I feel the same about you, Ethan?' He reached across the table and took her hand. 'I hope it is.'

'Oh, it is,' she said.

He let go of her hand and clasped the sides of the table in open delight. 'That's out of the way, then!' he said in obvious relief. 'And now I suggest you eat that poor cake before it's reduced to crumbs, and then we'll get out of here.

There's something I've got to do, and I don't want to shock these good people by doing it here.'

He turned to the waiter, asked for Louise's coat and the bill, and stood up. While the waiter was helping her into her coat, he dropped a pile of notes on the tray.

'Many thanks,' he said, and he caught hold of Louise's hand and dragged her, laughing, out of the restaurant.

'This won't wait a moment longer,' he said as they reached the pavement, and he spun her round to face him, pulled her to him and kissed her hard on the lips.

Oblivious to the faces staring through the large restaurant window, to the glances of the people walking past, to the hoots from cars driving by, they clung to each other, tighter and still tighter.

'I'm taking you back to your place right now,' he said, pulling abruptly away from her. 'I don't want to damage what we've got—what I hope we've got—by moving too fast. But we'd better go quickly or I might lose my scruples. Come on.'

His arm around her shoulders, they headed back to his car. He opened the passenger door for her, and then went round to the driver's side, got in next to her and put the key into the ignition.

'I can't think of anything you could do that would damage what we've got,' Louise said, and she leaned across the steering wheel, covered his right hand with hers, and stopped him from turning the key. 'I don't want the evening to end yet.'

He turned to her, and she saw the hope that lay deep in his eyes.

'I'd hate you to think I expected you to come to bed with me on a first date,' he said.

'But this isn't our first date, is it? We had ten days in the

States. This is about our eighth date, and each of the first seven dates was the length of several dates rolled into one. We've actually waited for ages. At least, it feels as if we have,' she added lightly.

'Are you sure, Louise? I want to get things right with you.'

She glanced through the window. 'You live in Belsize Park, don't you? Belsize Park is closer than Camden Town.' She gave an embarrassed laugh, took her hand from his and slid lower in her seat. 'I must sound as if I'm gagging for it, as Terri Lee would so elegantly say.'

'As a description of how I feel right now, that'd be spot on. Belsize Park, here we come!' He turned the key in the ignition, depressed the accelerator and the car sped off.

STANDING NERVOUSLY in the centre of Ethan's apple green bedroom, Louise stared at the large bed standing between two tall, white-shuttered windows. The lower half of the white cotton bedspread covering the bed was partially hidden by an open suitcase that had been thrown carelessly on top of the bed. A jumble of clothes spilled out of the case. A second suitcase, unopened, stood on the floor at the foot of the bed.

Biting her lower lip, she watched Ethan go across to the bed, gather the suitcase and clothes in his arms and drop them next to the woven Lloyd Loom armchair in the corner of the room. Then he took off his coat and threw it across the back of the chair. Picking up the green scatter cushions banked against the white pillows, he threw them one by one in the direction of the armchair.

And then turned to her.

Trembling, she was unable to move.

He came up to her, put a finger under her chin and raised her face to look into his. She saw sudden realisation fill his eyes.

'This is your first time, isn't it?' he said quietly.

She nodded.

'Are you sure you don't want to wait till we've been out a few more times?'

She took a step back, and with her eyes on his face, slowly unbuttoned her coat, slipped it off and threw it on to a chair behind her. Raising her arm, she unzipped the back of her vintage black velvet dress, eased it down over her shoulders and let it fall to the floor.

'That's my answer,' she said, her voice shaking as she stood before him in her bra and pants. 'I love you, Ethan.'

'And I love you with all my heart, Louise,' he said, and he swept her up in his arms and carried her to the bed.

21

What a nothing week it was going to be, Terri Lee thought irritably, and she reached for the sheets she'd been given to type. She slid her chair forward to be closer to the typewriter, glanced at the top sheet, saw rows of figures and groaned inwardly—it was going to be one long, boring morning. And judging by the thickness of the pile, it was going to be followed by an equally long, boring afternoon.

At least she'd be seeing Hugh that evening, and she wasn't going to be forced to endure another evening of listening to the others bang on about how wonderful their men were!

It wouldn't have been quite as bad if she and Hugh had made a start on planning their future together, but they hadn't. And although he'd hinted the previous weekend that he was ready to get down to brass tacks, and had talked about doing so that Monday evening, the plans had changed and they were going to meet his gruesome friends again.

About the only time she seemed to get him to herself was in the car. As a result, a couple of times recently, she'd tried to bring up the subject of the future while they were driving to their destination. But as he'd correctly said, he couldn't give the matter the attention it deserved as he had to concentrate on the road.

It was no wonder they were no further ahead than they'd been months ago.

Of course, he might be planning to surprise her with a ring at Christmas. In fact, he'd bloody well better be! If he didn't ... well, she didn't like to think about what she'd do if he didn't. But the more she thought about it, the more likely it seemed that he was waiting for Christmas. And that wasn't that far away.

Her mood began to lift.

What's more, even though they were meeting his friends later that evening, they were going to have a drink together first, just the two of them. As she didn't usually see him at all during the week, with or without anyone else, it could be a good sign that they were meeting on a weekday.

And another cheerful thought was that, being surrounded by shops, she'd be able to go out in her lunch break and buy something new to wear that evening. Being stuck in an accountant's firm for a week was gonna be dead tedious, and hard work with all the figures she'd have to type, not to mention audit working papers, but being in Knightsbridge *did* have some compensating advantages. She was minutes away from Harvey Nicks and Harrods, to name but two of them.

What's more, although such shops were normally way beyond her budget, Hugh had said he was tired of seeing her in the same old clothes, and she should find something suitable for a club or a party, and he'd pay. It was true that he hadn't suggested she update her wardrobe in Harrods, but nor had he actually said she shouldn't. Those Marcus

Shaw escorts probably shopped in Harrods, she thought defensively, and she had to hold her own against them.

She picked up the first of the schedules to be typed. Yes, she'd definitely pop out at lunch.

'It's Terri Lee, isn't it?'

She looked up in surprise. A tall man in a dark grey suit was standing by her desk, looking down at her. He was smiling as if he knew her. He seemed vaguely familiar and she frowned slightly, trying to remember where she'd seen him before. Probably at one of the parties, she thought, and she gave him her practised smile.

'Yes, it is,' she purred. 'How lovely to see you again.'

He laughed. 'You don't remember who I am, do you?'

'Yes, I do,' she said quickly. He raised his eyebrows questioningly. 'No, I don't,' she said with a giggle. 'Are you one of Hugh's friends?'

'While I met Hugh fleetingly outside your house on one occasion, I don't know that I'd class myself as that. I'm Robert, Caroline's friend. I had a very pleasant meal at your house one evening a few weeks ago. We met then.'

'So we did! How stupid of me to forget. Yeah, that was a good evening.' She smiled warmly up at him. 'Of course! You're an accountant, aren't you? Is this your company?'

'It is indeed, and I hope you're being extremely well looked after.'

'I am, thank you. Everyone seems very nice.'

'Is it the first time the agency's sent you here?'

'Yes. I'm here for a week.'

'Well then, we must celebrate your first day here. Perhaps you'd let me take you to lunch. I know a good place nearby: excellent food and very quick service, but it never feels rushed. Ideal for the working man and woman. How does that sound?'

'That's very kind of you. That would be lovely, thank you.'

'I'll collect you from your desk at one, then. See you later,' he said, and he moved off in the direction of a side office.

Lucky Caroline, Terri Lee thought, staring after his retreating figure.

She looked back at the schedule, skimmed along the first line and wished that Hugh would occasionally suggest them meeting up in the day. But lunch with Robert promised to be fun, and the day had certainly gone up a notch, even though a trip to Harrods was no longer on the cards. She'd find something in her wardrobe that she could wear that evening, and Hugh would have to lump it.

A smile on her face, she hit the space key with force.

'At least it's a dinner tonight and not another party. That's something, I suppose.' Terri Lee leaned back against the leather seat in the bar. 'Those parties are so bloody boring.'

Hugh opened his mouth.

'And don't say that the next party will be the last,' she said sharply. 'I'm fed up with hearing it. I've well and truly done my bit to help you get your backing, and enough's enough. I'm not going to any more parties.'

He put his arm around her shoulders and pulled her close to him. The strong scent of Guy Laroche aftershave almost overpowered her. 'I know you have, lover, and I respect that,' he murmured, and he kissed her lightly on the side of her forehead. 'You've been wonderful to have done as much as you've done, and I couldn't be more grateful. One glimpse of that luscious body, and Charlie and co are putty in my hands.' He nibbled the lobe of her ear and slid his hand under her pale pink angora sweater.

Giving his hand a light slap, she pulled away from him and straightened her sweater. 'The trouble is, they've had too many glimpses of it!' she retorted. 'We've been hanging around with them for months. I can't remember when we last went somewhere by ourselves.'

'We will do soon. Believe me, babe.' He edged closer.

She backed away from him. 'And we never seem to talk about anything these days. I'm not just a body, you know— I've got a mind, too. You never show the slightest interest in what I think about things or in what I do during the day.' Pouting her shocking pink lips, she folded her arms across her chest.

He trailed his hand down the side of her face. 'You silly little goose,' he murmured. 'Don't you think I want it to be just you and me? Of course I do. There's nothing I want more.' He pulled her into the crook of his shoulder, and rested the side of his face against her hair.

'Do you really, Hugh?' she asked, her voice forlorn. 'I sometimes wonder.'

'I swear I do, babe. And believe me, it won't be long before it *is* just us. The plans for the consulting room are in their final stages.' He glanced at the watch on the wrist that hung over her shoulder. 'We've got another half hour before we need set off. Why don't you tell Hughie what you're doing this week?'

'Actually it's not gonna be that bad a week,' she said, nestling closer. 'You'll never guess who I'm working for.'

'I thought you were temping for the agency. Isn't that what you do between auditions?'

'What I meant was, guess whose office I'm working in?'

Hugh shrugged his shoulders. 'I give in.'

'Robert's.'

'Robert who? You'll have to fill me in. Who's Robert?'

'That just shows how much you listen to me,' she retorted indignantly. 'A few weeks ago, Caroline asked her new boyfriend to come to the house, and did a dinner for us all to meet him. You were invited, too, but you couldn't come as you were with some medical bod or other.'

'So she's no longer with that overgrown schoolboy, then —Tom, or whatever his name is?'

'I told you she wasn't ages ago. Robert's the man of the moment. He's an accountant and she's really keen on him. He's our landlord—that's how she met him.'

'I vaguely remember.' His eyes wandered around the lounge. 'So you've had a good day at his office, have you? You ready to go?'

'Not yet! I haven't finished my drink and the half hour isn't up. As I was saying, when I got to the office this morning, I didn't know it was Robert's firm, did I? But he spotted me as soon as he arrived and he came over at once and said hello. If you want to know, I was quite flattered that he remembered me.'

'Who wouldn't remember you, babe?' Hugh said. He slid his arm out from behind her and adjusted his sleeve. 'You're a stunner. But I think we ought to be off now.'

'Anyway, he took me to lunch,' she said, beginning to stand up. 'All the people in the office were dead impressed I knew him and that he was so friendly. I'm quite looking forward to the rest of the week now. And he said he'll ask the agency to send me again.'

'That's nice. Come on, babe, let's go. You can tell me what you had for your lunch on the way to Henry's—we're picking him up. Now move that cute little butt.'

22

J*anuary, 1979*

'I LOVE Fridays and I loved 'Days of Heaven'. I adore romantic films. Thank you for a lovely evening, Robert,' Caroline said happily, leaning back against the leather seat in Robert's car as they headed out of Central London for Hampstead.

Robert glanced at her sideways. 'Did you know that the shot of the locusts ascending to the sky was filmed in reverse? The helicopter crew threw peanut shells down to the ground, and the actors walked backwards.'

'How inventive of them! It always amazes me how you know as much as you do,' she said, putting her hand lightly on his knee. 'How on earth did you know about those peanuts, for instance?'

'I'm brilliant, that's how.' He glanced across at her in

amusement. 'And my brilliance was helped by the fact that I read up about the film when it originally came out!'

They both laughed.

'Happy are they who've time to read anything other than books that need marking,' she said in a tone of woe. 'Heaven knows how many red biros I get through in a month! I could buy a house with what I spend on them.'

'Just as well, then, that you don't need to buy a house, isn't it?'

'I might need to one day, though. Funnily enough, I don't plan on sharing a house in Camden Town for the rest of my life. God forbid!'

She turned and glanced idly through the passenger window. They'd left the main road and were driving along-side the canal, she noticed in surprise. 'Where are we going?' she asked, sitting upright. 'This is Blomfield Road! We're in Little Venice. I thought we were going straight back to Hampstead.'

'That had been the plan, but I changed my mind.' He drew the car to a stop and switched off the engine. 'I thought we'd make a slight detour and have a drink before going home, if that's all right with you. Don't worry, though; we won't be late. I know you're always tired on Fridays.'

'It's very all right by me,' she said with a smile. She got out of the car, put on her dark brown alpaca coat and buttoned it up. 'I can always lie in tomorrow.' She strolled over to the water's edge and stared down at the black still-ness of the sleeping canal. 'I bet the water will be frozen solid in the morning,' she said, and she shivered.

'The idea of a morning in bed is very appealing,' he murmured, coming over and putting his arm around her. Together, they stared down at the water. 'Right; let's get that drink,' he said after a few minutes.

Their arms around the other, they strolled along the towpath, past a line of colourfully decorated barges and houseboats, and then turned off the path and went in the direction of a brightly lit pub.

'How was your Christmas?' Caroline asked as they walked along. 'You haven't said anything about it.'

'Not much to tell. Small town Kent isn't the most exciting of places, and my parents aren't the most exciting of people.'

'What about your brother? Did he go back home, too?'

'God, no! He doesn't go near the parents if he can avoid it, and I don't entirely blame him. He's years older than I am, seventeen years to be precise, and he's got his own family on the other side of the country.'

'That's a bit hard on your parents.'

'Life's a bit hard on my parents! In romance novels, my mother would be described as a faded beauty, who was completely unable to run a household, which is about the only thing she's ever been required to do. Our home was always chaotic, and not in a nice way. From a very early age, I've known that I wanted a very different sort of home for myself. The words 'piss up' and 'brewery' spring to mind whenever I think of my mother. She's the total opposite of you, my sweet, well-organised Caroline.' He stopped, drew her to him and hugged her.

Caroline giggled. 'You shouldn't talk about your parents like that,' she said as they started walking again. 'But since you are, what's your dad like?'

'Worn out. He has been for as long as I can remember. He's a civil servant who's been left in the lower ranks and who feels bitter about it. In his case, the phrase that springs to mind is rising to the level of one's incompetence. Sadly for him, it wasn't much of a level. He blames my mother for his lack of promotion as he was never able to invite his colleagues into the mess that was our home, which is what other ambitious types used to do. If he'd been able to do so, he would have been promoted further, he always says. I'm not sure he's right, but who knows? As I say, I want something very different for myself. And on that note, we've reached our destination.'

Caroline looked up at the sign hanging above the pub. 'Why, this is where we came on our second date, isn't it?' she said, turning and smiling at him.

'So it is!' he exclaimed, and he opened the door and went in ahead of her. Seeing two people getting up from a small table in the far corner, he made a beeline for the table. 'We're in luck! You sit here and keep the table while I go for the drinks.'

He vanished into the crowd of people lining the bar, and re-appeared a few minutes later, empty-handed.

'One of the nicest things about going out with someone over a period of time is that they know exactly what you like to drink,' she said as he sat down opposite her. 'Are they bringing the drinks over?'

'Spot on,' he said. 'Since they've got waiters here, we might as well use them.'

As he spoke, a waiter approached with a silver ice bucket, which he stood next to the table. A bottle of something fizzy was embedded deep in the shavings of ice. The waiter disappeared and returned a moment later with two champagne flutes. Then he lifted the bottle out of the ice, unwound the wire mesh covering the cork, held a small white towel over the stopper and gently eased the stopper out of the neck of the bottle.

'Champagne!' Caroline exclaimed, staring at Robert in surprise. 'Are we celebrating something?'

The loud explosion of the cork as it shot into the air drew the attention of everyone near them, and a number of eyes were turned in their direction. With a flourish, the waiter poured the sparkling liquid into each of their glasses, replaced the bottle in the ice bucket, wished them an enjoyable evening and left their table.

'In answer to your question, there's at least one thing to celebrate,' he replied. 'It's Friday today and we don't get have to get up early tomorrow. That's worth celebrating, isn't it?'

'Oh, Robert,' she said with a laugh. 'Of course it is. Two days of no school is always worth celebrating. But champagne—that's really pushing the boat out.'

'Maybe it *is* a bit of an extreme way to celebrate the fact that it's Friday,' he mused. 'Perhaps we ought to come up with another reason, too.'

'There *is* something else, isn't there? I bet you've bought another house!' Her eyes shone in excitement.

'Better than that, I hope. But it *is* to do with acquiring another chattel.'

'You mean you've purchased a different kind of property? Something in the commercial market maybe?'

'In a way. But I haven't actually got it yet, Caro. Whether I acquire it or not rather depends upon you.'

She stared at him across the table, and felt a sudden rush of blood to her head. Her spine prickled.

'The restaurant I've booked for dinner tomorrow evening is where we had our first date,' he said. 'I thought it would be the most romantic setting for what I wanted to say to you—to ask you—but I realised in the car that I couldn't bear to wait another twenty-four hours before knowing your answer. So I'm afraid you're having to put up with the site of our second date for what I want to ask.'

'Oh, Robert,' she whispered, and her heart seemed to stop.

'I love you, Caroline, and I want to spend the rest of my life with you. I missed you so much over Christmas, and I never want to feel like that again. I'll go down on one knee, if you want. Even if it means ruining my favourite suit,' he added with a wry grin. 'If that's what it takes to make you agree to marry me.'

'Of course, I'll marry you. I've loved you since the moment I saw you on the doorstep that day. There's nothing I want more.'

He grasped her hands in his. 'I'll never let you down, Caroline,' he said, his voice taking on a serious note. 'You're the most important thing in life to me, and you always will be.' He picked up his glass. 'Well,' he said with a broad smile, 'I think we've enough to celebrate now, don't you? Let's polish off this champagne before it goes flat.'

23

S *aturday*

THEY STOOD OUTSIDE THE CAR, alone on the deserted street, the cold air stinging their faces.

'I wouldn't ask if it wasn't necessary, and it'd be this once only. Please, baby, do this one last thing for me,' Hugh said, his voice pleading. He put a hand on each of her shoulders. 'I'm begging you.'

Terri Lee stared up into him, her face white, her eyes full of anguish. 'I thought you loved me,' she stammered.

'I *do* love you. You know I do. This has nothing to do with how I feel about you. Nothing can change the fact that I love you to bits.'

'Yet you want me to sleep with that revolting slob, Charlie Forbes Brown! That's love, is it?' Her voice started to rise. 'You want me have to touch his horrible flesh, to lie there while he breathes his stinking breath in my face, and leans on me, slobbering all over me, digging his filthy hands inside me. And I'd have to do to him whatever he wanted. That's what you mean by love, is it?' she accused, her voice shrill.

He hugged her tightly to him. 'Of course not, babe.' He kissed her on the forehead. 'You'd be showing me how much you love me by helping me in this way. He's said that if you go to him tomorrow night, on Monday morning he'll sign on the dotted line, and give me exactly what I want without strings. All he wants is one Sunday night with you. And afterwards, I'll show you how much I love you.'

'Oh, yes? And how you gonna do that exactly? Ask me to sleep with Alastair, too? And Henry?' she cried, distraught, tears rolling down her cheeks.

He gave a dry laugh. 'Not quite. I had in mind something more along the lines of asking you to spend the rest of your life with me. I want us to be together for always.' Gently, he wiped away her tears with his hands.

She gulped, took a step back and stared at him, startled surprise written across her face. 'What are you saying, Hugh? Are you asking me to marry you?' A tremor of hope shook her voice.

'I am, you lovely creature. I intend to tie you down so you can never leave me. I've almost asked you on several occasions in the past few weeks, but each time I've pulled back as I couldn't yet offer you the earth. And you deserve nothing less. But now that I've got the money for my prac-tice,' he went on, 'well, almost got it—I just need Charlie's signature—I can think about our future together. So, will you marry me, Terri Lee Taylor?'

A flush of pleasure spread across her tear-streaked cheeks, and she flung her arms around him. 'Oh, yes! Yes, I will. I love you so much, Hugh. We're going to have such a wonderful life together. I can't believe how happy I am.' She laughed out loud in gleeful delight, and hugged him even tighter to her.

Firmly, he extricated himself. 'We'll sort Charlie out tomorrow night, lover, I'll get the all-important signature on Monday morning, and we'll go shopping next weekend for something for your finger, just you and me together. How does that sound?'

'Couldn't we get the ring sooner? Please, please,' she begged.

'I'd love to, doll, but I'm off to a medical conference after I've seen Charlie on Monday, so I'll be away for a few days. It's a damn shame, but I've no choice.' He paused. 'Of course, you could always pop down to Tiffany's while I'm away, pick out something and we'll collect it next Saturday.' He ran his fingers slowly through her hair. 'If you want to, that is.'

'Tiffany's!' she said with a gasp of wonder. 'Really, Hugh? Tiffany's?'

'Why not? We're going to be flush with Charlie's money behind us. So, yes, Tiffany's. Only the best for my girl.'

'Oh, I love you so much, Hughie,' she cried, sliding her arms around his neck and kissing him again.

His lips brushed hers, and then he lightly pinned her arms to her sides. 'Charlie said he'd take you to a hotel, to a real nice place. After that's over, we'll decide where we want to live and things like that. Is that agreed, Mrs Hugh Waverley-to-be?'

She hesitated. 'Oh, all right then. But only because I love you so much.'

He smiled at her in satisfaction. 'I knew I could count on you, lover. You won't be sorry, I promise.'

24

S *unday morning*

'YOU'RE lucky to live so close to Hampstead Heath, and Camden Town isn't exactly far away,' Louise said as she and Ethan crossed Pond Street and made their way along a gravelled path to the pond at the bottom of the Heath. 'This is my favourite part of London.'

'Mine, too,' Ethan agreed.

'So, are you sure about me doing three days a week at your place? It would really help with my dissertation, and I'd enjoy it, too. I've missed going into the office and seeing the girls there, not to mention the work. The students at the business school are nice, but we don't really have much contact with each other.'

'It's more than all right. I wouldn't have suggested it otherwise.'

'And it wouldn't be a problem that I'd be working for you

while we're going out with you? Though obviously I wouldn't tell anyone at the office.'

'Even then.' He grinned at her. 'The best thing about being your own boss is that you make the rules, so you can break them if you want.'

Beaming, she tucked her arm into his as they strolled past the first of the ponds. Several young children were clustered at the water's edge, their hands full of bread for the ducks.

'Don't they look cute,' she said, smiling in their direction. 'I remember Markie at that age. He was absolutely adorable. And still is.'

Ethan's arm tightened around her shoulders.

'You'll be a terrific mother one day, Louise.'

'I just hope I'll be as good as Nicky. She's terrific with Mark. But what about *your* family? Did you have a good Christmas? You haven't really said anything about it.'

'It would've been better if I'd spent it with you. But I had to go home—I don't see my folks enough as it is. Herefordshire isn't the easiest place to get to from London.' Louise opened her mouth. 'Don't tell me,' he said with a rueful grin. 'I should make the effort more often, and my New Year's Resolution is to do just that. And the next time I go, I'd like you to come with me. After all, I've met your family, so now you must meet mine.'

'I'd like that,' she said with a smile, and they turned to look ahead at the path they were walking along.

'Did I tell you that Caroline's getting married?' she asked a few minutes later, seeing a young couple coming towards them, their arms entwined. 'Robert proposed on Friday night. We all thought he would, so no surprises there. I wonder how Tom will take the news. He'll find out tomorrow.'

'I've never met Tom. Does she still see him these days?'

'She has to—they teach at the same school. He'll be really cut up as he was ever so keen on her. And from one or two things she's said in passing, I suspect he still is. I thought they were good together, and even after they'd finished, I used to think she'd end up marrying him. I was obviously wrong. But she's good with Robert, too.'

'When's the wedding?'

'Not for a year and a half. She wants to get married in July, at the start of the summer holidays. She doesn't want to have to rush back to school immediately afterwards. They're marrying in Cheshire as that's where she's lived for most of her life. She's already thinking about wedding venues. Reading between the lines, I don't think Robert's that keen on the idea of Cheshire. He's lived in London for years, his firm's in Knightsbridge, and he's got lots of friends in London, and so has Caroline. He'd rather get married here.'

'That would seem to make good sense.'

Louise nodded. 'I can see both points of view. I expect they'll have a clearer idea when they get back from Cheshire. They'll be going up to see her parents quite soon as Robert hasn't yet met them. They don't even know she's engaged. Robert's going to ask Caroline's father for permission to marry her.'

'He's going the whole hog, then,' he said in amusement.

She laughed. 'He certainly is. I'd love to be a fly on the wall when he speaks to her father.

He grinned at her. 'Me, too.'

'I haven't a clue whether they'll finally decide on marrying in London or Cheshire,' she continued, 'but one thing's for sure, she won't wait long to start a family.'

'She shouldn't be in too much of a hurry. They need to get used to living together first. At least, that's what I'd want to do.' He stopped suddenly. 'Hey, look at that! An ice cream van on a freezing day like today!' He pointed to a white van standing at the place where two paths crossed. 'Talking of children, why don't we treat ourselves to the biggest ice cream they sell, complete with a chocolate flake and all the trimmings?' And he started walking briskly towards the van.

She trailed after him, her heart thumping fast in sudden anxiety.

Talking of children, he'd said. But that was one thing they'd never really done. From what he'd just said, though, children weren't at the top of his wish list at that moment in time, and certainly not when they hadn't spent time living together. Her getting pregnant would be the last thing he'd want, and the last thing she'd want for some time, too! She'd still got a few months of studying ahead of her, and she wanted a career at the end of it.

So far, she'd left the matter of contraception up to Ethan, but condoms weren't that reliable, as two girls in her year had recently proved, and she must go on the pill at once.

25

M onday morning

As SHE WRIGGLED into the tight crimson sheath dress, which Charlie had almost torn off her the night before, Terri Lee glanced at him over her shoulder. He was sitting on the edge of the hotel bed, which was sagging beneath his weight, and pulling on his socks. His boxer shorts were gaping and his shirt was open. Folds of white flesh hung loosely around his body.

She felt nauseous.

Shuddering, she quickly zipped up the back of her dress. She couldn't wait to get out of the hotel, back to the house and into a shower where she could rid herself of his smell, of the feel of his touch. She'd scrub herself inside and out. He'd said she could use his shower, but there was no way she was going to risk him coming back for a second helping. The very thought made her want to throw up.

With Charlie's eyes hot on her back, she pushed her toes into the first of her high-heeled sandals.

'You've got a beautiful tush, honey,' he said, his voice thick. She could hear the leer in his voice, and she hastily pushed her foot into her second shoe. 'Has anyone ever told you that?'

'I seem to remember hearing it before,' she said acidly. Bending down, she started adjusting the strap on each sandal.

'Yeah, baby; real beautiful. That Hugh's a lucky man.' She felt his eyes boring into her, and she speeded up.

'Was I good, honey?' he asked. She straightened up and stared at him. His eyes went straight to her cleavage. 'As good as Hugh?' he asked. His tongue moistened his full lower lip.

She gave him a weak half smile and picked up her bag. 'You were okay, Charlie.'

'Only okay?' He scowled. 'What d'you mean by okay?' His voice went up a notch and he sat upright.

She looked at him nervously. 'You were much better than okay, Charlie,' she said, and she tried to laugh it off. 'You know how we girls can be coy, talking about such things. You were really good. I promise you, babe: the best. You sure know how to hit the spot.'

'Yeah, well; that's more like it,' he growled. He leaned forward. 'But if I'm the best, how come you're in such a hurry to leave? Maybe old Charlie should treat you again. Huh?'

'I'm dressed now, Charlie. It's a work day—I've got things to do.'

'I'm sure you can make the time to go the round again. What d'you say?' He rubbed his stomach, and then slid his hand lower.

'I've gotta get off. I wanna see Hugh before he leaves.'

'What you mean is, you wanna see what I'm gonna show you,' he said nastily, and he stood up and faced her. 'There's something here I'm bursting to show you right now.' He pulled down his boxers and stood there.

She went cold. 'Like I said, I've gotta go.' She could hear her voice shaking. 'It's been great, it really has, but I need to get off now.' She took a step towards the door.

'Like hell you have,' he said belligerently. 'I'm not done yet, woman.'

'Well *I* am. I'm dressed now so that's that.'

'You'll do what I say,' he said, walking towards her. 'You want your Hugh to get his money, don't you? Huh?'

Their eyes met. Her shoulders sagged. He reached out his hand, grasped her shoulder, and pushed her to her knees.

HER EYES BLINDED by tears and shaking uncontrollably, Terri Lee stumbled from the taxi to the front door, turned the key in the lock and ran into the house, letting the door bang shut behind her.

'What's going on?' Caroline cried, running out of the kitchen.

She stopped short at the sight of Terri Lee standing in the centre of the sitting room, her hair dishevelled, crying hysterically. Black mascara ran in channels down her cheeks.

The blood drained from Caroline's face. 'Whatever's the matter?' she cried in alarm, and she ran across to Terri Lee, her arms outstretched.

· · ·

TEN MINUTES LATER, Caroline had phoned the school to say she was sick and had made them both a strong cup of tea. She'd insisted that Terri Lee lie on the sofa, and had covered her with a tartan rug that she'd fetched from her room.

As she drank the tea, Terri Lee's tears gradually slowed.

Sitting opposite her, Caroline waited patiently until Terri Lee was calmer. Then she went across and perched on the edge of the sofa next to her.

'What's wrong?' she asked gently.

'I can't tell you, Caroline. You'll hate me so much,' Terri Lee whispered, her eyes filling again with tears. 'You'll think I'm low-life trash, and you'll despise me.'

'Don't be silly,' Caroline said. Impulsively, she leaned over and squeezed Terri Lee's hand. 'I know you, don't I? Nothing you've done could possibly make me hate you or think that way about you. You're my friend. And I can see you're unhappy, so you must let me help you.'

'I can't tell you,' Terri Lee wailed. 'I want to, but I can't. I'm so ashamed.'

'You'll feel better when you've told me.' She paused. 'Is this about Hugh?'

Terri Lee nodded.

'So, tell me. What's he done or said to upset you like this?'

Tears rolled down Terri Lee's cheeks. Then she gulped hard, opened her mouth and the words poured out.

She began with Hugh's proposal and how excited she'd been when he'd finally asked her to marry him. Caroline started to say it was wonderful news, but Terri Lee vigorously shook her head and stopped her. 'That's only the start of it,' she told her. 'There's more, and it's awful.'

Then she told Caroline about Hugh begging her to sleep

with the revolting Charlie Forbes Brown, telling her it was the only way he'd get Charlie's money.

Caroline went white. 'No!' she whispered.

'He swore he loved me very much, and was only asking me to do such a thing because Charlie wouldn't back him if I didn't. That's what Hugh told me, and I believed him. It was then he asked me to marry him. I thought he really loved me, Caro. He told me I could go to Tiffany's and look for a ring.'

'To Tiffany's,' Caroline murmured. 'That does sound serious.'

'I thought so, too. I was so happy. You know how much I love Hugh. You do, don't you? I couldn't let him down. I knew he wouldn't have asked me if there'd been any other way. Or so I thought. Anyway, I agreed to go to a hotel with Charlie last night.'

She fell silent and smoothed down the tartan rug.

'We all know how much you love Hugh,' Caroline said, stroking the back of Terri Lee's hand. 'No one's going to judge you for anything you did.'

'I haven't got to the worst bit yet,' Terri Lee told her, her voice shaking. 'You'll think I'm so stupid when I tell you. Yes, you will,' she insisted, as Caroline opened her mouth to deny it.

She took a deep breath and told Caroline that when she'd finally done absolutely everything that foul slob had ordered her to do, both at night and in the morning, she'd felt sick to her stomach and had grabbed her things and run to the door.

She paused and looked at Caroline, her blue eyes dark in her tear-stained face.

Caroline nodded encouragingly. 'And then?' she prompted.

'And then Charlie told me something,' Terri Lee said flatly.

Caroline waited.

Terri Lee swallowed. 'Charlie told me that he'd signed the money over to Hugh a month ago,' she said slowly. 'A whole month ago. You should've seen him—his eyes looked really mean and nasty as he spat in my face that he'd already backed Hugh.'

Caroline put her hand to her mouth. 'Oh, Terri Lee,' she gasped.

They'd just been having fun with her, she'd told Caroline—a thank you for Charlie thrown in by his old pal, Hugh. Apparently, they went way back and Hugh had known all along that Charlie would invest in his surgery.

'I didn't have to do any of that, Caro, or go to any of those foul parties. Hugh was always going to get the money. He and his slobbish friends have been laughing at me all of the time. I've been such a fool.'

Caroline squeezed her hand again. 'No, you haven't. You're the victim here. How could Hugh have done that to you?'

'Quite easily, it seems.'

Telling her about the money hadn't been the only thing that Charlie had told her, she continued.

He'd told her that Hugh had been dating someone else for some time, someone classy with money, who didn't have cloth-ears, and he was going to marry her. He was with her at that very moment. A man of Hugh's standing would never marry a tramp like her, Charlie had sneered.

'Yes, he called me a tramp,' she told Caroline, ashen-faced. 'But I was just trying to help my Hugh. Or I thought he was my Hugh. I told Charlie he was lying, but deep down I knew he wasn't. It explains why we never went out in the week, or anywhere by ourselves, and why he never wanted to be alone with me, except when he wanted sex. I was someone for him and his friends to use and laugh about. Nothing more. A tramp, as Charlie said.'

'They're wrong, Terri Lee. What you did, you did for love. That's not being a tramp.'

'No, they were right. I'm thick, thick, thick. I must be thick to have been so wrong about everything. Only an idiot would think that a clever consultant, with a Harley Street practice, and who could have anyone he wanted, would choose someone like me above everyone else.'

'He doesn't know what he's lost by letting you go,' Caroline said gently, stroking Terri Lee's hair. 'You're worth a million Hughs, Terri Lee. He's the loser, not you, and don't you ever forget that. You've got a heart of gold.'

'You mean like a tart!' She tried to laugh.

'Of course I don't, you ninny. You're a warm and sincere person. Everything you've done for Hugh has been done selflessly, and that shows you're a loving, caring person. But because you're like that, you expect everyone else to be the same, but unfortunately, not everyone is.'

'But to go with Charlie like that...' Terri Lee's voice trailed off.

'What you did with Charlie, you did for the man you love. And who's to say we wouldn't have all done the same for the person we love? You've got to put it behind you now. Hugh's shown himself to be a real shit, and although you might not agree with me at the moment, you're better off without him. One day you'll see that, I promise you.'

'You're right about Hugh, of course,' she said, her tears drying up. 'And I do feel much better now. Thanks for not saying I told you so. You and the others have warned me often enough about Hugh so you'd have been entitled to say that. And I'm glad it was you who was home, not Emily. I bet she would've gloated. She always said Hugh would never marry me. Louise would've been all right about it, though.'

'You're wrong about Emily—she would have been sympathetic, too. I know she's got a brittle exterior and can seem self-centred, but I suspect that's only a veneer. None of us would ever rebuke you. We're friends and we feel for each other, and we'd never deliberately hurt each other.'

Caroline passed Terri Lee the box of Kleenex and she wiped her eyes.

'Now, go and have the shower you talked about,' Caroline said firmly. 'You'll feel better afterwards. Then we'll go out and have a late breakfast—but not where I'm likely to bump into anyone from school. Up you get now, Terri Lee. This is the moment when you begin your new life.'

26

M*arch*

JOHN AND EMILY leaned back on their elbows and surveyed the lake. The remains of their picnic lunch lay on the grass around them.

'What a glorious day,' she said, staring at the sparkling water, 'and so peaceful. I don't want this afternoon ever to end. What an excellent idea it was to come to Blenheim.'

'I thought you'd like it here,' John said with a smile.

'And you were so right.' She looked up at the clear blue sky and inhaled deeply. 'Mmm, this is lovely.'

'I love picnics,' John told her. 'They remind me of when I was young. My parents used to take my brother and me for a picnic every Sunday during the summer holidays. We'd go by bus, and when we got where we were going, my parents would hire deckchairs and flop in them for the afternoon. My father was a real stereotype: he'd cover his head with a handkerchief that was knotted in all four corners to keep it in place. And while they dozed, my brother and I would see who could do the best cartwheels. Something better done before eating rather than after,' he added with a laugh.

She sat up and glanced at him in surprise. 'I didn't know you had a brother, John. You've never mentioned him in all this time. Where does he live? And why didn't you tell me about him?'

'Probably because we never seem to talk about our families,' he said, taking off his glasses and adjusting the frame. 'He lives in Los Angeles. He went there shortly after leaving university, met an American girl, fell in love with her and married her almost at once. They've now got a couple of all-American sons. He loves it there and would never want to move back to England.'

'How often do you see him?'

'Not as often as I'd like. LA's a long way from England, and it isn't easy to get sufficient time off to make it worthwhile to go there. As I expect you've already found out, there're elements of unpredictability in our work, which makes forward planning difficult. If you want to be given the most interesting cases, you can't be seen to be taking too much time off. I take August off as the courts are shut, but that's about it, apart from a few odd days here and there.'

'You could go in August, then.'

'Too hot for me, I'm afraid. Los Angeles is effectively reclaimed desert. Admittedly, everywhere there is air-conditioned, but you have to get to and from your car, and to and from your house, and I prefer not to be there in such intense heat.'

'Does he ever come back on a visit?'

'He and his wife came over not long after they married. That was the one and only time. It's more difficult now

they've got children. But you're right in your silent criticism
—I should make more of an effort to see him.'

'You're totally wrong about what I'm thinking. I don't
think you should do anything for the sake of it. If you
wanted to see more of your brother, you would. Obviously
you don't. That's not to say you're wrong, but you and your
brother have your own lives, and they don't impact on each
other. End of story.'

'There may be some truth in that.' He paused. 'You're an
only child, aren't you?'

'That's right.'

'Are you, too, from a picnic-loving family?' he asked.

'No, I'm not. Here, there's one apple left—you have it.'

He took the apple from her. 'Thank you. But I won't let
you change the subject, Emily. I've told you something
about my family, and now I'd like to hear something about
yours. All I know is that you come from Weymouth.'

'There's not much to tell. My parents are not interesting
people, and I never go home.'

'I did begin to wonder. I know you didn't go home for
Christmas, for example, despite the fact that you strongly
implied you'd be doing so.'

'How d'you know?'

'Terri Lee let it slip by mistake when I was waiting for
you one evening not long before Christmas.'

'Trust her.' She looked at him curiously. 'Christmas was
ages ago. Why didn't you say anything at the time?'

'I respected the fact that you preferred not to tell me.' He
paused. 'But since we're talking about families now... Was
anyone else a lawyer, for example?'

She laughed. 'Absolutely not! I'm the first, and I'll
certainly be the last.'

'So it falls to you to found a legal dynasty, then,' he said with a smile, and he leaned back again, resting on his elbows.

'That's not going to happen,' she said, and she fell silent.

'Doesn't the idea of founding such a dynasty hold any appeal for you?' he asked after a moment or two.

'No, because that would necessitate me having children.' She pulled up some blades of grass. 'I don't like children and I don't want any.'

He rolled over on to his side and stared up at her in amazement.

'I'd sensed that you weren't keen on children, but to say that you never want them is an unusual thing to say at your age,' he said slowly. 'You can't know for certain at your young age how you'll feel in the future.'

'I do know,' she said bluntly. 'I hate children.'

'Isn't it a bit sweeping to dismiss all children? It's not like you to generalise thus. Surely, they're not all objectionable, just as not all lawyers are crooked shysters, much as the public would like to believe they are.' He attempted to laugh.

'I've never wanted children. I don't like them and I don't want them anywhere near me. When I see a baby, I never go into melting mode. On the contrary—I run a mile. I don't have a single maternal bone in my body. Some women don't. I can't imagine I'll ever feel differently.'

Seeing the bewilderment in his eyes, and an emotion she couldn't identify, she turned away.

'Apart from anything else, they're a huge responsibility,' she added, her gaze on the lake. 'If you get it wrong, you mess with their heads. That's a responsibility I'm not prepared to assume.'

John sat upright. Side by side, they stared ahead of them, their backs rigid.

'We must make sure we don't leave any litter behind,' she said at last to break the silence.

'You're right; it's time to go.' He stood up and brushed the grass from his light brown corduroys.

As they bent over to pick up the debris from their lunch, the afternoon silence was shattered by shrill screams. Startled, both straightened up at the same moment and stared across to the other side of the broad expanse of shimmering water.

Several young children were chasing each other around the water's edge, laughing and shrieking as they went. As they watched, the boy at the front of the group lost his footing and tumbled to the ground. The rest of the children fell on top of him in an untidy heap.

'Ouch! That hurts! Get off me, you wankers,' they heard the boy at the bottom of the pile wail, and the sound of his cries filled the air.

Emily turned to John. 'I rest my case,' she said.

27

Having looked quickly in both directions, Terri Lee hurried across the Fulham Palace Road and walked swiftly in the direction of the Thames Wharf.

Although it was only March, it had turned out to be quite a warm day and she was fast beginning to wish she'd done as Marcus Shaw had suggested and taken a cab. He'd told her he'd pay for it, but not wanting to be indebted to him in any way, she'd taken the tube to Hammersmith and walked from there. Unfortunately, the restaurant was further from the station than she'd realised, and what had seemed a good idea at the time, seemed distinctly less good as she became increasingly hot and flustered.

When she turned the corner, she saw the back of a brick building on the opposite side of the road. Looking up at the wall, she read the name of the restaurant. This was it! Pulling a small mirror from her bag, she swiftly checked her appearance.

She still looked okay, she thought in relief, even though she had a faint glow on her cheeks. All she needed was a light touch of lipstick. She'd piled her hair on top of her head that morning and a few curls had escaped. But they framed her face so she decided to leave them there.

As soon as she'd applied a little more lipstick, she put the mirror away, crossed the road and walked down the side of the building.

Coming out into an open area, she saw the river wall ahead of her and an expanse of grass to her right. Turning sharply to the right, she went up to the glass doors that led into the building and started to pull them open. As she did so, her reflection was thrown back at her.

The skirt of her new deep-blue linen suit clung to her hips, showing off how slim she was and hinting at the length of her legs. The jacket hugged her tightly, the severity of its style being offset by a low cut neckline that suggested cleavage without being too revealing. The final touch—the pearl choker necklace she'd borrowed from Caroline—added a touch of real class, and went brilliantly with the cluster of pearls that Louise had lent her to hang from her ears.

She smiled to herself—she knew she looked more than just okay. Her look was a combination of sexy and classy, a look that not everyone could achieve, and it was a look that could make her money. Marcus Shaw would see that the moment he saw her again.

But if she *did* decide to join his agency, she'd do it on her own terms.

She felt a sudden rush of nervousness. Suppose he wasn't there and everyone stared at her, sitting on her own. Suppose he *was* there, but hadn't been serious when he spoke to her in that club all those months ago. He might just be planning to have a bit of fun with her, and knowing men, hoping to get her into bed for the price of a lunch.

What made her think he was any different from all the other men she'd met?

But nevertheless, she did.

Or, at least, she had done when she'd phoned him.

Half turning away from the door, she took a step back. It had seemed easy enough at the time, ringing Marcus Shaw and telling him she wanted to discuss being taken on as an escort for his agency, but now that she was on the verge of meeting him again, she was beginning to regret ever picking up the phone.

Why, oh why, had she done it?

ON THE FRIDAY evening that had ended up with her phoning him, she'd found herself alone in the house when she returned from her latest tedious temping job. She'd poured a glass of wine and had settled in the sitting-room, hoping that one of the others would soon get back and would join her for a drink. And if they weren't doing anything that evening, maybe they could go out for a Chinese together. Even having Emily for company would be better than nothing, she was feeling that low.

Maybe not so much low as restless.

After the Charlie episode, she'd felt numb for weeks. She'd rushed home at the end of each working day, and refused to go out. Recently, though, the numbness had started wearing off and was being replaced by a yearning for change. It meant that she must've finally put that ghastly experience behind her, she thought in relief. Taking a sip of her wine, she stared at the door, hoping that one of the others would walk in.

But the clock had ticked on, and she'd still been alone when darkness had fallen.

She mentally kicked herself. Why had she thought for one minute that any of the others would be spending a Friday evening at home? Caroline would be with Robert, talking about weddings as usual; Louise would be with Ethan, talking about her boring dissertation, and Emily would be with that drippy John, talking about God knows what. She was the only one who didn't have anyone to talk to. It really was time she did something with her life.

That man, Marcus Shaw, had pointed out that she was the only one at the party who wasn't getting a thing for the hours spent humouring one boring old fart after another. He hadn't actually said that made her pig-thick, but he might as well have done.

Well, she wasn't pig-thick any longer.

And as she'd sat there that Friday, alone in the darkening sitting-room, she'd looked realistically at the facts of her life.

Fact number one: she was going to have to provide for herself. She didn't have a bloke and she didn't want one—she'd had enough of men to last her lifetime.

Fact number two: her acting career was a non-starter. She was a good-looking girl with no experience among a lot of good-looking girls, most of whom had experience. And after the months she'd wasted on Hugh, she felt much too jaded to consider joining a repertory company in order to get that experience.

Fact number three: being a temp was a shit-awful job and she'd no intention of doing it for much longer. The only decent thing it had thrown up in the past few months had been meeting Caroline's Robert. She'd now been to his firm a number of times as his company had started asking specifically for her, which was quite flattering, and she'd had the occasional coffee or lunch with him, but as the highlight of several months' work, it was hardly a big deal.

Decision: she was going to change her life. But that was the easy bit. Deciding how to do it was the difficult part.

More immediately, though, she must get back to her room before the others returned with their boyfriends, assuming they came back at all that evening. She wasn't in the mood to see people being happy.

Leaving her glass on the draining board, she made her way upstairs to her room, dumped her bag on the floor and threw herself on to her bed. Lying on her back, she looked around her room. Her eyes came to rest on her waste paper bin, and she sat up sharply.

Why not, she thought, and felt a sudden burst of excitement.

She swung round on the bed and pulled open the top drawer of her bedside table. The business card that Marcus Shaw had given her months before stared up at her. She picked it up, smoothed out the creases and read his number. Glancing at the clock, she saw that it was almost ten. That would be early for a man like him, she thought, and there was no time like the present. He was probably out, but it was worth a try.

Before she could chicken out, she ran downstairs, picked up the receiver and dialled his number.

The phone rang twice only before he answered. Thrown by a sudden attack of nerves when she heard his voice at the other end of the line, she stumbled over identifying herself.

He didn't sound at all surprised to hear from her; in fact, he sounded very pleased. He'd instantly taken over the conversation, telling her how delighted he was that she'd phoned and saying how much he was looking forward to meeting her again, and that they should make that meeting very soon.

She'd stammered something about being equally keen to see him again, and he'd suggested that she join him for lunch the following Sunday. As she'd hung up the phone, she realised how much she wanted the job—but just the escorting bit; no more than that.

And for the first time in months, she felt alive.

SHE STARED at the glass door in front of her, the door that might lead the way to a better life. She could do the cowardly thing—go home right now and find another way to improve her life, one she'd yet to come up with. Or she could open that door.

Taking a deep breath, she grabbed the handle, pulled the door open, walked into the restaurant and told them she was meeting Marcus Shaw.

Panicking inwardly as she was led through the dining-room to the outside terrace, where they told her he was sitting, she worried that she might not recognise him again, or that he might not recognise her. After all, it was months since she'd seen him, and they'd met so fleetingly.

She need not have worried.

When she stepped out on to the terrace, she saw him at once. He was leaning casually back in his chair, staring across the grass towards the river, looking cool, but distinguished a lightweight stone-coloured suit, his styled hair streaked with grey.

She realised in that moment that she hadn't forgotten a single thing about him.

His eyes turned towards her. Instantly rising to his feet, he was standing by the time she reached the table, smiling in obvious pleasure at seeing her. He took her hand in a firm handshake, and told her how delighted he was that she'd agreed to lunch.

'Truly delighted,' he murmured, as the waiter pulled out her chair and she sat down. Then he took his seat opposite her.

'It *is* nice to see you again, Terri Lee,' he said. 'I always hoped you'd get in touch with me. But before you tell me why you *did* finally give me that call, I think we should order.' He turned and indicated to the waiter to come to them.

'YOU DON'T KNOW what you missed by not having any dessert, Marcus,' Terri Lee said, pushing her empty plate away from her. 'That was yummy. But it must've been a thousand calories a mouthful.'

He smiled at her. 'I don't think you need to worry on that score,' he said. 'You have a perfect figure. Quite perfect.'

She blushed and gave a nervous giggle. Lifting her hand to her head, she pushed a tendril of hair away from her face and fixed it behind her ear.

'Ah, here's our coffee,' he remarked. He waited as the waiter removed her empty plate, poured them each a coffee and left the table. 'I think this is the moment to get down to business, don't you?' he said, stirring his coffee. 'I presume that it *is* a matter of business that brought you here?'

She cleared her throat. 'Actually, yes, it is.'

'I rather assumed it might be. I don't flatter myself that someone of my age would be sought out by a young lady such as yourself for the purpose of romantic dalliance, delightful though that thought might be.'

'You look ever so good for your age,' she said quickly.

'Ouch! That hurt,' he said with a laugh.

'I'm sorry! It sort of came out all wrong. I meant to say that you're not old. I've probably had a bit too much wine.'

'Don't worry; I know what you meant,' he said. 'Yes, wine certainly loosens the tongue. Not that it matters as this is just a social occasion. And a very pleasant one, I might add.'

'I've enjoyed it, too,' she said.

'But of course,' he went on, picking up his cup, 'when you're working, you'll have to be careful about how much you drink. It's nothing to worry about, though. There are clever little ways of making it look as if you're drinking more than you actually are. You'll learn them in due course.' He took a sip of his coffee.

She stared at him in surprise. 'But you haven't interviewed me, and we haven't talked about anything, not about my experience, or money, or hours or anything. Or about what I'd have to do.'

'Haven't we? Take experience. I've watched you in action on numerous occasions, transfixed each time by your beauty, your vivacity, your skill with people. Money? You'll make a lot of it. How much exactly will be up to you. Hours? If you don't want to work, don't work. You'll work when you want to, which is much in the way that you work as a temp.'

'How d'you know I'm a temp?' she asked in amazement.

'As I believe I've told you before, I make it a point of knowing everything about the people I'm interested in.'

'What else d'you know about me, then?'

'Just about everything,' he said with a wry smile. 'I knew Hugh long before you met him. He's used my girls on a number of occasions—that is, until he met you. From that point on, he no longer needed me as you were doing it for free. I also know that he's about to fetter himself to a woman with a face like a horse.'

'He's welcome to her,' she said quickly. 'He belongs to the past. It's the future I'm interested in.'

And most importantly, the thorny issue of what exactly she'd have to do to make her money. She nibbled her thumb nail as she wondered how to frame the question.

Marcus sat back, an air of waiting, a smile of amusement playing on his lips.

'There's something I want to make clear,' she said at last. 'I've heard about escort agencies from some of the girls I met at auditions. I know what men expect escorts to do, and if they don't put out, punters won't ask for them again and they're soon out of work. I'm not a ... well, I'm not like that. I wouldn't want to ... You know.'

'I wouldn't expect you to do anything you felt uncomfortable with. Trust me, Terri Lee. I make my money from the large fee I'll be paid for you escorting someone. You will be paid by me for being an escort, but not for anything else.'

'I see,' she said slowly.

He leaned forward. 'I'm not saying that some of the girls don't put out, as you express it, as that would make me very naïve. Some of them do, I'm sure, but it's their business, not mine, and I'm in no way involved. As I told you once before, I'm not a pimp.'

'And the men who book the girls—do they know what's what?'

'All of my clients know the score. They pay a lot of money for my girls because they want the best. They know that they can rely on my discretion, and on the discretion of my girls. And by the same token, if any client went too far, he would find himself blacklisted, not only by my agency, but by every other reputable agency in town.'

'You make working for you sound irresistible.'

'Correction. You'd be working for yourself. I think of

myself as a facilitator. I facilitate your ability to make a huge amount of money.' He sat back and laughed. 'But it's not totally altruistic on my part—we both do very well out of the arrangement.'

She gave a sigh of relief. 'It all sounds fine. Well, then, I'd like to join your agency, if you'll let me.'

'Indeed, I will. I rather hoped you'd want to.' He paused for a moment. 'Perhaps I may be so bold as to make a suggestion. I hope you don't take offence as none is intended. Your name is very much that of an actress or, dare I say it, a stripper. Perhaps you'd prefer to use a different name?'

She thought for a moment. 'It's a tempting idea as the old Terri Lee had to put up with a load of shit, but I think I'll stick with the name, thank you. It'll remind me of things I wish had never happened, and it'll help me make sure they never happen again. Is that okay? It won't put anyone off hiring me?'

'It certainly won't do that; on the contrary. But I think you're strong enough to handle any client who gets hold of the wrong idea.' His smile broadened. 'So that's it, then.' He nodded in the direction of their waiter and then looked back at her. 'Welcome to the firm, Terri Lee. The waiter's bringing us champagne as we speak, so that we can seal our agreement in the customary manner.'

'You were very confident of everything,' she remarked, seeing the waiter approach them with a tall silver bucket. He stood it at the side of their table, and then picked up the bottle of champagne lying on a cushion of ice chippings. Moments later there was a loud explosion as the cork flew into the air. When he'd filled their flutes with a stream of effervescent gold, he disappeared.

'You're right,' Marcus said, holding up his glass, his clear grey eyes looking steadily into her face. 'I *was* confident that we'd be needing champagne today, and I'm equally confident about something else that will eventually come to pass, unlikely though it might seem to you at present. I propose we drink to that something else.'

He touched her glass of champagne with his, and then, his eyes still fixed on her face, he very slowly put his glass to his lips.

Terri Lee felt her toes tingle.

28

'What's the matter, Em?' Louise asked. 'You haven't been your usual self for several days now. In the past, the old Emily would've been working on a Sunday evening like there's no tomorrow, or getting ready to go out with John. But you've been sitting there for ages, staring at that book, and you haven't even turned a page.'

Emily glanced quickly at Louise, and then back at her book.

'Whatever it is, you'll feel better if you talk about it,' Louise urged.

Emily snapped the book shut. 'If you really must know, I'm not sure how things stand with John. But that's between you and me. I don't want it getting back to the others.'

'You know I wouldn't say anything. What's happened, then?'

'Well, nothing as such. It's just that when we went out a week ago and had a picnic at Woodstock, the subject of children came up. I said I didn't want any, and John seemed a bit shocked. That's all.'

'But you've seen him at work since then, and you went out last night, so it can't be a big deal, can it?'

Emily frowned. 'That's what I don't know. Things definitely aren't the same as they were. I can't put my finger on it, but John's different towards me. He may not even be aware of it, but I can feel it.' She picked up her mug of coffee, and shrugged. 'Just ignore me. I can hear how silly I sound. I'm sure we'll be back to normal soon. It was probably just a bit of a shock, learning I wasn't the maternal kind.'

She ran her finger morosely around the rim of the mug.

'D'you think he could be really keen on having children, then?' Louise asked after a minute or two. 'Men can get hooked on the idea just like women.'

'I'm sure that's true of some men, but I wouldn't have thought that John was one of them. He's always seemed more interested in books and the fine points of law than in anything else. It's one of the things I really like about him.'

'Then it seems unlikely that your ideas about children could be a problem, but just in case there *is* something worrying him, why don't you ask him outright what the matter is?'

Emily nodded. 'That's good advice, Louise, and I may well do that. But there's no real urgency.' She finished her coffee and stood up. 'And now I'm going up to do the work you were surprised I wasn't already doing.' Forcing a smile, she went out.

But as she made her way slowly up the stairs to her bedroom, she knew that there *was* a degree of urgency. She was no longer able to concentrate properly on her work because of a growing alarm that John's feelings towards her had materially changed, and it was vital she got back her focus.

The subject of children had never before come up as there hadn't been any need for it to do so.

Emily's university years had been filled with work, and with the world of intellectual debate finally open to her wondering mind, she'd had no interest at all in boys.

The first time she'd felt the desire to go to bed with anyone had been when she'd been out with John. After she'd been on a number of dates with him, her body's urges getting stronger each time, she'd gone to the doctor before matters went further, and had hesitantly asked for help in avoiding having children. He'd given her the pill, and when John had brought up the subject of taking precautions, she'd told him it was all sorted, and that had been that.

She opened the door to her room and switched on the light. Her eyes fell on the small photo of John that stood on her bedside table. It had been taken at the end of a brilliant day at Regent's Park Zoo, and he was laughing into the camera, the sunlight bouncing off his glasses.

She stood motionless, gripping the door handle, staring at his face. Realisation struck her with force—she couldn't lose him. She just couldn't. She loved him. The fear of losing him was devastating.

Her eyes filled with tears. She kicked the door shut behind her, turned off the light, walked into the welcome darkness and sat down heavily on the edge of her bed. She, Emily Bycroft, who'd thought she was impervious to romantic love, had fallen deeply in love with that gangly, kind, gentle, lovely man.

Did he know how strongly she felt about him, she wondered.

Neither of them had ever put their feelings for each other into words. Maybe he didn't know how much she loved him. She'd only just realised it herself, after all.

But the last few months had been the best in her life, with her work, her home, her housemate-friends and, above all, with John. She didn't know what she'd said or done to upset him, but whatever it was, she must find out what it was and put it right. She'd take Louise's advice and speak to him as soon as she could.

EMILY GLANCED at the clock on her desk: four o'clock. The clock had hardly moved since the last time she'd looked at it. This must be the longest Wednesday afternoon ever.

John had been tied up on both of the last two evenings, and when she'd come into work that morning, she'd known that he was going to be busy that evening, too. Depressed, she'd been wondering if she'd ever get a chance to speak to him.

She knew about him working that evening as the previous day, she and Paul had bumped into Venetia on their way to the library, and Venetia had been moaning about John expecting her to stay late on a Wednesday evening. It was her tennis evening, she'd complained, and by the time John released her, it'd be too far late to get to the club in time for a game.

'That man should get a life,' she'd grumbled. 'All he ever does is work, work and more work. But then again, who'd want to go out with him? He's hardly dynamic, is he? It wouldn't hurt him to think about other people, though— people who might have something better to do than stay in Chambers for half the night.'

Emily had speedily looked away, anxious to prevent Venetia from seeing both the dislike in her eyes and the relief that she and John had decided to keep their relation-ship secret until she'd finished her pupillage. She'd have hated Venetia to have had ammunition to poke fun at them behind their backs, which she would've done for sure.

At the end of the Wednesday morning, the three pupils had met up again when all three had taken their sandwiches out to a bench in the nearby gardens.

Venetia's sunny mood had been very different from the day before, and her eyes had sparkled as she'd regaled them with a description of the gorgeous barrister she'd met at the small claims court that morning, who was going to take her for a drink after work that evening.

'Divine eyes,' she'd murmured dreamily. 'He's one beautiful man. And he's keen on tennis, too. I can't wait to see him in his tennis whites.'

'I thought you and John were working late tonight,' Emily said in surprise.

'Oh, John's a pussy cat,' Venetia said with a dismissive wave. 'When I told him my mother wasn't well and wanted me home as early as possible, he insisted I leave whenever I wanted. He said he could manage without me. He wasn't doing anything special this evening, so he didn't mind how late he worked.' Her laughter tinkled around the courtyard and bounced off the surrounding stone buildings.

'He's a good guy, John is,' Paul said, glancing at Venetia with a degree of irritation. 'You shouldn't take advantage of him like that. You don't know how lucky you are to have him as your pupilmaster. He's the best of the three of them, although Andrew's a close second. Emily's the one who's drawn the short straw. I wouldn't want to be Gordon's gofer for anything.'

'It's all in the way you handle your pupilmaster,' Venetia stated with an air of supreme confidence. 'Gordon's human like anyone else. You just don't know how to play him,

Emily.' She laughed again, and tossed her sleek blonde hair back from her face.

Emily didn't attempt to hide her dislike.

It was only when she was back at her desk that she'd seen that Venetia's lie had given her the moment she'd been waiting for. This might be her only opportunity that week in which to ask John what had gone wrong between them.

Admittedly, he was staying late in order to work, but she was sure that he'd be able to focus better on his work once the air had been cleared, just as she would. He must be as bothered as she by the atmosphere between them.

Once they'd sorted out the misunderstanding, for that was all it could be, she'd stay on and help him finish his work. Then perhaps they could go somewhere to unwind with a drink, just like they used to do before that Sunday at Blenheim. All she had to do was wait for the time when Venetia had said she'd be leaving.

A dread at what might happen settled heavily in the pit of her stomach.

She moved her clock to a position where she could see it more easily, picked up a red-ribboned brief from the top of the pile, untied the ribbon, and tried to fix her mind solely on the brief in front of her.

TAKING A DEEP BREATH, she knocked on John's door.

'Come in,' she heard him call. She opened the door, took a hesitant step into the wood-panelled room, stopped and stood there, her hand on the door handle.

He glanced up, and she saw a look of anxiety cross his face.

Her heart started racing. 'I'm sorry to disturb you, John,' she began nervously. 'I wanted to talk to you, and I knew you'd be working late, and didn't think you'd have anyone with you.'

He took off his glasses, put them on the desk and looked slowly around the room. 'No, no one here,' he murmured. 'Perhaps you'd like to come in and tell me what this is all about. Have a seat, will you?' He gestured to one of the chairs on the other side of his desk.

She released the door handle, let the door swing shut behind her and went and sat down. 'This feels so formal,' she said, and tried to laugh as she faced him across an expanse of dark mahogany.

He nodded. 'It does, doesn't it. Ridiculously so.' He got up, came around his desk and sat down on the chair next to hers. She moved slightly in her seat so that she faced him. 'What is it, Emily?' he asked quietly.

She gave him a weak smile. 'That's the coward's way out, pretending you don't know why I'm here. Of course, you do. It's because of something I said or did, though I don't know what that was. You should be telling me what's wrong, not pretending you don't know why I'm here.' She looked into his face. 'What is it, John? What have I done that's made you change towards me?'

'You've not done anything at all,' he said mildly.

'That's splitting hairs. What have I said, then?'

He was silent for a moment, and then he reached across for his glasses and put them back on. 'I was somewhat taken aback by the way you felt about children,' he said eventually. 'That's all. It's nothing more than that.'

'But not everyone's maternal. It doesn't automatically come with being a woman—God standing there with a tick list—breasts, womb, ovaries, maternal instinct. It doesn't work like that. Why must I want a child because I'm a woman?'

'No reason at all,' he said. 'It's just that most women seem to want children, so I was rather surprised to meet one who didn't.'

'Rather surprised! That's an understatement, considering the way you've been towards me since the subject came up. Does it really matter that much to you that I don't like children? Is this about you longing to be a dad and unable to contemplate going through life without achieving that status?'

'That's not what I'm saying.' He moved closer to her and stared at her intently. 'What makes you so anti-children, Emily? I know you're an only child, and I know you're not close to your parents, but neither fact satisfactorily explains why you affect to hate children so much.'

She shrugged. 'Everyone's made the way they are.' Her eyes filled with tears. 'I didn't think it'd matter. Lots of men say they'd have preferred it if they hadn't had to share their wives with a child. They're often jealous of their children and their wife's preoccupation with them.'

'I believe that is, indeed, true,' he said calmly.

'I'm offering you my exclusive devotion, and the ability to go wherever we want, whenever we want, and do exactly what we want without considering anyone but ourselves. Isn't that enough for you, John?' Tears trickled down her cheeks.

John took her by the hand. He cleared his throat. 'What are you saying, Emily? Are you asking me to marry you?'

She pulled her hand away and dug in her pocket for a tissue. He waited while she blew her nose. 'I've done it again,' she said, trying to smile though her tears as she put her tissue away. 'I've made a complete hash of this.'

He shook his head.

'Yes, I have,' she insisted. 'It's come out all wrong. But

since I've got myself into this mess, I might as well go ahead and make even more of a fool of myself. I love you, John, and the only reason I'm not asking you to marry me is that I know you'd refuse and I couldn't bear that.'

She started crying again.

John got up, put his arms around her and hugged her. 'Emily, Emily,' he said softly. 'You know I love you. I've never had to say it. Just as I know you love me, and you've never had to say it.'

'And you still love me?' Her voice lifted in hope.

'Of course, I do. It's because I love you that I want to understand you. If we're going to spend the rest of our lives together, we need to understand the things that are important to each other, and why they're important. The underlying reason can be even more important than the effect.'

Staring up into his face, she saw the love and concern in his eyes.

'What are you doing on Saturday?' she asked.

He pulled his desk diary over to him. 'Nothing,' he replied.

'Then you can pick me up at eight o'clock in the morning, with a full tank of petrol. If we leave at that time, it shouldn't take more than two hours to get to Weymouth.'

29

A*pril*

EMILY SIGHED with relief as the sea came into sight.

It was several hours since John had picked her up in his dark green Saab and they'd left London. Traffic jam after traffic jam had stalled them, and she was more than ready for the journey to end. As for John, who was doing the driving, he must want to see the back of that dreary road even more than she did.

But it would all be worthwhile if she could make John understand why she felt as she did. It wasn't going to be easy —sometimes she wasn't even sure that she understood it herself—but she had to get through to him if she was going to save their relationship. And she wanted that more than anything in the world.

The closer they'd got to Weymouth, the more her memories had crowded in, and the quieter she'd become.

John had glanced at her a couple of times, opened his mouth to speak, closed it again and returned his eyes to the road.

He'd only once broken the silence.

They'd been travelling for about an hour and a half, seemingly making little headway, and he'd suggested that they stop a while to let the traffic die down. But Emily had assured him that things would be even worse later in the day. They were travelling south on a major route, which was why she'd suggested an early start, she'd told him, and she'd sunk back into her thoughts.

As they neared the seafront, Emily directed John to take the road leading to the harbour roundabout, and then to go right towards the North Quay.

'Weymouth is more built up than I'd expected,' he remarked as he drove along the series of roads that led away from the centre of town and into the residential area.

'We're nearly there. In fact, you can stop right here.'

He put his foot heavily on the brake and the car came to a shuddering halt at the top of a hill. Leaning forward in her seat, she stared through the windscreen, her gaze travelling down the hill to a distant cluster of small shops.

'Welcome to my childhood, John,' she said, scanning the row of grey stone terraced houses on the right hand side of the road. 'We're all products of our past. I want to introduce you to *my* past. Starting with my parents. This is the road I lived in till I left for university, and I'm sure my parents will still be in the same house. They'll be taken out in their coffins.'

'When did you last see them?'

'The day I left for university. That must be the best part of five years ago. No, I tell a lie. I've seen them once since then, but not in the way you mean. Come on,' she said decisively, and she opened the car door and got out. 'Let's say hello to mummy and daddy.'

He got out, locked the door and came round the car to stand alongside her. She turned to look at him, her mouth forming a smile that didn't quite reach her eyes. He took her hand, gave it a slight squeeze and together they started walking down the hill.

Halfway down, Emily stopped in front of a house. 'Here we are,' she said, indicating the house to the right of her. She looked up at it. 'It's certainly seen better days. The front door could do with a fresh coat of paint, and so could the rest of the woodwork. But my parents aren't into material things, as you can tell.' She disentangled her hand from John's. 'Well, here goes.'

She walked up the short path to the front door, with John just behind her. She knocked on the door and took a step back.

'They're home. That's lucky!' John exclaimed, glancing towards the downstairs window. 'Someone looked out.' He smiled in the direction of the window. The net curtain dropped back into place. 'They've gone, so they're probably coming to the door.'

'I wouldn't be too sure of that,' she remarked drily. She bent down to the letter box, pushed it open it and called through it, 'Mother! Father! It's Emily—I mean, it's Prudence.' There was no sound from within the house. She tried again. 'Mother! Father! Open the door, would you, please? I've missed you. I want to see you again, and I want to introduce you to a friend of mine.'

She straightened up, and waited. But nothing happened. She went forward and knocked again.

'It seems as if they're not going to open the door, Emily,' John said gently after several minutes. 'It might be an idea if we found somewhere to have lunch and you told me all about it.' He put his arm round her shoulders and led her back to the pavement.

She stared at the house for a moment or two longer, and then turned away. 'We'll walk this way,' she said, pointing down the hill. 'You must see two other places. We can think about food after we've been to them. I'll tell you about my parents as we go.'

Walking past the terraces of grey houses, Emily told John about her childhood, about the clothes she was forced to wear, her difficulty in getting a formal education, the restrictions on her life and that of her parents, about the rules imposed by the austere religious community to which her parents belonged.

'They chose that so-called religion for themselves, and they chose it for me. I was never taught about other beliefs. I had to put on blinkers and accept what I was told without question. And when I couldn't do that, I was cast out.'

'That's true of many fundamentalist religions, I'm afraid,' John said, shaking his head. 'Believers can behave with great cruelty towards each other.'

'And they're not the only ones! You've no idea how desperately I wanted to be friends with the children who used to walk past the house. But they mocked me and jeered at me when I tried to get close. I learned the hard way how very nasty kids could be, and how mean and spiteful. Even now, sometimes at night I can hear them laughing at me.'

She stopped walking and turned to look at the house to their right. John stood beside her, his arm firmly around her shoulders.

'I did have one friend, though, called Patience,' she went on. 'But the community ordered her to turn her back on me, and she wasn't the sort of person who could stand up to them. Assuming she wanted to, that is. She may not have wanted to—she was happier with the whole religion thing than I was. I think she got married, and they live here with her parents.' She nodded towards the house in front of them.

'Why don't we leave Weymouth right now?' John suggested. 'I know enough about such sects to appreciate what your childhood will have been like. You must possess a tremendous inner strength to have been able to break free from it.'

'That's the point, John—I won't ever be free from it,' she said, her face distraught. 'It's a part of me, whether I like it or not. I've been conditioned by my childhood, directly and indirectly.'

'Let's go home, Emily. Let's go back to London and the people who love you.' His arm tightened around her.

She looked back at the house. 'They know we're here. I can sense it. But it would be pointless to knock on Patience's door,' she said, as if she hadn't heard him. 'At least one of them will have heard us by now, but no one's come to the door. It's a shame as I liked her. And I liked her mother— she used to teach me some of my lessons.' She raised her eyes to the upstairs window. 'I would've liked to have seen Patience for one last time. I'll never come back to Weymouth again.'

'I wish there was something I could say to help you,' John said. 'I can feel your misery.'

'Mind you, I wouldn't have known what to say to Patience, our lives are so different, and have been for so long,' she went on. Then she turned to him, her vision blurred. 'Final stop, the Meeting Hall, and then food.' She moved his arm from her shoulder, took hold of his hand,

and they continued walking down the road. 'I wonder if Preacher Madson's still in charge. I was terrified of him.'

As she led the way along the road to the Meeting Hall, she told John about how she'd always felt uncomfortable when Preacher Madson was near her, but hadn't really understood why.

'Looking back on it,' she said with a wry smile, 'I think my apprehension might've been owing to something that's never much talked about, but should be.'

As the low white building came in sight, her steps slowed. 'For a religion that notionally doesn't believe in hierarchy, and claims not to have idols or icons, it's somewhat contradictory that the community made that horrible man into a sort of god. Whatever Preacher Madson said, the faithful accepted without question. He was more infallible than the Pope!'

'That's often the way it is with exclusive sects,' he said.

'He'd go on and on about the importance of the Lord's family,' she said, her voice bitter, 'but he'd break up a human family simply because a person wanted to use her God-given brain.'

They reached the hall, and John stopped walking. 'Don't go any further, Emily,' he said, gripping her hand tightly. 'Let's go back to the car, and leave Weymouth and the past behind us. Being here is making you too unhappy. I don't need to see any more to understand your background.'

She stood still, staring at the Meeting Hall. 'You're right,' she said at last. 'I've seen enough.'

Turning round, they walked briskly back along the road and up the hill.

Neither spoke until they reached the car.

John unlocked the car.

Pausing by the passenger door, Emily glanced at him

across the top of the car. 'You do understand why I hate children and don't want a child, don't you?' she asked, a note of desperation in her voice. 'It's too easy to damage a child's mind, even if you don't mean to and you love that child. I don't want that kind of power over anyone. I'm not comfortable enough in myself to want to be responsible for someone else.'

'That could explain your reluctance to have a child of your own, I suppose,' he said thoughtfully. 'I'm not sure, though, that it fully accounts for your hostility towards all children.'

'The other children were hateful to me, simply because I was different. Children can be really mean.'

'But you were a child, too, Emily, and you weren't mean. Therefore, not all children are mean.'

'I wouldn't describe myself as typical, coming from the home I did. Apart from Patience, who came from the same background, all the children I met were nasty. It completely put me off children for ever, and I don't want any in my life, not now, not in the future. You can see that, can't you?' She opened the passenger door and slid into her seat.

'To a certain extent, yes,' he said, getting into the car. 'I may not agree with you, but I can understand your reasoning. It *is* possible, though, that this visit will have exorcised the ghosts of Weymouth for you, and that at some point in the future, you may feel differently about children in general, and possibly even about motherhood.'

'I doubt that.'

He gave her a half-smile. 'Don't let yourself become a prisoner of your past, Emily. If you do, the religion you so despise will have won.'

'But it hasn't!' she exclaimed. 'Look at my life—I've escaped the religion. It's just that it's left me hating children.' She paused. 'Knowing that, d'you still want to go out with me, John?' She suddenly felt acutely nervous. 'Well?' she asked, and she held her breath.

'Yes, I do. I love you, and nothing you've told me has changed that. It's helped me to understand certain things about you, but it doesn't stop me from loving you.'

She released her breath.

A feeling of joy welled up within her. She fell back against her seat and sighed with audible relief. John glanced across at her and smiled. Then he removed his glasses, wiped them with a cleaning cloth, put them back on again, and switched on the engine.

'We'll stop at the first pleasant place that we see and have something to eat,' he said.

MUCH LATER, as they were sitting in a long traffic jam in Buckingham Palace Road, John turned to Emily. 'I'd thought I wouldn't be able to see you next Saturday,' he said, 'but I'm wondering if perhaps you'd care to join me on my outing. I think it only right that *I* now open a window on my past. Would Saturday suit you?'

She stared at him, her forehead furrowing in vague anxiety. 'That sounds ominous,' she said, and she pushed her hair back from her face. 'Of course, I'll come with you. But should I be worried?'

'I hope not.'

30

Terri Lee looked up at the sparkling glass chandeliers which hung from the silver-leaf ceiling. Then she gazed casually around the lounge, her eyes lingering on the sleek serpentine bar that was dramatically offset against lacquered mahogany walls, and on the well-heeled clientele, who looked at ease in the opulent surroundings. She smiled in quiet satisfaction. This was the sort of place she'd be happy to get used to.

And she intended to do so

The night before, she'd earned the first real money she'd ever made, and she'd earned it doing something she could do well, which was right up her street, and which she'd enjoyed. And she was confident there'd be more such jobs.

And what's more, she thought happily, she'd be using her acting ability.

It wasn't the acting profession, strictly speaking, but it wasn't that different. She'd had to put on an act the night before, just like she'd had to do when she was at the parties with Hugh, and just like she'd done when she'd gone on auditions.

But from now on, when she put on an act, it would be altogether different—she'd be working for herself.

And it had been fun to have a reason to dress up again, and go somewhere nice for a change. Emily had been in Weymouth with John, Caroline had been getting ready to go to Cheshire with Robert, and Louise had been doing something or other with Ethan. She would have felt dead low if she'd had to spend the whole evening by herself, or go on a date with someone just for the sake of it.

Instead, Marcus had sent her on an escorting job. Her first such job. And she'd had a really good time. She was surprised by how much she'd genuinely enjoyed herself.

Inwardly aglow, she leaned back against the plush dark brown leather banquette and smiled across the small mirrored table at Marcus.

The American, Ted, whose escort she'd been, hadn't been riveting company in himself, but he'd been polite and charming, and he'd been very ready to find her entertaining. And she knew that she *had* been entertaining. The fact that the evening had gone so well was down to her. It certainly hadn't been down to the couple with whom she and Ted were dining.

On the way to meet the couple, Ted had told her that the man was a big importer, who bought a large amount of merchandise through Ted's export company in the States. Ted came over twice a year in order to keep alive the sense of a close social relationship. He was sure that it was good for business to do so, and these were competitive times.

Each time he came over, he took his client out to dinner, and the client's wife came, too. As Ted didn't have a wife, he always made sure that he had a woman on his arm. To balance the numbers, he'd said, and also to keep the conversation going in the way that women managed so well.

The client's wife was a mousy woman, Terri Lee had thought, with no visible interest in spending her husband's obvious wealth on stylish clothes, and little to say for herself. But she, Terri Lee, had managed to keep a conversation going that had seemed to engage their interest, and at the end of the evening, Ted had been so pleased with the way the evening had gone that he'd told her he'd be throwing in a little extra to show his satisfaction.

And even more important, he was going to ask for her the next time he came over to England. To her intense relief, he hadn't made the slightest attempt to suggest anything further for the evening, but had bid her a polite goodnight and sent her home from the restaurant in a pre-paid taxi.

'You're very quiet,' Marcus said. 'How was yesterday evening?'

'Absolutely fine,' she told him, her eyes shining. 'In fact, it was better than fine. He was a total sweetie, and his friends were boring but harmless. He said he's going to ask for me next time he's here.'

'And that, indeed, is what he told me when he rang this morning,' Marcus said. 'He's used us for years. He always contacts me in advance of coming over.'

'What's more,' Terri Lee went on, 'he didn't make a pass at me at all. He behaved like a perfect gentleman all evening.' She frowned slightly. 'It's really strange, isn't it, that someone would come all the way here just to have dinner with a client? That's crazy.'

Marcus laughed. 'You'll find it's not as unusual as you might expect. Many expenses can be put down to business, so businessmen and dignitaries are able to live in far more extravagant way than we poor workers.'

Terri Lee's eyes took in the expert cut of Marcus's deep blue suit, the crisp ice-blue shirt beneath, the heavy silver cuff links, the carefully styled hair. 'There's nothing poor about the way you live, Marcus,' she said firmly.

'And nor will there be anything poor about you for much longer, Terri Lee, if you stick with me. But as for Ted; it wasn't surprising that he didn't make a pass at you.'

'Well, thank you very much,' she said in a playful huff.

'Aha! Here comes our wine!'

The waiter approached them carrying a tray with a bottle of red wine and two long-stemmed crystal Chianti Classico glasses. He placed the tray on table, and showed the bottle to Marcus, who nodded and said, 'Just pour'. Then he filled each of their glasses and left.

Marcus raised his glass to Terri Lee. 'To a prosperous relationship and, more importantly, to a long friendship.'

She raised her glass to his, and then both took a sip of their wine.

'No, Ted's restraint was nothing to do with the way you look,' he continued, his eyes skimming her low-cut black top. 'Not at all. Our Ted comes over twice a year for a week of passion with his Derek. Derek has been the love of his life for the past ten years.'

Terri Lee stared at Marcus, open-mouthed.

'Derek's married,' Marcus went on, putting his glass back down on the table, 'and won't leave his wife. Ted's had to accept the situation. Coming to England is how he copes with it. And Derek, I believe, visits the States whenever he can. Mr and Mrs Homophobic Client would be ultra-shocked if they knew about Ted's sexuality, which is why he always has one of my girls on his arm. A lack of commitment is preferable in their bigoted eyes to the abomination of man on man, as they see it.'

'Well, well,' Terri Lee murmured. 'I certainly didn't pick that one up.' She took a few sips of wine. 'But tell me,

Marcus,' she said, easing back in her pencil-slim black skirt and crossing one stockinged leg over the other. 'You've a lot of girls in your stable, as I think you once called it. How come you're spending so much time on me? D'you go out of the way like this every time you take on a new escort?'

'I try to make everyone feel at home, of course. That's good business. But I admit that I might be seeing you more often than I'd normally see my girls.'

'Why's that?'

'It's a good question, and I'm not sure I know the answer. Maybe it's that I rather think we both come from the same place. Obviously I don't mean where you were born—I've no idea where that is, although I'll find out when you fill in the forms that'll regulate this for tax purposes. We'll deal with those forms another time—maybe over lunch next week. No, I think I sense that like me, you haven't had an easy start in life. We've both been let down by people we'd reason to trust, but we've come out fighting. It gives us something in common. But also, more than that, I genuinely like you.'

'You're right about my life. There was only my mother when I was little, and she was a prize bitch. She treated me like no normal mother would. You don't want to know. I left home the minute I could. Being an actress didn't work out, and then there was that scumbag Hugh, but you know about him. This escorting business is the first good thing that's landed my way, and I'm sure I'll be good at it.'

'You're a natural, Terri Lee, believe me.'

'Yes, that's what I think,' she said happily. She leaned forward to pick up her wine, the low cut of her neckline revealing breasts that were spilling over the cup of a black lace bra. 'I'm going to love this work, Marcus. I just know it.'

'You won't get a Ted every time, but I'm sure you'll cope.'

He gave her a rueful grin. 'I think you'd better sit upright. I'm no Ted and what you're doing to me by bending over like that, doesn't bear thinking about. It's fortunate that the table isn't made of clear glass.'

Her wine glass in her hand, she straightened up and met his steady gaze. They smiled slowly at each other. Then she took a sip of her wine, and again replaced her glass on the table, bending very low as she did so.

31

I t was the right time for Robert to meet her parents, Caroline decided. She knew he wanted to make a formal request for her hand, and she thought that a lovely idea. She liked the idea of things being done correctly and so would her parents, and she felt safe enough in her relationship with Robert not to fear that the ordinariness of the home into which she'd been born would damage the image of sophistication she aspired to.

The closer it got to their weekend in Cheshire, the more she found herself looking forward to going home—she, who hadn't been able to get away from the grocery shop on the outskirts of Northwich fast enough. Not only would she see her parents again, but she'd be able to parade her well-off, ambitious, very good-looking fiancé in front of her friends.

Robert, too, seemed to be looking forward to the trip. He'd been starting to wonder if she actually had any parents, he told her, as he'd heard so little about them, and he expressed himself keen to meet them.

Excited though she was, she was nervous, too. What

Robert would think of her parents, and the tedious provinciality of their lives, she wondered.

She fervently hoped they would make an effort with the way in which they presented themselves so that she didn't feel ashamed of them, and that her younger sister, Margot, who was going to try to get away from her polytechnic for the weekend, would be on her best behaviour.

Both she and Robert had been in high spirits when they set off for Cheshire early on the Friday afternoon. Unfortunately, it turned out to be a truly awful journey, with one traffic hold-up after another, and they didn't reach the grocery store until six thirty in the evening, by which time both were tired and fed up.

'Drive round to the side of the shop and park there,' Caroline told Robert as they approached the corner shop. 'We live above and behind the shop, but we try not to go in and out through the shop door. Instead, we use the door in the garden wall.'

'Thank God,' he said as he drew up alongside a red brick wall, and switched off the engine. 'What a god-awful journey! We should've taken the plane, and hired a car at the airport. What wouldn't I give for a drink! D'you think we can say hello and then escape to a pub on our own, and leave all the social stuff till tomorrow? I've just about had it for today.'

Caroline pulled a face. 'Mum and Dad are bound to have got a meal ready for us. But if there's a chance of slipping out when we've eaten, we'll take it. Whatever we can or can't do, though, please don't be in a bad mood, Robert,' she begged. She slid closer to him and ran her hand down his arm. 'We're here now, aren't we,' she said, cajolingly. 'Let's make it a good weekend. I want my family and friends to see how wonderful you are.'

He sighed loudly. 'You're right, lovely Caro; as always. I promise I'll be a good boy.' He gave her a quick kiss, and then got out of the car, walked round to the boot, opened it and started lifting out their weekend bags.

Caroline followed him. As she did so, the black painted door in the brick garden wall opened and her mother came through the doorway, closely followed by Caroline's father. Her mother held out her arms to Caroline, who went quickly over to her and hugged her warmly.

'How are you, Mum?'

'I'm fine, pet. All the better for seeing you.' Patsy Redway took a step back and held her daughter at arms' length, studying her face. 'You do look bonny, pet. Doesn't she, Father?' she said, glancing back at her husband. Releasing Caroline's arms, she reached in her pocket for a handkerchief. 'We've missed you, Caroline,' she said, wiping her watering eyes.

Arthur Redway stood and beamed at his daughter. 'My, you do look a picture,' he said, shaking his head in wonder. 'You're right about that, Mother.'

Caroline went across to her father, gave him a quick hug, and then stepped back and held out her hand to Robert. 'Mum, Dad, this is Robert.'

'I'm delighted to meet you, Mrs Redway.' Robert stepped forward and shook Patsy's hand. 'And you, too, sir,' he said, taking Arthur's hand in a firm grip. 'It's a pleasure to meet you both at last. Caroline's told me so much about you.'

Caroline glanced at Robert in surprised amusement, and hastily switched to a more neutral expression.

Arthur Redway looked gratified. 'Welcome to our home, Robert,' he said ponderously. 'Any friend of Caroline's is a friend of ours. Isn't that so, Mother?'

'Indeed, it is,' Patsy said. 'But why are we all standing

here? Let's go in and have something to drink. You must both be tired after your long journey. Father will help you with the bags, Robert.'

'Thank God for that word drink,' Robert hissed to Caroline under his breath as he bent over to pick up the weekend cases. Arthur made a movement as if to help him.

'Don't worry, Mr Redway,' Robert said quickly. 'I can manage both cases—we travelled light.'

A suitcase in each hand, he straightened up, and he and Arthur followed Caroline and her mother through the wooden door into the small manicured garden at the back of the house, and along the paved path that led to the kitchen door. They went straight through the kitchen to a small room that led off the kitchen.

'This is where we live, Robert,' Patsy told him, gesturing vaguely around her. 'That door there leads to the hall. There's a door from the hall directly into the shop, and also doors leading into the dining-room and front room. And there's the staircase, too, of course.'

'Leave the cases by the door, Robert. That's it. You can take them up when you've had a rest. Sit yourself down, there's a good chap. You must be tired after your long drive.' Arthur indicated the sofa facing the fireplace, its floral upholstery protected by a lace antimacassar. 'Caroline, you go and sit next to your young man. Unless of course,' he added quickly, colouring slightly, 'either of you would like to visit the small room upstairs.' He gave a little cough.

'I'm fine, thank you, sir,' Robert said, sitting down.

'Will Margot be able to get back home this weekend, Dad?' Caroline asked as she sat down next to Robert.

'She will, indeed. She'll be home tomorrow. There's a dance at her polytechnic tonight so she's not coming till the morning, but she'll be here in time for lunch. I don't understand you girls—you're always off to some dance or other.' Sighing, Arthur sat in one of the two leather chairs that flanked the fireplace.

'That's partly what a poly's for, Dad,' Caroline said, a hint of impatience in her voice. 'You go there to meet people as well as to study.'

'If you say so, Caroline. Now, Mother,' Arthur called to Patsy, who was hovering in the doorway, tying her pinafore apron behind her. 'I think we could all do with that drink, don't you?'

Robert brightened visibly.

'You're right. A nice cup of tea is just what we need,' Patsy said. 'I'll put the kettle on.'

'That will be perfect, Mother.' Arthur settled back into his chair in satisfaction.

Robert threw Caroline an anguished plea.

'Just a moment, Mum. Rather than tea, why don't we have something a little stronger?' Caroline said quickly.

Her parents looked at each other in surprise.

'Well,' Arthur said uncertainly, 'if that's what you'd prefer. We've got a bottle of sherry, haven't we, Mother? We normally save it for Christmas and special occasions, but I suppose this *is* a special occasion, meeting one of Caroline's friends from London.' He smiled at Robert. 'Yes, why don't we push the boat out?' He stood up. 'Go on, Mother. You bring us something to keep us going until it's time for tea, and I'll get the sherry and glasses. You'll like it, Robert—it's a nice sweet sherry.'

Arthur went over to the low teak sideboard running along one wall of the room, and bent over to open the cupboard door. Robert glanced at Caroline and rolled his eyes. She stifled a giggle.

A moment later, Arthur returned with the bottle of

sherry. He wiped the dust from the bottle with the sleeve of his maroon-coloured cardigan, put the bottle on the teak coffee table that stood in front of the sofa, and went back to the sideboard. Returning with four sherry glasses, he put them on the table and very carefully filled each glass half-full.

Patsy came in with a plate of custard creams and bourbon biscuits, which she placed next to the glasses, and then went and sat down on the chair opposite Arthur's.

Arthur handed the glasses around and remained standing. 'I feel as if we should have a toast,' he said, holding up his glass. 'To Caroline. It's a pleasure to have you home again.'

'He's right, pet,' Patsy said, beaming with pride at her daughter.

Caroline murmured something unintelligible and they all took a sip of their drink.

'So, Robert,' Arthur said, sitting down. 'Are you interested in bowls? There's a very nice green not far from here.'

32

'Oh, my God,' Robert said with a groan, and he stretched out on his back on Caroline's narrow single bed, fully dressed, and put his arm around her. 'I never in my life would've believed that one short evening could have seemed as long as that one did. I began to wish that the journey had taken us nine hours, rather than a paltry four and a half. If it had, we wouldn't have had time for quite so much mind-numbing trivia.'

'Ssh! You don't want them to know you're in here, do you?' Caroline whispered. 'They'd never get over the shock.' She nestled into the crook of his arm. He rested his head on the top of hers.

'How come you've turned out to be such a modern woman?' he murmured. 'Or is yours a thin veneer of sophistication in order to reel the man in, and then, when he's hooked, out will come that tantalising wrap-around apron?'

'So it was tantalising, was it?' she said, leaning up to kiss him. 'In that case —'

'Don't you dare,' he cried in mock horror. 'I'd live in fear of an important part of my anatomy mistakenly finding its way into one of its capacious pockets.'

Caroline giggled and squeezed closer to him. They quietly lay there in each other's arms for a few minutes. 'I'm sorry we couldn't slip out this evening,' she said, breaking the companionable silence.

'Don't worry about it. I realised pretty soon that it wasn't going to be possible, and resigned myself to an evening of tedium. I'll grab your father tomorrow morning if I can. Or will that be difficult?' He moved slightly back to look down at her. 'Is he likely to be working in the shop tomorrow?'

'I expect both of them will pop in and out to keep an eye on things, but they've got a couple of teenagers who work in the shop at weekends, and occasionally in the evening, too. The kids know what to do, so Dad will be able to leave them to it,' she assured him, and she pulled him close to her again.

'Good. What I'll do is slip out early on, and try to get hold of some champagne or washing-up liquid—anything we can use for a toast that will save us from the dregs of a bottle of sherry that must've been opened in Noah's day. If sherry could go green, that would've done. I'll catch your dad before lunch.'

'That's a fabulous idea. It'll get it out of the way before everyone else arrives. Apparently, the aunts, uncles and nosy neighbours are coming at about three. But Mum's fine with us going out in the evening. I thought we could go to a club in Warrington and you can meet those of my friends who haven't escaped the area. I'm afraid Margot will probably want to come with us, though.'

Robert sighed loudly. 'I'd forgotten about the jollity planned for the afternoon. And that your sister was coming. What's she like?'

'Very different from me. She's shorter than I am and quite thin. We've never been particularly close as we like different things. She hates cooking—can't see the point of it when you can buy fish and chips. She's not into marriage and the whole family thing. Why become someone's legal slave, is what she says. She's doing Business Studies, and said she'd hate teaching.'

'What's she planning to do at the end of her course? I can't see any obvious way of transforming your father's shop into a multi-national concern.'

'She's no intention of staying around here. Or she hadn't when I last spoke to her. She wants to work in the City, which was a real surprise as she's never seemed to be into anything serious. She's a die-hard clubber, or at least she used to be. That's about all I can tell you, I'm afraid. I've not seen her since Christmas, and we were home for such a short time then that we hardly spoke to each other.'

'She certainly sounds very different from my sexy, voluptuous, stunning fiancée,' Robert murmured, 'who's going to make me a home that's the envy of everyone who crosses its threshold, and who's going to produce children of utter perfection, the creation of whom is going to give me endless pleasure.'

Leaning towards her, he lightly kissed her forehead, the tip of nose, her mouth.

'You sexy thing,' he whispered, and he eased himself on top of her.

The bed beneath them creaked.

She pushed him off her. 'Not now; not here,' she said with a giggle. 'If my parents heard us, they could easily expire at the thought of hanky-panky taking place under their roof.'

'While hanky-panky with you sounds pretty good to me,'

he said, rolling on to his back, 'you're right about this being the wrong place. I'll go to my room, but I'll leave it a minute or two before I do. If I left now, I might bump into your parents with the front of my trousers standing to attention, and that would certainly give them a shock.' He grinned at her. 'But be warned, I'll expect compensation for my enforced celibacy when we're back in London, and for the lack of sleep I'm about to have, with you being so near and yet so far.'

'And I can't wait to compensate you.'

'With that galvanising thought in my mind, I'll get back to my monastic cell. When I get into bed, I'll think about tomorrow afternoon, which should rapidly cool my ardour. The thought of having to smile for several hours is sure to have a depressing effect, in every sense of the word.'

'But we'll have fun tomorrow evening,' she said with confidence.

THE FOLLOWING MORNING BEGAN WELL. Her parents were clearly thrilled that she was going to marry Robert.

'He's an important man,' her father said to her gravely, a note of awe in his voice. Her mother wept silent tears of joy.

They gathered in the room off the kitchen, and Caroline watched happily as Robert eased the cork from the champagne that he'd bought from a small off-licence a few streets away, and started pouring the sparkling liquid into the water glasses they were using in the absence of champagne flutes.

As Arthur raised his glass in what was obviously going to end in a toast, a sudden sound from the kitchen startled them all. He paused, and they all stared at the door.

'I'm home!' screamed a female voice.

It was followed by the owner of the voice bursting in,

loud, colourful and exploding with energy. She stopped abruptly at the sight of the bottle in Robert's hands.

My God, is that champagne!' she shrieked, and dropped her orange travel bag on to the carpet. 'Has some kind of revolution taken place in this Memorial to the Past?' Her eyes travelled up from the bottle in Robert's hands to his face. 'And who are you?' she asked, her voice several octaves lower.

'Assuming you're Margot, I'm your brother-in-law to be,' he said with a grin. 'We were about to drink to that. Will you join us?'

'Indeed, I will,' she said brightly, and she stepped forward and took the glass that Robert held out to her.

Caroline's gaze ran down the length of her sister's body, from the outrageous purple and magenta streaks in her short spiky brown hair, to the deep red lips that were curved in a seductive welcome, to the cropped, lime-green ribbed top, to the expanse of naked stomach that disappeared into low-slung denim hipster jeans.

What *does* she look like, she exclaimed inwardly, and then she saw the answer on Robert's face.

Her stomach turned over.

She should never have plumped for her yellow cashmere twin-set that morning, and a string of pearls, she thought, in sudden anger at herself.

THROUGHOUT THE LUNCH of sliced ham with beetroot, spring onions, cucumber, radishes, tomato and lettuce, Robert and Margot teased each other, each vying to outdo the other's witty barbs. Caroline was so busy seething that she didn't even have time to feel embarrassed when her mother put a bottle of salad cream in the centre of the table.

'Did I tell you that old Mrs Kennedy died a few months ago, Caroline?' Patsy asked as they were finishing their salad. 'She owned the little baker's shop that Caroline passed on her way home from school, Robert, and she used to give Caroline the broken biscuits at the end of the day. She was a martyr to her leg ulcers, poor Mrs Kennedy. Nasty they were. But she always had a soft spot for Caroline. She'd have been so happy to know you were getting married, pet.'

'And poor Mr Kennedy didn't last long after that,' Arthur added. 'Grief it was that took him. It was a sad day when we buried him next to his wife. They're turning the shop into a house now. We're one of the few shops left in the area, Robert. I don't like to think what the pensioners will do when we're gone.'

'You're right, Arthur,' Robert said, turning his attention from Margot to Arthur. 'The spread of supermarkets, and the way they've been bribing customers with their Green Shield stamps, is going to make it very difficult for small shops to survive. Supporting small shops and communities is essential. The government needs to look at the rental and rates imposed on small shops, and to act swiftly to ensure that those who are serving a local community are not so heavily taxed that they can't hold their own against the threat posed by the larger stores.'

Arthur sighed. 'I wish everyone thought like you, Robert. You are so right. Isn't he, Mother?'

'He is, indeed. Are you sure you don't want another radish, Robert, before I take the bowl away?'

THE MINUTE they finished their lunch, Caroline dragged Robert into the garden.

'So what was all that about with my sister?' she

demanded, her green eyes blazing with fury as she faced him.

'Nothing at all,' he said, raising his eyebrows in surprise. 'I was trying to inject some liveliness into the occasion, and Margot was playing along with that. That's all it was. Don't let your imagination run riot and make something out of nothing. But if I like her,' he added, looking down at her with a lazy smile, 'it's because she reminds me of you.'

'She's totally different from me!' she exclaimed. 'In every way.'

'She's shorter, less elegant, less beautiful, and she's louder than you. But she has a look of you about her eyes. And in the few moments when she was relaxed and in quiet mode, there was something very Caroline about her.'

Frowning slightly, she opened her mouth to protest again, but he wrapped his arms around her and kissed her hard on the lips. Then he drew back a little.

'I'm just trying to get on with everyone, Caro,' he said quietly, gazing deep into her eyes. 'I like your sister, but I love *you*, and I always will.'

Turning, their arms around each other, they walked back to the house, with Caroline feeling much better and scolding herself for being over-fanciful.

And by the end of the afternoon, she had almost forgotten the misery of their lunch.

Robert's behaviour towards the guests had been faultless.

He'd become more and more engaging as the afternoon had worn on, and her parents' faces had glowed with pleasure and pride as they received the heartfelt congratulations of everyone who came within striking distance of Robert's charm.

Caroline, too, received hugs and warm congratulations

as she stood side by side with Robert, making small talk
with whomever was standing in front of them, and
colouring slightly at the many references to Robert's good
looks, and coy hints about the future offspring of two such
handsome parents.

The stress of the morning had soon become a thing of
the past.

This was a dream come true, showing off a wealthy,
good-looking fiancé, who had buckets of charm and who
loved her, and by the time they set off for the club that
evening, she was completely relaxed.

BUT WHILE ROBERT'S behaviour towards the afternoon
guests had been faultless, his behaviour at the club with her
sister hadn't.

Margot had behaved shamelessly, and so had Robert—
he hadn't held back one little bit, Caroline thought grimly as
she sat in silence in the taxi taking them back to the shop.

The moment they'd arrived at the club, Margot had
flung herself into the heart of the writhing mass on the
dance floor, and stayed there. Swaying sensuously to the
throb of the loud music—sometimes alone, sometimes with
friends who'd come over to dance alongside her—she was
the object of many an eye, but her eyes continually sought
Robert.

And his were on her all of the time.

From his seat next to Caroline at one of the tables to the
side of the dance floor, he'd followed Margot's every movement, downing one glass of wine after another, virtually
ignoring those of Caroline's friends who'd wandered over to
meet him, but who drifted away when they couldn't engage
him in conversation.

'How on earth did Patsy and Arthur produce such a hot piece?' he'd muttered to himself at one point.

Caroline glared at him. 'Don't you think you should slow down with the drink?' she suggested acidly.

'No, I don't,' he snapped. 'I was a good boy last night and I've been a good boy all morning and afternoon. I'm bloody well going to do what I want now. And what I want to do is dance with my fiancée.' His mood changing abruptly, he stood up, smiled down at her and held out his hand. 'So dance with me, fiancée.'

The last thing she wanted to do was dance with him in the state he was in, but she wasn't sure how he'd react if she said no, so she stood up and let him take her hand and lead her over to the dance floor. As he turned to face her, he started to sway with the music, his hips rotating suggestively. She smiled up at him in what she hoped what a seductive way and did her best to move in time with the music.

Out of the corner of her eye, she saw Margot dancing towards them, never missing a single beat of the music. Closer and closer Margot came, until she was shoulder to shoulder with Caroline and face to face with Robert. Catching Robert's rhythm, she pursed her deep red lips, thrust her hips forward and gyrated provocatively, her eyes on his face, his eyes on hers.

Caroline could have burst into tears. Robert was being bloody-minded and Margot was being a cow. And there was nothing she could do about it.

She did her best to keep pace with them both, but furious with herself at having forgotten what a good dancer Margot had always been, and at having unwittingly given her a chance to show off, she kept on losing the beat. How she wished she'd suggested anything other than a club!

And it got worse.

Margot started singing along with the numbers that were beating out loudly, waving her arms above her head in a way that emphasised the line of her body, her bra-less nipples standing out beneath the stretchy material of her top, and her black lace thong clearly visible above the top of her tight hipster jeans.

Helpless, Caroline watched them in misery, longing for the evening to end.

FORTUNATELY, they were able to set off for London early on the Sunday afternoon.

The day before, while Robert had been formally asking Arthur Redway for Caroline's hand in marriage, Caroline had been impressing upon her mother how urgent it was to leave before the build-up of the Sunday traffic going south. The earlier they were on the road, the better, she'd stressed. To her relief, her mother had risen to the occasion and had managed to serve the Sunday lunch at noon, instead of at the usual one o'clock, and Caroline and Robert set off soon after amid a flurry of hugs and tears.

Margot had been subdued at lunch.

Hung over, Caroline thought to herself, and hoped she would have a stinking headache for the rest of the week. Her sister had trailed out to the car with her parents to wave them off, but hadn't attempted to cling on to Robert, or thrust her tongue into his mouth, as Caroline had feared she might.

Sitting beside Robert in the car as he pounded down the M6, Caroline stared tight-lipped at the road ahead, unshed tears of humiliation, misery and anger brimming her eyes.

'Are you going to keep this up for the whole journey,

Caro?' he asked her as they drove past one of the many exits for Birmingham.

'I've no idea what you're talking about,' she replied. Giving a little sniff, she turned away from him and stared pointedly out of the window.

'Of course, you haven't,' he muttered, his eyes on the road. 'But let's just pretend for a minute that you have. You're making too much of a bit of fun. That's all it was—a moment of fun.'

'What's so funny about you flirting with my sister?' she stormed, turning back to him, her eyes green shards of ice. 'And what's so funny about my sister publicly throwing herself at you, practically begging you to screw her in the middle of the dance floor? What must my friends have thought? I've never felt so embarrassed.'

She turned back to face the road, her cheeks flushed.

'Come on, Caroline. It wasn't as bad as that, and you know it. I admit that Margot somewhat came on to me and I rather played up to her, and shouldn't have done. But it was no more than light-hearted fun. You must admit, your parents are quite heavy-going. All that domestic stuff is stultifying, and I guess I jumped at the chance your sister gave me to have a bit of fun. But I love *you*, Caroline, and only you. Now and forever.'

Her lower lip trembled. 'Well, it didn't look like that last night.'

'I promise I'll never be a bad boy again, or do anything to cause you to be unhappy. I can't promise never to make you angry again, though,' he added, a note of amusement creeping into his voice.

Frowning, she looked at him questioningly.

'No, I can't,' he continued. 'You've no idea how sexy you are when your eyes are flashing in fury. I'd like to see that again, but only when I'm in a position to take immediate advantage of the situation.'

'Oh, you're impossible,' she said. Her shoulders relaxing, she sank back into her seat, and neither spoke again until they reached London.

'If you ever do anything like that again, Robert, we're through,' Caroline said as they drove across the Marylebone flyover. 'I'll never again put up with being humiliated in such a way.'

'You'll never have to, I promise,' he said emphatically, and he turned left into Lisson Grove, pulled up alongside the curb and put the car in neutral. He turned to her. 'I'm genuinely sorry that I behaved like a shit and hurt you, Caro,' he said. 'I don't know what came over me. You're the most important thing in my life, and I can't believe I behaved like that.'

'Am I really, Robert?'

'Yes, you are, and I'll be proving that to you over and over again throughout the coming years. I love you, Caroline, and July next year can't come soon enough. I intend to be the very best of husbands.'

He leaned across and kissed her on the mouth.

Then he slid back into his seat, glanced in the wing mirror and swung the car into the road again.

week later

CAROLINE PULLED two slices of burnt bread from the toaster and threw them angrily into the dustbin beneath the sink.

'I do wish people would leave the toaster settings where they're meant to be,' she snapped, staring pointedly at Terri Lee, who was stirring porridge oats into boiling milk. 'Surely it isn't too much to ask.'

Terri Lee glared at her. 'Don't look at me—I didn't alter the settings. What's got into you, anyway? You've wasted two bits of bread. So what? Toast two more. It's Saturday so you don't have to get off to school.'

'Oh, do shut up.'

'From the foul mood you're in this morning, I take it the weekend in Cheshire wasn't much fun, and last week wasn't much better.'

'Cheshire was fine, thank you. Anyone would be fed up

if they were faced with a huge pile of marking that was going to take the whole weekend.'

'There've been other weekends when you've had marking to do—quite a lot of them, in fact. But you've never been as stroppy as you've been all week.'

'Make your breakfast,' Caroline said, walking out of the kitchen. 'I'll leave it till you've finished.' She threw herself into one of the armchairs, picked up a magazine from the coffee table and opened it.

Louise looked up from the newspaper. 'I couldn't help overhearing, Caroline. Terri Lee's right—you've not been yourself all week. If it's to do with last weekend, it might help you to talk about it.'

'We had a lovely time,' Caroline said tersely, flicking through the magazine. 'They thought Robert was perfect. And he is.'

Terri Lee came into the sitting room with her porridge, and sat down at the table.

'I'll sit in Emily's favourite seat as she's not here,' she said, starting to eat. 'I hope she won't go mad if she comes down and finds me in her chair. I'd rather not be at the receiving end of someone else's bad mood again, thank you very much.'

'She's in the bathroom,' Louise said, 'so you're okay. She and John are going somewhere today.'

Caroline threw the magazine down, got up and left the room. A moment later, they heard her bedroom door slam shut.

Louise and Terri Lee glanced at each other. Louise looked quickly back down at the newspaper.

'I'd love to have been a fly on the wall of her parents' shop last weekend,' Terri Lee remarked cheerfully. 'I had a really good weekend, but I've a sneaking suspicion that if I'd been that fly, I'd have had an even better time.'

CAROLINE SAT on her bed and stared miserably around the room. If only she could turn the clock back to earlier that morning, to the moment before she'd snapped at Terri Lee for something that wasn't her fault at all! She'd known as she spoke that she was being unreasonable, but she hadn't been able to stop herself. She'd apologise as soon as she saw her again.

She glanced around the room.

Normally, its calm and order would relax her, but not this morning, and her eyes moved restlessly from the aubergine satin throw on her bed and the aubergine cushions carefully positioned in front of the crisp pale green pillows, to her light oak table. Two silver-framed photographs stood on the table, one of her with Robert, her arm tucked into his, and one of her with her parents and sister, which had been taken the day before she went to university. Her parents' faces showed the pride they felt at the first in their family going to university.

Above the table, there was a wooden shelf that she'd painted pale green to match the walls. At one end of the shelf were the books she used for her teaching, and at the other end the books she read for pleasure, or would do if she had the time. Her favourite books were her cookery books, and they were stacked neatly on the shelf beneath the drawer of her bedside table.

Her gaze went back to the photo of her with Robert. She'd been so happy before they went to Cheshire. How she'd love to be able to go back to the days before she'd taken Robert home. She'd do everything so differently. She wouldn't have worn a twinset with pearls, for example.

But she couldn't. She stared down at the cookery books, and her eyes filled with tears.

The phone ring downstairs and she glanced towards her door. A moment later, she heard Louise call up to her that it was Robert.

Swallowing hard, she rushed down to the front hall, and took the receiver from Louise, who went back into the sitting-room, closing the door behind her.

'Hello, Robert,' she said, clutching the receiver tightly.

'I'm so sorry, Caroline. I don't know what came over me. I've been desperately unhappy all week. That just wasn't me. I behaved appallingly.'

'Yes, you did,' she said, a catch in her voice.

'Please forgive me. I love you so much.'

'And I love you, too, Robert. That's why it hurt so much.' And she started to cry.

'I'm coming round,' he said quickly. 'I'm going to take you to breakfast, and I you must tell me what I can do to prove how sincerely sorry I am.' He paused. 'Would that be all right?'

'I suppose so.' Hearing the nervous hesitancy in his voice, the anguish that had been her companion all week, began to dissolve.

EMILY SHUT HER EYES, leaned back, looked up at the sky and let the wind brush her face and her hair fly freely. After a while, she leaned forward, took a paisley-print headscarf from the depths of her bag, and tied it around her head, knotting it at the nape of her neck.

'Is the wind too much for you?' John called across to her.

'I'll put the top up if it is.'

'No, it's lovely, provided you don't mind what I look like when we get to wherever we're going,' she said. 'The effect of the wind is marvellous—I feel so free. It was a brilliant idea to come out for a drive.' She paused. 'Is this what you do on the Saturdays when I don't see you—clear your mind by just taking off? I've often wondered.'

He smiled at her, and then turned back to the road.

It had been a good week, Emily thought, closing her eyes again and angling her face towards the sun. They'd almost been back to their old selves. Almost. She wasn't sure whether or not it was her imagination, but she'd wondered once or twice if there wasn't still a trace of reserve in John's behaviour towards her, and a vestige of disappointment, if disappointment was the right word, in his expression whenever he looked at her.

She so hoped it *was* her imagination.

She was desperate for everything to be normal between them again, and there really shouldn't be any reason why it wasn't, not now that John understood why she felt as she did. But if anything potentially harmful *did* still linger between them, hopefully whatever he'd planned for that day would clear the air once and for all.

She felt the car change direction. Opening her eyes, she saw that they were no longer on the motorway, but were following the signs for Oxford.

'Are we going into Oxford?' she asked.

'Not right into the city—just off the ring road. With luck, we won't meet too much traffic. The road can be a nightmare.'

'You seem to know the area—d'you come here often?'

'Yes, quite a lot,' he said, and he fell silent.

'Where're we off to exactly?' she prompted. 'We're

almost there now, so there's no reason not to tell me.'

He kept his eyes firmly on the road. 'We're going to a pleasant village on the outskirts of Oxford. There's a good pub there, which looks out over the river—not the Thames, contrary to what a lot of people think, but the Cherwell. We're going to have lunch there.'

'That sounds nice.' She settled back in her seat, and wondered what it was that John wasn't telling her.

Not long afterwards, he took a slip road leading from the ring road, and minutes later, he was driving the car carefully down a narrow lane and into a large car park.

'You certainly know your Oxford well,' she commented, undoing her seat belt. 'But then I suppose you would, having been at university here.'

'That's so,' he said, bringing the car to a stop. 'Right, Emily, out you get. We'll go straight into the garden. We don't want to sit inside on a lovely day like this.'

'Yes, sir,' she said, and gave him a mock salute. 'You're very authoritarian today, John, which is not like you at all,' she added with a smile.

Without replying, he led the way past the pub and into the garden. Pausing just inside the entrance, he scanned the wooden tables and chairs.

'Are you looking for someone?' she asked, hovering next to him. 'If not, there's a table for two over there.'

'We'll take the larger table on the other side,' he said, and went across to a table for four. 'Yes, we *are* meeting someone, Emily.' He gave her a slight smile as he sat down. Taking the seat opposite him, she looked at him questioningly. 'Given everything we've been talking about recently,' he continued, 'I'm rather surprised you haven't worked it out. But obviously you haven't. Can I get you a drink while we wait?'

'Daddy!' a voice cried out.

John spun round in his chair, and Emily was aware of rapid movement and a rush of air. And of John's face as he jumped to his feet and held out his arms for a small girl to run into them.

'Daddy!' the little girl cried again, and John hugged her tightly, lifting her off the ground. 'I've been waiting for you all morning. I've got a new dress on.'

'And very pretty it is, too,' he told her, gently lowering her to her feet. He glanced above the little girl's head to the woman coming up behind her. 'I thought for a moment you might not turn up, Angela.'

'I promised I'd bring her, didn't I? I wouldn't go back on my word,' the woman replied.

In a daze, Emily tore her eyes from the little girl, and stared at the woman.

She was very pretty, she thought—not beautiful, but very pretty. There was a touch of petulance about her face that stopped her from being beautiful. Impeccably groomed, she was a little shorter than John, with sleek brown hair that fell to just above her shoulders in what was obviously an expert cut. The ice-blue linen trouser suit she was wearing skimmed her slender body, and was set off by the single strand of large pearls that hung around her neck, and the identical creamy pearl that fell from each ear.

The woman turned towards Emily, her cold blue eyes appraising her. Then she turned back to John.

In bewilderment, Emily looked from the woman to John, and then to the small child whose hand John was holding and whose eyes were the mirror image of John's.

'Becky, this is Emily,' John told the little girl. 'Emily is a friend of mine. Emily, I'd like you to meet my daughter, Becky.'

34

He'd been in his first term at Oxford University when he'd met Angela, John told Emily as they sat with a coffee on the near-deserted garden at the end of the meal, Becky having been collected by her mother and taken home, protesting loudly all the way out of the pub that she wanted to stay with her father.

He'd been swept off his feet by Angela.

Painfully shy as a teenager, he'd been more interested in books than girls, and having been at an all boys' school meant that he'd met very few women prior to going to college. Angela was about the first woman he'd ever really spoken to, apart from his mother.

They'd literally bumped into each other in a coffee bar in Oxford half way through his first year of reading Law. Some of his coffee had spilt on her white shirt. He'd been mortified, but she'd made light of it. Laughingly she'd told him that in order to atone, he had to take her out for a drink. He'd gone scarlet with embarrassment and had started to stutter. Somehow or other, she'd understood that he was agreeing to her suggestion, and she'd told him she'd see him outside the Turf on the following evening at seven.

That had been the start of their relationship.

She, too, was in her first year, but hers was a French degree.

Despite their different subjects, they found they had lots to talk about, with each sharing with the other the surprising things they were discovering about their subject, and with her showing great interest in the fine points of law in the cases he was studying.

It had been a pleasure to be with her, he said, and soon they were seeing each other every day, sometimes only for a few minutes, sometimes for a few hours and, before very long, sometimes for the whole night.

From the moment he'd met Angela, he'd gone about his life in Oxford as if in a trance, unable to believe that such a beautiful woman, who could've had the pick of any student there, had fallen in love with him.

But loving Angela, as indeed he now did, didn't cause him to neglect his studies. On the contrary, he was even more determined to do well. A woman like Angela deserved to be given the best of everything, and he was going to do whatever he could to make that happen. It meant that he had to study even harder than he'd been doing, but he didn't mind—he loved his subject, and he basked in the approval of Angela, who'd encouraged him all the way.

To the great misery of both, just as John was beginning his third year in Oxford, Angela had to embark upon a year in France, a compulsory element of her degree course. She'd been found a placement in a school in a small town, and was going to be their English assistant. At the end of her time in France, she'd return to Oxford for her final year.

With it being the final year of his Law degree, he

couldn't go with her. Missing her enormously, he threw himself into his work, and the minute the Michaelmas Term was over, he flew to France to join her, fully intending to stay for the whole of December and into January. But the visit to which he'd long been looking forward, wasn't a success and he'd come home after two weeks.

He'd known from the moment he'd met her again that there was something different about her.

It was as if she was playing a part and getting the words wrong on occasions. And at times, she seemed preoccupied and distant towards him, almost irritated with him. Also, whereas in the past, she'd always been keen to discuss his work, wanting to know the minutest details of the cases he was studying, it was as if she could no longer be bothered to listen to him.

In the end, he'd plucked up the courage to challenge her outright, and ask what the matter was. She'd promptly burst into tears and told him that while she still loved him dearly as a friend, and always would, she'd fallen madly in love with a Frenchman, a viscount who lived just outside the small town in which she was teaching. He owned a lovely château with a vineyard, and he'd completely swept her off her feet.

She'd assured John that at first she'd resisted the advances of Gaston, which was his name, but that he'd persisted with flowers, declarations of love and little surprises that he'd sprung on her. In the end, lonely without John at her side and worn down by Gaston's pursuit, she'd given in and gone out with him. And she'd fallen in love with him.

She hadn't meant to, she told John, but it had happened. She and Gaston seemed to be made for each other and were planning a future together. He wanted them to marry as soon as her contracted year at the school was over, which would be in July, and then move into the château as its mistress.

Much as she would have preferred to return to England to complete her degree course first, she'd no intention of delaying her wedding by a year to do so.

With a huge château to run and a vineyard to supervise, Gaston would have been able to pay only the briefest of visits to England, and although she knew that he truly loved her, and she trusted him completely, her instinct told her that she'd be mad to leave such an eligible bachelor alone for so long a period.

And Gaston's mother, the dowager viscountess, who lived in a wing of the château, had hinted as much to her.

The dowager viscountess had confided in her that it was pure chance that Gaston had not already been caught by someone looking for a handsome husband who came with a title and an impressive house of historic significance. She explained that because he'd been so involved with his study of viticulture, there hadn't been time for matters of the heart, but now he was ripe for love and ready to commit to a suitable person.

Angela had wondered what she'd meant by a suitable person, but she hadn't wanted to ask.

She didn't much like his mother, she told John—she found her a rather cold woman. But she was very elegant, and was vocal in her admiration for Angela's stylishness, frequently expressing amazement at Angela's impeccable sense of dress. So many Englishwomen, the dowager viscountess had said in disdain on several occasions, appeared in clothes that not even a French maid would wear.

John wasn't at all surprised to hear that Angela's fashion

consciousness had caught the eye of Gaston's mother. She was always beautifully turned out. Back in their early days together in Oxford, she'd told him how she spent every spare penny on clothes, and preferred to have a few expensive outfits rather than a number of inexpensive ones.

Her parents didn't have much money, she'd confided to John, but what they *did* have, they spent on her their much-adored only child. With a natural flair for knowing exactly what suited her, and just how to wear her clothes, Angela made her limited funds go far.

Gaston's mother had obviously been curious about Angela's background and her ability to afford such clothes, and Angela had giggled a little when telling John that she'd got somewhat carried away in her description of her home and her background.

The dowager viscountess wouldn't have been particularly impressed to have learned that Angela's parents lived in a small two-bedroomed Cotswold-stone house that had been left them by Angela's grandparents, and it was none of her business, anyway. So Angela had merely said that the family home was in the countryside outside Oxford, with the odd hint or two that it was quite grand. She'd added for good measure that she was an only child, and that her parents hadn't wanted her to work, but that she'd disliked the idea of a life of idleness.

That had seemed to satisfy Gaston's mother, who'd murmured that it was most fortunate that Angela was so very stylish and spoke such excellent French as she would be able to involve herself in the renovation of the château, which would begin soon after the wedding.

Two weeks after he'd arrived in France, John had returned to England, a confused mixture of devastation and relief.

He was devastated to have lost the woman he loved and who'd loved him, and he couldn't believe that he'd ever again love anyone in the way he loved Angela. But in a strange way, he was also relieved. A part of him had never truly believed that such a sophisticated woman could love such an ordinary man as he, and he'd always felt that one day she'd wake up and see how unworthy of her he was. He could now stop waiting for that day.

At first, settling back into Oxford life, knowing he'd lost Angela, had been quite difficult, he told Emily, but gradually he rediscovered his enthusiasm for study, and after sitting his final exams, he decided to stay on for a fourth year to study for a Master's in the field of Property Law, his great love.

He began his research during the summer recess, and by the time that the new term began, he was once again happy and relaxed, and totally absorbed in his work. And then, a week after the new term had started, Angela turned up at his room in Oxford.

He'd been completely taken aback to see her standing there when he'd opened the door, and not particularly pleased. But she'd thrown herself at him, begging his forgiveness, and he'd taken her into his room—there was nothing else he could've done—and sat her down and made her some tea.

Over the tea, she'd wept pitifully that she was desperately unhappy and that she'd been so terribly stupid. 'Stupid! Stupid!' she kept saying. He assured her that whatever she was, she wasn't stupid, and he'd asked her to explain.

In between tears and self-reproaches, he'd gathered that Gaston and his mother had been labouring under the illusion that Angela's family had serious money. Not a gigantic fortune, but more than sufficient to help with many of the much-needed repairs to the château.

It had all been her fault, Angela sobbed. She should never have embroidered the truth as much as she had. She'd known that she was giving them the wrong impression, but had thought that it didn't matter: Gaston loved her and she loved him, and there could be no better basis for a marriage than that.

But there could be, the dowager viscountess had haughtily declared when she came to Angela's apartment to tell her that her engagement to Gaston was over. It was the duty of a French nobleman, with a large estate and people who depended upon him, to ensure that the heritage entrusted to him was maintained and passed on to his heir, ideally in an enhanced condition.

Building upon one's heritage was possible only if there was a fresh injection of funds at regular intervals in the life of a great family. Angela's marriage to Gaston was to have provided that much-needed injection of funds.

Angela begged to see Gaston, to hear him tell her for himself that he no longer wished to marry her, but his mother declared that impossible—Gaston had already left for a wine growers' meeting in Paris. Thereafter, he had business in Paris to attend to, and he wouldn't be back for a month or so. By that time, Angela's contract with the school would have reached its conclusion, and she would have been required to leave her apartment.

How had Gaston and his mother discovered the truth, John had asked.

Once more it had been her fault, she told him, and she started to cry again.

During her year in France, she'd made several friends in the area, mainly other English girls who were also on their compulsory year out of university, and they used to go out as a group at times. On one such occasion, they'd bumped into several Frenchmen they knew.

Bored, she'd amused herself by flirting with one of the men, although she was well aware that one of the other girls, Trixie, had been trying for some time to get the man to ask her out. It was a harmless flirtation, a bit of fun, nothing serious—she loved Gaston, and she'd no interest at all in the Frenchman. But at the end of the evening, when the men had left, Trixie had rounded on her in a jealous fury, and had called her a cow and worse.

Angela had apologised at once. Trixie had forgiven her, and it had all blown over and been forgotten.

Or so she'd thought.

Not long after that, a couple of months or so before their year in France was up, the girls were having a drink together outside a café-bar not far from the château, and they began taking it in turns to tell each other what they were going to do at the end of their year in France. The spotlight finally fell upon Angela.

They knew she'd be marrying Gaston in the autumn and they clamoured to hear the wedding details. She was pleasantly tipsy, and the late afternoon sun was really hot, so feeling relaxed and secure, she started describing the grand plans she had for the wedding reception, which was to be held in the château.

'Your parents must be loaded to be able to pay for all that,' they'd said enviously, as she described the decorations she envisaged and the food and the musicians.

'Not exactly!' she laughed. 'We'll be breaking with tradition—the groom's family will be paying for it, although they don't know it yet. That's where the money is—with Gaston's family, not mine.' And she told them that her parents had nothing.

She saw the surprise on their faces.

The way she dressed and spoke shouted out that she came from a moneyed background, they'd said, stunned. With a sly smile, she reminded them that looks could deceive, and she'd told them a bit about her background. For a moment there was complete silence, and then they'd all burst out laughing and had enthusiastically toasted her for her success in creating such an illusion.

On her way back to her apartment, she'd wondered whether she should have been quite so open to the girls about her parents' lack of money. Probably not, she decided, but they'd soon be going back to England, so it didn't really matter.

But it *did* matter. And looks *were* deceptive, just as she'd reminded her friends.

Whatever Trixie said, she hadn't forgiven Angela for flirting with the man she fancied, and she'd hot-footed to the *épicerie* a few streets from the château to tell the town gossip who owned the grocer's shop that Gaston would be marrying into poverty. Wouldn't it be a hoot when his family found out, Trixie had trilled.

John could work out the rest, Angela had said, her voice little more than a whisper.

She'd returned to England, moved into a student flat in the centre of Oxford and started on the final year of her degree. There'd been only one thing left for her to do, she told John through her tears, and that was to tell him how desperately sorry she was for allowing herself to be swept off her feet by Gaston. She'd been carried away by the magic of France, and had made the biggest mistake of her life when she'd turned her back on John, the only man she'd ever truly loved.

He'd accepted Angela's apology, assured her that he didn't bear any grudge, and had then assumed that they'd return to their very different lives and, being in different faculties, wouldn't meet up again.

But Angela had kept on popping round to his room to see him, and had started turning up in the coffee shop he liked to frequent for his morning coffee.

One day he'd bluntly asked her if she was pursuing him. She admitted she was, saying that she really missed being with him, and she'd begged him to give her another chance. She swore that in spite of the way it looked, she'd never loved anyone but him.

Eventually, they'd started going out together again, but it wasn't the same as before. He was no longer a naïve undergraduate, and given the history between them, he understood her well enough to know what was in her mind. Although a bright woman, she wasn't a natural academic and her main purpose in coming to Oxford had been to find herself a husband who could provide her with a life of comfort. A Chancery lawyer was a pretty safe bet for someone wanting financial security.

But he was still fond of her for old times' sake, despite what had happened in France and despite what he'd learned about her character, and he'd been willing to let the relationship drift on, knowing that he didn't love her any more, and knowing that one day either he would end their relationship or she'd meet someone more suitable for her, who'd be equally able to give her the life she wanted.

They'd even occasionally slept together, always initiated by Angela, and, as usual, she'd taken care of the matter of birth control.

They went on in that way for several weeks until John forced himself to face the fact that increasingly he was resenting having to stop working in order to spend time with Angela. His thesis was absorbing, and having to break off in the middle of studying an interesting judgment had become an intolerable interruption.

He decided that when they got together on the following Saturday morning, he would tell her that there was no future for them, and that he wanted to end their relationship.

When the day came, they met as arranged in front of the Carfax Tower in the heart of Oxford, and started to stroll down St. Aldates. After a nervous few minutes, he plucked up the courage to broach the subject, but as he opened his mouth, Angela had spoken first.

She'd turned to him, her eyes huge in her pale face. 'I'm pregnant,' she'd told him.

'So you married her, I take it,' Emily said in a flat voice.

'No, I didn't.'

'You didn't!' she exclaimed. 'You mean, you let her get on with it on her own?'

'No, I didn't do that either. I was obviously stunned and wanted to know how it could have happened since she was on the pill. She claimed to have had food poisoning a few weeks earlier and said that she must have vomited the pill. I don't know if I believed her or not, but whether I did or didn't was immaterial. She was pregnant with my child.'

'Did she want to marry you?'

'Yes, but I made it clear that I'd no intention of marrying her. I told her that I'd support the child financially and in every other way, and that Angela could always count upon me as a friend, but not as a husband.'

'What did she say to that?'

'Not a lot. She didn't like it, but what could she do? Unlike you, Emily, I had an extremely happy childhood, with parents who very much loved each other, and I wanted to replicate that for myself. Angela didn't love me. I don't think she ever did. And I think that what I originally felt for her was infatuation rather than love. I never for one minute felt about Angela as I feel about you. Her pregnancy would have been no basis for a marriage. I wanted better for myself than that, and I still do.'

Emily stared back at him, ashen-faced.

'What did Angela do?' she asked.

'She married a city broker three months after Becky was born. That was eight years ago. They have a lovely house not far from here, and things seem to have worked out well for them. Becky's a happy child, which rather suggests they have.'

He watched Emily's face, and waited.

'Do you see Becky a lot?' she asked at last.

'Whenever I can.' He leaned forward across the table, his eyes lighting up. 'I wish I could describe for you what it felt like the first time I held her, the feeling of intense love that came over me, but I can't. There are no words.' Shaking his head in wonder, he took off his glasses and wiped them. 'I shall always love Becky,' he said, a tremor in his voice. 'She'll be a part of my life forever, and I want to see her as often as Angela will allow, and as often as Becky wants to see me. Now that she's getting older, I'm hoping Angela will soon start letting her stay with me.'

Emily made a slight movement, but didn't speak.

He put his glasses back on, and looked at her, his eyes full of hope. 'And when that happens, I should like to have a wife, who'll have made a home in which Becky feels comfortable, and who'll share with me the pleasure I get out of her.'

'Then shouldn't you marry Caroline?' she blurted out.

The hope faded from his eyes.

'I had rather wanted that wife to be you, Emily,' he said quietly.

35

Emily woke early the following morning.

Lying motionless in her bed, she stared across her room to the window. Her curtains were taking on a soothing creamy translucency in the early morning light, but at the top of the curtains, a harsh bright glare was forcing its way through the irregular gaps between the wide tabs, bringing the new day into her room before she was ready for it.

If she would ever be ready for it.

She, who'd always felt so sure of herself, so certain of what she wanted, suddenly felt so bleak, so disorientated and so distraught. But was she distraught because she regretted her decision of the day before and now wished she'd answered differently, or because she'd lost John?

She didn't know.

She mentally pulled herself up. Decision was the wrong word. She hadn't decided anything—she'd reacted instinctively. She'd known for years what she wanted and what she didn't want. It was very simple. She wanted a legal career, which she had; she didn't want children, which she didn't have and was determined never to have.

Before she'd met John, if anyone had asked her if she'd wanted a husband, she would have said quite possibly, but not necessarily.

She would have seen herself as having sexual relationships, and she might even have tried what it was like to live with someone for a period of time, and to have to consider them as well as yourself in every decision you made. But she was confident that she'd always be able to do very well on her own, and she'd no intention of surrendering her valued freedom to anyone unless she was certain that to do so would enhance her life.

A man with a child was a man with baggage, and that sort of baggage would not enhance her life.

But John wasn't any man. John was John, and she loved him.

They shared the same interests and the same love of silence. And each seemed to know intuitively what the other was thinking. He was a loving, gentle, very intelligent man, and she'd begun to take it for granted that they'd marry one day. Or they might simply move in together. After all, neither was religious and they didn't need a certificate to prove their love.

John was everything in a man she wanted. But with one unwelcome extra.

She remembered the hurt on his face when she'd made the comment about Caroline, and the growing despair in his eyes as he'd come to accept that although she loved him, she'd meant it when she said that she wouldn't allow any child in her life, not even his, and she couldn't be swayed from that.

'You've defined the nature of your love very clearly,' he'd

said, staring at her face as if he didn't know her. 'Becky's my flesh and blood. She's part of my life. You can't expect me to turn my back on her, to pretend she doesn't exist.'

'Only you can decide what's most important to you,' she'd told him. 'You know my views about children and why I think as I do. Becky has a mother and a step-father. You've said she's a happy child, so she doesn't need rescuing from anything. Obviously you could see her as often as you wanted, just like you've been doing. It's just that I wouldn't want to join in all of that, or have her staying in my home.'

'I see,' he'd said quietly.

She'd leaned across the table, her voice softening. 'That doesn't mean I don't love you, John; you know I do. Don't let's fall out over this—I couldn't bear it.'

'I'm afraid you're going to have to bear it, Emily. Your love is a flawed love. It's selfish and conditional. I accept that it's the best you're able to offer anyone, but such a best isn't good enough for me.'

'But you know about my parents,' she'd said, her voice rising in urgency. 'And about the awful children in Weymouth. Their legacy to me is a hatred of children. I can't help it.'

'But that's not entirely so. I see in you a woman who never felt truly loved as a child, whose upbringing never taught her how to love in a generous, unselfish way, and who isn't prepared to try to learn. The last of those three is your fault.'

'I love you wholeheartedly, John.' Her voice had shaken. 'Really, I do.'

'No, you don't. You love me within the constraints of your inherited character. Your parents will have loved you in their way, but they were unable to cast aside their blinkered beliefs and think about what was best for you. In your character, you are, indeed, their daughter. You are as certain of the rightness of the strictures you've placed on your life, as your parents were certain of the rightness of living according to a narrow religious doctrine. You're deaf to any voice other than your own, just as your parents were.'

'That's not true,' she said tersely. 'I'm nothing like them.'

'You say you love me,' he continued, 'but you aren't prepared to modify your stance in the light of events that happened well before I met you and which cannot be ignored. That's not love. You're not prepared to unbend and act in my best interest any more than your parents were prepared to unbend and act in yours. That shows the limit of your sort of love. That's your true legacy from Weymouth, Emily.' He had stood up and looked down at her. 'I'm sorry for you,' he said. 'I'm sorry for the life we could have had together. I'm sorry for the person you could have been, but won't let yourself be. I could've loved that person very deeply.'

'John, please—'

He'd shaken his head to stop her, taken some notes from his wallet and put them on the table in front of her. 'The bartender will call you a cab to take you back to London. That will more than cover it. I'll see you in Chambers, but this is effectively goodbye. I wish you happiness in the rest of your life. I hope the choices you've made will bring you satisfaction.'

He'd turned and walked across the patio.

She'd opened her mouth to call after him to come back. But to say what? She'd closed her mouth and had sat there, numb.

.   .   .

SHE ROLLED on to her back and stared at the shadowy ceiling.

Sounds of movement from down below were breaking the silence of the house. She heard the other girls go downstairs, one by one, and then she heard the three of them wandering between the sitting-room and kitchen, preparing their breakfast, and talking and laughing as they did so.

But being in her room was infinitely preferable to going downstairs and listening to Caroline going on about Robert, Louise going on about Ethan and Terri Lee generally wittering.

She turned on to her side.

Perhaps she was being a little unfair to Terri Lee, she thought. She was no longer quite the pain she used to be. With that smug bastard Hugh well and truly out of the picture, she'd considerably quietened down. In fact, it suddenly struck her, Terri Lee had recently been abnormally quiet.

She'd been so preoccupied with what had been happening between her and John that she hadn't really paid attention to what was going on around her. While she knew that Terri Lee and Hugh had split up, she hadn't given the situation more than a passing thought. But Terri Lee must have been as devastated at losing Hugh as she was at losing John, and it had been really bad of her not to have made any attempt to help Terri Lee through her distress.

That sort of omission could've been what John had meant when he'd described her as selfish and self-centred, and unable to change her ways. Well, he was wrong, and to prove it, she was going to make more of an effort with the others in future, starting with Terri Lee.

A burst of laughter sounded in the sitting room. If she went downstairs, she would have to snap out of herself, which would be no bad thing. And as she was going to have to tell them at some point about what had happened with John, she might as well get it over with there and then.

Another gale of laughter reached her.

She threw back her duvet, jumped out of bed, pulled on her dressing-gown and headed for the bathroom.

'AND YOU REALLY DON'T THINK YOU could come to any arrangement that would keep you together?' Caroline asked in concern when Emily's voice trailed off at the end of her account of the day before. 'You and John seem so well-suited to each other.'

'I think we are, too. But it's not the sort of thing you can compromise about. Oh, God, I'm sorry!' she exclaimed as her eyes filled with tears. 'I hadn't meant to be so weak.'

'You're not being weak—you're being human,' Louise said, putting down her glass of water, and going across to Emily. She squeezed into the armchair next to her and put her arm around her. 'Anyone would be upset if they'd lost someone they loved. You'd be very strange if you didn't cry.'

Terri Lee got up from the sofa, went and got the box of tissues from the kitchen worktop, came back and put it in front of Emily. 'Here,' she said. 'I think you're gonna be needing these.'

'But surely you can come to an agreement with John. For example, have the child just once a month?' Caroline persisted, her forehead creasing as she struggled to balance her instinctive sympathy for Emily's obvious misery with her disapproval of Emily's stance. 'He can hardly ignore the fact that he's got a child. And it's to his credit that he doesn't want to.'

'Of course I don't expect him never to see her,' Emily

said, wiping her eyes. 'But the occasional weekend would just be the tip of the iceberg. There'd be more and more times that he'd want to have her over, such as in the holidays. We'd never be able to drop everything and take off if we felt like it—we'd always have to fit what we did around Becky. I'd be giving up my freedom and spontaneity for a child when I don't even like children. He can go and see her whenever he wants—I've no problem with that—but I don't want her in my home.'

Terri Lee sat back on the sofa and stared at Emily. 'I'm not that keen on kids myself, but I must say I think you're being dead unreasonable. I'm sorry but I do. You don't want him to let his daughter into his home, and presumably you also expect him to give up any idea of having any more kids.'

'That's right. And if John can't accept the way I am .... Well, he can't, and that's why we're no longer together. He mustn't love me enough.' Tears filled her eyes again.

'I'm afraid it rather looks as if *you* don't love him enough,' Caroline remarked, a trifle coldly.

'What on earth makes you dislike children so much that you'd lose John over one little girl, who'll spend most of her time somewhere else, anyway?' Louise asked, looking bewildered. 'Surely it's worth letting her stay on the odd occasion in order to remain with John. You love him. And who knows, you might even become quite fond of her.'

'I really don't see what the big deal about her staying is,' Emily said shortly, and she dried her eyes. 'She's got a home, and John can see her there or take her out.'

'That's right, of course,' Louise said. 'It's just that it sounds quite, well ... lacking in empathy, maybe ... not to appreciate that he might want her to stay in his home at times, and be a part of his family. He won't always want to be a guest in her home, or have to meet her outside somewhere.'

'Well, he can do what he wants now, can't he?' Emily said, getting up from the armchair. 'I didn't expect you to understand, but I thought you ought to know. And now I've got to get changed. I'm going to work in Chambers this morning. I'll pick up something to eat on the way.'

And she walked out.

THEY LISTENED as Emily stomped up the staircase.

'Wow!' Terri Lee exclaimed, as they heard her slam the bedroom door behind her. 'She must really hate kids.'

'She must at that,' Caroline agreed. 'It beats me how anyone could lose someone they love over a thing like that. Not if they really loved them.'

'She *does* love John,' Louise said. 'I'm sure of it. And he loves her. You only have to see them together to know that. No, this is clearly about the daughter. I'm wondering if deep down Emily's jealous of her and doesn't want her to get too close to John. I read somewhere that the father-daughter syndrome can make the mother feel really left out. If John's daughter visited them a lot, that could happen to Emily.'

'If Emily had any sense, she'd agree to have the girl for the weekend, and then always find an excuse to be out. She could say she had work to do, for example,' Terri Lee volunteered. 'It wouldn't be for long. Eventually, John's bound to stop wanting to have his daughter to stay. Kids aren't as cute when they get older. Just think of any teenagers you know. Would you want to have them around you out of choice?' She grimaced.

'Not everyone's like you, Terri Lee,' Louise said sharply. 'Emily isn't devious.'

Caroline shook her head. 'No, this comes from a deep dislike of children, and from her nature. It's not the first time we've had a glimpse of a stubborn, self-righteous streak in her, and this business has just brought it out even more. There's no compromising with her. She feels what she feels, and if the other person doesn't feel the same way, tough luck. When you mentioned empathy, Louise, you went to the heart of the problem. I think she's completely unable to empathise with John.'

Terri Lee stood up. 'Well, I guess we'll never know what makes her tick, and to be honest I don't much care. I've gotta get dressed now—I'm working today. See you all later,' she said, moving towards the door.

'But today's Sunday, Terri Lee!' Louise called after her. 'Surely you don't have to work on a Sunday? What's this new job you've got? Isn't it time you told us?'

Tapping the side of her nose, Terri Lee left the room.

36

The front door closed behind Terri Lee.

Louise picked up her newspaper and went and sat opposite Caroline. 'D'you know where Terri Lee's working?' she asked.

Caroline shrugged. 'Your guess is as good as mine. Whatever it is, she seems happier than she's done for a very long time. Since we've known her, in fact.' She sighed and stretched her legs out in front of her. 'I can't wait for the school year to end. What a year it's been—from the sublime, which was meeting Robert, to the ridiculous, which is me trying to control a class.'

'Are you going to stop working as soon as you're married? If so, you've only got one more year at the chalk face, plus the next few weeks.'

'I'd love to, and I know Robert can afford it. I don't like to suggest it, though. It sounds a bit lazy as we won't have any children. But fear not, I'm subtly working on him,' she added with a laugh. 'I've signed up for a weekly *cordon bleu* evening class that starts in September. I don't quite know how I'll fit it around my marking and preparation, but I will.

I'm hoping that the thought of a yummy meal every night will make him insist that I leave school as soon as we're married, and focus solely on his stomach.'

'Don't mention stomachs,' Louise said with a groan. 'Mine's all over the place at the moment.'

Caroline sat up in concern. 'You know, I thought you hadn't been looking your usual self for the last week or two. And you were a bit sharp with Terri Lee just now, which isn't like you. Have you seen a doctor?'

'There's no need to. I'm sure it's just a bug. But we'd better not start talking about food or I'll start feeling sick again. Have you managed to decide where to get married—Cheshire or London?'

Caroline beamed. 'Robert's agreed on Cheshire at last. There's a super hotel in the countryside near Nantwich and we're taking it over for two days. It's idyllic. It's got gorgeous gardens that'll be perfect for the photos. You three will obviously be my bridesmaids. In fact, we'll have to start thinking about our dresses soon.'

'But of course! It's almost May, and you're marrying in July next year. You're right, there's not a moment to lose.'

'You can laugh. We were only able to get the hotel as soon as that because there'd been a cancellation. Everyone seems to plan such a long way ahead, so I'll obviously have to do so, too, if I want the best of everything. I want my wedding to be a day to remember for as long as we live.'

'I'm sure it'll be wonderful,' Louise said, standing up. 'I must have a shower, and then I'm off to Nicky's for lunch. Ethan was going to come, too—he really likes Nicky and Jim, and he's great with Markie—but he's leaving today to go to the Cardiff branch. He'll be there for a week. He asked if I wanted to go with him, but I've got to hand in my dissertation soon, so I'm staying put. What are you up to today?'

'Going to Robert's to look at travel brochures. We want to go away for a couple of weeks in the summer—hopefully to somewhere that's not too hot, with the colour hair I've got. And we're going to talk about possible honeymoon destinations. It'll be fun.' She stared hard at Louise, and frowned. 'Are you sure you're all right, Lou? You really don't look it.'

'I must admit, I feel a bit queasy.'

'You couldn't be pregnant, could you?'

Louise laughed dismissively. 'Of course not. Like I said, it'll be a bug. Or I've just eaten something; that's all. Oh, my God!' Her hand to her mouth, she ran to the downstairs cloakroom, and reached it just in time to throw up.

LOUISE SANK on to the worn pink and green Sanderson-covered sofa.

'D'you need a hand?' she asked Nicola, who was carrying the ironing board into the sitting-room.

'I'm fine,' Nicola said, setting up the board. As she switched on the iron, she glanced across at Louise. 'You're as pale as a sheet. Lou. Why don't you go up and have a lie down? This won't take me long, not with Mark and Jim out. Thank heavens for some sunshine at last, and a nearby park and a football.'

'I don't need a rest, thanks all the same.'

'Then at least put your feet up. And you can start talking at the same time,' Nicola added, pulling a shirt towards her.

'What about?' Louise asked.

'About whatever's bothering you.'

Louise tried to laugh, but nothing came out. 'I don't know what you're talking about.'

Nicola stopped ironing the shirt and looked at her sister, her face serious. 'Don't tell me there's nothing wrong, Lou, when there obviously is. You don't look well, you didn't eat any lunch and you've been unusually quiet since you got here.'

'I don't feel brilliant. Mystery solved.'

'No, it's not,' Nicola said firmly. She stood the iron on its metal rest and went across to her sister. 'Tell me what the matter is,' she said, sitting down next to Louise. 'For a start, I can tell that you're unhappy. It might help you if you told me why.'

'You're wrong, Nicky; really you are.'

'Is this about Ethan?'

'No, not at all. Everything's fine between us. He's gone to Cardiff for work or he'd have come with me today.' She picked up one of the scatter cushions and hugged it to her stomach.

'Please tell me what's wrong,' Nicola begged, and she put her arm around Louise's shoulder. 'Please, Lou.'

Louise turned a wan face towards her sister, and then looked away. 'Oh, Nicky, I think there might be something wrong, and it's terrible,' she said, and she buried her face in the cushion.

Nicola hugged her sister. 'There's nothing so terrible that you can't tell me about it. Jim and I love you, and nothing can alter that. Are you ill?'

'Oh, no. It's nothing like that,' Louise said quickly.

'You being ill would be the worst thing possible, so it can't be that bad,' Nicola said, a lift in her voice. 'That's a good start, isn't it?'

'I suppose so.' She looked up at Nicola, her face stricken. 'It's just I keep throwing up, Nicky. I thought it was just an upset stomach, but something Caroline said this morning has made me think, and I realised my period was late. I'm never late.'

Nicola hugged her harder. 'People are often late because they're stressed or working too hard. Doing a dissertation at the same time as you're working in Ethan's office, could be working too hard. It might have thrown your system out.'

'I wish you were right, but I don't think you are. Looking back, I realise I can't stand the smell of coffee any longer. Me, not able to drink coffee! That's never happened before. I hate even to say the word, but I think I might be pregnant.'

Nicola frowned. 'But surely you took precautions?'

'Of course, we did—we used condoms. I was going to go on the pill, but never got round to it.'

'Condoms aren't a hundred percent reliable. The pill should've been a priority. But anyway, what's done is done,' Nicola said briskly. 'First of all, you can get home pregnancy test kits from the chemist's now, and you might want to get one. But if you do, whatever it says, you must also go to the doctor's as you don't know how reliable the tests are. And then we can take things from there.'

'I'm going into work tomorrow, so I'll make an appointment to see the doctor afterwards, but I'll pick up a test on the way to the office,' Louise said, lacing her fingers together and squeezing her hands tightly. 'I'd like to have an idea of what's what as soon as possible.'

'Would you like me to go to the doctor with you?'

Louise shook her head. 'I'll be fine. But thanks, anyway. I'd rather go on my own.'

'Fair enough. You know,' Nicola said, getting up and going back to the ironing board. 'While being pregnant at this time wouldn't be ideal, it wouldn't be that awful, either.'

'Yes, it would!' Louise exclaimed. 'It'd be the worst thing possible.'

'Why? You and Ethan love each other. He's financially

okay and he's the right age to become a dad. He'd probably be delighted by the idea—you've seen him with Mark.'

Louise sat up and gazed at Nicola in horror. She wiped her eyes with the back of her hands. 'If I *am* pregnant, there's no way I'm telling Ethan. It's the last thing I'd do.'

Nicola stopped ironing and stared at Louise in amazement. 'Why ever not? You must give him the chance to do the right thing.'

'To do the right thing! Would *you* want someone to marry you because it was the right thing to do? You wouldn't, and nor would I.'

'You would if you knew they loved you and genuinely wanted to marry you.'

'And how would you know that if they hadn't already proposed? Ethan's never so much as mentioned marriage. So if it turns out that I'm pregnant, I'm not going to tell him, and you mustn't, either.' Louise leaned forward, her eyes glittering. 'Promise me, Nicky.'

'Okay, I promise, then,' Nicola said. 'But I think you're wrong. He should be given the opportunity to stand by you. And also, he's got the right to know.'

'I told you what he said in America. He's never dated employees because of what happened with that woman years ago.'

'So?'

'So he'd feel trapped by me, just like he felt trapped by her. Only more so. He was able to get rid of the woman with a court case, but me being pregnant would be a life sentence for him. I can't do that to him.'

Nicola gestured helplessness. 'But he loves you, Louise. I've seen the two of you together. What happened in the past was a very different situation. He's well-established now, and not vulnerable.'

'Maybe he does love me now, but being trapped into being a father, whether or not we were married, could make him come to hate me. I don't want to risk that happening.' She gave a loud gulp.

'From what I've seen of Ethan, he wouldn't let himself be trapped. If he didn't want to marry you, he wouldn't, but he'd support you. Give him the chance.'

'The chance to regret ever meeting me. Never! You're reading Ethan wrongly, Nicky—I think he'd feel morally bound to marry me. And I can't think of anything worse than someone marrying me because I was carrying their child. I want them to marry me because they really want to. If *I* won't settle for less, why should I put Ethan in the same position as I'd be in?'

'You'd marry him even if you weren't pregnant, and you know it. And he's the same. I could understand it better if you'd only met him a month or so ago, but you've been together considerably longer than that.'

'One month, six months—what's the difference? If I find out I'm pregnant, and I tell Ethan and he proposes, I'll never know if he'd have proposed to me if there hadn't been a baby. I don't want to live with that.'

Nicola visibly hesitated. 'If you won't tell Ethan, and yet you still want to stay with him, which I'm guessing you do, surely, if you go ahead and have a baby, there's a weeny chance that he might notice. Or are you thinking of trying to get an abortion? You'd still be within the time limit.'

Louise shook her head with vigour. 'Never!'

'That's a relief. Well, you must do what you think is right, but I hope you change your mind about telling Ethan,' Nicola said. 'We'll have to stop now—I can hear Jim and Mark. Ring me after you've seen the doctor, won't you?'

The door swung open.

'I'm hungry,' Mark said, marching into the room in a red and white Arsenal shirt, the white sleeves of which were stained with grass. 'When's tea?' he asked.

'Who got the most goals, Mark, you or Daddy?' Louise asked brightly. 'Come and tell me about the game.'

Taking a biscuit from the jar that Nicola held out to him, Mark went across to Louise, who wrapped her arms around him.

'Daddy got an own goal,' he told her.

37

An ashen face stared back at Louise from the mirror in the ladies' room.

Outside, she could hear the chatter of the office girls as they caught up with what they'd all done over the weekend. And then she heard footsteps coming towards the ladies' room. But she wasn't yet ready to talk to anyone yet, and she hastened back into the nearest cubicle. Before she did anything else, she needed to get her feelings under control.

Despair swept through her, followed by panic. What on earth was she going to do? The doctor that evening would only confirm what she now knew for certain. She ran her hand across her stomach. It was as flat as ever, with no hint of the baby within. But there was a child there nevertheless, curled up, its heart beating, waiting to come into the world.

But what sort of world could she give it on her own? Not much of one, that was for sure. Her hand tightened protectively on her stomach. Maybe she *should* tell Ethan.

She started to imagine what she would say to him, and stopped short.

Her mind jumped back to their last night in Sausalito, when they'd sat staring at San Francisco across the bay and he'd told her about what happened in his past. She remembered the haunted expression in his eyes as he'd re-lived the experience, and she knew she couldn't bear to be the person who trapped him for a second time.

No, she would have to settle for having a part of Ethan with her for the rest of her life—his baby—but not the man himself. And that meant she must leave the job she loved, and the house she was sharing, and do both before Ethan found out.

She felt a wave of anguish. She didn't even want a child. One day, yes, when the time was right, but it wasn't right now. Oh, why hadn't she gone on the pill weeks ago as she'd intended!

But there *was* a way out, as Nicola had indicated the day before.

When she'd told her she'd never do that, she'd still had a hope deep down that this was no more than a bug. But things were different now that she knew for certain that it wasn't. It was still early days and there was a chance, albeit a slim one, that the doctor would be sympathetic and help her to get an abortion. If he was, Ethan need never know, and things between them would be able to take their natural course.

If she could bear to go through with it.

Nicola would be horrified, and disappointed in her, but it wasn't Nicola's baby—it was *her* baby.

But it wasn't just *her* baby—it was Ethan's, too. Could she really end the life of Ethan's child, his flesh and blood? Could she seriously end the life of any child? She felt ice-cold inside.

And she knew that the answer was no.

She didn't even know why she'd bothered to ask herself the question. Like it or not, she was stuck with her pregnancy. She pushed open the cubicle door and stepped outside.

'Good gracious me, what *is* the matter, Louise?'

Ethan's private secretary, Barbara Cooper, was standing next to one of the washbasins.

'You look awful, my dear, if you don't mind me saying so. You're as white as a sheet. Is it a headache?' Barbara asked, her face full of concern. Louise shook her head. 'Then, whatever's the matter, dear? Let me help you if I can.'

At the kindness in the secretary's voice, Louise let out a dry sob. Barbara put her hands on Louise's shoulders.

'Nothing can be as bad as all that,' she said gently.

'Yes, it can.'

'I take it you're having a baby. That's it, isn't it?' Barbara asked.

Louise nodded.

'What about the father?'

'He doesn't know.' Louise's eyes watered. 'This wasn't planned.'

'Well, I expect he'll be thrilled. Now don't you start crying. A baby's something to be happy about, even if it doesn't feel like it right now.'

'You won't tell anyone,' Louise said, looking at her in sudden alarm.

'No, of course not, although they'll all have to know at some point. You can't keep a thing like that hidden for ever, can you?' Barbara laughed encouragingly.

'I guess not,' she said, her face white.

'Why don't you go home now, my dear?' Barbara said, patting her on the shoulder. 'You're not really in any state to work today, are you? Go home, wash your face, put on some war paint and talk to that boyfriend of yours. You'll find that things will look a whole lot better tomorrow.'

'I think I will. Thanks, Barbara. Will you tell Patrick I'm not well, please? I'm meant to be meeting him this afternoon to talk about the food for the promotion we're working on.'

'Of course, I will. Patrick will manage. You need to sort yourself out. And don't worry too much, it'll all work out perfectly, I'm sure.' The secretary patted her again on the shoulder.

Giving Barbara a watery smile, Louise left the ladies' room and went back into the open office, her head down. A few minutes later, clutching her bag and jacket, she hurried out of the building. Barbara was right, she thought as she ran down the steps—a pregnancy couldn't be hidden for long. She'd have to decide very quickly what she was going to do.

Obviously, the first thing was see the doctor that evening. The next would be to write a formal letter resigning from Ethan Ford Electronics. In fact, she'd do that as soon as she got back from the doctor, she decided as she hurried along the road. It was a stroke of luck that Ethan was out of town that week as it meant she'd be able to take the letter into the office the following morning without any risk of running into him.

Once she'd done that, she'd decide on the next step.

AFTER A SLEEPLESS NIGHT, Louise was up early and was in the building the following morning even before Barbara had arrived.

She went straight to the desk she'd been using.

Pausing for a moment with her hands on the back of the

chair that she wouldn't be using again, a lump rose in her throat. Impatient with herself, she pushed it back by a frenzy of activity. When she'd emptied the contents of her desk drawers into the large canvas bag she'd brought with her, she stepped back, stared again at her desk, and then turned away. There was just one thing more to do before she left Ethan's company for ever.

Taking a deep breath, she walked across to his private office, pushed open the door and went into the large airy room. Her eyes fixed rigidly on his desk, she walked forward, took a slim brown envelope out of her bag and placed it in his personal in-tray.

'Good bye, Ethan,' she said quietly. Then she turned round, walked unsteadily out of the office, down the stairs and into the morning light.

As she reached the steps leading down to the underground station, she suddenly stopped. She hadn't specifically asked Barbara not to tell Ethan she was pregnant—she'd only asked her more generally not to tell anyone else. Perhaps she should ring her when she got back to the house, and mention that she'd rather Mr Ford didn't know, just to be on the safe side.

Or perhaps not.

She and Ethan had tried to keep their relationship to themselves, she thought, heading for the underground station. However, there was a slight chance that Barbara, who worked closely with Ethan and saw his diary daily, might have had a vague suspicion in the past that they were seeing each other. If she made too much of Barbara not telling Ethan, Barbara might put two and two together and come up with four. It was probably safer not to say anything to her, and just hope that Barbara included Ethan in the not telling anyone else.

In fact, the more she thought about it, the more she realised that it was highly unlikely that Barbara would mention her pregnancy to Ethan or to any of the girls in the office. It wasn't something you'd talk to your boss about, especially not someone like Ethan, who didn't like tittle-tattle. And Barbara wasn't into gossiping, either. She'd been cuttingly disapproving on one occasion when she'd come upon the women talking about one of the men in the office, and they'd all been careful what they said around her after that.

No, her secret was safe with Barbara. She must stop worrying about that, and concentrate on the future. Obviously the first thing to do was talk to the others when they got back from work that evening. They might have some ideas about what she could do, especially Caroline.

Some suggestions about how she was going to pay the rent for the following year would be a start.

Glancing ahead, she saw a woman with a small child in a pushchair coming along the platform in her direction, and a frisson of fear ran through her.

38

Thank God there are only three weeks left to the half-term, Caroline thought, walking out of school at the end of what felt like one of the worst Tuesdays of her life. The holiday couldn't come quickly enough. Apart from urgently needing relief from her daily torture by pupils, she desperately needed a break from seeing Tom.

It had been incredibly difficult working alongside him, especially at the start of her relationship with Robert. He'd looked so forlorn every time she'd seen him that she'd felt quite awful. He'd obviously really cared about her, which was flattering, she had to admit, but it also made her feel guilty, and she didn't like feeling that way at all. After all, she'd done nothing to feel guilty about.

She and Tom had only been together for a short time.

It was true they'd had a sexual relationship, but if they'd both been honest with themselves, they'd have seen that their relationship grew out of friendship rather than passion. And it was built upon need: one person's need for help in the early days of teaching—hers—and the other person's ability to give that help, which had been Tom. That wasn't the basis for a lifelong commitment, and she shouldn't be made to feel bad that she'd stopped seeing Tom.

Yet, she did feel bad whenever she saw him, and she felt angry with him, and also with herself, although she wasn't quite sure why.

She shook herself mentally. She was her own worst enemy, letting herself get bothered about a relationship that had ended months before. She'd far more important things to think about, such as wedding arrangements. With planning her lessons and marking them, teaching them, and writing reports all taking a huge chunk out of her life, it wasn't too soon to start working on the details of the big day. And that's what she would do, she resolved, striding purposefully towards the underground station. Dwelling on anything else was just a waste of time.

'We seem to be going the same way,' a voice from behind her said.

'Tom!' she exclaimed, springing round. 'You made me jump. I was just thinking about you.'

'You were?' he asked in surprise. Pleased surprise, she noted. And she could've sworn there was a trace of hope in his eyes. But if it *had* been there, it swiftly passed.

'I was thinking how grateful I am to you,' she said hastily, 'that I've managed to reach the summer half-term without murdering any of the pupils.'

They both laughed.

He shrugged his shoulders. 'It's hard for everyone when they're on their own for the first time,' he said. 'You're no different from anyone else.'

'It's kind of you to say that, but don't swear to it on the

Bible, will you? I'd hate to see you perjure yourself in such a way. I'm a lousy teacher and you know it. So, too, does everyone in the school who's got eyes, not to mention ears. The noise that blares forth from my classroom daily deafens me, and God knows what it does to everyone else in earshot!'

They laughed again.

Their laughter died away and they stood on the corner of the street, looking awkwardly at each other.

Tom thrust his hands into the pockets of his green corduroy trousers. 'Look,' he said hesitantly. 'D'you have to get off home at once, or could you come for a coffee, or maybe something stronger? Just for old times' sake.'

She smiled at him. 'Why not? That sounds great, Tom. But after the day I've had, make it the something stronger, will you?'

'So, how've you been?' she asked when they'd settled themselves at a window table in a small wine bar tucked behind the tube station, and the waiter had brought them a bottle of red wine, filled their glasses and left, leaving the bottle on the table.

'You see me nearly every day, if not every day, so what kind of strange question is that?' he asked with a half-smile.

'You know what I mean. I'm truly sorry things turned out the way they did, Tom,' she blurted out on a sudden impulse.

'Don't be. If it hadn't been Robert, it would've been someone else. I was never going to be able to give you what you wanted from life. Better for both of us that the parting was sooner rather than later.'

'Well, I *am* sorry anyway. We always had a good time together. And I was really fond of you. I still am, in a way.'

'I know you were, Caroline,' he said quietly. 'At times I even wondered if you felt more for me than you realised. If you'd been able to let go of that dream of yours, and looked clearly at what we had between us, we might've been in a totally different place right now. But that's all in the past,' he said with a slight lift of his shoulders. 'These days you're having a high old time with your Robert. So let's drink to good times for you and Robert. I really do wish you both well.'

'Thanks, Tom,' she said, and they each took a sip of their wine.

'Will you leave school when you get married? Next summer, isn't it? Or will you work till children come along?' he asked.

'I haven't given it a single thought.'

He laughed in her face. 'Come on, Caro. This is me—Tom. I know you better than you know yourself. I didn't really have to ask the question. You're planning to do one more year at the school, and will have resigned from teaching before you've even tied the knot. Yes or no?'

'Knowing how much I hate teaching, I suppose that's a pretty obvious supposition.'

'Then I'll go one step further, shall I? You'll be pregnant when you get married. Not too far gone, mind you—after all, we wouldn't want to spoil the line of the dress or ruin the photos, would we—but just far enough along to make you able to hand in your notice on the last day of the summer half-term next year, which is the deadline if you want to leave at the end of the summer term.'

'That is so scary,' she said sitting back in amazement. 'It's uncanny, Tom. How did you guess I was going to try and get things to work out like that?'

'I didn't need to guess—I know you. I know you better than Robert will ever know you,' he said steadily, his voice suddenly serious.

'Yes, I think you do,' she said slowly, and she smiled at him with genuine warmth.

His face broke into a broad grin. 'This is getting too heavy. We're meant to be celebrating.' He filled up their glasses. 'Drink up. We'll forget about the future and talk about the present, or rather the immediate past. Starting with what happened in the assembly this afternoon. I was walking along the corridor and I heard the upper school explode with laughter. A moment later, you came scurrying out of the hall, bright red in colour. You charged off like a bat out of hell, your head down, so you didn't notice me there.'

'Oh, my God!' she exclaimed. 'I don't ever want to think about that assembly again! That was the most ghastly moment of my life! I've had the most embarrassing after-noon because of it.'

'What on earth happened?'

'It was my turn to do the assembly and I did some sort of talk about being true to yourself, finishing up with a quote from Polonius to Laertes in 'Hamlet'. You know the one—to thine own self be true, et cetera, et cetera. The talk had gone quite well, I thought, so I was very relaxed when it came to reading out the notices. The final notice was about next year's French Exchange.'

'Is it really that time again?'

'So it seems. Anyway, it was about pupils collecting a letter about the Exchange. Time was moving on, so I decided to paraphrase the message for speed, and I announced very loudly and clearly that anyone who'd been absent last week should go to Madame Gilbert if they wanted a French letter.' Tom threw back his head and laughed. 'As I said the words French letter, I realised what I was saying, but I'd gone too far to be able to stop myself.'

'I don't believe it!' he cried in delight.

'You may well laugh. I shall die when I go into school tomorrow. Madame Gilbert's hardly a little ray of French sunshine at the best of times. I can't imagine what she'll say when the kids all troop up to her over the next few days and ask for what you can be sure they'll ask. And I bet they all begin with Miss Redway said.' She looked at Tom in horror, and then collapsed into a fit of giggles.

'Only you, Caroline!' he exclaimed in delight. 'How I'd love to be a fly on the wall in the Languages' department tomorrow!'

'You'd have to be a French-speaking fly in order to appreciate the richness of Madame's response, I'm sure,' Caroline said, and both broke into laughter again. Wiping the tears of laughter from her eyes, she looked at her watch. 'I suppose I really ought to be going,' she said.

'Are you seeing Robert tonight?'

'Yes, but just for a drink later on. Which I now need like a hole in the head. What about you? Are you seeing anyone at the moment?'

'No, no one special. You've rather spoilt me for everyone else. They all pale into insignificance next to you.' He gave her a rueful smile.

'Don't be silly,' she said with a nervous giggle.

'Silly or not, it's true. But don't worry. I'm not going to spoil our friendship by going on about it. Just know that you've got a friend if you ever need one. My number's on the back of that photo I gave you, if you recall. If you lose it, just ring the school. I'll let the office know that they can give you my number if you ever ask for it.'

She reached across the table and put her hand on his arm. 'Yes, we *are* good friends. Hopefully, that'll never change, not even when I've left the school.'

'We'll see, but that sounds a bit over-optimistic, even to me. Anyway, that's far off in the future. Let's drink to the present.' He filled their glasses with the last of the wine, raised his glass and waited for her to join him.

'To the present!' she echoed, and their eyes met.

For a moment, neither moved. Then Caroline looked quickly away, finished her wine, and put her glass down on the table. She stood up. 'I'm really going to have to go, Tom,' she said, reaching into her bag.

'Give me a minute,' he said, getting up from his chair. 'This is on me. I'll settle up and walk you to the station.' He went over to the bar and paid for the wine. 'Okay,' he said, coming back a moment later. 'That's done. Let's walk.'

'Gosh, it's bright!' she exclaimed as the strong light outside hit their eyes. 'I suddenly feel quite woozy. I think we drank more than we should've done. I'll have to stick to water when I meet Robert.'

He put his arm around her shoulders. 'Sometimes when you've had a bit too much to drink, it makes you able to say and do what you wouldn't be able to say or do if you were stone cold sober. Don't you think?'

She glanced uneasily at him. 'What're you talking about?'

He stopped and turned to her. 'I don't live far from here,' he said, running his fingers through her auburn hair. 'Come and be woozy at home with me, Caro. For old times' sake. I know I shouldn't suggest this, or even so much as think it, but I can't stop myself. I still love you.'

'I might be a bit tipsy,' she said, wobbling slightly, 'but I do know what I'm doing. I'm an engaged woman.'

'So? You're not a married woman and that's what matters. Or are you scared to sleep with me because you still care about me? Is that it?'

'That's rubbish and you know it. I don't want to sleep with you because I'm engaged to someone else.'

He gave a dry laugh. 'That's a lousy reason for not sleeping with someone. Being engaged means that you intend to enter into a marriage contract at a later date. It doesn't mean any more than that.'

'It *does* mean more than that. It means I love Robert and he loves me. I'd hate him to sleep with anyone else, so I'm not going to do that to him. What better reason could there be than that?'

'That you don't want to sleep with me,' he said quietly, looking into her darkening green eyes. 'That would have been a better reason, Caro.'

Their eyes held each other, and Caroline paled.

'Fond as you may be of Robert, Caroline, if I could support you in the way you wanted, I suspect you might be marrying me, not him.'

She opened her mouth to protest, but he cut through her. 'I don't blame you for it. You hate teaching and want to get out as soon as possible. Robert can give you a way out. And I believe you truly think you love him. But I'm worried that you don't, that you've kidded yourself. I think you *want* to love him because he's what you've always dreamed of. If so, you could finish up by being miserable. I love you, and I hate it to come to that.' He paused, and gave a dry laugh. 'Ignore me, Caro. What do I know, after all? It's probably just sour grapes talking, and me kidding myself about your feelings for me because I wish with all my heart that you did feel that way.'

She looked up into his face, and saw despair, and love.

'Goodnight, Tom,' she whispered, and she turned and walked unsteadily into the station, her vision misting.

39

'I've no idea where Caroline can be,' Louise remarked, leaning back on the sofa in the sitting-room. 'She's never normally this late home in the week. I can't think what she can be doing.'

'You and me both.' Robert glanced at his wristwatch, and settled more comfortably into the armchair. 'Maybe it wasn't such a bright idea, turning up early like this, but I was nearby and I thought Caroline might like to go for a drink sooner rather than later. And perhaps have a bite to eat afterwards.'

Louise hastily stood up. 'D'you want one while you're waiting for Caroline?'

He raised an eyebrow. 'Want one? What exactly are you offering, Louise?' He gave her a lazy smile.

'Wine, Robert. We've got wine of every colour. Or coffee, if you'd prefer,' she said, laughing.

'I'll settle for the wine, thanks. Make it the red variety, would you, please?'

She felt his eyes follow her as she went into the kitchen.

'You're not joining me in the strong stuff?' he asked, as

she came back into the room carrying a glass of wine for him and an orange juice for her.

'Not this evening, I'm afraid. I've one or two things I want to talk to the others about and I need a clear head for it.'

'Well, here's to whatever it is that needs a clear head,' he said, and he raised his glass in a toast. He took a sip of the wine, and grimaced.

'Sorry,' she said, giggling. 'It's pretty foul, isn't it? It was on offer at the supermarket.'

'I'm the one who should say sorry—that was rude of me. It's lovely, really it is.' He took another sip. 'Or it will be when I've drunk so much of it that I can't taste it any longer.'

They smiled at each other.

'So, you're going to have a female conference this evening, are you? That sounds ominous,' he remarked conversationally.

'Not really. It's just nice to have a chat once in a while. We don't do it often enough these days—we hardly see each other from one week to the next.'

'Such is life, I'm afraid. But tell me, how're you getting on? Caroline told me you're doing some work for Ethan again. Any more trips to California in the offing?'

'I've been doing three a days a week at the office. Alas, no more such trips ahead, though. But as my dissertation's due in soon, it's just as well. What about you? Bought any more houses recently?'

He settled more comfortably into the armchair. 'Funnily enough, I've got my eye on a couple of properties. One of them's a commercial property, which would be a new venture for me.'

'Sounds exciting. I imagine that in the long run there's more to be made from commercial than residential.'

'You could be right there.'

The front door slammed. Both glanced towards the sitting-room door as it opened.

Emily came into the room. 'Hi, Lou,' she said. 'And hello, Robert! What a nice surprise. And wine, too!'

'You should ask Emily's advice about the legal side of things, Robert,' Louise suggested. 'She does a lot of things to do with property; don't you, Emily?'

'I suppose so. Why, what's this about?'

'It's probably better left for another occasion, in view of the girlie chin-wag ahead,' he said. 'Tell Caroline I'll ring her later. As you've something to discuss, we can leave our drink till tomorrow.'

'That's really nice of you. Thank you.' Louise started to get up. 'Sorry about the wine.'

'Stay where you are, Louise. I'll see myself out. And don't worry about the wine—the company more than made up for it.' Giving them both a warm smile, he went out.

A moment later, they heard the front door close behind him.

'It was nice of Robert not to hang around,' Louise said. 'Caroline might be ages yet.'

Emily slumped into the armchair that Robert had been in. She glanced at the almost-full glass of wine on the table. 'I see he didn't think much of our wine,' she remarked in amusement. 'He's hardly touched it. For someone used to vintage, it must have been a weeny shock.'

'You should've seen his face when he tasted it! I wish I'd had a camera. He took a second sip out of politeness, and that was that.'

'At least you were wise enough not to join him. Unless yours is an orange-coloured wine.'

'I fancied an orange juice; that's all.'

'You must be pregnant,' Emily said with a laugh.

Louise went scarlet. Emily caught her breath sharply and sat upright. 'Oh, my God, Lou! You aren't pregnant, are you?'

Louise leaned back against the sofa. 'I was going to tell you and the others this evening, and ask for your advice. Mind you,' she added with a wry smile, 'I can well imagine what *your* advice would be!'

'Don't be so sure. Horses for courses, and all that. What really bad luck. Look, why don't I make us something to eat while we wait for the others? I know it's early, but it means we won't have to break off later for food.' She got up. 'By the time I'm done, Caroline should be back. Terri Lee's an unknown—her hours are so erratic these days.'

'*You* make us something to eat? God, You must think me a pretty desperate case.'

'Don't get carried away! I was thinking along the lines of either cheese or beans on toast, or maybe both together. Even *I* can't screw that up!' The front door slammed. 'I wonder which of them that is. If it's Caroline, you might be in with the chance of a decent meal.'

The sitting-room door opened and Terri Lee stood in the doorway, holding several carrier bags in one hand, and supporting Caroline with the other. 'Look who I found staggering from the station,' she announced. 'Our Miss Caroline! And she's more than a little bit merry.'

'I am so not,' Caroline said, and dissolved into a fit of giggles.

'We need to sober her up,' Emily said, and she went into the kitchen and pressed the switch on the kettle. I'll make her some coffee. I'll do instant for speed. And she must drink as much orange juice as she can hold. As for dinner, it'll be cheese on toast tonight.'

She took a jar of coffee from the cupboard, and reached up to the shelf on the wall for a mug and a tall glass. Then she took a carton of orange juice out of the fridge and filled the glass with the juice.

'Here, Caroline, get this down you,' she said, going back into the sitting-room with the juice. 'It'll help more than the coffee will. You need plenty of Vitamin C inside you. Get her on the sofa, Terri Lee, will you? I'll bring the coffee in a minute.'

'Trust you to be uptight,' Terri Lee snapped. Glaring at Emily, she dropped the carrier bags on to the floor next to the armchair. 'Getting tipsy once in a blue moon isn't a criminal offence, you know. Everyone needs to let their hair down at times. You should try it.'

'Don't blame Emily—it's my fault,' Louise cut in, moving across to the armchair so that Caroline could lie on the sofa. 'I need some advice from you lot.'

'Give me a minute, then,' Terri Lee said, picking up the bags. 'I'll drop these upstairs. I won't be long.'

'There's no immediate rush,' Emily said, looking at Caroline's pale face.

'I'M PREGNANT,' Louise said bluntly, 'and I don't know what to do. I've already told Emily.'

Caroline was the first to speak. 'Well, that's certainly sobered me up.'

'What do you know!' Terri Lee exclaimed. 'Louise is going to be a mummy! I'd have put money on Caroline being the first.' She paused, and stared hard at Louise. 'I must say, you don't look exactly overjoyed. Are you thinking of not going ahead with it?'

Caroline scowled at Terri Lee, and then turned back to Louise. 'What did Ethan say? I imagine he's thrilled.'

'I haven't told him, and I don't intend to,' Louise said firmly.

'What!' Caroline exclaimed in disbelief. 'Why not?'

'Because I don't want him to know,' Louise said, a stubborn note in her voice.

'We're all different, Caroline,' Emily said hastily, 'and we all handle things in our own way. I'm sure the most helpful thing for Louise would be to run through her options. Am I right, Lou?'

Louise nodded. 'It would be.'

Caroline drank some more of her orange juice, and lay back.

'Well, abortion could be an option, but you don't know if you'd be allowed one, and you wouldn't know till you'd asked,' Emily began. 'Having it adopted is another. Marriage or moving in together is another, and that's the most obvious thing to do as you clearly love each other. But if you don't want Ethan to know you're pregnant—'

'I don't.'

'Then you've presumably ruled that out. It must mean that you can't see a future for your relationship. Which brings me to the final option, and that is going it alone. I wouldn't have thought that ideal, given how hard it must be, and also there's some shame attached to having a child and not being married, but people do make it work. Have I missed anything?' She looked around at the others.

'You can rule out abortion and adoption,' Louise said. 'I'm having the baby, and I'm keeping it.'

Caroline sat upright. 'Then why aren't you telling Ethan? Surely he's got a right to know?'

'I wouldn't marry him under these circumstances.

Maybe we'd have married at some point in the future, I'll never know now. But he's never mentioned marriage, and I'd never want anyone to marry me just because I was pregnant, which rules out marrying him or living with him.'

'That's nuts,' Terri Lee said bluntly.

'Maybe it is. But I refuse to live with the life-long uncertainty of not knowing if we'd have stayed together if there hadn't been a baby. I'd hate that. And I'd always feel I'd trapped him. I've discussed this with Nicky, and I'm not going to change my mind.'

'If you stick around here, he's gonna find out at some point, though. A stomach that's bigger every time he sees you will give him a tiny clue,' Terri Lee said drily.

'That's why he mustn't see me—I handed in my notice this morning. He's in Cardiff till the end of the week so he won't find my resignation until he returns. By then I'll be long gone. I just don't know where,' she added miserably. 'I'm hoping you've got some ideas.'

'I don't know why you don't give some serious thought to adoption?' Emily said. 'If you had it adopted, you'd only have to disappear for nine months.'

'I'm keeping it.'

Emily opened her mouth to speak.

'Louise isn't like you, Emily,' Caroline cut in. 'Whatever she might think in advance, the minute she held the baby in her arms—Ethan's baby—she'd want to keep it.'

Emily shrugged. 'And she isn't like you, Caroline, either. In career terms, this couldn't be a worse time for her, and believe it or not, some people's careers matter to them. She needs to get established in what she wants to do before she's lumbered with kids.'

'Be that as it may, one thing's for certain—if Louise secretly had a baby and gave it away, Ethan would find out,'

Caroline retorted. 'Things have a way of coming out. He'd be unbelievably hurt. And personally, I think that'd be a truly unkind thing to do to him.' She turned to Louise. 'But if you're determined that he shouldn't know, and want to move away, isn't Nicola's the obvious place?'

'And it'd be obvious to Ethan, too, so that's no good. And it's too close to here. Even if Nicky was able to convince him I wasn't there, he'd be bound to bump into us at some point. I'll have to leave London.'

'Of course, you could always tell Ethan you're going on a lengthy religious retreat, and stay holed up here for the next eight months or so,' Terri Lee remarked, a trace of impatience in her voice. 'When the baby was born, you'd leave the kid in an upstairs room and reappear, all spiritual-like. We could stuff a dummy in the baby's mouth every time Ethan came to take you out, and hope he'd proposed to you by the time the child needed to leave its room to go to school.'

'Be sensible, Terri Lee,' Emily said caustically. 'You're not helping at all.'

'Well, I think Louise is making a problem for herself that need not be there,' Terri Lee said defensively. 'She's got limited choices. Whether she leaves now or stays here for the next few months, she'll need to bring in some money—I can't see Robert or any other landlord letting her live rent free. And she'll have to buy food and nappies and things like that. It means she's gotta work, and once she's had the baby, that won't be easy. Or she'll have to be kept by someone. So she's gotta tell Ethan and give him a chance to put his hand in his pocket. He *is* fifty percent responsible, after all.'

'That's a fair point, Louise,' Caroline said. 'It takes two to tango, and he should help you financially. The fact that Ethan's involved doesn't mean you have to marry him. As

Emily said earlier, it's possible to bring up a child by yourself. And if Ethan knew about the baby, there'd be no problem about you moving in with Nicola.'

'I agree with Terri Lee and Caroline. That's the best option,' Emily said decisively. 'Tell Ethan what's happened, but refuse to marry him if he asks. That way you wouldn't be trapping him, to use your words. You could do some temping till you got too enormous.'

Louise shook her head. 'I know Ethan. Yes, he'd support the baby financially, but he'd also insist on being a part of the baby's life. That would never work. I love him too much to cope with seeing him regularly, but not being with him. I'll only truly get over him if I move away and never see him again. If he doesn't know about the child, we can both start again, so to speak. It means I must be gone before he returns from Cardiff.'

'At least you've got a few days in which to give some more thought to this. When the shock's worn off, you might see things differently,' Caroline said.

'And I can give her another thing to think about,' Terri Lee said, getting up. 'She can ask herself what sort of person she is. Is she really a selfish cow, who's going to stop Ethan from knowing what he's a right to know, all because of some crackpot ideas, a selfish cow who's thinking only about what *she* wants, not about what's best for the baby. Being the child of a single parent is far from ideal, take it from me.'

'That's a very good point, Terri Lee,' Caroline said. 'It's not just about you, Louise—it's also about what's best for the child.'

'I need to go and put my things away.' Terri Lee stared down at Louise. 'Forget all that crap you've been spouting. You know in your heart whether or not Ethan loves you, and I think you know he does. It means that there's only one thing you should do, and if you don't do it, he deserves better than you and he's had a lucky escape. He's a really nice man, and he needs a really nice wife. If you don't tell him, that wouldn't be you.' And she turned away.

'Good God,' Emily murmured as they heard Terri Lee go up the stairs. 'I do believe she's actually growing up.'

'She's absolutely right. You all are,' Louise said. 'I don't have to marry him, but he does have the right to know, and I'm going to tell him at the weekend. He'll know I've resigned by then, and when I tell him what's happened, it'll explain why.'

40

W hat a bore the teas were, Emily thought gloomily as she trailed towards the room where most of the barristers in her Chambers gathered each afternoon at about four thirty. But at least it was better than being in Louise's position. The tedious tea would be over within an hour—Louise's problem would last a lifetime.

This would be the first afternoon tea she'd gone to in the weeks since she and John had broken up.

She hadn't known whether or not John was going to the teas—probably not as he disliked the polite formality of such occasions as much as she did—but she hadn't been prepared to take a chance. Instead, she'd made sure that she'd always been in the middle of urgent research when the clerks had called for the pupils to go along to the tea room, or writing an important Statement, or reading a set of papers she had to get through before the evening. It didn't matter what, so long as it was a valid reason not to attend.

It wasn't as if they'd miss her being there. All the pupils were expected to do was be an audience for the barristers when they spewed forth an endless flow of anecdotes and reminiscences. They weren't expected to open their mouths for any reason other than to laugh at the barristers' jokes, funny or not, and to sip their tea.

That morning, however, the Head Clerk had waylaid her as she was entering Chambers, and had pointedly reminded her of the wisdom of some degree of attendance at the afternoon teas if one was hoping to be made a tenant. Since she most definitely wanted to stay in those Chambers, she promptly decided to go to the tea that day, and she'd been hoping since then that John wouldn't be there.

She pushed the door open and went into the room.

The first person she saw was John.

He was standing on the far side of the room. It was the first time she'd seen him at a social occasion since the Becky day, and her heart gave a sudden lurch of longing. He'd seen her, too, she sensed, although he appeared to be engrossed in a conversation with another of the senior barristers.

Her eyes straight ahead of her, she crossed to the table where the cups had been set out, and took one.

'Don't you hate these occasions?' she murmured, sitting down next to Venetia and Paul.

Venetia shrugged. 'I don't really think about it. It's just something you have to do. It's all about making the right contacts.'

'I hate them, too,' Paul said, leaning in front of Venetia to speak to Emily. 'I avoid them whenever I can. How are you, Emily?' he asked, and he got up and moved to sit on the other side of her. 'I've hardly seen you for weeks. But on the rare occasions when I *have* seen you, you've looked decidedly down. Is it to do with Gordon?'

Venetia got up, her cup in her hand, and made her way across to the Head Clerk.

'Typical,' Paul said, watching her go.

'In answer to your question, I'm fine,' Emily said. 'It's nothing to do with Gordon. I've got used to him now and, anyway, my year as his pupil is almost over. No, I've had a bit of man trouble, that's all. But it's now in the past.'

'D'you want a shoulder to cry on? We could go off to Carey Street after work, have a drink, get a bite to eat maybe. We really ought to celebrate the fact that it's looking likely that all three of us will be offered a tenancy. We'll all have been very lucky if we are.'

She nodded. 'True. And Chambers will be very lucky, too, if they get us.'

'Hello, Emily.'

She looked up. John stood in front of her.

Paul looked from Emily's face to John's, excused himself, got up and moved away.

John sat down. 'How've you been?'

'Fine, thanks. And you?'

'Lonely,' he said. 'I've missed you.'

'And I've missed you, too,' she said flatly. 'I really have.' Neither of them said anything for a few minutes. 'How's Becky?' she asked eventually.

'Thank you for asking. She's doing well, thank you. She's going away to an American-style camp next week for the whole of half term. She's very excited. And so is Angela. She and her husband are going to the Seychelles while Becky's away. I'm on emergency stand-by. I'm secretly hoping for an emergency as it'll give me a chance to see Becky.' He gave her a wry smile. 'In the vernacular of today, how sad is that?'

'I hope it works out as you want. Perhaps Becky will get homesick and they'll call for you. Nothing too serious, but something that means she'll need to be taken home by you.'

'Good thinking.' He paused. 'She could always come

home to the two of us, you know, Emily,' he said quietly. 'I could accept not fathering any more children in order to keep you in my life, but I can't change the fact that I already have Becky. If you felt like being on emergency stand-by with me, you'd be very welcome.' The grey eyes that were turned to her were full of hope.

'I'm sorry, John. I can't do kids.' She stood up. 'I really *am* sorry, John,' she said gently, looking down into his face. 'I do still love you, and I know that I always will. But I can't do what you want.'

Taking a deep breath, she went across to Paul, who was helping himself to another cup of tea from the side table. 'Don't drink too much, Paul, or you won't have room for that drink later.'

'Hey, are you accepting? That's great, Emily.' His face broke out in a delighted grin. 'I'll stop by your room when I leave. If you're not ready, I'll hang on till you are.'

'Fine. See you later, then.' She put down her cup and walked to the door.

When she reached the door, she started to open it. Then she paused and turned back to look at John.

He was still where she'd left him, sitting by himself, staring dejectedly into his tea cup. She wondered if he was thinking of her, and wishing she was at his side.

But that was what she wished, too.

She found herself releasing the door handle and starting to walk back into the room, her gaze fixed on John.

Then she stopped abruptly.

It might be Becky he was thinking about. The memory of Becky's face, so like John's, flashed in front of her eyes.

He might be regretting how little he saw of her, and hoping he'd see her more frequently as she got older and it became easier for Angela to leave her with him and go off with her husband to exotic places. Yes, this might be about Becky, not her.

She turned sharply, went back to the door, opened it and walked out into the hall.

Any form of compromise would inevitably mean that she'd have to look after a child for a period of time each month, and she was no more prepared to do that now than she'd ever been.

It meant that she truly had to accept, which she recognized that she hadn't yet managed to do, that she and John were finished for all time. He must be relegated to the past, and she must look to a future without him.

41

Ethan leapt from his car, bounded up the steps from his parking place to his office, patted his jacket pocket to ensure that nothing had fallen out, and entered the building in long strides. It was a pity that his first meeting with Louise after several days without her was going to be on a Friday afternoon at the office—hardly the most romantic of places—but she'd be working that day, so it was unavoidable. Their real reunion would have to come later. And he couldn't wait!

The only plus point about his enforced absence for the week had been that it had given him time to get something done that he'd been meaning to do for a while. But very much on the down side, it had been a week since he'd spoken to Louise, and every minute had felt an age.

He'd rung the house on several occasions, and left a couple of messages, but she hadn't rung him back. In the end, he'd come to the conclusion that their system for leaving each other messages must be badly flawed. And surprisingly, she hadn't called his hotel as she usually did, despite him having made sure before he left that she had his number.

At one point, he'd come close to ringing the office just to hear her voice, but he'd pulled back at the last moment. The women there had amazing antennae, and he hadn't been prepared to risk Louise becoming the subject of gossip.

He nodded to the receptionist as he passed her, went into the main area and headed straight across it to his private office.

'Hello, Barbara,' he said as he walked past his secretary's desk. 'Can you give me five minutes and then come into the office?' Going into his room, he took off his jacket, hung it over the back of a chair, walked round his desk to his black leather chair, sat down and opened his desk diary.

A few minutes later, Barbara hurried into his office, her notebook in her hand.

'Would you check with Patrick if it's convenient for me to have a word with Louise Crawford?' he asked, looking up. 'It's nothing serious, but there're a couple of things I need to ask her as soon as possible. And would you ask Sharon to get me a coffee, please? When I've spoken to Louise, we'll make a start on the mail. Don't worry, I won't keep you late —we'll just do anything that looks urgent. You must be as ready for the weekend as I am.' He leaned across to the in–tray.

'Of course, Mr Ford. I'll arrange for a coffee at once, but I'm afraid that Louise has left.'

'Left? What do you mean left?' He stopped mid-action and stared at Barbara.

'Just that. She's resigned. There's a letter for you in your tray. She phoned at the beginning of the week to tell me what she'd done. Here.' She pulled Louise's envelope from the in-tray and handed it to Ethan. His face bewildered, he took it from her, stood up and moved across to the window.

'That's a surprise,' he said at last, staring at the unopened envelope. 'I thought she was happy here. Her work has been excellent.'

'Patrick's very disappointed, too, Mr Ford. He thought she was a girl with tremendous ability, and he was looking forward to her joining the company after she'd finished her course.'

He stood motionless, looking down at the brown envelope in his hand, his brow furrowed.

'Let me get your coffee,' Barbara said.

'Thank you.' His gaze still on the envelope, he dismissed her with a wave of his hand.

She went out of the office, and closed the door behind her.

Swiftly slitting open the envelope, he read through the contents of the letter, scarcely able to take in a word. Louise had resigned, just as Barbara had said. She hoped he didn't mind, but she wouldn't be working for him any longer. The arrangements for the product demo she'd been organising with Patrick were effectively complete, and that made it a good time for her to go.

There was nothing else—no explanation, nothing.

He looked up from the letter and felt cold. Louise hadn't called him while he was away, despite the messages he'd left for her. And now her resignation for no obvious reason. The silence suddenly seemed ominous.

He stared through the window at a world that seemed very far away.

People walking along the street, talking and laughing; people in cars and buses, chatting to each other as they hurried home—all of them getting on with their lives, completely oblivious to the overwhelming sense of desolation that was sweeping through him.

Hearing Barbara open the door, he turned away from the window, went back to his desk and sat down.

She put his coffee next to him, and sat down, her notebook open on her lap.

He stared at his in-tray, his eyes unseeing, his coffee untouched.

'Is anything wrong, Mr Ford?' she asked, anxiously. 'Are you worried about Louise leaving so unexpectedly? If you think there might be a problem with something she was working on, I could ask Patrick to come in.'

He shook his head. 'No, it's all fine, I'm sure.'

'Well, you don't look too good, if you don't mind me saying so,' she ventured hesitantly. 'Maybe you should go home. I've worked for you long enough to know when you're not feeling well. You've probably overdone it this week.'

He caught her look of sympathy, and knew he had to get out of the office fast. He wasn't going to waste another minute. He was going to go to Louise and find out exactly what was wrong.

He stood up.

'You might be right, Barbara. It's been a very busy week, and I've a lot on my mind as a result. I'm sorry about the coffee, but I think I'll leave now. The mail will have to wait.' He went round his desk and took his jacket from the chair. 'It's a funny thing, though,' he remarked as he slipped into the jacket, 'Miss Crawford leaving so suddenly.'

'In a way, I suppose it was understandable,' she said, getting up. 'The poor girl was completely thrown by finding out she was pregnant.'

'Pregnant!' He stopped wrestling with the sleeve of his jacket.

'Yes, she was so upset about it,' Barbara continued, 'that I couldn't help but feel sorry for her. I came upon her in the ladies' room just after she'd found out, and she was in a real state. But really, with everything there is to stop girls from getting pregnant these days, you wonder at the stupidity of some of them.'

And she went out, shaking her head.

Louise pregnant!

Ethan put a hand to his head. Louise carrying his baby! He was going to be a dad! He felt stunned. And thrilled. And desperate to see her.

He loved her, and he'd always intended to ask her to marry him. But she'd know that, of course. Having a baby just meant that they'd marry sooner than they might've done, and that it wouldn't be long before he'd have to share her with someone else. But none of that mattered—they'd have plenty of time for themselves in the future, when their children had grown up and flown the nest.

His head spinning with relief and excitement, he grasped the back of the nearest chair to steady himself, drew in a deep breath, and slowly exhaled.

She must've resigned from the company as suddenly as she'd done, he thought as he finished putting on his jacket, because she was suffering in the early weeks of her pregnancy. She could easily be feeling nauseous every morning. If so, the last thing she'd want to do would be to drag herself off to work when there was no need. By resigning as she had, she'd done a very sensible thing.

And she wouldn't have phoned him as she'd want to tell him the news in person, and might be afraid that it would slip out on the phone. In her place, he'd probably have held off phoning, too. She couldn't possibly have known that Barbara would tell him about the pregnancy.

Frantic to see her again as soon as possible, he grabbed his bag and left his office, said goodnight to Barbara, hurried past the receptionist, ran down the steps and turned left into the car park next to the building. In a matter of minutes, he was putting his car into gear and heading north.

Half an hour later, he was standing in front of the Camden Town house. His heart beating fast, he rang the doorbell. After what felt like an eternity, he heard footsteps coming towards the door.

HER FACE PALE, Louise led the way into the sitting-room and then turned to face him.

'Would you like coffee?' she asked,

'I thought you'd never ask,' he said, suppressing a desire to fling his arms around her and hug her tightly. 'It's been a very strange day, and a shot of caffeine would be most welcome. I didn't stick around the office long enough for coffee.'

'I can guess why.' She gave him a weak smile, and went through to the kitchen.

Unbuttoning his jacket, he sat down in one of the armchairs and waited for her to return.

'I'm sorry the room's such a mess,' she said when she appeared with a mug of coffee for Ethan and a glass of water for herself. She gave him his drink and sat down on the sofa opposite him.

'I can't see the room,' he said quietly. 'I can see only you, and you look beautiful to me.'

'Then Cardiff must have damaged your eyesight!' She

attempted a laugh. 'I look even more of a mess than the room.' Her hand went to her hair.

'So,' he said, sipping his coffee. 'I understand you want to stop working for me, or so you wrote. May I ask why? You didn't give a reason in your letter?'

'It's complicated.'

'Then why don't you let me help you uncomplicate it? If you start at the beginning, we can unravel it together.'

Biting her lower lip, she stared at her glass of water.

'To start the ball rolling, then,' he said, leaning slightly forward. 'You've resigned from the firm. And you've not contacted me all week, although I left you some messages. Are the two things connected?'

She nodded.

'So it doesn't matter which we start with, does it, the resignation or the silence?' he said with a smile.

She stared at him across the coffee table, her eyes filling with tears.

'I suppose not,' she said at last, a catch in her voice. '

'Well?' he asked gently.

'I'm pregnant,' she said with a sob.

'I know,' he replied. His face broke into a wide smile. 'I know, Louise, and I think it's the most wonderful news. I guessed you wanted to tell me yourself so I didn't say anything.'

He jumped up and went quickly across to her.

She looked up at him, bewildered, as he sat down on the sofa next to her. 'But how did you know?'

'Barbara told me,' he said, putting his arms around her. 'I couldn't be more thrilled. You must know how much I love you. And I'm delighted that I'm going to be a dad—it's bloody marvellous! We'll marry as soon as we can. If you'll have me, that is.' He hugged her tightly.

She pushed his arms away from her, and stared at him in disbelief. 'You can't really want that. You don't have to pretend. We didn't plan this and there's no way I'm going to let it ruin your life.'

'Ruin my life!' he exclaimed. 'It's—'

'No, let me finish, Ethan,' she said, her voice shaking. 'I've thought it all through. That's what I've been doing ever since I found out. I can bring up the baby on my own. You can always be part of the baby's life, but you don't have to be any more than that. What I mean is, we're not getting married.'

He moved slightly back, bewilderment spreading across his face. 'I don't understand,' he said, shaking his head. 'I love you, and I'm certain you love me. So why won't you marry me?'

'I'd hate someone to marry me just because I was pregnant.'

'And I wouldn't dream of marrying you just because you were pregnant. That would be an appalling basis on which to get married, especially as I can easily afford to support a child while also maintaining a harem of ladies. We wouldn't be marrying because you're pregnant—we'd be marrying because I absolutely adore you and want to spend the rest of my life with you. And I know you love me. That's why.'

She shook her head. A tear trickled down her cheek. 'I'm sorry,' she said, 'but I'd never be able to believe that we would've married if it hadn't been for the baby. I'd always worry that you'd felt you had to do the right thing, even if you didn't realise it. And at some point, you might start to resent me for what had happened, and to feel trapped. I love you too much to want to put you in such a position.'

'Feel trapped? But there's nothing I want more than I want to be trapped with you for the rest of my life. With you, with our baby, and with all the other babies that are going to follow.' He took her hand. 'In fact, Louise, I'd actually intended to propose this weekend.'

She gave him a watery smile. 'Oh, Ethan. I think you're just saying that, and as I can't see into your head, I'd never know if it was true. You must admit it's a tall order to expect me to believe in such a coincidence, much as I might want to.'

'But what if I can prove what was in my head, Lou?' he asked quietly, feeling a rising sense of excitement. 'What then?'

'I don't understand.'

He put his hand into one of his jacket pockets, and pulled out a small box.

She gave a little cry, and stared at him, her eyes wide.

'I bought this for you this week,' he said. 'But I'd rather intended to produce it somewhere a little more romantic than your sitting-room. And before you say that I could have bought it between the office and here, I'll show you the order if you want. It's dated the day I arrived in Cardiff—it's from a jeweller's there.'

He opened the small box, and sank to one knee beside the sofa. 'Please, please, say you'll marry me, Louise? I love you so much.'

She took the ring from his fingers and stared at it in wonder, the sparkle of the large solitaire diamond glittering in her eyes.

Then she looked at him, her eyes filled with love. 'I believe you, Ethan.'

He slipped the ring on her finger, took her into his arms and buried his face in her dark brown hair. 'I adore you, Louise, and will do so for as long as I live.'

42

J *uly*

THE FLIMSY CURTAINS that hung in front of Caroline's bedroom window shimmered gold as they blocked the early morning sun from her room.

It was Saturday morning, which meant no school. She yawned, sighed with happiness and rolled over to look at the clock on the bedside table. There were still four hours before she was meeting Robert, so she could allow herself the luxury of another hour's sleep, if she wanted.

She closed her eyes. Thoughts of her wedding day meandered through her mind, and she smiled into her pillow.

What a day it was going to be!

How different it was going to be from Louise's wedding in Marylebone Town Hall, which was very low key. Admittedly, it was what she and Ethan had wanted, and they'd seemed happy enough about it both on the day and after, but she wanted something much more memorable for herself.

In several ways, her wedding in exactly a year's time would be marking the end of an era, as well as the beginning of a new one.

It would be the end of them sharing the house together. Louise had already moved into Ethan's flat, and they'd be looking for a house once the baby was born. Terri Lee and Emily had both said they'd be buying places of their own the following year, and she would be moving in with Robert.

Fortunately, although Louise had moved out, they didn't need to replace her.

Robert, with his usual kindness, had insisted that the three of them should each continue to pay the same amount of rent as they'd been doing, and shouldn't attempt to make up Louise's share, nor to get anyone for Louise's room. It would've been a real drag to have had to get to know a new person for so short a time, and it would've been difficult for anyone to come into such a close-knit group of friends, so they'd all been relieved.

Her wedding, therefore, would mark the beginning of new lives for them all in their new homes.

Although the wedding was a year away, she'd already started on the preparations. The church and hotel were confirmed, her dress ordered, the photographer and the in-house catering booked. They'd settle on the final menu nearer the time. There was still masses left to decide, though, such as what the bridesmaids would be wearing, the cars, the flowers, the cake, and the wedding favours, but she had plenty of time to do so.

She mustn't be complacent, though, not if she wanted

everything to be perfect, and she did. She must bear in mind that her work for school, the *cordon bleu* cookery class into which she'd enrolled, and the dreamy hours she'd be spending with Robert, would eat up a lot of that time.

And she'd obviously have to go up to Cheshire a few times during the coming year. For a start, she didn't dare risk her parents buying their wedding outfits on their own. There'd be no need for Robert to go with her, though, which was bound to please him—he'd clearly had more than enough on the one and only occasion he'd met her parents.

Her mind leapt back to the weekend she'd taken Robert to Cheshire—that awful, excruciating weekend. She still shuddered at the very thought of it. But it had been months ago, and since then he hadn't given her any grounds on which to feel alarmed. On the contrary, he'd been the best fiancé a woman could have—loving, attentive, generous. Everyone was entitled to get it wrong at least once in a relationship, and she'd long put that episode of his behaviour out of her mind.

All the same, she intended to go to Cheshire alone in the future.

She turned on to her side and stared towards the window. The one thorny issue was the little matter of getting the timing right for her pregnancy—she fully intended the next teaching year to be her last, which meant she'd have to hand in her notice before the last day of the summer half-term next year.

Fortunately, Robert was happy to spend as many hours in bed with her as there were hours in the day, so with careful planning, she should be able to arrange it that she was about four weeks pregnant by May. If she was, she was confident that Robert would agree it was pointless for her to start a new school year when she wouldn't come close to finishing it, and he was sure to be in favour of her leaving the school at the end of July, just before they got married.

And Tom had known she'd plan it that way!

She smiled to herself. How clever of Tom to know her well enough to second guess what she'd do.

But she'd have to be careful what she told Robert.

She'd have to say she'd suffered a memory lapse or had food poisoning or something like that. She wouldn't want him to think she'd manipulated things, though he probably wouldn't mind if he knew. After all, he'd said often enough that he wanted a house full of children, and he'd never suggested they leave it a few years before starting their family.

And it would be much more pleasant for him, as well as for her, if she were at home all day. She'd have the time to put a woman's touch to the house, and she'd be able to wait on him hand and foot. She'd have the energy to create wonderful meals each night, and to entertain Robert's clients and their friends with a gourmet cuisine that impressed them all. Things would slow a little in the first few months after the baby had been born, but once she'd got the child into a satisfactory routine, normal life would be resumed.

She sighed and stretched herself in satisfaction.

She was such a lucky woman. Her last year of teaching was going to culminate in the most perfect of weddings, which would be followed by a happy ever after life.

43

ONE YEAR LATER

S *aturday, 29th July, 1980*

WAKING EARLY on the morning of her wedding day, Caroline lay in the executive suite, listening to the birds singing outside the open window while she waited for the start of the day she'd dreamed of for so long. At the end of the day, she would be Mrs Robert Chesterton, the wife of the most wonderful man in the world.

Theirs was going to be a supremely happy marriage, she just knew. She'd make sure that the next eight months or so, when it'd be just her and Robert, were magical. And then there'd be three of them.

She smiled to herself and ran her hand over her stomach. Happily, it'd be a while before anything showed as she was little more than a month overdue. It wasn't long, but it was long enough for her to know that she was pregnant.

But that hadn't been the reason for her resignation in May. Tom had been wrong about that.

Despite sleeping with Robert nearly every evening in the weeks leading up to half-term, delighting him with her appetite for sex, there'd been no sign of a pregnancy by half-term, and she hadn't been able to hide her despair.

On the first evening of the half-term holiday, realising that something was bothering her, Robert had taken her to the pub where he'd proposed, and there he'd coaxed out of her what was making her so unhappy.

She'd had no intention of telling him the whole truth as she wasn't sure that it showed her in the best of lights, but when he'd persisted in wanting to know the reason for her dejection, she'd known she had to say something, and she'd tearfully confessed that she was rather panicking about how she'd be able to balance the demands of teaching once they'd got married with her desire to make him the most wonderful home.

She'd added in a joking sort of way that if she'd been pregnant, it wouldn't have been a concern as she'd probably have been handing in her resignation that week, ready to leave in July, but she wasn't.

'I wanted our life together to be perfect from day one,' she'd sobbed, taking the handkerchief he'd offered her. 'I wanted to cook you a delicious meal every evening, and not have to dash something off while correcting piles of useless books.'

'Is that all it is?' he'd exclaimed, and he'd laughed, pulled an envelope out of his pocket, removed the contents and started writing a few sentences on the back. Drying her eyes, she'd tried to see what he was writing.

'There,' he'd said a few minutes later, 'I've written your

notice for you. You can sign that if you like and hand it into the school tomorrow.'

She'd stared at him, open-mouthed. 'What do you mean? I'm not pregnant.'

'You may well be by then. We're going back to the house just as soon as we've finished our wine, and we're going to have a shot at changing the situation,' he'd told her with a grin. 'But even if we don't hit the bullseye this side of July, I rather like the idea of you waiting on the doorstep for me each evening, my slippers in one hand, a whisky in the other, and a voluminous paisley apron wrapped around that beautiful body.'

'Robert!' she'd cried out in joy and she'd jumped up, run round the table and hugged him hard.

And it was probably because she'd been so much more relaxed about everything that she'd got pregnant fairly soon after that. Robert would be thrilled when she told him, which she'd do after their honeymoon.

Being pregnant had clearly already had an effect on her, though.

When Louise and Ethan had arrived the previous afternoon with nine-month old Georgie, she'd felt overwhelmingly maternal as she'd gazed at Georgie's little face, and she'd carried him around the room, pointing through the windows to the flowers and the birds, telling him their names. She'd so enjoyed herself that she'd been genuinely reluctant to hand him back to Louise when it was time for Georgie to be taken upstairs to have his nappy changed.

As she'd been putting him into Louise's arms, the little boy had turned to look at her, his large brown eyes fringed by long dark eyelashes, and he'd suddenly given her the widest of smiles. Feeling quite emotional, she'd clutched his

chubby little hand, and run her fingers down his smooth
cheek with her other hand.

'He's lovely, Louise,' she'd whispered.

'We think so, too. Don't we, Ethan?' Louise had said,
smiling up into Ethan's face.

That'll be me soon, Caroline had thought.

The light in the suite was brighter now. It was time she
got up. The ceremony was at three o'clock and there was a
lot to do before that, the first thing being to have a good
breakfast.

She threw back the bedclothes, jumped out of bed,
pulled open the curtains and gazed at the sky. The weather
couldn't have been better. The sun was shining and the sky
was clear blue. She could tell that it was already quite warm,
but it wouldn't be uncomfortably so owing to a light breeze
that was stirring the air.

She'd quickly slip into something and go down to breakfast. She'd decided against room service as she thought it'd
be more fun to sit with the others. Having a laugh with them
would stop her from getting too nervous about the day
ahead. With luck, at least one of the girls would be at breakfast by now.

The hairdressers would arrive at her suite at nine
o'clock, and the girls were coming along at that time, too.
The four of them were going to have their hair done
together, accompanied by the first champagne of the day.
The make-up artists would arrive at ten, and the photographer was booked for not long after that. From then on, it
would be non-stop last-minute activity.

Her mother had chosen to have her hair done at her
favourite hairdresser's in Northwich before they'd set off the
previous afternoon, bringing Margot with them. As soon as
they'd reached the hotel, Margot, seeming somewhat

subdued, had gone off to the spa, leaving Caroline with her parents. She'd been greatly relieved to see that the hairdresser had persuaded her mother to let her take out a little of the yellowing grey and to have her hair done in a slightly more modern style.

'You look gorgeous, Mum,' she'd told her as she sat with her parents in the crimson plush lounge, waiting for an afternoon tea of homemade scones, jam and clotted cream to be brought to them, along with a pot of English tea. 'It's a shame the hairdresser couldn't persuade Margot to tone down those streaks, though.'

'Are you sure it looks all right, pet?' her mother asked, fiddling with the back of her head.

'It looks really lovely, Mum,' Caroline told her. 'It knocks years off you. But you must leave it alone or you'll spoil it.'

'Caroline's right, Mother. You look a treat,' Arthur said, patting his wife's arm. He looked around him, and shook his head. 'This must be costing Robert a pretty penny or two,' he murmured. 'Your mother and I would've done our best for you, Caroline love, but we couldn't have afforded this.'

'I know you would, Dad, and I appreciate it.' She leaned across and squeezed his hand.

Her parents had been quietly happy throughout the wedding rehearsal that followed, their gaze fixed admiringly on Robert, and also at dinner that evening. They'd chosen to sit at one of the smaller tables at the side of the room, and Margot had joined them, having turned down the invitation that she sit with Caroline and her friends. Her parents clearly been overawed by the luxury of it all, and Caroline wasn't in the least surprised that they retired to their room soon after finishing their meal.

Margot left the dining-room at the same time, disappearing in the direction of the bar.

'You're lucky Robert's parents didn't feel up to the journey,' Emily remarked as she watched Patsy and Arthur leave the dining room, nodding apologetically to everyone they passed. She turned back to Caroline. 'Your sister's not that friendly, is she?'

'She's all right, I suppose, but she can be moody. She's a few years younger than I am so I don't really know her well. I asked her to be a bridesmaid, but she didn't want to. We're very different.'

'You can say that again!' Terri Lee said with a laugh. 'I can't exactly see you in a bright pink leather jacket and tight black trousers.'

After dinner, Robert left for the nearby hotel where he was going to stay the night, and Ethan went with him to keep him company for the rest of the evening. Louise took Georgie up to bed, telling the others she'd ring the hotel baby-sitting service as soon as Georgie had fallen asleep, and would come back down, and she'd joined them again soon afterwards.

'He went to sleep at once,' she said. 'So miracles can happen.'

Finding themselves alone, the four girls picked up their liqueurs and moved into the lounge to continue their conversation.

'It's certainly very different from my wedding,' Louise said. 'I thought my wedding lovely, but it was nothing compared with this.'

'I don't know how you've succeeded in being as happy as you are, Lou,' Terri Lee said in mock seriousness. 'No wonderful embossed invitations, no endless bridesmaid fittings, no hen night in Champneys, none of this opulence.' She gestured around.

'Wasn't the weekend in Champneys terrific!' Caroline

exclaimed. 'You were a revelation, Emily. I never thought you'd enjoy yourself as much as you obviously did. I wouldn't have thought that pampering your body was your thing.'

'That just goes to show how wrong you can be about a person,' Emily retorted. 'I've joined a health spa in Islington —it's quite near my flat. I'm earning good money now and I'm having fun spending it. There's only me to spend it on, after all.'

'When are you moving into the flat?' Terri Lee asked.

'Next week. Robert said I could stay on in the house till the end of August if I wanted. The new tenants aren't moving in till mid-September, so there'd still be time for the house to be decorated and anything fixed that needed fixing. But I want to move in while it's quieter at work, and that means moving in August when the courts are closed. And also, you and Louise have already moved out, and so's Caroline now. I'd be the only one living there, and I think that'd feel quite strange.'

'But that means you'd be moving during the holiday month,' Terri Lee said in surprise. 'Don't you want to get some sun or whatever?'

'I still can if I want. I might just move into the flat, dump everything and take off. That's the great thing about being free—you can do whatever you want.'

'D'you ever see John these days?' Louise asked.

'Nope,' Emily said. 'I'm too busy dating other people— people without baggage—and that's how I like it.' She paused. 'I think he may have met someone else, but I don't know for certain. I hope so. I'd like to think he was happy.'

Louise turned to Terri Lee. 'What about you, Terri Lee? You never say much about what you're doing these days. Are you still seeing that Marcus?'

'Not in the way you mean. We're just good friends, and that's all there is to it—well, except for occasionally,' she added with a giggle. 'I don't know why, but he seems to enjoy my company, and I certainly enjoy his. He's staying with some friends near Manchester tonight, but he'll be here in time for the ceremony. I don't think I've ever been as happy as I've been this last year. Thanks to Marcus, I now feel that I'm worth something as a person. I don't think I've ever really felt that before, or at least not since I was very little.'

'That's wonderful,' Caroline said with genuine warmth.

'Ditto from me,' Louise added.

'And I love my flat,' Terri Lee went on, 'even though I actually prefer Camden Town to Regent's Park—Camden Town is more me. But if you're wondering about men, apart from Marcus, the only names in my little black book are purely work names.'

'I doubt there's much that's pure about your work,' Emily said drily.

'Believe it or not, there is! I'm very lucky to be doing what I do. I've got a job I love, and it gives me a brilliant income. You've seen my flat—it's awesome. I've got a view from the balcony to die for and everything about the flat is the last word in luxury.'

'Well, you know what you're doing,' Emily said, a trace haughtily.

'And I also know what I'm not doing, Emily. I'm not doing what you're implying. Being an escort isn't anything to be ashamed of, whatever you might choose to think. Just because some slappers give the job a bad name, it doesn't mean that all escorts are the same. Ask Robert if you don't believe me. His firm uses my agency from time to time, just like loads of other good firms.'

'Robert uses your agency!' Caroline exclaimed, sitting up. 'I didn't know that. Why?'

'For the same reason as any other company—they want extra girls when they put on business functions, girls who look the part and who can talk to the people there. It helps with keeping their guests happy, and it makes a company look good.'

'He's never mentioned it to me,' Caroline said, looking hurt.

Terri Lee shrugged. 'There's no reason why he would. It's a normal part of business life. How much of his business *does* he discuss with you?'

'None of it really.'

'There you are, then. Anyway, I go to all the top places, meet lots of interesting people, make pots of money and only work when I want to. And what's more, I've got a great future ahead of me. Marcus is a little older than I am—'

'Which is par for the course, I'm sure,' Emily cut in.

'—and he doesn't want to carry on working till he drops dead,' Terri Lee continued, ignoring her. 'In about a year, he's going to sell me the business at a knock-down price. And in fact, he's already started showing me the ropes. Whatever you choose to think, Emily, I've made something of myself, and I've got a future. In just over a year, I'll be running my own business and then I'm gonna start investing in property, just like Robert does.'

'That sounds fantastic, Terri Lee. I'm really pleased it's worked out so well for you,' Caroline said warmly. 'I'm sure we all are, even if we can't all bring ourselves to say it,' she added, frowning slightly in Emily's direction.

'And it's working out okay for me, too,' Louise volunteered. 'Georgie's now in a routine, and we've got an *au pair* starting in September when we get back from France. I really miss working so I'm going back to the PR department in Ethan's company in October. Just for a few hours each week at first, but that'll be ideal.'

'That's wonderful, Louise,' Emily said with genuine pleasure. 'It would've been such a waste if you'd stayed at home all day and done nothing.'

'Looking after a small child is hardly doing nothing,' Caroline remarked, a touch acidly. She turned to Louise. 'It *is* good news, Lou, but you could always go back to work when Georgie was a few years older, you know. If you did, you wouldn't need to have another woman living in your house. That could be a little unwise.'

'Why would it be unwise, Caroline?' Emily asked. 'Are you afraid that Robert might play away if you hired an *au pair*?'

'Of course not,' Caroline said quickly. 'I'm just saying; that's all.' She turned to Louise. 'It's just that Georgie's so sweet, I don't know how you can bear to think of leaving him.'

'It'll only be for a few hours each week. And there's sufficient flexibility in my job for me to be with Georgie when he needs me. But I'm desperate to kick my brain back into action. I spent last year being pregnant, ironing shirts, baking cakes, singing 'I'm a little teapot'. Much as I love Ethan and Georgie, I want more in my life than that.'

'Well, I'm glad it's working out for you,' Caroline said. 'After all, I'm getting what I want, and so's Terri Lee. Why shouldn't you have what you want, too? And what about you, Emily? Long term, what's your dream?'

'I'm living it now. My job, which I love, is endlessly fascinating, and I've sufficient money to pay someone else to deal with all my domestic trivia. I want to spend what free time I have with like-minded people, people with whom I can go out if I want, and against whom I can close the door if I so wish. Which I can do now.'

'Aren't we all so different,' Terri Lee said, smiling as she looked around at the other three.

'Perhaps we're such good friends because we *are* so different,' Caroline suggested.

'Maybe,' Louise said. 'But sharing a house creates a huge bond. I may not have seen that much of you recently, what with being married and having Georgie and all that, but I feel just as close to you as I always did.'

'I'm sure we'll always be close, no matter where we live,' Caroline said firmly.

'Yes, but with me in Belsize Park,' Louise said mournfully. 'Terri Lee in Regent's Park, Emily in Islington and you in Hampstead until you find a place in Hertfordshire, I've a feeling it won't ever be the same again.'

Terri Lee clapped her hands. 'Time to change the subject, girls. This is Caroline's last night of freedom. Don't let's end it by blubbing.'

aroline's wedding day was, indeed, a day that would be remembered by everyone there.

To the sound of the Wedding March, she floated down the aisle, a vision of loveliness on her father's arm.

Wearing a strapless ivory Thai silk gown, of which the hem and bodice were edged with a wide band of delicate pearl beading, she looked stunning. Tiny pearl buttons ran down the back of the fitted bodice, leading into a skirt that gently filled out as it fell to the floor. Her ivory bridal slippers were embroidered with the same pearl beading that bordered the bodice.

In her hands, she carried a posy of full-blown creamy white ranunculus that had been tied with a ribbon of the palest ice-blue silk. Her auburn hair had been swept up into a tiara formed by a cluster of tiny pearls, from which fell a filmy two-tiered creamy-white veil.

The ice-blue of the ribbon was picked up by the ice-blue

silk dresses of the three bridesmaids, whose sling-back shoes were in the same shade of blue.

Walking ahead of Caroline, Louise scattered creamy rose petals in her path, the aroma of which blended with the fragrance from the clusters of full-blossomed cream roses tied at the aisle-end of each pew. And coming behind her, Terri Lee and Emily carried a single white ranunculus encircled by a narrow ribbon of ice-blue silk.

Waiting at the front of the church, looking stylish, handsome and confident, was Robert.

Wearing a charcoal-grey formal dress suit over a cream silk waistcoat embroidered with ice-blue and grey, with a matching cravat and pocket handkerchief, and sporting a single ranunculus in his lapel, he looked every inch the successful man he was, Caroline thought with pleasure as she stepped up to his side in front of the altar.

Smiling over her shoulder at Terri Lee, she handed her the posy, and turned again to Robert. Their eyes met.

'You look lovely,' he said quietly. 'Absolutely stunning.'

'And you do, too,' she whispered, and they turned to face the altar.

THE EVENING WAS FALLING as Caroline moved among the tables that were covered with a crisp white linen cloth, exchanging light-hearted words with one group of guests after another, a champagne flute in her hand.

She felt deliriously happy.

Night had fallen, and every so often, her reflection stared back at her from the large windows as she neared them—tall, slender, graceful. When she reached the table closest to the window, she went right up to the glass and peered through her reflection into the illuminated darkness.

The dense blackness that was slowly consuming the world around the hotel was being held at bay by the golden light that streamed through the hotel windows, and by sparkling spotlights that had been hidden amongst the dense green foliage that lined the patio. Beyond the foliage, tall trees flanked the long drive that wound into the invisible distance, their fronds painted a brilliant green by the up-lights that crouched among the leaves.

Above the fronds, the tips of the trees were silhouetted in sharp relief, jagged and mysterious against the black-ening sky.

She shivered, turned back to the warmth of the dining-room and walked across to the table where Louise was sitting with Georgie, who was playing with a white linen napkin. Terri Lee and Emily were swapping banter with Marcus and Ethan. Seeing them all, she was filled with an overwhelming sense of joy.

What a day it had been!

From the romance of the ceremony, crowned by the excitement of signing the register and walking back up the flower-strewn aisle as Mrs Robert Chesterton, to the flashing lights of the photographer, to the clouds of confetti and rose petals that fell upon her and Robert as they ran laughing to the ribbon-covered Rolls-Royce that was to return them to the hotel, to the elegant dinner beneath stunning crystal chandeliers, and the toasts—confident and amusing on the part of Robert and his best man; nervous, but adequate, on the part of her father—the day had surpassed her wildest dreams.

Every single minute was going to live in her memory forever.

'If it isn't the bride herself,' Marcus said, smiling at Caro-line as she reached the table and sat down next to him. 'You look beautiful, Caroline, but I'm sure you've been told that many times today. Should you ever want a job ... ,' he murmured.

They all laughed. 'I have a job, Marcus, thank you,' she said lightly. 'One that I can't wait to get down to.'

Marcus wagged his finger reprovingly. 'Pray, don't put us to the blush,' he chided with feigned severity. 'A bride should be the epitome of virginal modesty and restraint about such matters.'

She leaned forward, picked up a *petit four* and made as if to throw it at him. He covered his face in self-protection. 'Don't hurt me, please,' he begged in a little-boy voice.

'I see that my wife's rehearsing for domestic bliss,' Robert remarked with a smile, coming up to the table and sitting down between Caroline and Ethan. Caroline put the *petit four* down on the plate in front of her and slid closer to Robert.

'Hello, darling husband,' she said. He wound his right arm around her, and with his left arm, picked up the bottle of champagne from the wine stand next to the table. 'Empty,' he said, turning it upside down and putting it back into the ice. 'We'll get some more.'

Minutes later, a waiter was at their side, uncorking a fresh bottle. There was a loud explosion, and the champagne flowed over the neck of the bottle.

'Only a little for me till I've put Georgie down,' Louise said quickly. 'I'll take him up soon—it's already well past his bed time. I'll call the baby-sitting service when he's asleep and come back down.'

'He looks far from ready for bed to me,' Robert said, smiling at the baby. 'In fact, I've never seen anyone look more awake.' He waved at Georgie across the table. Georgie chuckled gleefully and waved back.

'I know,' Louise said with a sigh. 'That's the trouble. He fell asleep during the speeches. Not for long, but for long enough to take the edge off his tiredness. I should've forced him to stay awake.'

'Since I don't have to worry about a baby, I'll have a refill, thank you, Robert,' Emily said, pushing her glass forward.

'Perhaps Georgie should have a little champagne, too,' Robert suggested with a grin. 'The odd drop might work wonders. What d'you say, Ethan?'

Ethan laughed. 'He'll take a rain check, thanks. You can give Georgie's share of the champagne to his father instead. I should take him upstairs now, Lou. You'll probably find that he falls asleep in a minute or two.'

Robert filled the empty glasses.

In the distance, they heard the sound of the band starting up on the dance floor that led off the dining-room. Having quickly downed his champagne, Robert stood up and held out his hand to Caroline.

Smiling, she gave him her hand and let him lead her between the tables and the guests, who rose to their feet as they passed and clapped, to the middle of the dance floor. Taking her in his arms, he held her tight, and began to lead her around the floor to the strains of 'Unchained Melody'.

'IT'S NO GOOD, Ethan—he won't go to sleep. I've been up there for more than half an hour, and every time I go to leave the room, he starts screaming. He's just not tired,' Louise said wearily, standing next to the table with Georgie in her arms. Dressed for bed in his Mr Happy pyjamas, Georgie stared at the table, his eyes wide open.

'Of course, he's tired, Louise. Just look at his face. If anything, he's over-tired,' Ethan said, taking a sip of champagne. 'Take him back to the room, tell the babysitting service he's there, and leave him. It won't hurt him to cry for a bit. And it'll give the service something to do, which'll stop them from being bored.'

'I'm hardly going to leave him screaming, am I?' she remarked testily. 'And you're not meant to do that, anyway. As soon as he's asleep, I'll let them take over and come back down, but I can't till then. I'll leave it another half an hour, and then try him upstairs again.' She sat down and put Georgie on her lap.

'That's not on, Lou. He can't stay down here any longer,' Ethan said. 'It's time for the grown-ups now. The others won't want a baby in their midst.'

'I'm sure that nobody minds,' Terri Lee said.

'I could be stuck up there for hours, waiting for him to drop off,' Louise said in annoyance. 'If that sounds okay to you, Ethan, I suggest that *you* take him up and sit with him.'

Ethan stood up suddenly. 'I've had a brainwave,' he said. 'Here, give him to me.' He lifted Georgie out of Louise's arms. 'He always drops off in the car. I'll take him for a quick spin, and as soon as he's asleep, I'll bring him back and we'll take him straight upstairs. What say you to my master plan?'

'I say that it's an inspired idea,' she said, 'except that you can hardly ask them to get the car out at this time of night. And more importantly, you've been drinking fairly steadily throughout the day, and are way over the limit. We've both drunk far too much to drive.'

'Come on, Lou. Yes, I've had some wine and champagne, but it was over a period of several hours and they've had time to be absorbed. I'm stone-cold sober now. And it's not as if I'll be going out on the road. I'll just drive around the hotel grounds till he drops off, which won't take long, I'm sure. What d'you say?'

'I'm not that keen to be honest. Whatever you say, you've had too much to drink, and that'll affect your reactions.'

'Tell her, Emily, Terri Lee,' Ethan begged the girls. 'If Robert and Caroline were here, they'd agree with me. I really don't want to spend the rest of the evening with Georgie, and if *I* don't want that, then I'm sure you want it even less.'

'Whatever it is, give it to the man,' Robert said, coming up behind Ethan, holding hands with Caroline. Both looked flushed and happy. 'Why aren't you on that dance floor, all of you?'

'What d'you say, Louise?' Ethan repeated. 'I'd rather have you in my arms than Georgie, much as I love my son.'

'Oh, all right then. But be careful, won't you? And if he doesn't go to sleep pretty quickly, bring him back and I'll take him up, anyway. Promise?'

'I promise.' With the baby in his arms, he started to walk across the room. Louise jumped up from her seat and ran after them. 'I'll come with you,' she said.

'No, you won't. You've done sterling babysitting duty all day, and there's a limit. I'll let you wave goodbye to us from the hotel steps, but then you're to come back in here and start having fun.' He stopped walking, leaned over and kissed her gently on the lips. She put her arm around him and Georgie, and together they went out of the hotel and out to the stone steps.

'Goodnight, Georgie,' she said, and she gave him a kiss while they waited for the parking attendant to bring them their car. 'Be a good boy for Daddy, which means you must go to sleep at once.'

The car drew up in front of the steps. The parking attendant got out and held the driver's door open.

Still holding the baby, Ethan opened the door to the

back seat, turned to Louise and took Georgie's hand in his. 'Wave to Mummy,' he said, and he waved Georgie's hand up and down. Then he lowered Georgie into his carrycot and strapped him in.

He straightened up. 'I'll be back in no time,' he called to Louise. 'Believe me, he'll be asleep by then.' He got into the driver's seat, and the attendant shut the door and walked away. Then he put his foot on the accelerator.

Louise watched him pull sharply away from the steps, swing the car round and head towards the long drive. She waved, and then turned to walk back up the steps and into the hotel.

A loud crash shattered the still of the night. Followed by silence: a heavy, eerie silence.

She stopped dead.

Blood rushed to her head, and pounded in her ears. As if in a fog, she heard the sound of footsteps running through the hotel towards her, and footsteps running past her, down the steps and on to the drive.

A massive explosion ripped through the air.

Slowly, shaking uncontrollably, she turned to look towards the long drive.

Ravenous, all-consuming flames were hungrily wrapping themselves in and around a skeletal dark metal frame that stood out stark in their midst.

Above the ball of fire, the black sky blazed a crimson-red.

45

T*hursday, 10th August*

B*eneath an overcast sky*, they huddled together at the front of the small red-brick building attached to the cloister in the heart of the crematorium.

Louise, tiny in a tailored black suit, stared around her with unseeing, red-rimmed eyes that were half-hidden by the short black veil that hung from her cloche hat. Wearing a black dress and short black jacket, Caroline stood on one side of Louise, her arm around Louise's shoulders, supporting her. Subdued in a fitted, high-necked sleeveless black linen dress and a wide-brimmed black straw hat, Terri Lee stood on the other side, clutching a black Gucci bag.

Standing close to the three girls, but apart from them, were Ethan's distraught parents.

They'd arrived from Devon the day before. Wanting to be by themselves in their grief, they'd turned down Louise's invitation that they stay with her, and had chosen to go to a small hotel near Finchley Road.

They'd reached the crematorium that morning at the same time as the car bringing Louise, Nicola and Jim. As soon as Louise had got out of the car, they'd gone to each other, none of them able to speak. Ethan's mother had looked into Louise's stricken face, put her hand to Louise's cheek, and broken down. She'd been led gently to one side by Ethan's father, and they stayed there, clinging to each other, white-faced and disbelieving, as the mourners assembled.

Marcus and Robert stood slightly to one side of Caroline and Terri Lee, talking quietly to each other. When Patrick Grayson, who'd worked with Louise, arrived, he went over to the two men, and not long after that, they were joined by Barbara Cooper. Tears flowed unchecked down her face, and she clutched a handkerchief.

People gradually arriving gathered in small clusters throughout the area, some just inside the small brick waiting room, some outside it—men in dark suits and women in black; friends and colleagues who'd come to say goodbye to a man they'd liked and admired, and to a child most of them had never seen.

Nicola stood near her sister in floods of tears, with Jim awkwardly at her side, doing his best to comfort her. 'I can't believe it. I just can't believe it,' Nicola sobbed over and over again. 'Not Ethan. My poor Louise. Not Georgie, too.'

'Ah, here's Emily!' Terri Lee exclaimed, seeing Emily hurrying towards them, with John close behind. 'For a moment, I was worried she was going to be late.'

'Oh, Lou,' Emily said, and she went straight to Louise and hugged her. 'Oh, Lou,' she repeated, and she released her.

John stepped forward. 'I didn't know Ethan for long,' he told Louise, 'but I knew him for long enough to like and respect him enormously. As for your baby, there are no words.'

Louise nodded, unable to speak. The tears that had lain in the brim of her eyes rolled down her cheeks, and she pulled her veil further over her face. John put his hand lightly on her shoulder, left it there a moment, and then moved away to stand with Robert's group.

Caroline tightened her arm around Louise. 'We're here for you, Lou,' she said gently. 'And we always will be.'

Louise turned to look Caroline in the face. 'Some people never have the happiness I had with Ethan,' she said, shakily. 'I'm so lucky to have had him for any time at all. That's what I'm going to focus on today.' She turned to Emily. 'It's nice of John to come.'

'As soon as he heard what happened, he wanted to be here. He only met Ethan a few times, but he liked him. When he was around. When John was around, that is,' she finished lamely. 'I'm so sorry Louise,' she said, her voice catching.

'Marcus and I got here early and had a look at the garden,' Terri Lee said quickly. 'Ethan would have liked it here—it's lovely.'

Louise nodded. 'Yes, he would; you're right.'

'God, I can't stop crying,' Emily said, and she searched furiously in her small bag for a tissue. 'I was so determined not to cry. What use am I if I keep on crying?'

'You being here is of use, whether or not you're crying,' Louise said. 'Funnily enough, you being so emotional today, so un-Emilyish, it sort of helps.' Then she turned away and looked towards the red brick tower.

Hearing her draw her breath in sharply, they followed

her gaze. A stately black hearse was gliding between the red-brick pillars that stood on either side of the entrance to the crematorium.

Louise's hand flew to her mouth.

The low hum of people died away.

Motionless, her hand still in front of her mouth, Louise watched the hearse come to a halt in front of one of the buildings at the edge of the cloister.

Terri Lee stepped back to let Nicola move to Louise's side and put her arm around her sister's waist. Together with Caroline, Nicola lightly propelled Louise across to the place where the hearse was standing. Ethan's parents followed close behind, and then Emily and Terri Lee. The rest of the mourners came after them.

Most of the guests continued straight into the chapel. Soon, only Louise, her sister, Caroline and Ethan's parents, were left outside. They stood in silence, waiting while the coffin bearers carefully positioned the coffin bearing Ethan and Georgie on to their shoulders. The funeral director then indicated to Louise that she and Ethan's parents take their place behind the coffin.

A loud sob escaped Louise.

Caroline hugged her, and then she and Nicola helped her to take a step forward behind the coffin, and another step, and another. Faltering, Louise looked up at the lily-strewn coffin on the shoulders of the bearers in front of her, and at the tiny yellow flowers grouped into the shape of Mr Happy.

'No!' she screamed. 'No!' She stretched out her arms out to the coffin. 'No! This isn't happening. This isn't real. It's not happening.'

And sobbing loudly and uncontrollably, she followed the coffin into the small chapel, held upright solely by the arms of her friend and her sister, who supported her on either side.

THE DEBRIS from the post-funeral reception in Louise and Ethan's house having been cleared away by the caterers, only the cards and messages of sympathy that lined the shelves and the mantelpiece in the downstairs reception rooms, and the colour of the women's clothes, gave any indication of the event that had taken place earlier in the day.

Marcus, Robert and John left the Belsize Park house at the same time as the caterers, and not long after that, Ethan's parents declined the invitation to stay longer, said goodbye and began their long journey home. They were followed closely by Jim and Nicola, who had to get back to Mark. The rest of Ethan and Louise's friends and colleagues gradually drifted off, until the only people left in the reception room were Louise, Terri Lee, Emily and Caroline.

Still very pale, but dry-eyed, Louise sat on her upholstered Victorian settee, with Caroline next to her. Terri Lee and Emily had settled in the two Victorian wing armchairs that stood in front of the tall sash windows. All kept their eyes resolutely away from the silver-framed photographs on the mahogany table by the far wall.

'Are you and John back together again, then?' Terri Lee asked, turning to Emily.

'Trust you to ask something totally inappropriate for now!' Emily exclaimed.

'No, that's fine,' Louise said quickly. 'In fact, it makes me feel better, talking about normal things, and hearing you two snap at each other. Everything will be a lot easier if everyone goes back to the way they usually are. Feel free to be as rude to each other as you like.' She managed a smile.

'Well then, in answer to your nosy question, Terri Lee, no, I'm not back with John. We work in the same set of Chambers, but that's all. He really liked Ethan and when he heard about the accident—' She stopped abruptly and looked anxiously at Louise.

'Carry on,' Louise said quickly. 'I want us to be able to talk about Ethan and ... ' She drew a deep breath. '... and about Georgie. It was brilliant having them for any time at all—totally brilliant—and I don't want to pretend they weren't ever here.'

'We'll keep them alive with you, Lou, I promise,' Caroline said gently.

'They think he clipped one of the trees, you know. But he wasn't going too fast. A freak accident they said.'

'To bring the John issue to an end once and for all,' Emily said hastily, seeing Louise's face flush, 'it really is over. I will never play happy families, not even for John, and he knows that. And I now know for certain that he's met someone else. I'm really pleased about that. He should be with someone who truly cares for him, who'll look after him and who wants the whole family thing. I could never have been that someone. I don't think I'm into marriage any more than I'm into children.'

'When people say that, they usually get married the following week,' Terri Lee remarked with a wry smile.

'Not me,' Emily said cheerfully. 'I intend to go it alone.'

'I doubt you'll be allowed to, Emily.' Caroline said. 'You're far too attractive. To be honest, I never thought I'd say that, let alone think it, but you've really blossomed. You've got a very good figure and now that you know how to use make-up, you've brought out the best in your features. I'd be amazed if men didn't go for you.'

'You don't think she's a niche market?' Terri Lee asked with a grin.

Emily made as if to throw a scatter cushion at her, and Terri Lee ducked.

'Actually, Caro's right, Emily,' Terri Lee said, peeping through her fingers. 'I hadn't really noticed how you've been changing over the months, but now that she's pointed it out, I reckon you could hold a candle to some of Marcus's girls.'

Caroline leaned forward. 'Talking of work, I suppose it's too soon to ask if you've given any thought as to what you're going to do about work and everything, Louise?' she asked hesitantly. 'It probably is, isn't it?'

'I know that Ethan has left me the company, and I'm going to take advice about what to do. I'm hoping it'll be possible for it to continue pretty much as it is, but with a different person running it. That person won't be me, though. That's beyond me. While it's too soon to make any decisions, I know for certain that I want to work, even though I'll never have to worry about money.'

Her voice started to shake again.

'That's great, Lou. It means you can go at your own pace,' Caroline said quickly.

'I haven't yet thanked you, Caroline, and not just for your support today,' Louise said. 'It was unbelievably kind of you to put off your honeymoon. You didn't have to, you know—I'd have understood.'

'Being with you today was the most important thing to me, and to Robert. He really liked Ethan; we both did. We're friends, Lou, and there's nothing more important than friendship. Honeymoons can be taken at any time.'

'You *have* been a good friend to me. All of you have,' Louise said, looking around at her friends, her eyes glistening. 'I don't know what I would've done without you. And I don't just mean now, I mean for the whole two years we've known each other.'

'And we'll always be friends,' Caroline said. 'Look what we've been through together—finding our feet in our first jobs; meeting the men in our lives; our ups and our downs with our jobs and with the men; all of us learning the kind of future we want. That's a lot for two years, and it's made for very close ties between us—the sort of ties that'll never be broken.'

'That sounds like a cue for a toast,' Terri Lee said. 'Is there any wine left?'

Caroline stood up. 'Good idea. There's an open bottle in the fridge. Let's finish it with a toast to our friendship.'

She went and got the bottle, and then took four wine glasses out of a glass-fronted cabinet, divided the wine between the glasses and gave one to each of the girls.

Standing up, she held out her glass. The others rose to their feet and did likewise.

'We may not be sisters in blood,' she said, 'but we're sisters in spirit. And believe me, that can be the best sort of sister to have. To the four of us. May we never let each other down.'

46

NINE YEARS ON

S *unday, 18th June, 1989*

'You!' Caroline gasped. 'My God, it's you!'

Her face pale, Emily stared back at Caroline.

'Look, Caroline,' she began, and she stopped. She raised her hands in a gesture of helplessness, and then let them fall to her sides.

Frozen to the spot, Caroline stood there a moment, stunned, unable to speak. 'You bitch,' she choked out at last. 'You prize bitch.' She spun on her heels and ran back along the path and across the road to the car.

She threw herself on to the driver seat, fumbled with the seat belt, switched on the engine, swung the wheel to the right and made for the road out of Brighton. As soon as the town was behind her, and she was heading for Hertford-shire, she pulled into the first lay-by she came to, and burst into tears.

. . .

THREE HOURS LATER, the chimes of the doorbell resounded throughout the Hertfordshire house.

Her eyes swollen from crying, Caroline went to the front door. Keeping the chain on, she opened the door a crack. Robert stood on the doorstep, with Emily a little way behind him, a red spot high on each of her cheeks.

'Don't think you're coming in, Robert,' Caroline said flatly, 'because you're not.'

She started to push the door shut, but Robert swiftly put his foot in the doorway to stop it from closing.

She pushed the door against his foot, but he wouldn't move it.

'If you don't go right now, I'll call the police,' she threatened.

'Please let me in, Caroline. This won't get us anywhere. I don't want to do this on the doorstep.'

'There's nothing to do, you bastard!' Again, she pushed the door hard against his foot. 'You've already done it. And with that slut, too. You've left me and your children, and gone off with someone I thought was a friend. Some friend! She doesn't know the meaning of the word. And nor do you—you've both betrayed me, and there's nothing you could say that I'd want to hear. The facts speak for themselves.'

'At least give me a chance to explain. You've got to do that much. Let us both explain. Please.' He put his shoulder against the door and increased his pressure.

'I haven't *got* to do anything,' she snapped. 'I'll do want I want, no more and no less. And what I want is never to see you again. Either of you.'

'Please, Caroline. Surely we can talk about things in a

civilised sort of way—where to go next, what to do about the kids, and all that?'

'I know where I'm going next—to a divorce lawyer, that's where. As for the kids, thank God they've been away with the school all week. Screwing that skinny cow was obviously more important to you than them, but I'd hate them to know it.'

'I'm not going anywhere till we've talked,' Robert said firmly, his shoulder still against the door. 'I'll stand here all day if I have to, and I'll shout out the reasons why I left you. Even if you closed the door, you'd still be able to hear me loud and clear, and so would the neighbours. I'm sure they'd love that. I'm not sure what it'd do for your street credibility, though.' She hesitated visibly. 'Please, let me in, Caro,' he repeated. 'I really don't want a public slanging match.'

Caroline unhooked the chain. '*She's* not coming in,' she said, indicating over his shoulder at Emily.

Robert glanced round at Emily, and nodded towards the low brick wall that encircled their front garden. He turned back to Caroline. 'All right. It'll be just you and me, then.'

She moved away from the front door, leaving it open, went into the drawing-room and perched stiffly on the edge of the seat of one of the armchairs.

Robert came into the house, closed the front door behind him and followed her into the drawing-room. He stood uncertainly in the middle of the room.

'Make it quick, will you?' she said, and fixed her gaze on the floor.

He crossed to the armchair closest to hers, sat down and leaned slightly towards her. She shifted in her chair, angling herself away from him.

He cleared his throat. 'I'm sorry, Caroline.'

'Fine. You've said the necessary so now you can go.'

'I never meant to hurt you,' he continued. She gave a short laugh. 'I know that's a cliché, but it's true all the same. I really didn't want to hurt you. Nor did Emily.'

Her shoulders stiffened.

'Well, that makes it all right then,' she said, her voice shrill to her ears. 'You've ruined my life, and Heaven knows what you've done to the children. But you didn't mean to do it, so that's all right. A lame apology makes all the sneaking around, the lying, the cheating, the screwing with my so-called friend, just fine and dandy, does it? It's all hunky dory because you didn't mean to do it.'

'Of course, it doesn't. I've hurt you and nothing can make that right. Saying sorry doesn't come near it. You deserved better from me.'

'You're bloody right, I did!' She spun round to face him, her eyes glittering with tears of anger and pain. 'You couldn't have had a better wife than me. From the minute we married, I've made the sort of home you wanted. I've run the house, cooked you great meals, entertained your work colleagues, supported you in every way I could. You know I have. And I've given you two super kids, though you've hardly been around to see them.'

'That's not my fault, and you know it isn't. You know how hard I've had to work, expanding the property business while keeping a handle on the accounting side of things. You were pleased enough with the money I brought in.'

'But it wasn't just hard work that kept you out of the house, was it?' A sob escaped her. 'Unless, of course, you call getting into that cow's knickers hard work.'

He flinched. 'That's beneath you, Caro.'

'Well, I certainly know what's been beneath *you*, don't I? You, who've always said you prefer curves to skin and bone.

They don't come much bonier than her.' She indicated the window, and then looked back at the floor.

'I admit you're the perfect wife, Caroline,' he said softly. 'I did love you, and I still do.'

Her shoulders slumped. She stared at him, bewildered. 'So why did you leave me and go to that woman? I gave you what you wanted, didn't I?'

'But that's just it—it wasn't what I wanted.' She started to speak, but he put up his hand to stop her. 'This is all my fault—you've done nothing wrong. It's what I *thought* I wanted, but I was wrong. After a chaotic childhood, my ideal was to have the perfect wife and a well-run home full of children. But when I got my wish, I found I didn't really like it. It was too ... too... domestic is probably the best word. I don't blame anyone but me. You didn't put a foot wrong, Caro. But much as I loved you, and appreciated the home you made, I came to feel smothered by the perfection of it all.'

She drew back. 'Smothered? I *smothered* you?'

'You did, without realising it. It was the food, the house, the family, the kids—it was doing everything that should be done at the right time in the right way. I was overwhelmed —more than that—I was stifled by it all. More and more, I wanted to be free of all the baggage that comes with perfection.'

'Baggage! So we were baggage, were we? Well, I know who put those ideas into your head! When you talk about being baggage-free, I can hear her voice.'

He shook his head. 'You're wrong. I'd felt trapped in an unreal world for some time before I started seeing Emily. I was close to exploding with the tedium of it all when I met her that day.'

'What day?'

'Just over a year ago, when the company was celebrating its fifteen years. You remember—I held a drinks' party at the office to mark the occasion. I asked you to come, but you wouldn't. Daniel had a slight cold and you refused to leave him with a sitter.'

'That was hardly my fault. I did what any mother would do.'

'I know that. I'm not accusing you. I'm just telling you what happened. Anyway, as I often used to do, I asked Terri Lee to send along a few girls to give the party a bit of a buzz. Emily came with them. Apparently, she'd been out with Terri Lee the night before, and when Terri Lee said that she and a few of her girls would be going to my place the following day, and asked if Emily wanted to join them—not as a job, just for fun—she did, and you can imagine the rest.'

'But *Emily*. I can't believe that you'd go for someone like her. And not just once, but that you'd carry on doing so. And to go as far as getting a place together. A place with Emily, who wasn't into living with anyone. Having a thing for Terri Lee, I could've understood; for Louise, possibly; but for Emily, never! What's so special about *her*?'

'Perhaps it's that she's everything you're not. She's not into cooking; she's not into kids and all the paraphernalia that goes with them; she's not into anything to do with the house. There's a touch of free spirit about her, and that's very attractive. She doesn't believe in life-long commitment, and she's kept the Islington flat, but maybe we'll last. Equally, maybe we won't.'

'So she's totally lazy, irresponsible and self-centred! And that's attractive, is it?'

'Actually, yes. She's also very intelligent and extremely interesting. Her job is stimulating, which makes for good conversation that has nothing at all to do with anything domestic. She's lively and spontaneous, has a dry sense of humour and, something which was a pleasant surprise to me, she's full of fun. I feel liberated when I'm with her. But at the same time, I want to be with her as much as I can. I suppose you could rightly say that that's a strange sort of liberation,' he added with a wry smile.

'But you always said she was the least physically attractive of the four of us, and unless you've dramatically changed, that side of things matters to you.'

'Just as I was wrong about what I wanted from life, I was wrong about that, too. Her personality makes her physically attractive. You go on about her being skinny, but you don't need curves to be a knockout in bed.'

Caroline stood up. 'Well, that makes it okay, then. I don't think there's anything left to say. You'll hear from my lawyer in the next week or two.'

'I'm not going for any form of custody, but I shall want to see the children at times,' he said standing up. 'This isn't about them.'

'Of course, it isn't,' she said coldly. 'You've chosen to live with someone who'll never allow the children to stay over—not that I'd let them go near that bitch—and who'll never take any interest in them. Why on earth would I think that what you've chosen to do reflected your feelings for them?'

'I know you well enough to know that you won't take this out on them, Caroline,' he said quietly. 'I know you'll put this in the best light you can, because that's you.'

'I want you to leave now.' She walked out into the hall, opened the front door, and waited. 'We're completely finished, Robert,' she said, standing aside for him to go out. 'As far as I'm concerned, I hope I never see you again.'

He glanced at her distraught face, and nodded.

Then he went out of the house and down the three

white stone steps that led to the drive. Pausing a moment, he stared back up at the house. Then he turned to face Emily, who was sitting on the low brick wall, and started walking slowly towards her.

Caroline saw Emily stand up and look questioningly at him.

Leaving the door wide open behind her, she found herself following Robert, her steps speeding up until she drew level with him, and then overtook him. Reaching Emily, she stood squarely in front of her, her back to Robert.

'This is the last thing I'll ever say to you, Emily, but I want an answer. I deserve that much. I want to know whether at any time during your sleazy relationship with my husband, you gave so much as one minute's thought to the wrong you were doing to my children and me, and to the pain you'd cause me if I ever found out? After all, we were supposed to be friends.'

Emily stared at her. 'I'm truly sorry, Caroline,' she said.

'Answer my question, you cow. I don't give a damn about whether or not you're sorry.'

'Then the answer is no, I didn't think about you at all. I went out with Robert because he was good company, and then I fell in love with him. That's all. I didn't think about you or your children; not at any time.'

'Not even when we all met up? We may not have seen that much of each other during the past year, but we have met occasionally.'

'Nope, not even then.'

'You're unnatural! How can anyone be that unfeeling and hard?'

'I would say that you're fairly unfeeling and hard your-self, Caroline. Or perhaps determined is a better word for you. You knew what you wanted and you went after it with blinkers on. It was always about the perfect wife image with you, wasn't it?'

'There's nothing wrong with such an ambition.'

'There is, if it makes you tell yourself a lie. If you'd taken your blinkers off for so much as one minute, you'd be happily married to Tom right now. You genuinely loved Tom, and he loved you, but you wouldn't let yourself see that. Teacher Tom didn't fit into your nutty dream so you discarded him, despite the strong feelings you clearly had for each other. That's being pretty hard and unfeeling, I'd say. So to be honest, if I'd given any thought to the effect it would've had on you if you'd found out, I would've said that once your pride had got over it, you'd be just fine.'

'That shows how little you know about people.'

'But I know about you. You have what you've always wanted, which you rated above real love, and you'll continue to have that—a lovely home; children at a private school; friends you can cook for; a good income, which means that you've no need for a tiresome career. I think you'll be just fine after you've shed the appropriate number of tears for the occasion.'

'You heartless bitch!'

Robert looked from one face to the other. 'I think enough's been said for today by both of you. We'll talk some more when this isn't so raw, Caroline. You should know, though, that neither Louise nor Terri Lee are aware of my relationship with Emily.'

'Then I still have two friends. But I suspect *you've* lost three friends, Emily. Your existence really is baggage-free right now. I wonder how happy that freedom will make you when Robert realises that he's got it wrong this time, too, which he'll do.' She turned to Robert. 'There's nothing more to be said. In future, any communications must go through our solicitors. Goodbye, both of you. You're welcome to each other.'

She turned round, walked up the drive to the house and closed the door firmly behind her.

Fighting back the urge to break down in tears, she walked into the drawing-room, stood in the centre of the room and looked around. Its emptiness crowded in on her. Her gaze fell on the display of photos that stood on the white mantelpiece beneath a large framed mirror.

Coming from somewhere outside, she heard the sound of a car driving off.

She hesitated, and then crossed to the photographs, gathered up the three that were taken at her wedding, the one of the staff at her school-leaving party, a photo of her and Robert on their belated honeymoon, and one of Robert standing in a hessian sack on a sports' day at the children's school.

With the photos in her arms, she walked across the hall, into the kitchen, and went straight over to the large oval stainless-steel dustbin. Depressing the top, she dropped the framed photos into the bin. Staring down, she watched as the silver frames fell against each other, and the glass shattered.

Turning round, she started to leave the kitchen, and then paused and looked back at the dustbin. Going back to it, she reached down and carefully retrieved the frames from among the broken glass. She put the frames on the worktop, removed the photos one at a time and threw them back into the bin.

The last of the photos was trapped in a corner of its frame. She was about to throw both frame and photo into the bin, when she saw Tom's face smiling up at her. It was the photo of her with all of the teaching staff.

.

Straightening up, she ran a finger slowly over Tom's face. The thought came unbidden that maybe, just maybe, Emily had been right. Maybe she, as well as Robert, had got it very wrong.

Mentally, she shook herself. This wasn't the time to dwell on the past—there'd be plenty of time for that in the months to come. The children would be back from their trip the following day, and there were things she must do before then. Clutching the frames and the staff photo, she went back into the hall and put them on the small mahogany table by the wall, to be put away later.

She glanced again at the staff photo. Her eyes scanned the faces, but lingered on one face in particular.

Impulsively, she pulled open the drawer in the hall table and took out the wood-framed photo that Tom had given her years before. It had been taken at the Christmas Fair in the year that they'd dated.

She stared hard at it. Tom looked so happy. And so did she. She looked genuinely relaxed and happy at being with Tom. There was none of the anxiety that she'd felt at times in recent years at having to make sure that everything was perfect.

And her obvious happiness was despite her loathing of teaching.

She turned over the frame and saw Tom's phone number on the back.

Standing very still in the silent emptiness of the hall, she could hear the sound of her heart beating.

She wasn't in any state to think about the future now, but she would be one day. And when she felt ready, she must take one cautious step at a time. Having once blinded herself with her dreams, she must never let that happen again. This photo would always be a reminder of that.

Very carefully, she put the photo back in the drawer with Tom's face looking up at her.

Get over the next few weeks, she told herself, and then take stock.

With a last look at the photo, she closed the drawer, walked across to the wide central staircase, and went up the stairs and into the main bedroom. She must change the sheets on their bed before she did anything else.

No, she must change the sheets on *her* bed—it was no longer *their* bed.

Oblivious to the tears that were streaming down her cheeks, she went over to the bed, took hold of the continental quilt and pulled it to the floor.

Actually, Emily, you're right, she said inwardly, and she wiped her face with her hands.

I shall be just fine.

IF YOU ENJOYED THE BEST FRIEND

It would be very kind if you would take a few minutes to leave a review of the book.

Reviews give welcome feedback to the author, and they help to make the novel visible to other readers.

In addition, it's easier for authors to promote their books, given a number of promotional platforms today require a minimum number of reviews.

Your words, therefore, really do matter.

Thank you!

LIZ'S NEWSLETTER

You might be interested in signing up for Liz's newsletter.

Every month, Liz sends out a newsletter with updates on her writing, what she's been doing, where she's been travelling, and an interesting fact she's learned. Subscribers also hear about promotions and special offers.

As a thank you for signing up for Liz's newsletter, you'll receive a free full-length novel.

To sign up and get a free book, go to

www.lizharrisauthor.com

ACKNOWLEDGMENTS

Once again, a huge thank you to my cover designer, Jane Dixon-Smith, for a really striking cover. I love it! And also to my Friend in the North, Stella, who's always the first person to see my completed manuscripts, and who never fails to provide me with invaluable constructive criticism. Every author needs a Stella!

A thank you also to the members of the Romantic Novelists' Association. The many RNA friends I've made over the years have helped to make the writing process a highly enjoyable one.

In writing *The Best Friend*, I drew upon aspects of my experience, rather than on books. My Law degree inspired Emily's background; my teaching inspired Caroline's choice of career; my 6 years in California inspired parts of both Terri Lee and Louise's stories, and I love France, and go there often, which inspired a part of John's story.

Lastly, a massive thank you to my husband, Richard, who keeps the real world at bay while I inhabit my fictional world.

ABOUT THE AUTHOR

ABOUT THE AUTHOR

Born in London, Liz Harris graduated from university with a Law degree, and then moved to California, where she led a varied life, from waitressing on Sunset Strip to working as secretary to the CEO of a large Japanese trading company.

Six years later, she returned to London and completed a degree in English, after which she taught secondary school pupils, first in Berkshire, and then in Cheshire.

In addition to the six novels she's had published, she's had several short stories published in anthologies and magazines.

Liz now lives in Oxfordshire. An active member of the Romantic Novelists' Association and the Historical Novel Society, her interests are travel; the theatre; reading; cryptic crosswords. To find out more about Liz, visit her website at: www.lizharrisauthor.com

ALSO BY LIZ HARRIS

The Dark Horizon (The Linford Series)

Oxfordshire, 1919

The instant that Lily Brown and Robert Linford set eyes on each other, they fall in love. The instant that Robert's father, Joseph, head of the family's successful building company, sets eyes on Lily, he feels a deep distrust of her.

Convinced that his new daughter-in-law is a gold-digger, and that Robert's feelings are a youthful infatuation he'd come to regret, Joseph resolves to do whatever it takes to rid his family of Lily. And he doesn't care what that is.

As Robert and Lily are torn apart, the Linford family is told a lie that will have devastating consequences for years to come.

The Flame Within (The Linford Series)

London, 1923.

Alice Linford stands on the pavement and stares up at the large Victorian house set back from the road—the house that is to be her new home.

But it isn't *her* house. It belongs to someone else—to a Mrs Violet Osborne. A woman who was no more than a name at the end of an advertisement for a companion that had caught her eye three weeks earlier.

More precisely, it wasn't Mrs Osborne's name that had caught her eye—it was seeing that Mrs Osborne lived in Belsize Park, a short distance only from Kentish Town. Kentish Town, the place where Alice had lived when she'd been Mrs Thomas Linford.

Thomas Linford—the man she still loves, but through her own stupidity, has lost. The man for whom she's left the small

Lancashire town in which she was born to come down to London again. The man she's determined to fight for

The Lengthening Shadow (The Linford Series)

London, 1917

When Dorothy Linford marries former German internee, Franz Hartmann, at the end of WWI, she's cast out by her father, Joseph, patriarch of the successful Linford family.

Dorothy and Franz go to live in a village in south-west Germany, where they have a daughter and son. Throughout the early years of the marriage, which are happy ones, Dorothy is secretly in contact with her sister, Nellie, in England.

Back in England, Louisa Linford, Dorothy's cousin, is growing into an insolent teenager, forever at odds with her parents, Charles and Sarah, and with her wider family, until she faces a dramatic moment of truth.

Life in Germany in the early 1930s darkens, and to Dorothy's concern, what had initially seemed harmless, gradually assumes a threatening undertone.

Brought together by love, but endangered by acts beyond their control, Dorothy and Franz struggle to get through the changing times without being torn apart.

The Road Back

When Patricia accompanies her father, Major George Carstairs, on a trip to Ladakh, north of the Himalayas, in the early 1960s, she sees it as a chance to finally win his love. What she could never have foreseen is meeting Kalden – a local man destined by circumstances beyond his control to be a monk, but fated to be the love of her life.

Despite her father's fury, the lovers are determined to be together, but can their forbidden love survive?

A wonderful story about a passion that crosses cultures, a love that endures for a lifetime, and the hope that can only come from revisiting the past.

'A splendid love story, so beautifully told.' *Colin Dexter O.B.E. Best-selling author of the Inspector Morse novels.*

A Bargain Struck

Widower Connor Maguire advertises for a wife to raise his young daughter, Bridget, work the homestead and bear him a son.

Ellen O'Sullivan longs for a home, a husband and a family. On paper, she is everything Connor needs in a wife. However, it soon becomes clear that Ellen has not been entirely truthful.

Will Connor be able to overlook Ellen's dishonesty and keep to his side of the bargain? Or will Bridget's resentment, the attentions of the beautiful Miss Quinn, and the arrival of an unwelcome visitor, combine to prevent the couple from starting anew.

As their personal feelings blur the boundaries of their deal, they begin to wonder if a bargain struck makes a marriage worth keeping.

Set in Wyoming in 1887, a story of a man and a woman brought together through need, not love ...

The Lost Girl

What if you were trapped between two cultures?

Life is tough in 1870s Wyoming. But it's tougher still when you're a girl who looks Chinese but speaks like an American.

Orphaned as a baby and taken in by an American family, Charity Walker knows this only too well. The mounting tensions between the new Chinese immigrants and the locals in the mining town of Carter see her shunned by both communities.

When Charity's one friend, Joe, leaves town, she finds herself isolated. However, in his absence, a new friendship with the only other Chinese girl in Carter makes her feel as if she finally belongs somewhere.

But, for a lost girl like Charity, finding a place to call home was never going to be that easy ...

Evie Undercover

When libel lawyer, Tom Hadleigh acquires a perfect holiday home - a 14th century house that needs restoring, there's a slight problem. The house is located in the beautiful Umbria countryside and Tom can't speak a word of Italian.

Enter Evie Shaw, masquerading as an agency temp but in reality the newest reporter for gossip magazine Pure Dirt. Unbeknown to Tom, Italian speaking Evie has been sent by her manipulative editor to write an exposé on him. And the stakes are high – Evie's job rests on her success.

But the path for the investigative journalist is seldom smooth, and it certainly never is when the subject in hand is drop-dead gorgeous.

The Art of Deception

All is not as it seems beneath the Italian sun ...

Jenny O'Connor can hardly believe her luck when she's hired to teach summer art classes in Italy.

While the prospect of sun, sightseeing and Italian food is hard to resist, Jenny is far more interested in her soon-to-be boss, Max

Castanien. She's blamed him for a family tragedy for as long as she can remember and she wants some answers.

But as the summer draws on and she spends more time with Max, she discovers that all is not necessarily what it seems, and she starts to learn first-hand that there's a fine line between love and hate.

A Western Heart

(a novella)

Wyoming, 1880

Rose McKinley and Will Hyde are childhood sweethearts and Rose has always assumed that one day they will wed. As a marriage will mean the merging of two successful ranches, their families certainly have no objections.

All except for Rose's sister, Cora. At seventeen, she is fair sick of being treated like a child who doesn't understand 'womanly feelings'. She has plenty of womanly feelings – and she has them for Will.

When the mysterious and handsome Mr Galloway comes to town and turns Rose's head, Cora sees an opportunity to get what she wants. Will Rose play into her sister's plot or has her heart already been won?

Printed in Great Britain
by Amazon